Folktales
of
Iraq

Lili, the Baghdad Christian woman who told many of the
stories in this volume

Folktales
of
Iraq

Edited and Translated by
E. S. Stevens

with an Introduction by
Sir Arnold Wilson

ILLUSTRATED

Dover Publications, Inc.
Mineola, New York

Bibliographical Note

This Dover edition, first published in 2006, is an unabridged republication of
the work originally published in 1931 by Oxford University Press, London,
under the title *Folk-Tales of Iraq: Set Down and Translated from the Vernacular.*

International Standard Book Number: 0-486-44405-8

Manufactured in the United States of America
Dover Publications, Inc., 31 East 2nd Street, Mineola, N.Y. 11501

INTRODUCTION

IT is a privilege to introduce to the public a work which breaks, as far as I know, entirely fresh ground, for no writer, European or Arab, has attempted to collect the traditional fairy tales of Mesopotamia. A number of Kurdish stories have been published, notably by Soane, Edmonds, and Ivanow. In *Persian Tales* (1919) Lt.-Col. D. L. R. and Mrs. Lorimer have published a comprehensive selection of tales translated from Bakhtiari and Persian originals, whilst Mr. H. D. Barnham's amusing *Tales of Nasr-ed-Din Khoja* (1923) have their roots in Turkish soil, and are scarcely older than their author, who was Court Jester to Timur the Lame in the fifteenth century. To the student of folk-lore, however, Mesopotamia is almost virgin soil.

The stories here recorded are equalled in range and interest only by *Persian Tales*, and appear in some respects to be of even greater antiquity. They have been admirably translated, and in their present form should be no less welcome to antiquaries than to children. Ruskin once said: 'All inferior poetry is an injury to the good . . . and in general adds to the weight of human weariness in a most woeful and culpable manner.' These stories are exempt from such a charge, for the form in which they are told is as vivid as when they first fell from the lips of the narrator.

In 'Iraq as elsewhere such legends as have survived have in the course of centuries been polished by the stream of time. They owe their freshness in part to the qualities of clarity and conciseness that the Arabic tongue shares with Greek and Latin, and in part to the fact that the professional story-teller was wont to exercise an economy of words, supplemented with gestures the absence of which makes Englishmen seem so impassive to the rest of the world.

What memories do such stories call up from the past— memories of our own childhood, and of our own children

—and of every generation from the beginning of time! 'We know,' said Max Müller, Taylorian Professor in the University of Oxford, 'that all the most vital elements of our knowledge and civilization—our languages, our alphabets, our figures, our weights and measures, our art, our religion, our traditions, our very nursery stories, come to us from the East . . . but for the rays of Eastern light . . . Europe . . . might have remained for ever a barren and forgotten promontory of the primeval Asiatic continent.' This work is an important new contribution, which perhaps no one but the talented authoress could have made, to our knowledge of the undercurrents of Eastern life and thought.

The reference at page 254 to the mechanical man of iron, which was wound like a clock, may seem comparatively modern, but the story may well be a thousand years old, for Firdausi records the construction, by the order of Alexander the Great, of an iron horse on wheels, deriving its motive power from naphtha, which moving rapidly forward, struck terror into the ranks of the enemy and scattered the elephants. Elsewhere are enshrined references to practices, now long since forgotten, which were in vogue long before the days of Alexander.

I must, however, leave to scholars the task of collating these stories with Indian, Persian, and European collections, and perhaps with Semitic and Sumerian archetypes. Meanwhile, with the confidence born of personal experience, I place on record my belief that these stories will be as welcome in the nursery as in the drawing-room, and as valuable to the student of the East as any historical work.

A. T. WILSON.

PREFACE

R<small>EALIZING</small> one day that I was in the second decade of my sojourn in 'Iraq, I asked myself if I could make any useful contribution, however slight, to the sum of knowledge about the country. I have an advantage in being a woman, since my countrymen in 'Iraq are for the most part workers employed in official or commercial activities, and therefore with limited time and often little opportunity, to devote themselves to matters not vital to politics, business, history, or science. Moreover, as men, they are shut off from the family life of a large part of the community. As a woman I can enter where they could not, and so am free to study the country from an aspect denied to them.

I turned to notes I had made about 'Iraqi customs, occupations, crafts, superstitions, practice of magic, and much else, and found amongst them several stories written down as I had heard them. These reminded me that just as there is still below the soil of 'Iraq a wealth of archaeological material as yet untouched, so there is, on the lips of the people of a country which was up to the time of the world-war remote from Western influence, a folk-lore, hitherto uncollected, which must have its origins in the earliest times. 'Iraq has been termed the Cradle of Mankind, and if this is the case, one would expect to find traces of some of the stories which amused Mankind in his cradle, some of the lullabies which soothed him, some of the bogies which frightened him.

Folk-lore is the youngest of all the sciences: she is also the most modest, since she acts as useful handmaid to her elder sisters, history, anthropology, mythology, and kindred sciences, and intelligent analysis of folk-lore yields precious fragments of information which illuminate dark corners in our knowledge of the human family, its customs, beliefs, and wanderings.

I once saw a string of amber in a shop near the British Museum, each bead of which contained a fly. Similarly, in

the stories and legends of 'Iraq the skilled reader will
perceive embalmed amid all the nonsense and fancy, scraps
of mythology, religion, saga, and tribal custom far older
than the fable which clothes them. In the very fact that
such and such a folk-story appears in other countries may
lurk information as to a race migration, a foreign conquest,
a trade route, or the like.

The folk-stories of 'Iraq come from many varied
sources, for 'Iraq, lying as it does between Near East and
Far East, has been one of the world's highways and battle-
grounds.

Wave after wave of migration, conquest, and settle-
ment have surged over it, Sumerian, Chaldaean, Cassite,
Assyrian, Persian, Arab, and Turkish; each race in turn
contributing something of its religious beliefs, customs,
sagas, and traditions to the folk-lore of the country.
Merchant caravans in their slow progress from the
Mediterranean seaboard or cities of Cathay or India,
Jewish captives, negro settlers and slaves, travellers, and
wandering gipsies must all have added to 'Iraqi folk-lore
and distributed it. Stress must be laid particularly on the
instrumentation of imported slaves, for part of a slave's
duty is to entertain his owner by tale and song. Lastly, in
Moslem times, we have the yearly caravans of pilgrims
passing to and fro, and colonies of pilgrims in the holy
cities, such as Karbala and Najaf.

It is not surprising, therefore, if the folk-stories and
folk-lore of 'Iraq are of a very composite nature, and much
of the material gathered here is already familiar to students
of folk-lore, if only in translations from the Persian,
Armenian, and Turkish, not to mention the more universally known Grimm. In my notes I call attention to
a few of these parallels. It is rarely that a whole story is
transplanted from one nation to another; indeed, it would
seem rather as though incidents in stories were drawn
from the same lucky-bag. Intercourse between Persia,
Armenia, Syria, Turkey, and 'Iraq has been continuous,
and it would be surprising if there were not a common stock of legend. But it is useful to see what the

Gipsy entertainers in an encampment of tribesmen

individual genius of each people makes of the same raw material.

As soon as I concentrated upon this particular form of research I discovered how delightful the quest can prove. Not only did it bring me into touch with a great many interesting and pleasant personalities, but it gave me an excuse for wandering about the country, and experiencing the charming hospitality of tribal shaikhs and other persons.

The art of story-telling, an old one in the East, is declining in 'Iraq, and in the towns few, almost none, of the present generation possess it. Story-telling up till twenty years ago was a lucrative profession and a recognized accomplishment. Men story-tellers sat in the coffee-houses or sūqs and were paid, or received gratuities, for their recitations; women story-tellers were always welcome in the harems. Now, the cinema and gramophone have replaced the story-teller in the towns, and though in most families there is to be found an old slave, dependant, or relative who tells tales in the family circle, even these are becoming few, and much of the folk-lore which has been handed down by word of mouth from generation to generation will gradually be forgotten altogether. When wireless is added to the cinema and gramophone, the process will be accelerated, for the 'Iraqi is quick to profit by all such Western inventions, and before long the very tribesmen in the desert will be listening-in to concerts and possibly political propaganda broadcast from some Near or Middle Eastern radio station.

All the tales in this volume are in actual circulation to-day. Many of them are lacking in finish and construction, many of them show palpable gaps, but I have tried to reproduce faithfully as far as possible the spirit and manner in which they were told, and have striven throughout not to be over-free in translation but to follow the Arabic as nearly as I could. Some stories are verbally translated, but not all, for amateur shorthand, scribbled while the stories were being told, was only adequate when the narrators spoke slowly and paused sentence by sentence. These narrators included all kinds and classes of people: a Cabinet Minister, schoolmasters, Moslem and Christian ladies, their servants and slaves, tribesmen and tribeswomen. They were not all of equal skill. The best narrator I met with was a Baghdad Christian woman, though a Moslem lady of tribal origin, a charming woman of much artistic ability, came very near her in proficiency. The Christian, an illiterate, one-eyed woman of between fifty and sixty, became lost to her surroundings from the moment she squatted on the floor and embarked upon her tale. She was a good actress and employed gesture and change of voice to aid her graphic and racy speech. She had her stories, she said, from her grandmother, who was fond of relating them, and declared that these stories, heard when she was very young, were the only ones she could remember accurately. Among other stories I took down from her lips was the well-known classic from the *Thousand Nights and One Night* entitled 'The Story of Hasan of Al Basrah'. Space forbade me to include her version in this volume, but it was interesting to find how close the oral tradition keeps to the written word. I was careful not to read the original story until I had set down the tale as she told it.

I made my collection in Baghdad, Mosul, and the desert north of Mosul, but not, I am sorry to say, in Basrah or the South. I hope in the future to be able to gather some folk-lore in Southern 'Iraq. Mr. John Van Ess, whose *Spoken Arabic of Mesopotamia* is a standard work, and who knows 'Iraq and the 'Iraqis better than any living European or American, tells me that the South is rich in folk-tales and that the practice of voodoo amongst the black slaves there deserves study.

Now as to the form of the stories. At the beginning of the recital it is usual to utter some verselet such as (among Moslems),

Hnāk, ma hnāk	'Here, not here,
Ya ʿāshqīn an Nabi	Oh lovers of the Prophet,
Salluʿalaih	Pray for Him,'

to which the audience reply in chorus,

> *Elf as salāt*
> *Was salām 'alaik ya rasūl Allah;*

'A thousand prayers
And peace upon thee, oh Prophet of God;'

while both Moslems and Christians employ the formula:

> *Kān u ma kān* (or *kān ma kān*) [1]
> *'Ala Allah at Tuklān*

'It was and it was not.
(Our) reliance is upon God.'

Conventional tags and verselets occur in the course of the story, and at its conclusion comes another little jingle such as,

> *Kunna 'adkum wa jīna*
> *Wad daff umgarg'a wal 'arūs hazīna.*

'We were with you and came back
And the tambourine is rattling and the bride sad.'

or,

> *Hadhal hechāya*
> *Nusha chedhbāya* (*Nusfha kadhab*)
> *Wa lo baitna qarīb*
> *Kunt ajīb likum*
> *Tubeg hummus wa tubeg azbīb.*

'This story is half-lie,
And were our house near,
I'd bring you a dish of beans and a dish of raisins.'

These tags will appear from time to time in their proper places.

The matter of the tales is, as I have said, very varied. It might seem easy to classify the tales into groups of

---

[1] *Kān u ma kān*, or *kān ma kān*. It is difficult to find the true translation for this tag, the literal translation being somewhat unmeaning. A local name for folk-tales is 'Kān mā kān stories' and the tag may come from some classical source. Turkish and Armenian stories sometimes open 'There was was not' (a king, man, &c.), much as we begin 'Once upon a time'. I think the purpose of the rhyme is twofold, first to imply that the story is a fanciful one, and second to invoke God's name against malign influences which might be conjured up by the narration, especially when the jānn appear in it.

'nursery' tales, 'nursery' jingles, animal fables, tales of the Grimm *Household Tales* type, tales of the *Arabian Nights* type, and anecdotes told about supernatural beings by people who believe them to be true experiences; or they might be divided according to probable origin. But I found my attempts to arrange the stories into categories unsatisfactory, and so I have left them in no rational order at all, merely stating some particulars about the narrator of each tale at the end of the volume. At the end of the volume too will be found such notes as do not actually elucidate the text, but rather the matter of the stories, and references to a few collections of Persian, Armenian, and Turkish folk-tales which contain parallel stories.

Practically every tale set down here is of some type well known to folk-lorists, such, for example, as the stories in which *jānn*, or fairy-folk, don at will the appearance of birds, a type familiar to us in the legend of the Swan Maidens.[1] When one finds them in 'Iraq, one is bound to recall the bird-men of the early cylinder-seals, and the representations of men dressed in bird's plumage which one finds from time to time on Sumerian objects. Again, the description of the condition of the dead in the underworld in the Babylonian epic of the Descent of Ishtar into the dark realm 'where dust is their food and earth their eating', is significant:

> They see not light and sit in darkness,
> They are dressed like a bird with a garment of wings.

In short, the bird has always been symbolical of the soul, and the story of the Thorn-seller, with its other-world bridegroom coming in the guise of a bird, recalls both the Sumerian dwellers in the underworld and the legend of Lohengrin. The likeness to the latter and other folk-tales of the sort is heightened when the bird-man in the Arab story vanishes from the ken of his human bride the instant that his name and nature are proclaimed.

There is one great difference between fairy-tales told to an 'Iraqi child and those told in an English nursery. The

---

[1] Cf. *The Science of Fairy Tales*, by E. S. Hartland, Chap. X, 'Swan-maidens'.

English nurse or mother does not believe in the existence
of fairies or ogres, whereas the 'Iraqi story-teller very often
does. To the vast mass of the population of 'Iraq, excep-
tions being only found amongst the small educated
minority, the supernatural beings which appear in tale
and anecdote really exist. On the other hand, I have lived
over ten years in the country and have never heard a ghost
tale. I do not say that they do not exist, but I personally
never heard one, and when one hears of a house that is
maskūn, or haunted, it is never haunted by the dead, only
by *jinn*. I have asked some of the women the reason, and
their reply is usually something like this: 'Why should the
dead return? When they are dead, they go to their proper
place.' This is curious, seeing that Sumerian and Babylonian literature is full of belief in ghosts and of directions
how to propitiate them. But traces of the ancient ghost-
cult do linger in a few of the stories such as 'The Story of
the Boy and the Deyus', again proving the survival of
ideas in folk-stories after they have disappeared from
popular belief.

It will be necessary to say something of the various
supernatural beings which appear in these pages. Western
readers are already familiar with the *jinni*, '*afrīt*, and *ghūl*
which appear so often in the pages of the *Arabian Nights*,
but they may know less of other demons and ogres which
figure in the pandemonium of the 'Iraqis, such as the
s'ilūwa, the *deyu*, the *dāmi*, the *se'ir*, the *tantal*, the *tābi'a*,
the *ūm es sabyān*, and the *qarīna*.

I will only deal here with such of these mythological
beings as occur in the stories, for I hope to discuss the folk-
lore of 'Iraq more exhaustively in a future book.

The *s'ilūwa* occupies much the same role in 'Iraqi
legend as the witch or ogress in Western fairy-tales. She
is a water-spirit, for she dwells in the river or in caves near
running streams. Her body is covered with long hair,
her breasts are pendant, reaching her knees, and when she
wishes to suckle her children, whom she carries on her
back, she throws her breasts over her shoulder. In shape,
she is like a woman, but is represented sometimes as

having a fish's tail instead of two legs. She is fond of human flesh, but at the same time she has a partiality for human lovers. She is mortal like all the creations of Allah, except the angels, and she fears iron. Judging from some of the many stories about the *s'ilūwa*, I am inclined to think that this demon is a composite myth made out of some ancient river-goddess cult and the anecdotes which African slaves have told of the great apes.[1]

Another river demon is called the *ferij aqra'a*. He is fond of playing tricks on fishermen and river-dwellers, but does not seem to be such a dangerous being as the *s'ilūwa*.

Like her, he has either a fish's tail or weak legs. He resembles an old man, but his head is red and bald and the hair of his beard is green. A Shammari tribesman once told me that a shaikh camped beside the Euphrates, noticing that his mare which had formerly been tireless and strong, became weak and dispirited, had some pitch smeared one night on her back. The next morning they found a *ferij aqra'a* astride her, struggling in vain to flee away after his nocturnal ride. The shaikh's people fell on the monster and killed it with their knives. An appearance resembling this demon was reported in a Baghdad paper as lately as August 1922.

The *dāmi* is a half-bestial ogress which haunts the outskirts of towns. Like Babylonian and Assyrian demons,

---

[1] One day when speaking about *s'ilūwāt* to my head-servant, a Bahreini, I said to him, 'Are there such creatures near Bahrein?' He replied that there were, and that people were sometimes attacked by them in the desert. I asked, 'Have you ever seen one?' He replied, 'Yes.' I asked him to tell me how and where, and to my surprise, he answered, 'In London, when I went there with Faisal Ibn Saūd.' (The man had been attached to Faisal Ibn Saūd's suite when he visited London at the end of the War.) Pressed for details, he continued, 'Mr. Philby took us one day to a large garden where there were many animals. There were *s'ilūwāt*, two of them, male and female, in a box, and the box was adorned with adornment. No one was allowed to come near them but one, an Englishman, who guarded them.'

I said, 'What you saw were monkeys, Mubārak.'

He replied, 'No, *khatūn*, monkeys we saw there, too, many of them, but these were of the nature of man.'

The Arabic for gorilla is غول *ghūl* (anglicè, ghoul), indicating again that the Arabs take the larger apes for demons.

its usual food is dirt, refuse, and leavings of all kinds, though it has also a liking for human flesh. In 'Iraqi folk-tales it often takes the role assigned in European fairy-stories to the wolf.

The *qarīna* is a female demon. She will attach herself to a man, draw away his affection from his wife or bride, and even have children by him. An unmarried man is often thought to have a *qarīna*[1] as his wife. Amorous dreams are put down to intercourse with her. She is supposed to be very jealous and to injure any human woman on whom her human lover may have set his affections. She also steals or kills babies. It has been pointed out by Mr. Campbell-Thompson that she is probably the direct descendant of the Babylonian *ardat lilî*.[2]

The *deyu* is another rustic demon who haunts woods or desolate places. He and his female counterpart occur so often in these pages that their habits may be gathered from them.

The *se'ir* was described to me by a Shammar tribesman as haunting desolate places and ruins, especially Hatra. In appearance, he said, it was a very old man with a beard to its knees, one eye, very long teeth with iron on them, and toe-nails of iron. It devours human beings. I have only heard of this demon from the Shammar: in Baghdad and the south it is not apparently known. In Mr. Campbell-Thompson's *Semitic Magic*, p. 57, I find:

'It appears from several poetical passages of the Old Testament that the Northern Semites believed in demons of a precisely similar kind—hairy beings (*se'irim*), nocturnal monsters (*lilith*), which haunted waste and desolate places in fellowship with jackals and ostriches.'

To judge from the story told me by the Shammar, this ogre is related to the Cyclops of Greek legend.

I hope that 'Iraqis who read this book will be kind enough to furnish me with any information which may be in their possession about all these creatures of the night, for 'Iraq is a vast storehouse of folk-lore and legend. In

---

[1] In Armenian folk-tales she is called the Al.
[2] R. Campbell-Thompson, *Semitic Magic*, pp. 67 and 77.

offering these tales, drawn from my own imperfect and always growing collection, to a British public, I hope to prove how rich the country is in such treasure. I have not printed here stories which are obscene, but those given are unbowdlerized. I deemed it better to offer the stories in their natural form, without paraphrase or excuse.

I wish to thank most warmly those friends who have aided me in my work. The story-tellers head the list, and kind people like Madame Tatheossian, Shaikh 'Ajīl al Yawir, and members of the Naqīb's family who have put me into touch with them. Next comes 'Abd al Azīz Beg Mudhaffar, who was good enough to take a warm interest in the collection and to verify the correctness of the various tags of verse in dialect. To Sir Arnold Wilson, who was the first European to whom I showed this collection, I am most grateful, in the first place for his great kindness in contributing an introduction to this book, and secondly for much helpful suggestion and encouragement. I must also thank Professor Alfred Guillaume, for valuable advice on certain points of Arabic transcription and translation which were referred to him when the book was in proof.

CONTENTS

LIST OF PLATES

NOTE ON TRANSLITERATION

ALL the stories in this collection (with the exception of four, Stories XIV, XX, XXXIII, and XLV) were related to me in Arabic. The language was the vulgar colloquial dialect of 'Iraq, and as such I have tried to reproduce it in the verselets and quotations. An attempt to reproduce dialect must necessarily be exposed to criticism, and is far from easy. I have tried to reproduce Arabic and other Oriental words in the way that they were spoken, but in general have endeavoured to give the reader the clue to the literary word or root (where it exists). It is no service to truth to force these stories of the people into a mould which has been disused for centuries in common talk. There is not one dialect and pronunciation, but many. Even in Baghdad, the Christians, Jews, and Moslems all pronounce their words differently and employ their own corruptions of speech, and this is further accentuated because the women still further exaggerate differences and employ words rarely used by men. The leading characteristics of the dialect are as follows:

(1) *k* ك is rendered *ch.*

(2) *q* ق becomes *g* or *j.*

(3) The vulgar reverse their syllables in speaking, e. g. *ta* becomes *at*, *mu* becomes *um*, and so forth.

(4) Other vulgarisms are mispronunciations, e. g. *jīna* for *j'ina*, *khō* for *hadha al*, '*ad* for '*and*, &c.

(5) The use of Persian and Turkish words, such as *khōsh* and *chōl.* These are used throughout the country and by well-educated and ill-educated alike.

(6) A plentiful use of the diminutive, e. g. *shuwāiyib* (little old man).

The vowels also change in the spoken word, and more so in the South than in the North; for example Van Ess rightly gives the Basrawi *keteb* for the correct *kataba* (he wrote), while the Baghdad Moslem says *katab*. Everywhere *malik* (king) is pronounced *melek*, and it would be incorrect to transcribe the word in its literary form. For shortcomings in my efforts to reproduce tags and verselets as I heard them, I offer my apologies. I thought it better to risk writing rubbish than to force the verses into something which though grammatically correct, was certainly not what I heard.

For the transcription of Arabic I have, at the suggestion of my publishers, employed the system, slightly modified, to indicate dialect characteristics, recommended by the Royal Geographical Society. In the vernacular the difference between a heavy consonant and a light consonant is barely perceptible to the untrained European ear, and the Arabic scholar will readily perceive the letter intended. I have retained certain Arabic words in the text, e.g. *sūq*, as the words 'market' or 'town' do not convey the meaning. The Indian word 'bazaar' comes nearer, but to use the Arabic word is preferable. Similarly, 'cloak' and 'coat' do not translate '*aba* with any exactness.

I

THE CRAZY WOMAN

THERE was once a woman whose intellect was feeble. She was not possessed, but wanting. Her husband was a *raqq'a*, a cobbler, and he had a friend, a shepherd, who brought him one day two fleeces of wool from his sheep and said, 'Get an 'aba made with that for yourself.'

The cobbler replied, 'I am much obliged. Thank you!' and he took it home, and said to his wife, 'O woman, do you know who will spin this wool? I want to get it made into an 'aba.'[1]

Answered she, 'Yes! I know.'

He gave her the wool, and where did she go? She walked to the ditch outside the South Gate, which was full of green water, and the frogs croaking in it, qurrutch! qurrutch! qurrutch! Krk! Krk!

The woman called to them, 'Cousins! My cousins!'

They answered, 'Qurrutch! Qurrutch! kk! kk!'

She thought they answered her, and said, 'I have brought you some wool for you to spin into an 'aba for my husband, can you do it?'

They answered, 'K-k! k-k! qurrutch! qurrutch!'

Asked she, 'And when shall I come for it?'

Said they, 'Qurrutch! k-k!'

Said she, 'Aye, a month! Good, I will come for it!' And she threw the two fleeces into the ditch, and then returned home.

Said her husband, 'Did you leave my wool to be spun?'

Answered she, 'Aye, husband, I left it with my maternal cousins!'

He thought to himself, 'I never heard that she had cousins, but perhaps she has!' and he said to her, 'When will they bring it?'

She replied, 'I am going to fetch it in a month's time.'

[1] The universal outer garment of the Arab. It is woven either of wool or of silk, and is embroidered at the neck and on the shoulders with gold thread. It is square in cut, and has wide sleeves.

The month passed, and another month, and yet another month, and the man said to his wife, 'It is now three months and my 'aba is not ready, I will go with you and get it. Where do your cousins live?'

Said she, 'Near the South Gate!'

So they walked and walked, and came to the South Gate, and when the man asked where the house was, she pointed to the ditch, and said, 'My cousins live there!' while the frogs said, 'Krr-rr! kk-kk! qtsch! qurrutch!'

The man looked, and there he saw the two fleeces in the water, all green, and rotten, and spoiled! How angry he was! He beat her, crying, 'You crazy creature! You idiot! you fool!' and when they got back, he shut the door on her and went to bed, leaving her outside in the road, although it was growing dark. As for him, he went to sleep.

Dī! the night wore on until it was nearly midnight. The woman still sat by the road, and her husband was asleep inside. A cat passed by, and she thought that her husband had relented and sent the cat to fetch her in, so she said to the cat,

> *Fūti, fūti, mā āji!*
> *B'ath 'aleya pishpish*[1] *khātūn*
> *Mā āji!*
>
> 'Go away, go away!
> He has sent Miss Pussy for me,
> I won't come!'

A little after that, a dog went by. The woman cried:

Eyhu! b'ath 'aleya aūsh-aūshera
Mā āji, mā āji!
Fūt, fūt!

'Goodness gracious! he has sent a Bow-wow for me now,
But I won't come!
So go away!'

Now it happened that a thief had been at work that night in the Sultan's house, and presently he came walking

---

[1] 'Pish!' is the exclamation used in shooing a cat away.

with the stolen treasure on the back of a camel. The camel strayed from the path, and stopped in front of the woman who cried:

B'ath pishpish khātūn, mā ruhtu!
Aūsh-aūshera mā rūhtu
Hadha hōb-hōbera,[1] *lāzim ārūh wiyāhu!*

'He sent a Miss Pussy, but I wouldn't go!
He sent a Bow-wow, but I wouldn't go!
But now here is Mr. Hump! I must go with *him*!'

So she rose and knocked at the door, and called to her husband:

'You sent Miss Pussy, and I wouldn't come!
And you sent a Bow-wow, and I wouldn't come!
But now you have sent Mr. Hump, I must come!'

Now the man was beginning to feel sorry that he had left the woman out in the cold, and he opened the door, and there was the woman with a camel.

He said, 'Where did you get this camel?'

Answered she, 'You sent it to me!'

So he drove the camel inside into the yard, and said to his wife, 'It is cold, go in and sleep!'

And when she had gone, and he knew that she was asleep, he opened the saddle-bags, and found them full of treasure! He got a spade and made a hole and buried it all, then he killed the camel, and buried it too, only keeping a piece of the meat. This he took and made of it some kubbeh[2] and cooked it, then he went up to sleep.

Now there came some neighbours from a house near by, and they knocked at the door, and cried to the woman, 'We want to go down to the river to get water!'[3]

He heard the women knocking, and roused his wife and said, 'Go, wife, see who knocks at the door!'

She went, and they took her with them to go down to the river to get water.

---

[1] *Hōb!* is a cameleer's cry.

[2] Rissoles of meat, within a casing of rice or wheat.

[3] Women do not like to go out at night by themselves, or in twos or threes, they prefer a larger number for safety.

While they were gone the man took a dish of the kubbeh on to the roof, and as soon as his wife came back from the river, he threw some of the kubbeh at her; then he went back to bed and pretended to sleep.

Cried the woman, 'Come, neighbours! Come! It is raining kubbeh!'

The women picked up the kubbeh which he had thrown and ate it, and then they went away. Came the woman to her husband and roused him, saying, 'O husband! husband!'

He answered, 'What is it? You won't let me get any sleep!'

Said she, 'Come! It has been raining kubbeh!'

He looked at what she had brought, and said, 'Yes, it is indeed kubbeh! From whence did it come?' and ate of it.

She replied, 'It came from the skies: when we came back from the river, it rained kubbeh upon us!'

Said he, '*Suduq?*' 'Truth?'

Then they both went to sleep.

The next day the cobbler went to his work as usual, and the next day and the next, but on the third day, a crier went through the town, crying, 'Has any one seen a camel bearing the Sultan's saddle-bags on its back?'

The woman heard it, and she called to the crier, saying, 'The camel is in our house, come, come! My husband took it into our yard!'

She led them into the house, but they found nothing. Then they asked her, 'Where is your husband?'

She said, 'In the sūq,'[1] and sent a boy to show them where her husband sat in the sūq, mending old shoes. The police seized him, and bore him off to the serai, saying, 'The Sultan wants you!'

When he got to the serai they brought him before the mudīr of the police, and accused him saying, 'You have a camel, with saddle-bags on its back.'

---

[1] Place of shops. See note, p. xv. The *sūq* is usually a covered-in street with booths on either side. Trades are apt to congregate together, so that there is a *sūq* of the slipper-makers, another of coppersmiths, and so on.

He answered, 'No! By Allah!'

They said, 'Do not prevaricate, your wife has already confessed.'

He said, 'It is a lie, I have no camel. I am a poor cobbler, and every one knows me for an honest man. Where should I put a camel?'

They said, 'Your wife came to the crier and said that you took into your yard a camel with saddle-bags on its back.'

He replied, 'Will you bring my wife here, and examine her before me, and allow me to ask her questions?'

They answered, 'Yes, she may come,' and they sent for her, and said to her, 'Your husband has sent for you: he is in the serai. Come with us.'

She replied, 'Aye, I will come, but he told me to keep guard on the door, and how can I do that if I go to the serai? I had best bring the door with me!' So she took the door off its hinges¹ and put it on her head and went to the serai.

When she arrived, the mudīr said, 'What is this? Why is this woman carrying a door on her head?'

She answered, 'O my uncle, my husband told me not to leave the door of the house, so I've brought it with me!'

Said the cobbler, 'Tell the police all that happened the day you say I took the camel with saddle-bags into the house.'

She replied, 'That was the day you asked for the 'aba, and I took you outside the city to see if my cousins the frogs had spun the wool. Then you beat me and pushed me outside our door. And that night you sent Miss Pussy to ask me to return, and I would not, and then you sent Mr. Bow-wow to ask me, and I would not, and then you sent Mr. Hump, and I went with him, and you let us both in.'

Said the man, 'What else happened that night?'

Answered she, 'Why, yes, husband! That was surely the night when it rained kubbeh!'

¹ An 'Iraqi door is often made on the ancient Sumerian pattern and hooks into its hinges. Hence it can easily be removed if it is not closed.

The mudīr cried, 'What is this rubbish!'

Said she, 'But it is truth, O mudīr, I was coming back from the river, and it rained kubbeh from heaven and I ate some!'

Said they, 'The woman is crazy!' and then they said to him, 'Go! There is no accusation against you!'

And the man went home, and he divorced his wife, and after that he dug up the bags one night, and travelled away to another city, where he lived like a rich man on the Sultan's treasure.

II

THE GOAT AND THE OLD WOMAN

THERE was once upon a time an old woman who had a goat, and they lived in a little mud hut, and in the yard there was a well.

One day it began to rain, and it rained so hard that the roof leaked, and the old woman said to the goat, 'My goat, we can't keep dry here, let us get into the well.'

The goat replied, 'I won't go down.'

Said the old woman, 'You won't go down?'

Said the goat, 'No.'

Said the old woman, 'Shall I call the butcher to kill you?'

Said the goat, 'Go away!'

So the old woman went to the butcher and said,

Imshi īdhbah 'anūzi   'Go and kill my goat
Anūzi mā yirdha yinzal   My goat won't go down
  bil bīr!   the well!'

The butcher said, 'I won't come out in this rain, go away, go away!'

Said she, 'Shall I bring the smith to make your knives blunt?'

Said he, 'Go away!'

Then she went to the smith, and said, 'Smith, go and make the butcher's knives blunt! the butcher won't kill my goat, and my goat won't go down the well!'

The smith said, 'Go away, go away! I won't go out in this rain!'

She said, 'Shall I bring the river to quench your fire?'

He said, 'Away!'

So she went to the river and said,

'River, river, quench the smith's fire.
The smith won't blunt the butcher's knives,
And the butcher won't kill my goat,
And my goat won't go down the well.'

The river said, 'Away, away!'
She said, 'Shall I go and call the camel to drink you?'
The river said, 'Go away!'
Then she went to the camel and said,

> 'Camel, camel, drink the river,
> The river won't quench the smith's fire,
> And the smith won't blunt the butcher's knives,
> And the butcher won't kill my goat,
> And my goat won't go down the well!'

The camel said, 'Go away, I won't come in this rain!'
She said, 'Shall I bring rope to strangle you with?'
He said, 'Go away!'
Then she went to the rope, and said,

> 'Rope, rope, strangle the camel
> The camel won't drink the river,
> The river won't quench the smith's fire,
> The smith won't blunt the butcher's knives,
> The butcher won't kill my goat,
> And my goat won't go down the well!'

The rope said, 'Go away, go away! I won't come in such rain!'
Said she, 'Shall I call the rat to come and nibble you?'
He said, 'Go away!'
So she went to the rat and said,

> 'Rat, rat, nibble the rope,
> The rope won't strangle the camel,
> The camel won't drink the river,
> The river won't quench the smith's fire,
> The smith won't blunt the butcher's knives,
> The butcher won't kill my goat,
> And my goat won't go down the well!'

The rat said, 'Go away, go away! I won't go out in this rain!'
Said she, 'And if I bring the cat to come and eat you?'
He said 'Away!'

Then she went to the cat and said,

'Cat, cat! eat the rat,
The rat won't nibble the rope,
The rope won't strangle the camel,
The camel won't drink the river,
The river won't quench the smith's fire,
The smith won't blunt the butcher's knives,
The butcher won't kill my goat,
And my goat won't go down the well!'

Said the cat, 'Where is the rat? Lead me to it!'

The cat was about to spring, when the rat said, 'No, no! I am going to nibble the rope!'

The rope said, 'No, no! I am going to strangle the camel!'

The camel said, 'No, no! I am going to drink the river!'

The river said, 'No, no! I am going to quench the smith's fire!'

The smith said, 'No, no! I am going to blunt the butcher's knives!'

The butcher said, 'No, no! I am going to kill the goat!'

And the goat said, 'No, no! no!' and it went down the well, and the old woman after it.

III
THREE LITTLE MICE

Kān mā kān
'Ala Allah wat Tuklān
Kul men 'aleyhu dhanb yaqūl Istaghfar Allah!

'Was it, was it not,
Upon Allah, the Worthy of Reliance,
All who have sinned must say, "I ask pardon of Allah!"'

THERE were once three little mice, who were sisters. The eldest was called Hanni, the middle sister was Manni, and the youngest was called Tariaqsanni.

Hanni lived in a baker's shop and sat in it.
Manni lived in a butcher's shop and sat in it.
Tariaqsanni lived in a greengrocer's shop and sat in it.

Now one day, Tariaqsanni fell sick. A man came riding into the town to buy bread, meat, and vegetables, and the first shop he went to was the greengrocer's to buy some dates. When he entered the shop, he heard a tiny voice speaking to him:

Ya rākib al faras
Ya muchanchin bi jaras,
Qūl, li ūkhti, li Hanni, li Manni
Tariaqsanni qa [i.e. qad] tamūt!

'O rider on the mare
With jingling bells,
Tell my sisters Hanni and Manni
That Tariaqsanni is like to die.'

The man on horseback (*abul faras*) then rode on to the baker (*abul khabz*), and as he bought bread from him, he said, 'When I was in the greengrocer's shop just now, I heard a little voice coming from the shop which said,

"O rider on the mare with jingling bells,
Tell my sisters Hanni and Manni
That Tariaqsanni is like to die."'

Now Hanni heard his words, and no sooner had they left his mouth than she went running to her sister Manni and told her, 'A man came to my shop, and he told me that our sister Tariaqsanni is like to die!'

Then Hanni and Manni went together, running, running, running, to the greengrocer's shop to see their sick sister. They comforted her, saying, 'Please Allah, you will get well and we will all go out into the chōl[1] for a little change of air.'

And in time, Tariaqsanni got well. Then each mouse made provision for the journey. Hanni took some bread with her: Manni took some meat with her, and Tariaqsanni took some dates.

Then they set forth and journeyed into the chōl,[1] each carrying her food in her mouth. Presently they met a dog, who barked at them and pursued them. They ran away from him affrighted, and took refuge in a hole at the mouth of a well.

Then the dog came and barked over the well, saying thrice

Ūmm al bīr, ūmm al bīr[2]
Tisqa fi rāsech al kabīr!

'Well-mother, Well-mother,
Thou who givest to drink from thy wide mouth!'

Then crying, 'If you had had sense or forethought, you would not have come to the Mother of the Well!' he jumped in and ate Hanni, Manni, and Tariaqsanni—*all up!*

[1] *Chōl* (Turkish). This word, which occurs often throughout these tales, may be translated as 'desert', 'prairie', 'the wide world', 'the country', or 'the outskirts of a town'. In short, 'chōl' (pronounced to rhyme with bowl) is the townsman's word for whatever lies outside the wall of the city, and is always used in this sense in Baghdad. Just without the city wall, or just outside the door of house or tent—all is 'chōl'. To a townsman the chōl is a place of danger and fear, to a tribesman it is his natural surrounding.

[2] *Ūmm al bīr.* The dog is addressing the spirit of the well. A female spirit is supposed to haunt every well. See p. 120.

IV
THE SPARROW AND HIS WIFE

THERE was once a sparrow who was happily married and lived in a tree. One day he went out and bought seven grains of corn, for he wished to give a party. He brought the grains back to his wife, and then flew off to ask other sparrows to come to the feast. But he lingered on his errand, and when she had waited a long time for her husband to return, she was so hungry that she ate up all the seven grains, one after the other.

Just as she had finished, her husband flew back and his guests with him, and said to her, 'Bring the seven grains, for we are hungry!'

She answered him, 'Pardon! O my husband, you were so long away that I became weary and faint with hunger, and I ate the seven grains!'

He was very angry, and then and there before his guests he divorced her, saying three times, 'Woman, I divorce you!'[1]

Then she flew off to her people and the guests flew away to their houses, and the sparrow remained alone to repent his hastiness to his wife, for he loved her.

So after a little, he flew to the tree where she lived with her family and perched on a bough.

The wife-sparrow called out, 'Who has alighted on my father's tree?'

The sparrow answered, 'It is I, it is I! Little witch, little pecker! Little feathered and billed wife, I want you back! I want you home!'

> *Ana! ana!*
> *Bint as sāhira*
> *Bint an nāqira*
> *Bint ābul rīsh wal manqara*
> *Jīnā nsālah marrtna*
> *Ta'tūna illa naradd lil wara!*

---

[1] To say thrice before witnesses 'I divorce you' is a legal divorce. The story is a playful indictment of hasty divorce.

But she answered him, 'Go away! return whence you came!'

The next day he flew to her father's tree again, and she asked, 'Who has alighted on my father's tree?'

He answered as before: 'It is I, it is I! Little witch, little pecker, little feathered and billed wife! I came because I want you back, I want you home!'

But she answered, 'Go away! return whence you came!'

So it was each day.

But one morning, the sparrow went to the sewing-woman, and said, 'I want a green thread, a yellow thread, a blue thread, a red thread, and a lilac thread!'

And the sewing-woman gave him all five threads in five colours.

Then he took them in his bill and flew to the tree of his wife's father.

Cried she, 'Who is it that has alighted on my father's tree?'

Answered he, 'It is I, it is I! Little witch, little pecker, little billed and feathered wife! I came because I want you back, I want you home!'

She made reply, 'Go away! return whence you came!'

But he said, 'A red, and a green, a yellow, a blue, and a lilac (thread) I have brought. Will you give her to me, or shall I return without her?'

> *Bil āhmari, bil ākhdhari*
> *Bil āsfari bil māwi bil lilāqi*
> *Ta'tūna illa naradd lil wara?*

Then she uttered joy-cries and flew down to him, and took the threads in her beak, and flew back with him to their nest. She wove the threads into it:[1] then they bought some more corn and gave a party to all their friends.

---

[1] Threads of different colours interwoven are a charm against the evil eye. Cf. R. Campbell-Thompson, *Semitic Magic*, p. 164.

V

DUNGARA KHSHEYBĀN

THERE was once a man who had two daughters, and both grew up and married. The elder daughter married a wealthy man, but the younger chose a poor man.

One day, at a time when the younger was pregnant and near her delivery, she felt a longing to eat some lentil soup. She went to her elder sister, and said, 'Can you give me some lentils, for I have a longing for lentil soup.'

The elder said, 'I will cook you some lentil soup.'

So the younger sister sat, and the elder sister cooked soup, and while she was cooking it, she heated red-hot in the fire a skewer. When she brought the soup, and the younger sister sat to eat it, she ran the skewer into the other's thigh, and the younger sister fled away, hungry, leaving her soup uneaten.

She returned to her husband, and asked him to go and find some lentils for her, and he went off to try to get some.

While she sat in the house, waiting for him, her pains came upon her, and she was afraid, for there was no one there to help her. But, just as her need was greatest, the wall of the room parted, and out of it stepped five maidens, daughters of the jānn,[1] who came to her and helped her. When she had brought a daughter into the world, they washed it, and clothed it, and gave it back to the mother.

Said the first jinnīya, 'If God wills, a golden head-dress[2] shall crown her brow.'

Said the second, 'When she walks, myrtle and jessamine will spring from her footprints.'

The third said, 'When she speaks, a jewel will fall from her lips.'

The fourth said, 'When she weeps, the rain will fall, and when she smiles, the sun will come out.'

[1] The fairy folk, *jinni* and *jinnīya* are the singular forms, masculine and feminine. The plural forms are *jīnn*, *jānn*, masculine or collective, and *jinniyāt*, feminine.   [2] *tās*.

The fifth said, 'Each time she bathes, the water she has bathed in will turn to an ingot of silver and an ingot of gold.'

Then the wall reopened again, they stepped into it and disappeared.

The woman washed her baby that evening, and, just as the jinniyāt had said, the water in which she had bathed the babe turned into an ingot of gold and an ingot of silver. She bought food, and clothes, and hired servants, and a fine house, and had as much money as she could desire, for every day there was gold and to spare.

But all this while her husband had not returned, for he had gone everywhere in search of lentils and had been able to find none. So when she had moved into her fine house, the woman sent a slave in search of her husband, and ordered the man to take him, when he had found him, to the bath, and to clothe him in good new clothes.

The slave searched for him in the sūq, and there he found him.

Said the slave, 'Your wife has sent me to find you, and she wants to know why you have not returned to the house.'

Answered the man, 'I have looked everywhere for the lentils for which my wife was craving, and have found none. How then could I return to the house?'

Said the slave, 'Your wife has brought a daughter into the world, and wishes to see you, but first you must go to the bath.'

So the man went to the bath, and afterwards he put on the new clothes, and returned with the slave to the house. His wife was waiting for him near the door, and when he approached, she went to him, and told him all that had happened.

He was delighted, and from that day he and she lived in great comfort and wealth, and wanted for nothing.

Their daughter grew, and in course of time she reached the age of thirteen, and was of such rare beauty that every one who saw her was amazed.

One day, she went on to the roof to take the air. As she

walked there, the Sultan's son passed, and gazed upon her. He was bereft of his senses as he looked upon her, and as soon as he had reached the palace, he went to his father and said, 'I have seen the maiden that I wish to marry. I will take none other as wife.'

The Sultan asked, 'Who is this maiden, my son?'

Answered the youth, 'I saw her to-day on the roof of such and such a house.'

Said the Sultan, 'That cannot be, for we do not know the girl or her people.'

But the youth besought his father, and at last the Sultan gave in to his importunity, and sent women of his household to the household of the girl. They saw that the family was wealthy, and the Sultan's wife said to the mother of the girl, 'I have come to ask for your daughter. My son wishes to marry her.'

So the marriage was arranged, the marriage contract drawn up by the mulla, and the day appointed for the bride to go to her bridegroom.

Her mother's sister said that she would accompany her, and on the evening of the bride's departure, she and the bride went in a carriage to ride to the Sultan's palace. On the way her aunt persuaded her to stop the carriage and rest a little, and when they had left the road the aunt said to the girl, 'I wish to try on your bridal clothes, will you change with me?'

Answered the girl, 'Aye!' and she took off her clothes, and put on her aunt's. As soon as they had changed, the aunt seized her and tore out her two eyes, and left her there by the road. Then she got back into the carriage and rode to the Sultan's palace as the bride. None of the Sultan's household suspected that she was not the bride, but the bridegroom, when he saw her face, came out of the bridal chamber, and said to his mother, 'This is not the girl I saw.'

She replied, 'This is the girl you have married, my son,' and he was forced to accept her as his bride.

As for the real bride, she walked with blinded eyes into the desert, pricked by the thorns and stumbling over stones, and her dress was torn, and her feet were bleeding. When she had gone thus for some way, she met a poor thorn-seller, who was amazed by her beauty, and cried, 'Are you fairy or human?' *Ins ū jins?*

She answered, 'I am human.'

Then he pitied her plight, and took her home with him, and said to his four daughters, 'Here is a poor girl whom I met in the desert; give her food and tend her.'

The eldest daughter said, 'My father, we are hungry, and have not enough bread for ourselves! You must turn this stranger away; she will eat our bread and we shall have none!'

Said the thorn-seller, 'How can I turn her away? It would be a sin!' and his youngest daughter said, 'My father, she shall stay, and I will give her half my portion every day,' for as soon as she saw the girl she loved her.

So the bride stayed with them and shared the bread of the youngest daughter. When it was night, she said, 'Fetch me water, I want to bathe,' and a pearl fell from her lips when she spoke.

The youngest went to get her water, and the bride bathed, and when she left the water, in its place was an ingot of silver and an ingot of gold. These she gave to the thorn-seller, and told him that he should have the same every day, as well as the jewels which fell from her lips. So the thorn-seller became a rich man.

One day the bride said to the thorn-seller's daughter, 'Take some of this myrtle and jessamine that have grown from the ground upon which I have trodden, and go to the Sultan's palace. When you have come beneath the windows of the prince's bride, cry:

Yās ū yāsmīn	"Myrtle and jessamine
Bi 'ain al yamīn	For the right eye!"

until she looks out from the window.'

The daughters of the thorn-seller did as she had asked, and went below the window of the false bride, and cried:

'Myrtle and jessamine
For the right eye!'

The false bride looked out of the window, and said, 'What do you want?' They said, 'Here is myrtle and jessamine for the right eye!'

She was frightened, and threw the right eye out of the window to them. They returned, and the bride put the right eye in its socket, and it grew again, and she could see with her right eye.

Next she took a pearl which had fallen from her mouth when she spoke, and gave it to them, saying, 'Go as before to the window of the prince's bride, and cry:

Lūlū sār	"A pearl.
Bi ʿain al yisār!	For the left eye!" '

They went as before, and the false bride came to the window and said, 'What do you want?'

They answered, 'A pearl for the left eye!'

Then she threw them the left eye, and they returned with it to the real bride, and she put that into its place, and she could see perfectly with both eyes as before.

One day the girl asked the thorn-seller to bring some wood, and to carve her a dress from it, and to make her as well a wooden staff.

He did so, and made her a dress of wood which covered her completely from head to foot, leaving only holes for her eyes, and holes for her arms. Then she took the staff in her hand, and bade him and his daughters farewell. They begged her to stay with them, but she refused, saying, 'You are rich now, and I must go.' She gave them her blessing, and set out, and walked until she came to her husband's palace, where she seated herself by the door.

The servants noticed her, and came to the Sultan's son, saying, 'There is a man dressed all in wood sitting by the Palace gate!' Said he, 'Go and ask what he wants.'

They went to her, and said, 'What do you want?'

She answered, 'I want to become a servant in the prince's house.'

They answered, 'Come in, you shall help in the house.'

She entered, and so well did she do her work, that every one was amazed. At night she took off her wooden dress, but by day she always wore it, and they gave her the nick-name of 'Dungara Khsheybān'.

One day the prince gave a feast to his friends, and he said to the master of the household, 'This evening no one shall wait on us at table but Dungara Khsheybān.'

So when the guests came, Dungara Khsheybān brought the dishes to the table, and her movements in the wooden dress were so clumsy that she let the dishes fall, and they were broken.

He was very angry, and cried, 'Dungara Khsheybān! Take off that wooden dress of yours, or I will stab you with my dagger!'

At that, she lifted the wooden dress, and came out of it, and there she stood, beautiful as the moon from behind the clouds. He knew her at once for his own true bride, and bade her tell him everything.

She told him all that had happened to her, from the beginning to the end, and he embraced her, and took her for his wife, and as for the aunt, he ordered her to be burnt alive!

> *Kunna 'adkum wa jīnā*
> *Wa lo baitkum qarīb*
> *Kunt ajīb likum hafna[1] zabīb.*

'We've been to you and come back
And were your house near
I should have brought you a handful of raisins.'

---

[1] In Baghdad they give a *tubeg* (trayful), in Mosul, only a handful. Mosul people bear the reputation of being close-fisted.

VI

THE CRYSTAL SHIP

Kān u ma kān	It was and was not!
'Ala Āllah at Tuklān.	(Our) reliance is upon God.

THERE was once a merchant who had three daughters. One day he was obliged to travel to a far country in search of merchandise, and he said to his eldest daughter, 'When I return, what shall I bring you, my daughter?'

She said, '*Arīd lī bedli hilwi!* I want a pretty new dress!'

Then he asked the same of his second daughter, and she answered, 'I want a pretty new dress, too.'

Then he asked the youngest, who was but a child, and she went to her mother and said to her, 'O my mother, what shall I ask my father to bring me back when he returns?'

The mother said, 'Ask for clusters-of-pearl.'[1]

So she went to her father and said, 'I want clusters-of-pearl.'

He promised his daughters to bring them back what they had asked, and then he set forth, and travelled by ship to the distant country. When his business there was transacted, he went to the sūq, and he bought two lengths of silk for his two eldest daughters, but the youngest he forgot. Then he went to the harbour, and embarked on the ship. The captain came to him and said, 'Is all your business transacted, and is nothing left undone? For my ship will not sail if there is one on board who has left something undone.'

The merchant exclaimed, 'I have forgotten my promise to my youngest daughter that I would bring her a present!'

Said the captain, 'Then return to the shore and get it, else my ship will not move from the harbour.'

The merchant went ashore again, and went to the sūq of the jewellers, and said, 'I wish to buy clusters-of-pearl.'

---

[1] *Lulu 'anāqīdu.*

They answered him, 'Clusters-of-pearl is the name of a person: it is the name of the son of the Sultan of the Jānn.'

He asked them, 'Where is he to be found, this Clusters-of-Pearl?'

They told him, 'His father's palace is in such and such a place.'

The merchant went to the place they indicated, and he found the door of the palace and knocked at it.

A voice inside the door said, 'Who is it?'

He answered, 'I!'

Said the voice, 'What do you want?'

He said, 'I seek Clusters-of-Pearl.'

The door was opened, and there stood before him a beautiful boy, who said to him, 'My name is Clusters-of-Pearl. What do you want of me?'

The merchant answered, 'I have three daughters, and when I left my country to come here, I promised them each a present. To the two eldest, I promised new dresses, and to the youngest, I promised Clusters-of-Pearl.'

Said the boy, 'Take this small box. In it are three hairs. Give them to your daughter and tell her to sit in an empty room, near a bare threshold in a place apart, all by herself. This room you must build for her. When she is alone, let her rub the three hairs together. Whatever appears to her, she must not utter a word or cry aloud for fear, but must say "*Māshāllah!*"[1] thrice.'

The merchant took the small box, and said farewell to the boy, and then went back to the ship. It sailed with him and in time he reached his own country.

When he returned to his house, his daughters greeted him, and embraced him, and the eldest said, 'Where is my new gown?' He opened his box, and gave it to her, all broidered and sewn and ready to wear. The middle sister said, 'Where is my new gown?' and he gave it to her, all sewn and broidered and ready to wear. Then the youngest said, 'Where are my clusters-of-pearl?' And he

[1] *Mā sha' Allah* (literally, 'What God willed') is an exclamation which averts the evil eye and envy, and should be used every time one looks at anything beautiful or splendid.

replied, 'O my daughter, I forgot what you asked, so I have brought you nothing.'

But that night as he lay abed, he said to his wife, 'Wife, I do not know what to do and you must give me your counsel. Clusters-of-Pearl is the name of the son of the Sultan of the Jānn,' and he told her all that had happened, saying when he had done, 'What say you, wife? Shall we build a room and leave the girl alone in it, as the son of the Sultan of the Jānn said, or shall we not?'

His wife answered him, 'Build it, and you will see that good fortune will come of it.'

So the next day the merchant called builders, and built a new room, and put nothing into it: the threshold he left bare as Clusters-of-Pearl had ordered and, when it was finished, the little sister went to the bath, and they dressed her, and adorned her, and then her father and mother led her to the room and bade her wait there, giving her the box containing the three hairs. Her father bade her strike them together, and to forbear exclaiming at what she might see, only saying, '*Māshāllah!*' three times.

Then they locked the door, and left the girl alone. She struck the three hairs together as they had said, and as she waited there she looked at the threshold, and saw that it had become a lake, and upon the lake swam a ship of crystal. The ship approached her, and in it was a boy,

Subhān Allah al khalaquh   Praise to God who created
Wal khāliq ahsan!   him, and the Creator is
                             better than his creation.

and this boy was of the most perfect beauty.

The little sister was amazed, but she said no words but '*Māshāllah!*' thrice-uttered, as her father had bidden. The boy approached her and kissed her and she loved him and he her, and they stayed together in happiness and contentment until the morning. Then he said to her, 'If anything should happen to part us, and I am unable to come here, go and seek for me: but you must put on shoes of iron,[1] and carry an iron staff in your hand.' Then he bade her

---

[1] *Iron* is a protection against evil spirits. See the note on this story, pp. 293–4.

say nothing of what had happened that night to any one, and he took his departure, sailing away in the crystal ship. Then the threshold became as it was.

In the morning her two parents came, and she told them that she was happy and blessed, but more than that she did not say.

At night she returned to the room, unlocked it, and did as she had done the former night, and spent the time in happiness and contentment with Clusters-of-Pearl till the dawn. And so it was for many nights.

Now the eldest sister guessed what was happening, and was jealous of the little sister's happiness. One day, when all the sisters went to the bath with their mother, the eldest refused to take off her clothes.

They said to her, 'Come and bathe with us!' but she would not, saying, 'I do not wish to bathe to-day, I will wait for you.'

As soon as the others were bathing, she went to her sister's clothes, and stole the key of the room from her pocket. Then she returned quickly to the house, went to the room and unlocked it, and seated herself in her sister's place. There she saw the box, and when she had opened it, she found three hairs. These she took out and rubbed them together, and after she had done so, the threshold became a lake, and in the midst of it a ship of crystal, in which was the son of the Jānn. The girl was so astonished that she cried aloud, and at that, the ship flew into splinters and entered the body of the boy. Then he and the lake disappeared, and all was as it had been before.

She was frightened, and went out and locked the door, and when the rest had returned from the bath, she went secretly and put the key back in her sister's pocket, but said no word of what had happened.

That evening, the little sister went again to her room, and rubbed the three hairs together, but nothing happened, and though she waited all the night, nothing appeared, and the room was dark and empty.

The little sister wept and cried, 'Woe, woe! This is my sister's work!' and the next morning she went to her father, and told him that he must make her a pair of iron shoes, and an iron staff to carry in her hand.

She travelled, and travelled, walking over deserts and valleys, and after many days she came to a town. Upon the outskirts of the town there was a tree. She was foot-sore and tired from her journey, *khatīya*![1] so she sat beneath it to rest, and closed her eyes.

Now on the boughs of this tree there were two doves, (*cucūkhtiain*). Presently one began to coo to the other, and the little sister heard these words:

Cucūkhti! eyn ūkhti?	'Coo-coo, sister doo, where
Idha hadhal bint kānat	are you-u-u![2]
nāimi	If this maiden be sleeping
Hadha nasībha	Her fate is sealed.
Idha kānat qa'adi, min	If watch she is keeping,
nasībha!	Her fate is healed.'

When she heard this, the little sister kept her eyes closed, but she listened with all her ears.

The other dove replied:

Cucūkhti, eyn ūkhti!	'Coo-coo, sister doo, where
	are you-u-u!'

'This maiden was visited by the son of the Sultan of the Jānn, but one day when she was at the bath, her sister stole her key and rubbed the three hairs together, and when the boy appeared she cried out, and the ship flew into splinters and entered the body of the boy; and when this child came in her turn to rub the hairs, no one came to her, and she remained there sitting and weeping, and now she has come to seek him!'

Then the other dove took up the tale and said,

'And now that boy is sick unto death, and his father seeks everywhere for a medicine to cure him. Now, if that maiden were listening, she would seize us both, and kill us and take our blood and feathers and some of the leaves of this tree. With these she must go to the house

[1] An exclamation of pity 'What a sin!' 'What a shame!'
[2] A quotation from a popular rhyme imitating the cooing of doves. The rhyme is given in full in the note to this story, pp. 293-4.

of the Sultan of the Jānn. There she must cry, "A healer! A physician!" until they invite her within. As soon as she has entered, she must take the sick boy to the bath, and smear his body all over with our blood and feathers,[1] and all the crystal splinters will fall out of his body. After that she must wipe his body with the leaves of this tree, and the boy will be cured.'

As soon as the doves had ceased their talking, the girl rose quickly, seized them, and wrung their necks, and then she poured blood from their bodies into a cup, and their feathers she placed in a kerchief. Then she plucked leaves from the tree, and she went into the town, crying, 'A healer! A physician!' until she came to the door of the castle in which the Sultan of the Jānn lived. When the Sultan of the Jānn heard her voice without, he sent and had her brought in before him.

He asked her, 'Who are you?' and she answered, 'I am a healer, and if you will bring your son to the hammām,[2] and leave him there with me, I will cure him completely.'

The Sultan of the Jānn said, 'It shall be done,' and they took her to the hammām, and brought to her the boy, who lay there as if dead. She ordered them to leave her alone with him, and they left them alone in the bath. Then she took off his clothes, and dipped the feathers in the blood and smeared it all over his body. As soon as she had done that, the crystal fell out of the boy's body. Then she wiped his skin with the leaves of the tree, and the wounds closed and his flesh was healed, and he opened his eyes, and was completely cured.

Now when he gazed upon her, he did not know her in her man's dress, but he begged her, saying, 'Come, take off your clothes, and we will bathe together.'

She refused, saying, 'No, I will not bathe.'

Then the boy was angry, and said, 'I will not leave this bath until you have bathed with me!'

Then the little sister confessed, saying, 'I am she to

[1] Clearly a *fedu* or ransom charm. See p. 271.
[2] Hot bath. Hammāms are supposed to be especially inhabited by spirits.

whom you came in your boat of crystal: and when you came no more, I came to seek for you!'

Then the boy embraced her tenderly and took her to his father, the Sultan of the Jānn, who said to her, when he had heard all:

'Daughter of man! Had you not cured him, your life should have been forfeit, but as you have saved his life you shall marry him and dwell with us in the country of the Jānn.'

Then he made a wedding for three days and three nights, and the boy and girl were married, and they lived always in the country of the Jānn.

Kunna ʿadkum wa jīnā!

VII

THE OLD COUPLE AND THEIR GOAT

ONCE upon a time there was an old couple, and they kept a goat, of which they were very fond. Their house was of clay and their door of reeds, and they two and the goat lived there together.

One day a dāmi[1] who lived in the desert near by became hungry for human blood, and she said to herself, 'I will eat either that old man or that old woman!' So she went to the house and knocked at the reed door and said:

Yā bāb al qasab,	'O reed door!
Ăkassar ʿanak	I will break you down!
Lo ujāiz lo shwāyib bi	I will eat up your little old
ākul ʿanak!	woman or your little old
	man!'

Now the old woman was alone in the house, and when she heard this she was very afraid, but the goat was listening and she answered, 'With my horns I will butt you and with my teeth I will bite you!'

When the dāmi heard this, she was frightened of the goat and ran away back into the desert.

But she was still very hungry, so the next day she came again and knocked at the gate. The old woman who was alone said, '*Minu?* Who is it?' and the dāmi said,

'O reed door!

I will break you down!

I will eat up your little old woman and your little old man!'

And the goat answered, 'With my horns I will butt you and with my teeth I will bite you!' and the dāmi was frightened and ran away.

Now as the dāmi was going along the road, whom should she meet but the old man? She said to him, 'Every day I come to your house to give you some food from the Sultan's house, but your goat will not let me in!'

[1] See Preface, p. xii, and note, p. 295.

The old man went back and said to the old woman,'What is this? The dāmi brings us food every day from the Sultan's house and our goat will not let her in! I shall kill the goat!'

Answered the old woman, 'O husband, is your understanding wanting? The goat stands before the door because the dāmi wants to eat us! Don't kill the goat!'

The next day it was the same, the dāmi came and the goat would not let her in, and the dāmi complained to the old man.[1] But after the dāmi had complained for the third time, the old man took his knife and prepared to kill the goat. The old woman cried:

'O husband, do not believe the dāmi! She wants to eat us! She is hungry for our blood! Do not kill our goat!'

But the old man went to the goat and cut her throat.

The old woman wept and cried, '*Shlōn sowweyt!* What have you done!'

But as the goat was dead, she roasted some of the meat, and made *pācha*[2] of the head and oddments, and the rest she put in a pot of brine.

The next day the dāmi came and cried:

'O reed door!
I will break you down!
I will eat up your little old woman and your little old man!'

And from the pot of brine a voice came from the meat,

'With my horns I will butt you and with my teeth I will bite you!'

And the dāmi was frightened and ran away.

That night the old man ate up the meat that was left. The next day the dāmi came before he had gone out, and she cried to the door,

'O reed door!
I will break you down!
I will eat up your little old woman and your little old man!'

[1] Repetition, which I do not give in full.
[2] *Pācha.* Stew of sheep's offal and head and feet. A favourite dish in Baghdad, and the trade of *pāchachi*, or pācha-seller, is a remunerative profession in the poor quarters of the city. It is not, however, a dish that is set before a guest.

And this time there was no answer, but inside the house the old woman said, 'Now you hear for yourself! The dāmi wants to eat us!'

The old man ran off and hid in the clay oven, and the old woman rolled herself in some matting and hid in the room.

The dāmi cried again at the door, and there was no answer, so she pushed with her head, and the door gave way, and she entered and wandered about the *hōsh*.[1] The old man, in his fright, let a sound escape him in the oven.

Called the dāmi:

Menu darrat?	'Who made that noise?
Al hāyit darrat?	Was it the wall?
Al bāb darrat?	Or the door?
Al bait darrat?	Or the house?'

And she wandered about looking. *Dī!* She came to the oven. She looked in the oven, and there she saw the old man!

Said she:

Menu darrat?	'Who made that noise?
Ash shāib darrat!	The old man did!
Shlōn aktalak?	How shall I kill you?'

The old man said, 'Because I did not listen to my wife's advice, when she asked me not to kill the goat, now you are going to eat me!'

The dāmi took him and tore him in two halves, and ate him all up and returned to her lair in the desert.

As for the old woman, she brought some friends to live with her in the house, and the dāmi did not return there again.

[1] The *hōsh* is all the ground, including the yard, enclosed by the house-wall.

VIII

SHAMSHŪM AL JABBĀR

THERE was once a very strong man called Shamshūm the Mighty, and he married the daughter of a merchant, who was very beautiful. He loved her exceedingly, and she bore him a son. But although she was lovely to the eye, she was not faithful to him, but had forty deyus[1] as her lovers. Every day they visited her, and took her to their house in the desert, where she played chess with them. At last her son, who was grown to be a big lad, told his father, 'My mother goes out when you are absent.' So Shamshūm followed his wife, and went into the house of the forty deyus, and attacked them, and beat them and drubbed them and overthrew them, and brought his wife back to his house. Every day she went with them, and every day he fetched her and beat and maltreated the deyus, for he was so strong that they had no power against him.

At last the deyus said to the woman, 'Ask your husband whence he derives the strength with which he overcomes us and beats us.'

That night she rose in her bed and asked her husband, as he lay by her,

Whence do you derive your strength? How is it that you are so strong?

He replied, 'Why do you wish to know? And to what use will you put your knowledge?'

She said, 'It is only that I wish to know.'

He answered then, 'My strength is in the birds.'

The deyus then caught all the birds, wherever they might be flying, and killed them every one—there were none left in the world.

But for all that it was the same as before. Daily he beat them and overthrew the deyus in their house.

So they said to her, 'Lies! His strength is not in the birds! He continues to beat and torment us. Find out the cause of his strength.'

[1] For *deyu* (pronounced dey-u) see Preface, p. xiii.

So that night she asked him again, and pressed him to tell her whence he derived his strength.

He answered her, 'My strength is in my broom.'

Then the deyus collected all the brooms and burnt them in the fire. There was not one left in all the world.

Bōsh![1] Empty! No use! There was no diminution of his strength, and when she went to play chess with the deyus, he came as before and beat them and drubbed them and overthrew them.

That night she said to her husband:

'Verily you have deceived me! Where is your strength? Tell me the truth.'

He said in himself, 'She is a woman, what harm can she do me?' and he told her, 'My strength is in my hair.'

When she heard that, she laughed, and went and played chess with the deyus and said, 'His strength is in his hair!'

And they said, 'When he is asleep, cut his hair.'

That night she cut his hair.

This. And when he awoke in the morning he was sick and had not the strength to walk. Then the forty deyus came and seized Shamshūm the Mighty, and bound him with chains, and put him into a sack up to his armpits, and took him into the desert, and dug a hole, and put him into it up to his chest, and put a large slab of marble on his chest to hold him down. There they left him.

But his son came every day while his mother went to amuse herself with the forty deyus, and he sat beside him and asked his father how he did, and gave him bread. There Shamshūm the Mighty stayed for a space of forty days, and each day his hair grew, and as his hair grew, his strength grew. *Dī, dī, dī!* On the fortieth day he said to his son, 'O my son, give me help. With your effort and my effort we shall be able to throw off this stone.'

The boy answered, 'Yes, I will help you.'

And, *dī, dī, dī!* they strove and struggled, and made

[1] Turkish.

great effort, and at last they pushed the great stone from his chest, and threw it into the desert.

Then Shamshūm said, 'O my son, go to my house, and bring me my sword which hangs from the ceiling. Bring it with care, and do not flash it, or draw it, because it is very sharp and dangerous, but hold it by the hilt, and bring it here.'

The boy went, and as his father had ordered, he put a ladder on the table, and took the sword down from where it was hung on the ceiling, and bore it with care to his father. His father took it and cut open the sack, and severed the chains which bound him, and said, 'Now, I will go and slay the witch[1] your mother,' and he went to the castle of the deyus and stayed by the door.

As each deyu came out by the door, *dī!* he cut his head off, and the head of his wife he cut off also. Only the fortieth deyu had two heads, and when he had cut one head off, the deyu escaped with the other still on his shoulders, and so lived. Now this deyu, the father-of-two-heads, loved the Khalīfa's daughter, as you shall hear anon.

As for Shamshūm and his son, they went into the desert, and remained there, until one day they came to a sea, and beyond the sea was an island. On the shore there was a big serpent, which was coiled about a tree. This serpent lived upon the nestlings of an eagle which had its nest in the tree, and each year, when the bird hatched its eggs, he ate the young birds. When he saw the serpent, Shamshūm took his sword and slew it.

Then flew back the eagle, and she said,

'Woe, woe, son of Adam! Is it you who come each year and kill my brood?'

But the eaglets cried, 'Wiss, wiss, wiss! Our mother, this son of Adam did nothing to us, but he has saved us from the serpent which you see dead!'

And the eagle saw the serpent slain beneath the tree, and rejoiced, and said, 'Son of Adam, you have saved my children from death, ask and desire!'

---

[1] S'ilūwa.

And Shamshūm answered, 'I have no desire, but take my son and myself, and throw us on the island.'

She answered, '*Mā yukhālif!* Let it be so,' and opened her two wings, saying, 'Get you on one wing, and your son on the other.'

And she flew with them over the sea, and threw them down on the island.

They abode there, and Shamshūm, who was learned, and could read, taught his son knowledge and reading. But there was nothing to eat and drink in the island, and the boy became hungry and thirsty, and at last he fell sick and died.

Shamshūm rose, and dug a hole in the earth, and made a tomb for his son and buried him, then he sat down beside the tomb and read and read, and thought, and thus he stayed, reading and pondering for seven years.

And he said to himself, 'One day, I shall lie here beside my son!'

Now the deyu who had escaped with his life when Shamshūm slew his brothers, was the lover of the Khalīfa's daughter. And when he told her about Shamshūm the Mighty she longed to see him, and said, 'Where is Shamshūm the Mighty now?' The deyu replied, 'I do not know where he is hiding.' So the princess sent for magicians and sorcerers and wise women. And they read, and they read [spells], and they answered her, 'He is to be found, but he is very far.'

At last there came a very old and skilled witch, and the princess said to her, 'I want Shamshūm from you, and if you can find him, everything you want I will give it to you.'

The old and skilled witch read in the sand,[1] and took much trouble and read and read, and said, 'He is in an island behind the sea.'

---

[1] For divining in sand, see *Arabian Nights*, Haikāyat 'Ali Shār. It is practised still. A little sand is spread on a level surface and smoothened. The inquirer takes a little and holds it near his heart, and then, at the diviner's command sprinkles it on the rest of the sand. The diviner marks the sand at random with his finger-tips in four rows; adds the marks up to see if they are odd or even, then consults his book.

The princess said, 'Take me to him, for I wish to see him.'

The witch was very skilled in witchcraft, and she answered, 'Good, I will take you and put you on the island. There is no objection.' And she witched and witched and witched until the daughters of the jānn came before her. Then she ordered them, 'Take this deywa and throw her on the island which is in the sea beyond seven seas,' for the witch was ruler of the jānn, and what she ordered them they must perform.

Then she said to the princess, 'Shut your eyes!' and to the daughters of the jānn, she commanded that they should take the girl and put her on the island. So it was, and they flew with her fr-r-r-r! to the island beyond the sea that is over seven seas.

There, while she was yet in the air, the Khalīfa's daughter saw Shamshūm reading from an open book upon the tomb of his son, and he was now an old man. And she descended.

Shamshūm lifted his eyes and saw her sitting upon the other side of the tomb and he asked her, '*Nti ins, jins?* Are you human, or fairy?'

She answered, 'I am a human woman.'

He said, 'You have come here—why?'

She said, 'I want to know your story, and all that has happened to you.'

Said he, 'Why do you wish to hear my story?'

Answered she, 'I wish to know why you are here, for I too, have fallen into this island.'

Said he, 'I will tell you, but on one condition, that is, when you have listened to my tale, you will kill me and bury me beside my son.'

She answered, 'Good, let it be so.'

Then he told her his whole story, which you have heard and know, from the beginning to the end. When he had finished his telling, he said to her, 'And now I have told you, take my sword which is on my son's grave here, and cut off my head and bury me with him.'

She replied, 'No, how can I cut off your head! It cannot be!'

A corpse being taken to burial at Najaf

Digging a well in the desert west of Mosul. Water was not found

But he entreated her and gave the sword into her hand, and then she took the sword and cut off his head.

And she dug a grave so that he might lie beside his son, and buried him, and this is the end of the story of Shamshūm; at least, I heard this story from my grandmother, and this is all I know of it.

IX
HUSAIN AN NIM-NIM

Husain an Nim-Nim was a Tekrīti and a raftsman by trade. One day he and his companions loaded up a raft[1] and set off down the Tigris.

When he and his companions were at some distance from Tekrīt, the south wind began to blow and the river became rough, so, unable to proceed, the raftsmen drew the raft up to the foreshore and ate a meal there. As they were eating, a s'ilūwa[2] came up out of the water and seized upon Husain an Nim-Nim while his companions rushed to the raft and succeeded in getting away. Now, finding Husain a pretty fellow, the s'ilūwa did not eat him, but took him to her lair on the shore, where she made love to him, licking his legs so that they became thin and the bones lost their hardness and were like the wick of a candle. He was her paramour for three days and nights, and on the morning of the fourth day the s'ilūwa said, 'We have nothing to eat: I must go to the market to buy bread, rice, and meat.'

Answered Husain an Nim-Nim, 'Go, and I will await you here.'

She left him and he sat by the river alone. He had not sat long before he saw in the distance the raft and his three companions who had returned to seek for him. As they approached they said, 'Is the s'ilūwa here? We dare not approach!' but he answered, 'Do not fear, she has gone to the sūq!' Then he went down to them and his legs wavered and bent from weakness. They helped him on to the raft and pushed off.

---

[1] A *kelek* is a raft supported underneath by inflated skins. These rafts carry heavy loads of firewood, grain, &c. When the *kelek* reaches its destination, the load is delivered, the raft broken up and sold as firewood, and the skins are deflated by the *kelekjis* and packed in sacks, and taken back to the place from which they came by road. These skins are roughly tanned with powdered pomegranate peel and salt, and are sun-dried, and thus prepared may be used again and again.

The chief occupation in Tekrīt is making *keleks* and sailing on them, and the birthplace of this story may be in Tekrīt.   [2] See Preface, p. xi.

Building a kelek on the Tigris

But before the raft was far away, the s'ilūwa returned, and finding him gone, went to the river and saw the raft. She hurried to a point where the raft must pass, and called to her lover, 'You have played me false, but where I have loved, I cannot destroy. If you wish to leave me, you must leave me!'

Answered Husain an Nim-Nim, 'It is of the nature of a man that he should yearn for his home.'

Said she, 'I will give you a gift so that you may remember me,' and she spat. The spittle, streaming upon the wind, reached Husain an Nim-Nim. 'This is my gift,' said the s'ilūwa. 'To you and to your descendants will be the power to cure red eyes by spitting into them.'

There is another version, like the first up to the point where the s'ilūwa takes Husain an Nim-Nim into her cave and licks his legs. According to this version, he stayed with her many years.

After the first nine months she bore him a daughter. Then she again became pregnant, and assuming the disguise of a human woman by putting on an 'aba she went and sought a midwife,[1] saying to her, 'Come and deliver me. Last time I bore a daughter, and this time I want a son, and if you do not contrive that my child will be a boy, I will kill you.'

The midwife went with her, but before leaving her house, she slipped a candle into the bosom of her gown. In time the pains grew upon the s'ilūwa and a child was born, but it was a girl. The midwife was afraid to tell the mother the truth, so she slipped the candle between the thighs of the child, and holding it up, said to the s'ilūwa, 'You have brought a son into the world.'

The s'ilūwa rejoiced, and gave the midwife a piece of red onion-skin and a piece of white garlic. The woman went home and, disgusted at such miserly payment, threw the onion and garlic outside the door, saying '*Shinu hadha!* What is this!' But the next morning when she looked outside her door, she saw that the onion had become gold and the garlic silver.

---

[1] *Jidda*, literally 'a granny'. The trade is followed by many ignorant old women, but efforts are now being made to train midwives.

Meantime, the s'ilūwa had discovered that the midwife had deceived her, and that night she went to her house and beat at her door, calling her by name, 'Mother Bāji! Mother Bāji!' The midwife trembled and made no stir or sound. This happened every night until the s'ilūwa again became pregnant, and this time she was delivered of a boy. After this she had yet another boy.

But there came a day when the s'ilūwa tired of her human lover and mounting a raft, she went off down the river while her husband stayed on the bank and begged her to come back. Finding her deaf to his entreaties, he took their children and tore them in half, one by one, throwing her one half and keeping the other half on the shore. As to her, she spat and said, 'I give to you and to your offspring power to cure sore eyes.'

Thus in the Mosul version; another Baghdad version has it, like the first I quoted, that it was Husain who escaped. A third version is interesting as making the haunt of the s'ilūwa a forest and not the river.

Somewhere on the bank of the Tigris in Tekrīt there was a forest which belonged to the s'ilūwa: it was known as the Zōr[1] as S'ilūwa . When the s'ilūwa captured Husain an Nim-Nim with whom she had fallen in love, she took him to this zōr and lived with him there, licking his legs in order to keep him a prisoner until they became so weak that they were no longer able to support him.

Their first child was a boy: they called him Dabīb al Lail, Creeper of the Night. The s'ilūwa had a sister who lived on the opposite bank of the river, and this sister had five children whose names were, Saīda, Sumaida, Samad al Bahr, Makka, and Madīna.

One night Dabīb al Lail became ill. She shouted to her sister on the other bank asking for medicine to cure him.

Dāda, dāda, 'andech hawāij lil lawāij?
Dabīb al Lail tūl al lail ya'alij min fuaduh!

'Sister, sister, have you medicine for aching pains?
Dabīb al Lail is suffering from his heart all night long.

[1] The word *zōr* (forest) is used of a mere thicket of shrubs, such as tamarisk, or liquorice.

To this her sister replied, swearing by her five children, that she had not even the *dust* of a drug for Dabīb's complaint.

Wa hayāt Saīda	'By the life of Saida
Wa Sumaīda	And Sumaida
Wa Samad al Bahr	And Samad al Bahr
Wa Makka wal Madina	And Makka and Madina
Ma 'andi ghabaruh!	I have not (even) its dust!'

X

THE BLACKBEETLE WHO WISHED
TO GET MARRIED

THERE was once a blackbeetle who wished to take a husband. She

Kanasat al hōsh	Swept the yard,
Laqat bāra,	And found a farthing,
Kanasat at tarma	Swept the balcony
Laqat bāra,	And found a farthing,
Kanasat al gubbeh	Swept the room
Laqat bāra.	And found a farthing!

So she rose up and went her way to the sūq, and she bought paint and powder and antimony, and then she went home and

Athammarat	Reddened her cheeks
Atpowdarat,[1]	Powdered her face,
Atkhattatat	Pencilled her eyebrows,
Addeyramat,[2]	Coloured her lips,
Atkahhalat.[3]	And put black round her eyes.

and then she stood herself near the door of her house. Came by a pedlar of sweetmeats (*abul halwa*) with a tray of sweets on his head, who said to her:

Khunfisāna	'Beetle, beetle
Dūn fisāna,	Without feetle,
Leysh g'āda	Why do you stand
Bil bueybāna?	By our little door?'

And the blackbeetle answered: 'I want a little husband!' (*Arīd lī ferd zuweyjāna!*)

The sweet-seller answered, 'I will marry you!'

---

[1] *tapowdar* (vulg. *atpowdar* or *atbaudar*) has become an Arab verb (5th form of *padar* or *badar*—to powder).

[2] *deyram* is a tree (walnut?) the sap of which, if its peel or leaves be rubbed on the lips, leaves an orange stain. This is much used as a cosmetic in 'Irāq.

[3] Black (antimony) powder applied to the eyes with the end of a small pointed instrument. *Kahal*-boxes have this instrument attached to the screw-tops. The use of *kahal* is supposed not only to enhance the beauty of the eyes by blackening the rims of the eyelids, it is supposed to strengthen the sight.

Said the blackbeetle, 'And when you marry me, with what will you beat me?' (*Waqt tākhudhni, beysh tadhrubni?*)

Answered the sweet-seller, 'I will beat you with my sweetmeat-tray—*hard*!'

Said the blackbeetle,

> *Fūt, fūt, fūt!*
> *Al khunfus khunfus 'anak*
> *Wal baghla tarfus ūmmak!*
> *Wa ana beydha naqīya*
> *U ukhdūdi qarmazīya!*
> *Fūt, fūt!*
> 'Go away, go away, go away!
> The beetle can do without you!
> May the mule kick your mother!
> For I am pure white,
> And my cheeks are rosy red!
> Go away!'

Next came by a radish-seller, and he was crying, 'Radishes! Radishes!' He saw the blackbeetle by the door and said to her,

> 'Beetle, beetle,
> Without feetle,
> Why are you sitting
> By our little door?'

The beetle answered, 'I want a little husband!'

Said the radish-seller, 'I will take you to wife!'

Said the beetle, 'And when you marry me, with what will you beat me?'

> *Abul fijl, abul fijl,*
> *Yōm al tākhudni*
> *Beysh tadhrubni?*

He replied, 'With the radish root, *hard*!' (*Bi rās al fijl— heyl!*)

Cried the beetle,

> '*Fūt, fūt!*
> *Ana qishr al basal ma ahmilu!*
> Go away, go away, go away!
> I couldn't endure (to be beaten even with) an onion-skin!'

Then there came by an onion-seller, and he was crying, 'Seed-giving onion! Seed-giving onion!' (*Bādhūri al basal.*) When he saw the blackbeetle sitting by her door, he asked her,

> 'Beetle, beetle,
> Without feetle,
> Why are you sitting
> By our little door?'

The beetle answered, 'I want a little husband.'

Said the onion-seller, 'I will take you to wife!'

Said the beetle, 'And when I marry you, how will you beat me?'

Replied the onion-seller, 'With an onion, *hard*!' (*Bi rās al basal—heyl!*)

Said she, 'Go away, go away, I could not endure to be beaten even with the skin of an onion!'

Next there passed by a pickle-merchant, with a basin of pickles on his head. He glanced down and saw the blackbeetle by the door and said to her,

> 'Beetle, beetle,
> Without feetle,
> Why are you sitting
> By our little door?'

The beetle answered, 'I want a little husband!'

Said the pickle-merchant, 'I will take you!'

Asked the beetle, 'And when you have married me, how will you beat me?'

And the pickle-merchant answered, 'With this basin (*injāna*)—*hard*!'

She answered him,

> 'Go away, away, away!
> The beetle won't have you to-day!
> Bad luck to you, I say!
> For I am as white as dawn of day
> And my cheeks are crimson as roses in May!
> Away, away!'

And he went, and next there came by a big rat. He said to her,

> 'Beetle, beetle,
> Without feetle,
> Why are you sitting
> By our little door?'

Said she, 'I want a little husband!'

He answered, 'I will take you to wife!'

Said she, 'And when you have married me, with what will you beat me?'

He answered, 'I will beat you with my tail—*hard*!'

And she cried,

> 'Go away, away, away!
> The beetle won't have you to-day!
> Bad luck to you and yours, I say!
> For I am white as dawn of day
> And my cheeks are crimson as roses in May!
> Away, away!'

And he went. And after he had gone, there came by a tiny little mouse. And it said (in a small voice),

> 'Beetle, beetle,
> Without feetle,
> Why are you sitting
> By our little door?'

And the beetle answered, 'I want a little husband!'

Said the little mouse, 'I will take you to wife!'

Asked the beetle, 'And if you marry me, with what will you beat me?'

Replied the mouse, 'I will beat you with my tail—*g-e-n-t-l-y*!'[1]

Said the beetle, 'Aye! this one shall take me!'

So there was a wedding which lasted for seven days and seven nights, and when it was ended, the beetle said to her husband, 'O my husband, I am in the family way, and I want you to bring me some honey.'

Said he to his wife, 'Where shall I find honey?'

[1] *y-a-w-a-s-h.*

She replied, 'The Sultan has vats full of honey.'

And he to her, 'Give me a cup: I will go to fetch you some!'

So she gave him a cup and he went to the Sultan's house to get her some honey from a vat. And when he arrived at the palace, and found the vat, and went to open it, he tumbled in and died, and that was the end of him.

And the beetle looked for him in the street, and she waited and she gazed and she called, and at last she went out to search for him. And when she came to the Sultan's house, she saw him lying dead before the door, in a pool of honey, for when they went to get honey from the vat they saw that there was a dead mouse in it, and emptied it all into the street.

So she wept bitterly and mourned and wailed, and took his body up and brought it to their house and buried it. Then she called the beetles and the lizards and the mice to mourn with her, and lamented her husband in these words:

> *Mā khalleyt ʿattāra*
> *Mā khalleyt baqqāla,*
> *Shifet shaikh al chebīr*
> *Wa waqaʿ bil kawāra*[1]

> [2]'The chandler thou passed by
> And the greengrocer's shop,
> But higher wished to try
> And in the vat didst drop.'

Wa kunna ʿadkum wa jīnā!

---

[1] *kawāra*. A *kawāra* is a jar of non-porous earthenware with a lid, usually used for storing grain. Another form of *kawāra* is of woven reeds in jar shape, plastered over with pitch, like the *guffah*, or basket boat.

[2] Her lament, in the form of doggerel, is suitable to the mock-heroic manner of the whole tale. The words used for 'she lamented her husband' are ʿaddat ʿala zōjha. The ʿaddadāt are the professional mourners, who use such doggerel in their chanted laments over the dead. The word ʿaddāda means 'one who enumerates', and her duty is to enumerate the good qualities of the deceased and the sorrows of the survivors.

XI

THE THORN-SELLER

The trade of selling desert thorn is limited to the very poor, who send their women or go themselves, to cut the desert thorn and sell it for firewood.

THERE was once a thorn-seller who went every day into the desert to collect thorn, brought it into Baghdad, and sold it to buy bread for his children. Every day he did this; it was his only occupation, and he was very poor. One day there was a heavy rain, and the desert was deep with mire. He said to his wife, 'I do not think I can collect thorn to-day.' Said his wife, 'And what will the little children eat? *Khatiya*! Shame! What will the babies eat?'

Answered the man, 'Good, I will go out and see what I can find,' and he went out into the rain and mire with his axe on his shoulder, but he found no thorn to cut, for it was not worth cutting. So he went into Baghdad and began to hunt among the refuse which the vegetable-sellers and the fruit-sellers had cast into the road, saying, 'Perhaps I shall find some bruised leaves and egg-plant, and if my wife can wash them well and cook them (Allah is merciful!) my children will have something upon which to dine!' So he gathered up here and there the leaves and vegetables which had been cast away, and amongst them lay a little dry-looking gourd[1] which he picked up with the rest, saying, 'Perhaps if we plant this it may become a useful plant.'

He took home what he had found, and his wife made a little soup, and upon that they fed. But the dry gourd he put on a shelf in his room. That night at midnight, he woke, and he heard a voice calling him:

'*Yā ab! Yā ab!* O father! O father!'

He answered, '*Eyn yāb?* Where is he that calls me father? What do you want?'

And the voice came from the shelf where he had put

[1] *shejera.*

the gourd, saying, 'Will you take me to the daughter of the Sultan and betroth me to her?'

The thorn-seller laughed. He said, 'How shall I take you to the Sultan's house? I am only a poor thorn-seller, how can the likes of me look upon his house? *Shlōn akhtubak?* How then can I betroth you to the Sultan's daughter?'

And the gourd said, 'Open your lap!'

And he opened his lap, and tchringq, tchringq, tchringq! a hundred gold pieces came tumbling into his lap. When he saw that, his reason flew away, and he was beside himself for joy. The next morning he rose early and went to the sūq and bought bread, wheat, rice, meat, chickens, vegetables, clothes for his children, and he and his family rejoiced exceedingly. That night, at midnight, when they were sleeping, he was wakened by a voice from the shelf.

'*Yā ab, yā ab!*' And he replied, '*Eyn yāb?* Where is he that calls father?' And the gourd said, 'Did you go to ask for the hand of the Sultan's daughter for me?'

The thorn-seller replied, 'How could I go, a poor thorn-seller, and ask the Sultan for his daughter? I went and bought bread and clothes for my children.'

Said the gourd, 'Open your lap.'

And into the lap of the thorn-seller, tchringq, tchringq, tchringq! there fell two hundred pieces of gold.

Said the gourd, 'Go to the market and buy for yourself a mare, and fine clothing of the best that can be bought, and a black servant, and go to the house of the Sultan and betroth me to his daughter.' So the next day, the thorn-seller bought all that the gourd had ordered, and fine furniture and handsome rugs and ordered improvements to be made in his house. Then he went to the Sultan's house, mounted on his mare, and tried to enter the courtyard, but the door-keeper stopped him and said, 'No one passes here, this is the Sultan's house.'

He answered, 'Yes, my father, I know it is, and I have business with the Sultan, I must speak with him about a certain matter.'

The door-keeper replied, 'You have no permit to enter, you cannot go in.'

So he returned to his house, and that night, as he lay sleeping, he was wakened, and heard the gourd say,

'*Yā ab, yā ab!*' And he answered, '*Eyn yāb?*'

Then the gourd said, 'Did you betroth me to the Sultan's daughter?'

And the thorn-seller answered, 'Yes, my son, I went to the sūq, and bought what you ordered me to buy and went on the mare, with the slave following behind, to the Sultan's house, but when I asked to enter, they refused me.'

The gourd said, 'Open your lap.' And into the thorn-seller's lap there fell tchringq, tchringq, tchringq! three hundred gold pieces. And it continued, 'To-morrow, go to the town, and when you get to the Sultan's house, push the door-keeper aside without a word and go up the stairs, and you will see in the diwān of the Sultan, two chairs, one of silver and one of gold. He who has a petition to make sits on the silver chair, and he who is a suitor to the Princess sits in the gold chair, so seat yourself in the gold chair and speak boldly.'

The next day, the thorn-seller put on his fine clothes, and got on his mare, and went, and his black servant was behind him, to the house of the Sultan, and he did not wait by the gate but went in without speaking, and up the stairs and into the diwān and seated himself in the golden chair.

The Sultan was there, and his court and his Ministers. When the Sultan perceived it, he looked at him out of half his eye, and said in himself, 'Who is this fellow that wants my daughter?' Then he spoke to the thorn-seller and said, '*Eysh āku 'andak?* What's your business? Speak!' The thorn-seller answered, 'I want to betroth your daughter to my son.'

The Sultan was furious and turned to his wazīr, and said, 'Whoever this is that wishes to marry my daughter, I will cut off his head!'

The wazīr answered, 'That is not suitable behaviour for rulers! You cannot reply to him thus, but place impossible conditions before him, and say if he fulfils them he may marry her, but if he does not fulfil what you ask of him, you will cut off his head, and so your dignity will be preserved.'

The Sultan answered, '*Zein!* Good.' Then he said to the thorn-seller, 'If in the space of three days you can build a castle that will extend from your house to my house, each brick of gold, and the galleries and gallery posts of gold, and the knobs of diamonds, and the bed-steads of gold with bedspreads of pearls and emeralds, and the carpets embroidered with precious stones, your son shall marry my daughter, but if you fail to fulfil these conditions, I will cut off your head.'

The thorn-seller answered, 'Good,' and he turned and went out and returned to his house. He was cast down, his heart had gone out of him, and he sat down and wept, and his wife said to him,

'What is it?'

He replied and told her that he must die because of the Sultan's words, and informed her what had happened in the palace.

She replied, 'Why lose heart? Allah is merciful. Why not ask your son, the gourd up there on the shelf, perhaps he can help you. Ask this night.'

They had supper, and went to bed, but the thorn-seller could not sleep, he was too troubled to close his eyes. At midnight he heard the gourd cry, '*Yā ab, yā ab!*' and answered, '*Eyn yāb?*' And the gourd said, 'Did you go to the Sultan and betroth me to the princess?'

And the thorn-seller said, 'I went, O my son, and what a calamity, what a disaster! Since that time I have not eaten or slept! I can only think of what is before me.'

The son of the jinn who was in the gourd began to laugh, *qah, qah, qah!*

Said the thorn-seller, 'How can you laugh when I am doomed to die!'

He laughed yet more and answered, 'What the Sultan has asked is nothing, nothing at all! It is easy! Open thy lap!' And into the thorn-seller's lap there fell four hundred gold pieces. The gourd continued, 'Do not worry any more, do not think about the Sultan's conditions, they are *hīch*! Nothing!

The thorn-seller took the money, and went to sleep, and when he got up the next morning he looked to see if there were a castle, but there was nothing, all was as before. He began to fear again and could not sleep, but it was as before, the gourd gave him five hundred gold pieces and bade him not fear.[1] The next morning there was still no stone of a castle to be seen, and that night he was troubled, and wept, and the gourd spoke to him and gave him six hundred gold pieces, and bade him sleep and be unafraid. The third morning he woke, and there was a golden shining in his room, and he went, and looked out, and behold, there was a castle of bright gold stretching between his house and the Sultan's palace!

The Sultan got up, and said when he saw the light, 'What can this bright shining be?' and he looked out, and saw also. When he entered, he found everything as he had said, only yet more fine and dazzling. Then he sent for the thorn-seller, and said, 'It shall be as you wish, to-day we will have the betrothal.' Then he sent for the mulla, and there was a contract drawn up, and music and drums, and a feast, and guests, and all that was proper for the marriage of a great prince.

That night, when the gourd spoke to him, the thorn-seller told him that the betrothal was complete. Then the gourd said, 'Tell the Sultan that the bridegroom will come to the bride on Thursday. I wish to make her mine on the Thursday. But I shall not come until the guests have gone away, and the bride must sit with the door open.'

So on the Thursday all was made ready for the bride-groom: guests were invited, musicians came, a feast was cooked, and there were great rejoicings. When they had all gone away, the bride sat in the bridal chamber on a couch, alone, dressed gorgeously,

muzawwaqa, mulawwaqa

embellished and suitably attired

---

[1] Repetition.

waiting, waiting, waiting. At twelve o'clock a little bird
flew in at the door, fr-r-r-r! and sat on the bed, and in its
claw was a stick. It came to the ground, and struck the
stick on the floor, and took off its cloak of feathers, and
grew, and behold! a young man stood before her,

Subhān Allah, rabb al khāliqin
Wal khāliq ahsan!

so handsome that, were the moon absent, his beauty would
have illumined the sky. Then he struck the ground again
and it opened, and in the floor there appeared a large pool,
and out of the water came forty beautiful girls, one carrying a towel[1] embroidered with gold; another a loofah;[2]
another a golden basin;[3] another a golden comb; another
qīl;[4] another soap; another a massage-glove;[5] others
brought pumice-stone,[6] a bowl[7] to hold the jewels, bath-
clothes, every one something. Then they took off the
bridegroom's clothes, and led him into the water, and
washed him and his hair, and perfumed him and put on
his robe and put him on the bedstead beside the bride
and began to utter cries of joy. This done, he struck with
his stick, and they went into the water, the pool disappeared, and the floor closed up, and they were alone.
Then he made love to her, and she to him, and in sweetness and love the night passed and it was near dawn.
Then he said to her, 'I lay a command on you, that you
must keep silence about me. Do not say that I am handsome, or describe me or say that I come as a bird, or utter

[1] *manshafa*. Towels and bath-wraps embroidered with gold and silver thread
are used for a bride's bath.

[2] *līf*. The loofah in Baghdad is knitted into a bag, with a draw-string.

[3] *tāsa*. The bowl is for pouring water over the person who is being washed.
A bride's washing-bowl sometimes has a small domed receptacle in the centre
which unscrews. It is filled loosely with peas which rattle as it is used. This
is called a *tāsa khashkhāsh*.

[4] *Qīl* is a saponaceous earth, which is mixed with rose-leaves and rubbed into
the hair. Sometimes called *khāwa*.

[5] *kīs*. The massage-glove is of coarse, black hair-cloth stitched with white
thread.

[6] *hajer*. Pumice-stone is used for the soles of the feet.

[7] *salabché*. This is a round silver box resembling a football in size and shape,
into which the bather's jewels are placed when given into the bath-keeper's
custody.

one word about me, or I must go away and you will never see me any more.'

She answered, 'Good.' And he put on his dress of feathers, and flew away.

The next day was the *Subhīya*, or the Feast of the Next Day, and her friends and relations came, and the thorn-seller and his children, and there was music and feasting in honour of the married pair. They asked her, '*Shlōnuh?* What is the bridegroom like? Is he handsome, is he this, is he that?' But she only answered, 'Praise to Allah!' to all these questions.

And for every night for two years the bridegroom came to her, and they had delight of each other, and she was happy. But one day she said to her attendant, 'I want to go to the hammām in the sūq.'

Answered the handmaid, 'O my daughter, why go to the sūq! There is a hammām here, more beautiful than the bath in the sūq.'

She answered, 'But I wish to go outside to-day and bathe in the public bath.'

So when they perceived that she would go, they took a basin of gold, and bowl of gold, and a bath-robe of gold cloth, and clogs of gold, and all the bath things, and went into the sūq, and came to the public bath. When the princess entered, all the women there greeted her, and she sat there in her splendour. Then the women began to whisper about her maliciously,

Liweish! Hadha kubrīya, shinū?

'Why such display and grandeur? Every one knows that her husband is only a sparrow!'

She heard their murmurings, and was furious, and unable to stop herself she cried out, 'My husband is a man, fashioned like other men; he is not a sparrow!'

As she spoke, the sparrow flew down through the hole in the dome of the bath and perched on her knee, and said, 'Did I not command you not to say anything about me? Now you will never see me again!' And it seized in its beak her golden comb and her bracelet, and flew out again.

How she wept, how she lamented, how she bewailed
her folly! The tears ran, and ran, and her eyes were like
fire. There came to the castle the wife of the thorn-seller,
and she said, 'My darling, my daughter, do not weep,
Allah is merciful, perhaps he will come again!' But she
could not console her.

The princess mourned her husband as if he were dead,
and wept always, till *dī, dī!* a year passed. The princess
said to herself, 'There is no way out: I will set myself
something to do!' So she called an *usta*, a skilled work-
man, and said, 'Build me a hammām in fifteen days.'

He answered, 'Aye, I will.'

He and his fellows worked, and in fifteen days they
had built a fine bath. When it was complete, the princess
wrote on the door of the bath the following couplet:

> *Kul men yiji yaghsal bil hammām*
> *Yuhkiluh hikāya yughsil bilāsh wa yitla‘.*

'Who wishes a bath here a story must say,
Can be washed without price and then go away.'

For she said within herself, 'If every one who comes here
has to tell a tale, I may hear something about my husband.'

So she seated herself on a cushion within the door of
the bath, and became the *natūra* (doorwoman) of the bath,
and guarded the jewellery of those who went within, and
they paid her by telling a story.

One day there came to the bath an old, dirty woman.
She said to the princess, 'O honourable princess, I wish to
wash, my head is very dirty.' The princess said, 'You may
wash for nothing, if you tell me a story.' Now the old
woman knew no story, so she said, 'Grateful thanks, O
excellent princess! I will go away now, and wash my
clothes first in the river, for they are very dirty, and buy
myself a little soap, and return to-morrow, to wash my
head.'

So the old woman returned to her house. But that
night, when the moon came out from the clouds and shone
on the old woman, she woke and said to herself, 'The dawn
has come, I will go and wash my clothes!' And she

walked, *meshi, meshi, meshi,* till she came to the shore of the river. There she sat and she washed and washed her clothes, and put them on the ground to dry and waited beside them. While she sat there, she saw a cock come up out of the water with two water-skins on his back. He swam to the edge, and filled his skins and dived beneath the water again. The old woman marvelled, and said to herself, 'If he comes again, I will seize the cock by the tail.' Presently, he appeared again, with two skins on his back as before. He filled the skins, and when he had finished, the old woman seized him by the tail. He dived underneath the water, and she clung on to him and went beneath too.

And below, under the water, they came to a castle

Wa lā awwal	First in splendour,
Wa lā thāni!	Second to none!

And before the castle, a pool of water, and near the pool a long table, and upon it forty plates, and forty spoons, and forty forks, and forty knives, and forty goblets.

Said she, 'Here is a fine tale for me to tell the Sultan's daughter! Allah has sent me this adventure, so that I shall have a story for her!' And she thought, '*Bil qīr wal Jehannum!* By bitumen and Hades! I want to see all that there is to be seen here!' And she went into the castle and came to the kitchen, and there, on the fire, were dishes and meat boiling and frying, and roasting and sizzling, but no one there. Dishes were being taken to the table outside, but she could see no one carrying them, they moved in the air.

She stretched out her hand to eat of a dish, but as she did so, some one struck at her hand and a voice cried,

Jurri īdech
Sīdi mā yahibbech mā yarīdech!

'Draw back your hand
My master doesn't love you and doesn't want you!'

So she withdrew her hand. Then she said, 'I will hide under the couch to see who is coming to eat this feast.'

So she crept beneath the couch and hid herself, and no sooner was she hid than there flew down forty doves, and forty fair damsels came up out of the pool to them, each bearing towel, bathing-wrap, soap, friction-gloves, and all that was necessary for the bath. Then the doves took off their dresses of feathers, and there stood there forty beautiful youths, *Subhān Allah!* And the youths descended into the pool, and when they were washed and dried and clothed, they sat down to the table and ate. The food that was put by them appeared without hands, *awādim māku!*, and they ate, and finished, and washed their hands and mouths, and then each arose and went into the castle. Each went to his own room, for there were forty rooms. Said the old woman, 'I must go and see what is in these rooms.' So she followed them and went up the stairs, and entered one room and saw the first of the forty youths reading a book, another was sleeping, another was reading the gazette, and each one was doing something or was asleep. When she came to the fortieth room and looked in, she saw the youth who was in it sitting, and on his knees were bracelets and a golden comb, and he was sighing and weeping and saying,

> *Yā dār, yā dār!*
> *Abchi 'ala umm al mukhashkhash[1] wal aswār!*

> 'O house, O house!
> I weep for the lady of the anklets and bracelets!'

And the tears fell, and ran down.

The old woman said within herself, 'Surely this must be the husband of her who keeps the bath!' Then she was afraid that she might not be able to come into the world above again, and she returned quickly to the place where the cock had left her, and he came with two skins on his back. She seized his tail, and fr-r-r-r! he flew up and through the water, and came again to the bank. It was

---

[1] The *mukhashkhash* is a hinged anklet which is fastened with a chained pin. It is very Assyrian in design. I have also heard bracelets of the same pattern called *mukhashkhash*. The root means 'to rattle', e.g. a poppy is called a *khashkhash* because its seeds rattle in the pod.

dawn and the old woman picked up her clothes, and said to herself, 'What a fine story I have for the Sultan's daughter.' Then she spent a metallik on soap, and did up her bundle for the bath, and went there.

The Sultan's daughter said, 'Welcome my mother, welcome! Welcome, old woman of good omen.'

The old woman said, 'O my daughter, what a fine story I have to tell you!'

And the Sultan's daughter said, 'Aye, old woman.'

And the old woman said, 'Last night, I went to wash my clothes by the river, and I saw a cock come out of the water and on his back two skins. And I seized his tail, and went under the water, and saw a fine castle, and beside it a pool. . . . See, what a fine story! *Bāwi, ey khōsh hekāya!*'.

And the Sultan's daughter kissed her hand, and said 'Continue.'

And she said, 'Beside the pool was a table, and on the table were forty covers. Then there came flying forty doves, and they took off their dresses of feathers and entered the pool.'

Cried the Sultan's daughter, 'This is indeed a tale,' and she kissed the old woman's knees joyfully.

The old woman told her all that happened,[1] and when she had finished the princess embraced her, and said to the bath attendants, 'Take this old woman and wash her well, and give her fine new clothes.' It was done, and they brought her back to the Sultan's daughter.

Then the princess said, 'I shall not part from you, you must come back to my house, and to-night you can take me to the young man who has my bracelet. *Ānā aghnīk wa namaghni[2] Allah!* I will enrich you, and God will prosper me.'

Said the old woman, 'On my head, on my eyes, I will take you!'

At night, when it was dark, the old woman said, 'Rise, my daughter,' and they went to the river bank and waited.

---

[1] Repetition, omitted here.
[2] The narrator always said *namaghni,* a mistake for *al mughni,* the Enricher

Dī, dī, dī, dī! At midnight there came the cock, and the old woman said, 'When I seize his tail, hold you my dress!' And so it was, and when the cock had filled his water-skins, the old woman held his tail and the Sultan's daughter held the tail of the old woman's dress, and kh-sh-sh! They went through the water and came out at the bottom of the river, close by the pool and the castle. The table was spread as it was on the first night, and the old woman and the Sultan's daughter went into the kitchens and saw food a-frying and a-boiling and a-roasting, and dishes being carried to the table outside.

The princess stretched out her hand and put it into one of the dishes, and a voice cried:

> *Muddi īdech, muddi īdech,*
> *Sīdi habbech wa yarīdech!*

> 'Put out your hand, put out your hand,
> My master loved you and wants you!'

So she put her hand into the dish and took the food and ate it.

Then the old woman said to her, 'We must hide beneath the couch.' So they hid beneath the couch, and all that had happened the night before happened again. When she saw her husband, the princess could hardly restrain herself, and said to the old woman, 'That is he, that is he!' When the forty sons of the jānn had eaten, they washed their hands and mouths, and went up the steps of the castle, each to his own chamber. Then the old woman and the Sultan's daughter followed them, and looked into each room. One was studying, another was reading, another was sleeping, another was singing, and so they came to the fortieth room, and there sat the princess's husband, weeping, and on his knee the bracelet and the golden comb. And he was saying,

> '*Yā dār, yā dār,*
> *Abchi 'ala umm al mukhashkhash wal aswār!*'

This. And the old woman spoke over his shoulder and said, 'Do you want her? I will bring her!'

And the young man said, 'You are a human creature, how have you dared to tread our house?'

The old woman replied, 'Allah brought me here, and I have your wife with me.'

He said, 'Where is my wife?'

And she answered, 'Here!'

Then the young man rose and encaged his wife within his arms and embraced her.

Then he said to her, 'You must go, or I fear that my brothers and sisters will kill you for seeing our secrets here. Go quickly, and I will return to you in the guise of a man and will not leave you again.'

So they went below, and saw the cock with the skins on his back, and seized his tail and were drawn to the shore of the river.

The next night there was a knocking at the door of the princess's house, and, when she opened, there was her husband, in the likeness of a man, although he was the son of the Sultan of the Jānn, and he remained with her like a human husband always.

XII

THE BLIND SULTAN

Yōm min al eyām	A day of days
Wa sā'a min az zamān	And an hour of time!
Allah yunsur as Sultān.	May Allah make the Sultan victorious!

THERE was once a Sultan who had three sons by two wives, the one Arab like himself, and the other an Abyssinian. The time came when the sons were grown, and they went to their father and said, 'Why do you not get us wives?' And he said to the two eldest, 'Go on to the roof, and take your bows and arrows and draw.' And the two sons of the Arab woman went on to the roof and drew their bows. And the arrow of the eldest fell on the roof of an amīr who was abiding in the town. They sent to ask for the hand of the amīr's daughter, they performed the rites of betrothal and the eldest prince was married to her, and she came to his house. The arrow of the second prince fell on the house of the wazīr, so they sent to ask for the wazīr's daughter, and performed the rites of betrothal, and on the appointed day she came to the house of her husband. As for the third son, the son of the Abyssinian woman, he left his father's house and went out into the chōl.[1] He walked and walked, earth making, earth taking,

> *ardh athattu*[2]
> *ardh atshīlu!*

until he saw a lion. And the lion called to him, 'Come to me! *Beni Adam, la takhāf!* Child of man, do not fear! I will not hurt you. Approach, and help me.' For this lion had wounded his foot, and he held it out to the young man, saying again, 'Do not fear, I will not hurt you: only

---

[1] See p. 11.
[2] This tag the story-teller repeated some six or seven times to represent the length of the journey.

cure my foot, and I will enrich you and God will give me abundance.'

So the young man stooped and took the foot of the lion into his hand, and there was a thorn in it, and he pulled it out, and the abscess was eased, and the pain ceased. And the lion said to the young man, 'Pull out three hairs from my coat, and when you are in need, rub them together.' And he ran off into the desert.

The young man immediately took the three hairs and rubbed them together, and there straightway appeared before him three slaves, who said to him, 'Ask, and wish! What do you want?' (*utlub u temenna!*). The young man said to them, 'I wish for a mare that can fly (*timshi bil hawa*),' and immediately a beautiful mare stood before him. Then he asked for trappings for her, and for clothes for himself, and behold, the mare was caparisoned, and the youth richly dressed. He got upon her back, and thanking the slaves, he rode through the air, until he was near a city. Outside the walls he met a shepherd, and asked him for a sheep. The shepherd sold him a sheep, and the young man slaughtered it, and put the skin of the paunch upon his head, so that he appeared bald, and he bound it round with the intestines.

So disguised he went into the city, and coming to a garden near the Sultan's palace, he went to the gardener, and asked him if he might work for him. As he asked no pay, the gardener let him stay and work in the garden, and the young man abode with him. Now the windows of the Sultan's palace looked over the garden, and one day, when the youngest princess was gazing out, she saw a handsome young man, in fine raiment, on a beautiful mare,

> *Subhān rabb al khāliqin*
> *Wal khāliq ahsan,*

Glory to the Lord of creation,
He who creates is more excellent than his creatures,

for the young man, seeing her, had struck together the three hairs, and appeared to her in all his beauty. Her eyes rested on him with favour, and she loved him at sight.

The Sultan had three daughters, and as yet they were unmarried. One day they leant from the window and spoke to the gardener in the garden below, and said, 'O gardener, *sowwīnna ferd chāra!* Do us a good turn, and speak to the king on our behalf. It is time that we were married, and you must go to the king and tell him that we are marriage-ripe.' The gardener said to them, 'I am the gardener, and I am ashamed to speak to the king, but I will give him your message.' So he picked three melons, and the first was over-ripe, and the second approaching over-ripeness, but the third was at its perfection. And he placed these three melons in a basket and sent them to the king. When the king knew that the melons had been sent by his gardener, he lifted the napkin that covered the melons and looked, and saw that the first was far too ripe, the second over-ripe, and only the third just fit for eating. He was angry, and said, 'Why does my gardener send me melons like these from my garden?' And he ordered the gardener's head to be cut off. But the wazīr was with him, and said, 'Do not so, your Majesty! If the gardener has sent you these melons, it is to convey a meaning. Your Majesty has three daughters, who should be wedded, and their condition is like that of the three melons. They are marriage-ripe and husbands should be found for them. That is the meaning of the three melons, a meaning which your gardener has not dared to speak.'

The Sultan's anger was appeased, and he immediately sent for his daughters, and giving them each an apple, he ordered them to throw the apples at the men of their choice. The first to choose was the eldest daughter. She sat at her window and, by order of the Sultan, all the marriageable men were to pass beneath the window so that she might choose one of them. They assembled, and, *dī, dī, dī, dī*, the men of the city passed before her, the princes, the senators, the rich men, the ministers, and the merchants. She threw her apple at an amīr's son, while all the people clapped their hands. The betrothal was made forthwith, and the marriage completed before seven days had passed. The second week the second sister sat at the window, and it was the same with her, *dī, dī, dī*, wāly, pāsha, minister, all passed below her window. She threw her apple at the wazīr's son, and the people all clapped their hands. It was with her as with her sister, the betrothal took place at once, and they were married before seven days had passed. Then it was the turn of the youngest sister, and she too sat at the window. Wāly, pāsha, wazīr, senator, deputy, rich man, merchant, *dī, dī, dī, dī*, all passed beneath her window, and she did not throw her apple to one of them. The second day the procession continued, and the third, and still she had not thrown her apple. Her ladies came to her and said, 'All the men in Baghdad have passed before you. Choose one of these men, there is no one left in Baghdad now!' She replied, *"Abadan!* I will not throw the apple at any of those, and all have not yet passed; for I have not seen yet the gardener's apprentice.' They said, 'The gardener's apprentice is dirty, bald, and lame, a poor fellow that works without pay.' She said, 'Nevertheless, bring him.' So they brought him, and she said to him, 'Why did you not go out into the street, you, and pass beneath my window? I will choose you, and none other!' and she threw her apple at him.

When the Sultan heard what his youngest daughter had done, he was very angry, and said, 'Why has she refused all the wealthy men and chosen this lame, bald fellow? Throw her and her husband into the stable!' And they did so, and the youngest princess and the gardener's apprentice lived in the stables.

Now soon after this war broke out, and when news was brought of it to the Sultan, he went out to fight the enemy at the head of his troops. The young man, when he heard of it, went outside the city, rubbed together his three hairs, and when he had obtained the mare and the trappings and his fine clothes from the three slaves, he went *dī, dī, dī* over the desert till he came to where the Sultan was fighting with his army. Then he rushed into the fight with the utmost bravery: where the Sultan's soldiers killed a thousand, he killed two thousand with his own two hands. The Sultan asked who he was, but no one knew him, and the Sultan had him brought to him when the battle was ended and thanked him. Seeing that his hand was wounded, the Sultan, who was amazed by his beauty and his bravery, tore a piece from the embroidered shawl that he wore round his waist, and tied up the wound with his own hands, sighing as he did so, 'Why are you not my son-in-law?' And he would have honoured him further, but the young man retired, rubbed his three hairs together, got on his mare and flew back to Baghdad, and there pulled the sheep's paunch over his head and bound it with the entrails.

When the Sultan got back to Baghdad, he made inquiries of every one as to where the brave youth was who had disappeared so suddenly from his camp. He said to his court, 'There was a youth who rode a mare and fought with us (*Subhān rabb al khāliq, wal khāliq ahsan!*) and he was beautiful as the moon of the fourteenth night, and as brave as a lion! With his two hands he killed two thousand men! Who is he, from whence came he, how shall I find him again?' And his grief at losing the youth was so great that he wept and wept until he lost his sight and became blind.

Then all the physicians in that place were summoned and they all tried to cure him, but they could do nothing. At last there came a very old, wise doctor, and he said, 'I know of a certain cure, O Sultan! If your Majesty can procure a lioness's milk, contained in a lion's skin, and brought on a lion's back, and put some of this milk on your eyes, your Majesty will by the mercy of Allah regain his sight.'

The eldest daughter's son, the amīr's son, when he heard this, went to the Sultan and said, 'I will go in search of the lion's milk and bring it back.'

The Sultan replied to him, 'Do not go, my son. There will be danger in getting it and I am afraid that you will be killed.' But the young man insisted that he would go,

and at last the Sultan consented. Before going he went
into the sirdab¹ and took a bag of gold and then into the
stable to get a mare to ride. *Dī, dī, dī, dī, dī,* off he went
into the desert, until he came to a place where three roads
met. And there sat an old, decrepit man spinning the
thread of day and night (*shaikh kabīr gargūmaʿ qaʿad yaliff
al lail wan nahār*). And the young man said to him,
'God keep you, tell me the names of these roads, and
whither they go.' The old man made answer, 'This is
the Road *Sadd-u-mā-Radd* (Went-and-Returned-not), and
the other two are both called "Goes-and-Comes" (*Yarūh
u Yīji*).' The young man said, 'I will take the Road "Goes-
and-Comes",' and he went on and on and on, *ardh atshīlu,
ardh athattu,*² until he came to a town, and entered it,
and went into its streets, and stopped at a coffee-house.
There he tied his mare and sat down to rest. In that
coffee-house there was a man who approached him and
greeted him, 'Peace upon you! *Ahlan ū sahlan!* Welcome. How are you?' and other speeches of welcome and
courtesy. And he said to him, 'Will your honour come to
my house? All strangers who come to this place stay with
me, and I entertain them for three days and nights.'

The young man thanked him and the man took him to
his house, where they ate and drank and amused themselves for three days and nights. The third night the host
said to his guest,

'Do you play chess?'

The young man said, 'Aye.'

And the stranger said, '*Yālla!*'³

So they sat down and played chess, and they played for
money. The stranger won the first game and the amīr's
son gave him gold from his bag. Then he won the second
game, and the young man gave him more gold, and so it
went on until all the gold in his bag was gone. Then he
staked his mare, and then his clothes, all but his shirt and

¹ A basement room, or cellar. Most of the inhabitants of ʿIraq spend the hot
hours of the day in their *saradīb*. Some houses have several stories of *saradīb*
below their house, and Najaf is celebrated for the depth and extent of these
underground chambers. ² Repeated as before.
³ A vulgarism for 'Get on with it!' (literally 'O God, *Ya Āllah*).

drawers, but the stranger won every time, and at the end, when he had won all, the host rose and bade him begone in a rough voice.

The young man went into the sūq and asked a pāchachi[1] if he wanted a servant. The pāchachi said, 'I want a boy to help me, but I can only give you a little food for wages.' And the young man was glad to accept.

A year passed, and there was no news of him at the palace of the Blind Sultan. Then the second daughter's husband, the wazīr's son, came and said to the Sultan, 'For twelve months we have had no news of my brother, and your Majesty is still blind. Allow me to go in search of the lion's milk, and also for my brother-in-law.'

The Sultan said, 'No, don't go. Your brother-in-law must be dead, and if you take this dangerous journey you too will die. Don't go, my eye, you will die too, and both my daughters will be widows. Stay here.'

But the wazīr's son said, *'Abadan!* I will go!'

So he sent to the sirdab and got a bag of gold, and to the stables to get a mare, and he set off. He went by the same road as the amīr's son, and in time he came upon the old, decrepit man who sat where three roads met and span the threads of day and night. The wazīr's son spoke to him, and said, 'Guide me, and tell me the names of these roads, and whither they go.'

The old man said, 'The first is called the Road "Went-and-Returned-not" and the other two are both called "Goes-and-Comes".'

So, like his brother, the wazīr's son took one of the roads named 'Goes-and-Comes', and, like him, he came at last to the town, and entered it, and stopped at the coffee-house. There he was greeted by the stranger, *'Ahlan ū sahlan!* How do you do? Deign to come to my house, for I always entertain strangers who come to the town for three days and nights.' The young man went with him to his house, and there ate and drank and spent the time in amusement and pleasure until the third night. Then the host said, 'Do you play chess?' And the young man said

---

[1] A seller of *pācha*, or sheep's fry; see p. 28.

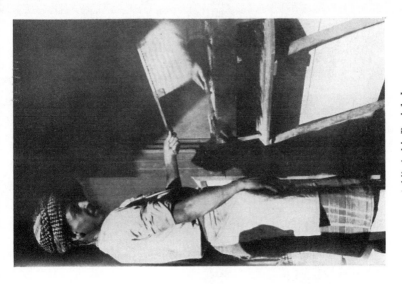

A kibabchi, Baghdad

Thorn-gatherers. The thorn is sold for fuel

'Aye!' And the host said, '*Yalla!*' And they sat and played chess until the wazīr's son had lost the gold in his bag, and his mare, and his clothes, all but his shirt and his drawers, and he was turned out of the house. He, too, went into the sūq to look for work, and a kebābchi[1] took him as servant, and gave him as wages a little food.

Another year passed, and the Sultan's youngest daughter said to her husband, 'You went to fight for my father in the war, now go and bring back my brothers-in-law and cure his blindness.' So the young man sent to tell the Sultan, 'I will go in search of the lost, and of the lion's milk.' When they told the Sultan what he had said, the Sultan became very angry, and said, 'I will not have that good-for-nothing brought near me, and I do not wish to hear the sound of his voice. Do not speak to me of him.'

But the young man took leave of his wife, and went into the desert, took the sheep's paunch off his head and rubbed the lion's hairs together. At once the three jinn appeared and said, '*Utlub ū temenna! Shey tarīd?* Ask and desire! What is your wish?'

And he asked for the mare that flies through the air. And she was there, and he mounted her, and went quickly *dī, dī, dī,* until he came to the cross-roads where sat the old, decrepit man who sat spinning the threads of day and night. And he came politely to the old man and asked after his health and his family (*Shlōn keyfak? Shlōn āilatak?*) and said, 'I am sorry for you that you must sit here day and night spinning,' and other pleasant speeches. After these politenesses, he said, 'I want to ask, my father, what these three roads are called, and whence they go.'

The old man replied, 'O my son, the first is called, "Went-and-Returned-not" and the other two "Goes-and-Comes".'

Said the youth, 'O my father, I will go by the first.'

Said the old man, 'O my son, do not so! Two youths have passed here, and both took the other two roads, which are easy and straight, and they did not return. If

---

[1] A vendor of *kebāb*, small pieces of meat threaded on skewers and grilled over a pan of charcoal, which is fanned to a bright heat by the *kebābchi*.

you take the road "Went-and-Returned-Not" which is perilous, you may perish. You are pleasant-spoken and intelligent, I should be sorry if you came to harm.'

Replied the youth, 'Nevertheless, I choose the Road "Went-and-Returned-Not".'

Said the old man, 'If you persist in taking this dangerous road, tell me why you are risking your life.'

And the young man told him all that happened to him from the beginning.

Then the old man said, 'My son, you are kind-hearted and soft-spoken, and clever too, so I will tell you what you must do. When you go along the road you will be attacked on all sides, and beaten, and hit with stones, but you must not turn round, or you will die. Go straight on, looking neither to left nor right, and at the end of the road you will find a large castle surrounded by a wall, in which are seven gates, each guarded by a deywa.[1] These deywāt are fierce and will eat you, should you try to enter, but I will give you seven hairs from my beard, and you must make nooses with them, to draw from the mouth of each deywa the gum which she is chewing.[2] As soon as the gum is removed she will fall asleep, and will not harm you. When all the seven deywāt are asleep, you can enter the courtyard of the castle, in which you will find lionesses in plenty. They will not harm you, for a lioness does not eat the children of Adam, it is only the male which does this. Kill and skin one beast, and milk another, then place the skin of milk on the back of a cub, and return by the road by which you came, taking care that you look neither to the right nor left when you are beaten and stoned.'

Then he plucked out seven hairs from his beard and gave them to the young man, who set off on the road 'Went-and-Returned-Not'.

It was just as the old man said: and the young man was thumped and dumped, and beaten and shaken, but he took no notice, nor glanced to right nor left, but went on, straight as a mile, *dī, dī, dī, dī*, until he came to the great castle. There it was, and round it a high wall, with seven gates. He went to the first, and at the gate a deywa was sitting chewing gum lest she should fall asleep. The young man made a loop of one of the hairs from the old man's beard, and came softly, softly, and slipped the noose into her mouth, and drew out the chewing-gum, and that instant the deywa fell asleep. He said, 'I have finished with that one, now I will go on to the second gate.' And he went on to the second gate, and softly, softly, he slipped a hair over the chewing-gum of the second deywa and she too fell asleep. He said, 'Praise to Allah, she is finished too!' And he went on to the third, and the fourth, until all the deywāt were asleep. Then he entered the courtyard of the castle, and there, in a big cage were many lionesses with their cubs. He opened the cage, took his sword and killed one lioness, and skinned her whole, then milked a second lioness into the skin. After that, he took one of the lion cubs, put the skin on his back, and drove it before him as if it were a donkey out of the castle. He returned by the road by which he had come, and this time it hailed blows faster than ever, and stones were hurled at him from right and left, but he did not turn his head, but continued walking straight on, until he came to where the old man sat at the cross-roads. When the old man saw him he was overjoyed, and said, 'Welcome, my son, I feared that I should never see you again, but I know now that you are as wise as you are brave, and deserve the good fortune which will be yours.' The young man thanked him and then said to him, 'My father, I came not only to get the lioness's milk, but to find my two brothers. Please tell me by which road they went.'

And the old man told him.

Then he asked the old man if he might leave the lion with him, while he went to search for his brothers, and the old man said, 'Leave it, and Allah be with you, my son.'

So the young man went on the road 'Goes-and-Comes' and in time he reached the town, and entered it, and stopped at the coffee-house near the gate. No sooner had he stopped there, than the stranger approached him and said, 'Peace upon you! *Hallat al baraka!* Blessing upon you! Welcome! Deign to come to my house, for I entertain all strangers who come to this place for three days and three nights.'

The young man thanked him, and went with him to his house, where he was received with honour, and feasting and drinking for three days and three nights. But on the third night, the host said, 'Do you play chess?'

Answered the young man, 'Aye.'

And the host said, '*Yālla!*'

So they played, and the host lost. They played again, until the host lost all his money, and his house. Then he said, 'This time, I will stake my soul.'

They played, and the host lost. So the young man drew his sword, and prepared to take the host's soul, but the host seized his hand and said, 'Do not kill me! I am not a man, but a woman.'

Then the young man said, 'I will not kill you, since you are a woman, but you should not have played chess with me. I do not play chess with girls. Tell me, where are my brothers?'

She answered him: 'There came two young men who played chess with me here, and their bags of money are hanging here in the room, and their mares are in the stable, but they went away, and I do not know what became of them.'

Said the youth, 'I will hunt for them.' And he threw her into the street, and went forth into the sūq to look for them. After a little he came to the pāchachi's shop, and there was the amīr's son, dirty, ragged, greasy, low, engaged in serving pācha to the pāchachi's customers. The young man knew him, but his brother-in-law, who had only seen him with the sheep's paunch on his head, did not recognize him. So the youth took a mejīdieh[1] from his pocket and went to the pāchachi, and said, 'Send your apprentice here to my house with a dish of pācha.' And the pāchachi said, '*Mamnūn!* Gratefully.'

---

[1] About 3s. 6d.

So the young man returned to the house, and the amīr's son behind him. When they got to the house, he bade his brother-in-law follow him upstairs, and said, 'Put the pācha on the table,' and he did so. Then he said, 'How long have you been with the pāchachi?'

The amīr's son said, 'Two years.'

And he said, 'What wages does he give you?'

And the other replied, '*Bi akil batni,* I get my keep.'

Then he said, 'Come, sit down and eat the pācha with me.'

The other said, 'I am only an apprentice, how can I eat with your Honour?'

But the youth said, '*Leysh?* Why, don't be ashamed, come and eat with me, for I shall not eat without you.' So they ate together, and when they had finished, the youth said, 'Take the plate back to the pāchachi, and then leave his service and come to me for your keep.'

And the amīr's son said, 'Aye.' And he returned to the pāchachi, and said, 'I am leaving you, and entering the service of the effendi who bought the pācha.' And so it was.

When he got to the house again, the youth gave him clothes, and sent him to the hammām, and they passed the evening in pleasure and amusement.

The next day the youth said, 'I will search for the other.' He went again into the sūq, and he looked, and looked, this way and that, and then he saw his other brother engaged in fanning the kebāb as the meat roasted on the skewers. So he went to the kebābchi and gave him some money, and said, 'Make me a plate of kebāb, and send your fellow with it to my house—it is such and such a street.' And the kebābchi said, '*Mamnūn!*' The wazīr's son followed the customer back, and when they had gone upstairs, the youth said to him, 'Come, let us all eat together,' for the amīr's son was there awaiting them.

The other two made answer '*Abadān!* Never! It is not seemly!' But the youth pressed them, and in the end they all ate together, but neither of his brothers-in-law knew who he was. At the end of the meal he bade his second brother-in-law take back the plate to the kebābchi, and leave his service. The other agreed, went back to the kebābchi, and said, 'I wish to leave you and enter the service of the effendi who bought the kebāb', and so it was. When he got back, he, too, was sent to the hammām and provided with new clothes. Then they spent three nights together in that house, feasting and amusing themselves. On the third night the youth said, 'I want to hear a story: tell me who you are, and whence you come.'

They answered him, 'We are from Baghdad, and our father-in-law the Sultan was blind, and needed lion's milk for his eyes,' and told him their adventures in that place, and how they had lost all they had in gambling.

The youth said, 'I will give you some lion's milk, and we will all go to Baghdad. Set you out first, and I will follow with the milk and give it to you.'

The next day the two brothers-in-law set out on foot, but the youth got on his flying mare, and came quickly, quickly to the cross-roads, while they were twenty days behind upon the road. There sat the ancient man, and the lion beside him. The youth thanked him and bade him farewell, and rode off on his mare, driving the lion before him. When he had gone some way in the desert, he rubbed the three hairs together, and the three jinn appeared, saying,

'*Utlub ū temenna! Shey tarīd?*'

He told them, 'I want a tent fit for a prince, and within it servants, and a golden chair, and about it soldiers to guard it.' And in the twinkling of an eye, they were before him. Then he mixed a little of the lioness's milk with some water, put it in a bottle, and waited until his brothers-in-law came up with him. When they appeared, he sent a servant to them, and said, 'The Sultan wishes to see you, please to enter his tent.' They followed him, and entered, and made obeisance, and saluted him. Then he said, 'Have you procured the lioness's milk for your father-in-law?' And they said, 'By Allah, until now we have not procured it.' And he said, 'I have some here for you.' And they kissed his hand, and said, 'God keep you! We are thankful, we are very grateful.' He said, 'I will give you this bottle, but on one condition: and that is that you will bend down and let me put my seal on your backsides.'

They answered, '*Abadān!* Never! That cannot be!'

And he said, 'Then the bottle will not be given to you.'

Then they consulted with each other apart, and one said, 'If we allow him to do what he says, who will know it? We are far from Baghdad in the desert, and shall never see him or his people again, and our shame cannot be known.' And the other agreed with him, and said, 'O your highness, we are ready.' They bent down, and the Sultan sealed their backsides with his seal, and having placed the bottle in their hands, he bade them travel in peace.

So after some days' journey, they returned to Baghdad, and there was music, and cheering, and great joy when the people knew them. They went to the palace of the Sultan, their father-in-law, and he rose to embrace them, saying, 'I thought that you were dead, that wild beasts had devoured you, that we should never see you more! Welcome, my sons!'

Then they told him that after many dangers they had procured the lioness's milk to put on his eyes, and gave him the bottle. He put in a drop. *Hīch!* Nothing! He was blind as before. Then another drop. *H-ī-c-h!* He could not see. Then all the bottle, but in vain, he remained blind.

Meanwhile, the youngest daughter's husband, the son of the Abyssinian, rubbed the three hairs together, and when the slaves appeared, he said, 'Remove all!' and soldiers, tent, servants, golden chair, all went: their place was empty. Then he went to Baghdad, and drew the sheep's paunch over his head, and drove the young lion before him into the stable. His wife met him with joy, and said, 'Where were you this long time! At last you have returned, and with the milk for my father's eyes. Go quickly and take the lion to my father, and tell him all that you have done for him, how you defeated his enemies, and killed two thousand of them, and how you procured this lion.'

He asked her, 'Your brothers-in-law, have they come?'
She said, 'Aye, they came.'
Asked he, 'Did they give milk to the Sultan?'
Answered she, 'They gave.'
Asked he, 'Were his eyes opened?'
Answered she, 'No.'

Then he went to the wazīr and asked to see him, and told him that he had the cure for the king's blindness. And the wazīr said, 'Your brothers-in-law have already brought milk, and it did him no good.' But he said, 'Nevertheless, I will go in with the lion.' And he struck the hairs together, and removed the paunch,

> *Subhān rabb al khāliq*
> *Wal khāliq ahsan!*

he became as beautiful as the full moon. So he went into the audience-room, and the lion cub with him, and took some milk from the skin and put one drop of the milk into the Sultan's eyes. He asked, 'Do you see?' The Sultan answered, 'Allah is great, I see a little.' After an hour, he put in another drop, and the Sultan saw more clearly, and another drop, after another hour, and the Sultan saw the wide world clearly and was overjoyed. He said, 'Who are you and whence did you come, and how did you procure this milk?'

And the young man answered, 'I am your son-in-law, husband to your youngest daughter.' And he told him the story from beginning to end, and how he had given the milk mixed with water to the other sons-in-law, and added, 'If you do not believe me, look at their backsides!' And the amīr's son and the wazīr's son were shamed. Then the youth said, 'It was I who fought in your army, and here is the shred of shawl with which you bound my hand.'

The king was very happy, and cried, 'It was you! and I did not know it, and put you in the stable! Forgive me!'

Then he called his people and they made great wedding festivities, and large feasts, and calling the Abyssinian's son, he took off his crown and placed it on his head.

And this is the end of the story of the Blind Sultan.

> *Kunna 'adkum wa jīna*
> *Ad duff mugargaʿ wal arūs hazīna!*

We were at your house, and we came back,
The tambourine rattles and the bride is sad! [1]

or

> *Kān akūsh telet ʿtufahaiyāt* (tufahāt)
> *Wāhida illi, wāhida lil tahchi al hechāya, wāhidi lil*
> *tismʿa al hechāya.*
> *Wal qishūr lil Sultān!*

There were three apples:
One for me, one for the story-teller, and one for the
   listener,
And the peel for the Sultan.

(Then, fearing that she had uttered *lèse majesté*, the story-teller said, quickly,

'No, not that! "*Wal qishūr lil feresi.*" And the peel for the mare.')

---

[1] A bride of modest character should always weep at her wedding: a smiling bride is thought bold. Tears also serve to keep away the evil eye.

XIII

JARĀDA

THERE was once a man whose laziness prevented him from rising in the world; in fact, he was a fellow with neither energy nor intelligence. He was married to a woman called Jarāda, or Locust, who was as quick-witted as he was slow. One day she said to her husband, 'We have no food in the house, you must get out and earn some money.'

He replied, 'How shall I earn money, wife? No one will give me work.'

She said, 'True, but you have not yet tried the trade of magician. That is a calling which brings in money. Go, sit in the market and tell the people that you are a white magician and will write them charms (*hijāb*) to keep off ill-fortune.'

Said her husband, 'O Locust, how shall I do that? I know not *alif* from *yay*—I cannot write.'

'Dense-witted man,' said Locust, 'is it necessary to write to make amulets? Make but a few scribblings on paper and they will take it for hidden writing.'

She gave him a pen-case[1] to stick in his belt, and paper, and forth he went to the market-place and cried that he was a *fatahfāl*[2]—a reader of secrets, a dealer in magic.

Wherever there is a deceiver there are always deceived, and the false prophet never lacks disciples. Locust's husband did a brave trade, and wrote charms against the Eye, amulets against bullets, protections against fevers, cures for the palsy, and other charms, and at the end of the week he found himself the possessor of more money than he had ever earned by honest work.

The fates which had given him a good wife had also contrived that he should prosper, for his fame quickly

---

[1] A belt pen-case is shaped rather like a pipe (if it is merely box-shaped it goes into the pocket). At one end is the ink-pot, in the other a spoon for the sand and a reed pen.

[2] The *fatahfāl's* cry is *Fatahfāl! aʻaddad nejm, ākhudh khīra!* I count the stars and take omens! This cry is heard in Baghdad to-day.

spread. People began to talk of the cures he had worked, of witchcraft he had brought to naught, and of other wonders he had wrought. One day as he sat in the market-place a woman came to him and said,

'O wise man, I am in trouble and seek your help. Can you be secret?'

'The wise are always secret,' replied the husband of Locust.

'Then my trouble is this. I am a servant in the house of the Khalīfa. One day I saw the Khalīfa's ring lying in his chamber, and Shaitān entering my mind, I took it. Now there is great hue and cry after the ring, and I want to consult the stars to know if I shall be discovered.'

Locust's husband pretended to consult his book and told her that the stars were against her. 'You must lose the ring.'

Said the maid-servant, 'Sooner the ring than my head. What must be done?'

The magician looked again at the book and told her that she must instantly put the ring into the cistern: otherwise, he warned her, her life would be forfeit.

'It shall be done,' said the woman, and she gave him a fee for his good counsel.

When he came home, he told his wife, and she commended him for what he had said, and putting on her veil, she went to talk with some of the women of the Khalīfa's household, telling them that her husband was a wonderful wizard, and that if the Khalīfa would only consult him, she was certain that he could find out from his magical book where the ring was.

They told the Khalīfa's wife, who mentioned it to her husband. The result was that the magician was summoned to the palace and brought into the presence of the Khalīfa, who ordered him to prove his skill by discovering the ring. The wizard opened his book, and after a little scribbling, he told the Khalīfa that if he looked in the cistern, the ring would be found. It was even as he said, and the Khalīfa was so pleased that he rewarded the wise man generously.

A short time after this there was a robbery in the palace, and a chest containing money and jewels disappeared. The Khalīfa sent at once for the magician, opened the matter to him, and instructed him to discover in his book where the chest was secreted. The charlatan was in the utmost difficulty, looked in his book and wondered what he should do. At last he said, 'O Commander of the Faithful, I do not see clearly in my book, and I must work my spells at home.'

It is a bad thing to disappoint princes. The Khalīfa frowned, and said, 'See that the spells do not fail, or it may cost you dear.'

The husband of Locust answered him, 'My spells will not fail, but I need time.'

'How much time is needed?' asked the Khalīfa.

'Forty days,' replied the charlatan, for he thought in himself that in forty days much might happen.

'Good,' said the Khalīfa. 'But if after the forty days you have not restored the chest, your life will be forfeit.'

'Hearing and obeying,' replied the magician, and he returned to his wife in great misery, and spent the rest of the day in weeping and in prayer.

Now the thieves who had stolen the box of treasure were forty in number, and when news reached them that the king had sent for the wise man who had discovered the lost ring so easily, they became disturbed in mind. The chief of the band decided to send one of their number as a spy to the wizard's house, to see if he could find out if the wizard were indeed on their track. So at nightfall he crept to the house, and laying his ear to the door he listened.

Presently he heard the magician within say to his wife with a deep groan, 'O Locust, my wife, one of the forty is passing!' He meant that one of the forty days left to him on the earth was drawing to its close, but the thief who was listening took the words to himself. He went back to the chief, and said, 'O chief, this man knows all! While I was hid, he said to his wife, "Here is one of the forty!" and I fled away.'

'We must discover more,' replied the chief. 'To-morrow night another of you must go to listen.'

The next night the second thief went to lay his ear to the door, like the first. The words he heard were, 'O wife, one of the forty has gone, and now another of them is passing!' and the thief made off as fast as he could and reported the words to the chief.

The master-robber beat his breast and cried, 'Without doubt he knows each one of us! And he may go at any moment to tell the Khalīfa.'

The thieves consulted together, and in fear of their lives they agreed to go to the wizard and throw themselves on his mercy, promising him a large sum of gold if he would forbear to betray them to justice. This they did that very night.

Locust's husband said to them, 'I know each one of you and his wickedness, but I am a man of clemency, and will do what I can to protect you. You must tell me, however, where you have hidden the chest, and nothing of the treasure must be missing, so that it can be restored to the Khalīfa.'

'Life is more precious than treasure,' said the robber-chief. 'We will show you where the chest is hidden and give you a handsome reward as well.'

The next day the magician presented himself at the palace and told the Khalīfa that the spells had worked more quickly than he had at first thought, and that he could lead him to where the chest was hidden. He took the Khalīfa to the spot which the robbers had shown him beside a bush in the desert, and when the Khalīfa's servants dug in that place, lo, the chest was laid bare, and none of its contents were missing.

The Khalīfa was very pleased and bestowed a fine house and much money on the soothsayer, whose fame was much increased thereby.

The Khalīfa boasted of the powers of his magician to all the princes that he knew, and one day Locust's husband was summoned to the palace, where a foreign prince was being entertained. The Khalīfa presented the magician

to the prince, and told the latter that he beheld a very
master of wonders. Said he, 'He can see through walls,
and he can see through the earth!' And to prove the
wizard's power, he asked him before his guest, 'Tell us
what I hold here in my closed hand!'

The soothsayer cursed the day that he had taken up
this trade, for he knew that if he failed now before the
foreign prince the face of the Khalīfa would be blackened
and that he would certainly die for his imposture. He
cast himself on his knees, and cried in despair, 'Caught at
last, O Locust!' of course meaning his wife.

As he spoke, the Khalīfa opened his hand, and a locust
flew out.

One of the princes then plucked a bunch of lentils and
went with it in his closed hand to the magician, and said,
'Divine what is here in my hand,' and the magician
exclaimed:

'*Al yidri yidri,*	Who knows, knows
Wal ma yidri	And who knows not
Jadhbat ʿades![1]	A bunch of lentils!'

and again he was right.

The foreign prince was astounded at the magician's
powers, and rewarded him by a purse of dinars.

However, when he returned to his wife Locust, the
soothsayer said to her, 'Chance has helped me three times,
but I fear that next time fortune will forsake me. I live in
constant fear that the Khalīfa will set me a task I cannot
perform. What shall I do, O Locust?'

His wife advised him to feign madness, and that as soon
as might be.

So the next day when his friends came to see him, she
told them that Allah had afflicted her husband and that
he was crazy. The news reached the Khalīfa and he sent
at once to know if it were true.

They brought the supposed madman, raving and singing, into the palace. To prove his madness, the soothsayer
pretended not to recognize the Khalīfa, when brought

---

[1] A symbol of despair. If one is in despair, they say of him *yakul ʿades*.

into his presence, but going up to him laid hold of him familiarly by the sleeve and sought to draw him from the room.

The Khalīfa humoured his whim, and the courtiers followed to see what the crazy fellow would do. No sooner had they left the audience-chamber than the ceiling fell in with a crash.

The Khalīfa turned to his courtiers and said, 'Even in his madness this fellow is wiser than ordinary mortals! He was surely sent hither by the Compassionate, so that our lives might be spared.'

And he overwhelmed his saviour with riches, so that the magician and his wife Locust lived in comfort all the days of their life.

Wa hadha hechāya
Nus[1] ha chedhbāya,
Lo enta qarīb
'Ateytak tubeq azbīb!

This story
Is half-lie,
If you were near
I'd give you a dish of raisins.

[1] *Nusf.*

XIV

THE STORK AND THE JACKAL

THERE was once a stork who was on friendly terms with a jackal. But being bested by the cunning of the jackal once or twice, he made up his mind to give him a lesson. So he invited the jackal to dinner, and when his guest arrived, he led him to a thicket of brushwood where peas were scattered. The stork could easily pick up the peas with his long bill, while the jackal pricked and scratched his tongue and muzzle. The next day the jackal invited the stork to dinner, and bought a bottle of milk, which he poured on a slab of marble. The jackal licked up the milk easily, while the stork, trying in vain to swallow a little, broke his bill. The stork, feeling his dignity injured by his broken bill, made up his mind to revenge himself, so he went to the jackal and said, 'Brother Jackal, I want to teach you how to fly! Ride on my back, and I will show you when we are in the air.' The jackal got on the stork's back and the stork flew up higher and higher with him. Presently, the stork asked, 'What does the world below look like?' The jackal answered, 'It looks as big as a carpet.' The stork flew yet higher, and asked the jackal, 'How big is the world now?' The jackal replied, 'It is as big as an orange.' The stork flew higher still, and asked again, 'How big is the world?' The jackal answered, 'The earth is so far below us that I cannot see it.'

Then the stork said, 'My shoulder is tired, will you please cling to the other?' While the jackal was doing this, he contrived to shake him off, and flew away.

The jackal fell towards the earth, and as he fell he kept crying and praying to Allah,

> *Ya rabbi la tiksar akrā-i*
> *Waqqʻani ʻala furwat ar rāi!*

> 'Oh Lord, do not break my fore-leg!
> Cause me to fall on the shepherd's sheepskin coat!'

And indeed, when he approached the earth, he saw that he was falling towards a flock of sheep tended by a shepherd. He fell on the shepherd, who, affrighted, flew off leaving his sheepskin coat and his fifty sheep behind him.

The jackal donned the sheepskin, and the sheep thinking him their shepherd followed him into his cave. Then the jackal offered banquets to his friends and relatives, and had the best of times with the provision he kept in the cave. Soon he was pronounced Shaikh of Wawīa,[1] owing to the dignity he had acquired by his hospitality and the wearing of the sheepskin.

One day when he went to drink, the jackal met the lion, who said to him, 'Ha, *Abul wīyu*, from whence this fur coat you are wearing?'

Answered the jackal, '*Ya, Abu Khumeyis*,[2] *leish, enta ma i'aref?* Why, Father-of-Five, don't you know? Making fur coats is our trade. My grandfather and father were both of that profession, and we have secrets of the trade which we keep in our family.' The lion said, 'Take my measurements and make me a fur coat.' The jackal took his measurements and said, 'Your fur coat will need twenty camels, fifty sheep, and a hundred and twenty hens.'

The lion said, 'Good! I will bring you the materials you ask.' When the lion came with the camels, sheep, and hens, the jackal drove them all into his cave and gave great feasts to his friends and relations while the lion waited for his fur coat.

Growing impatient, the lion went to look for the jackal, and said, 'Where is my fur coat? Is it not yet ready?'

The jackal replied, 'I am glad to say that your fur coat is a really fine one, the best we have ever made! but the materials you brought were not quite enough, and we need a little more for the buttons—a mere nothing—only twenty sheep and forty hens. Then I shall hope to send you your fur coat and you will wear it in good health,[3] please God!'

---

[1] Jackaldom.   [2] Lion's nickname, Father-of-Little-Five (claws).

[3] When a new garment is put on for the first time it is customary to say *Bil 'afya!* (Wear it in good health!) in order to keep off the evil eye.

The jackal got a new supply of provisions from the lion, and departed and spent the winter in his cave. Then the lion got angry and making inquiries discovered the trick which had been played upon him. He swore to give the jackal a good lesson, and lying in wait for him, he managed to catch him one day. The lion asked him, 'What has happened to my fur coat? Why have you not delivered it?' The jackal answered, 'A few threads are still lacking, and if you will bring me a little more material——' At that the lion burst in with a great roar and said, 'Am I to be the mock of you and your father?' and struck him with his paw.

The jackal was too quick for him, and escaped with his life, but his tail was torn off and he ran away tailless. The lion shouted after him, 'Now I shall recognize you! because you are without a tail!'

The jackal realized his danger and resorted to a trick. He went to a mound and shouted to all the jackals of the district that he wished to call a meeting. When they were all assembled, he addressed them, 'O my brethren! during my travels in other countries I learnt the most graceful and beautiful dance! I want you all to learn it, as it will cause you great amusement. It is very simple. Each jackal must take a partner, and must face one in one direction and the other in the other: and their tails I shall tie together. When you are all in place, I will teach you the first step.' He went round and saw that their tails were all tied fast one to the other, and then from his mound he gave a loud cry, 'Fly, my brothers! A gang of lions is approaching us to eat us!' The jackals in terror plunged for freedom, each in another direction, and in so doing pulled off their own tails. Next day all the jackals of the district were tailless like their shaikh.

When the lion sent out his messengers to arrest the tailless jackal, they returned to him saying, 'O Abu Khumēyis! All the jackals in this place are tailless!'

So the jackal effected his escape.

XV

'IT IS NOT THE LION'S FUR COAT!'

ONE day, Abu Khumēyis,[1] the king of beasts, was saun-
tering in the desert, when he came upon a well, and
stopped by it. And when he looked down into it, he saw
a wolf, and wished him good-day. Said the wolf,
'*Ahlan u sahlan, ya Abu Khumēyis!* Welcome, O Abu
Khumēyis!'

Said the lion, 'What are you doing down there?'

Said the wolf, 'I am making a fur coat.'

Said the lion, 'O wolf, the weather is cold, I should like
a fur coat, too.'

Said the wolf, 'Good, I will make you one, but I shall
want sheepskins.'

The lion agreed, and went away, and having caught
two fat lambs, he threw them down the well to the wolf.

Said the wolf, 'That is not nearly enough, I shall want
many—one or two at a time.'

So the lion came every day and threw him a lamb or two
daily, but each time he asked, 'Is the coat finished?' the
wolf answered, 'I want more skins.' At the last the lion grew
impatient, for each time he threw a lamb in the wolf had
an excuse why his coat was not ready, such as 'It is a
feast,' or 'I have not been well.' But the lion would hear
this no longer, and said that he must have his coat. The
wolf replied, 'In another two days.'

When the lion came after two days, he said, 'The coat
only needs a few stitches, and you shall have it to-morrow.
Come early and bring a rope.' So the next day the lion
came and threw a rope into the well and hauled upon it
as he was bid. As he hauled he thought that the coat
must be a fine one, for the weight that hung on the rope
was great. This was because the wolf, who had clung on
to the rope with a couple of the skins, had grown very
fat upon the lambs which the lion had thrown down. No

[1] See p. 81, note 2.

sooner had he been drawn to the top, than he threw the skins at the lion, and before Abu Khumēyis recovered his wits, he was off and far away.

And if in Baghdad a person who has ordered a garment of the tailor is met with excuses for its delay, he answers, '*Eysh sārē kho mū furwat es sebaʿ*!   It isn't the Lion's fur coat!'

XVI

TWO STORIES OF ABU NOWĀS, THE
BOON-COMPANION OF HĀRŪN
AR RASHĪD

ABU NowĀs sometimes tired of his continual attendance upon the Khalīfa, whose every whim he was supposed to humour, and one day, unable to endure it, he went off into the city, and hid himself. The Khalīfa missed him, and sent orders far and wide that he was to be found and brought to him. In time, some of his servants visiting the outskirts of Baghdad found Abu Nowās, who was in merry mood, a leathern bottle of wine slung to his waist. They apprehended him and brought him back to their master, who, in his joy at recovering his favourite, was disposed to forgive him for his truancy. However, he affected to be angry, and fixing Abu Nowās with a stern look, he asked, 'What have you in that bottle?'

'*Laban* (sour milk),' returned Abu Nowās readily.

The Khalīfa opened the bottle, and frowned.

'Is laban red, O Abu Nowās?'

'The laban saw your Majesty, and was bashful and blushed!'

The Khalīfa laughed and forgave the jester.

On another occasion, Abu Nowās, being weary of Court life sought permission from his master to journey into other parts of the country. Harūn ar Rashīd gave his permission, and Abu Nowās, when he went to pay his farewell visit, produced a document, which he begged him to sign and seal with the royal seal. It was a firmān, and in it was set forth that by order of the Khalīfa, every man who was afraid of his wife should give to Abu Nowās an ass.

In time, Abu Nowās returned, and lo! behind him was a train of some four hundred asses! Abu Nowās hastened to visit the Khalīfa, who declared to him that he had led a dull life since Abu Nowās had gone away.

Said Abu Nowās, 'Many a good jest have I enjoyed with your Majesty. Does not your Majesty remember that night when——?'

The Khalīfa looked apprehensively at the curtain and tugged at his sleeve. 'Not so loud, Abu Nowās, or Sitt Zobeidah will hear what may not be fitting for her to hear!'

Abu Nowās said, 'Your Majesty, I demand two asses.'

'Wherefore?' said the Khalīfa.

'Because your Majesty, being at the same time like and unlike other men, must pay a king's fine for being afraid of his wife. Lesser men pay one ass, your Majesty must pay two.'

XVII

A STORY OF THE KHALĪFA
HĀRŪN AR RASHĪD

ONE day the Khalīfa was walking in Baghdad with his minister, and they came to the river, where a fuller stood beating cotton-cloth in the river. It was winter, and the weather was bitterly cold, and the Khalīfa paused by the man and spoke to him.

Said he, 'You have twelve, do you need these three?'

Answered the fuller, 'For the thirty and two they are needed.'

Said the Khalīfa, 'And the far?'

Replied the fuller, 'Is now near.'

Spake the Khalīfa once more, 'If I send you a goose will you pluck it?'

And the fuller made reply, 'Yes, I will pluck its feathers and send it back.'

Then the Khalīfa and his minister passed on, and when they had gone a little way the Khalīfa turned to his minister, and said, 'Did you understand what I said to the fuller?'

The minister replied, 'O Khalīfa, lord of the age and time, I did not understand.'

Said the Khalīfa, 'I will give you a respite of three hours to find out the meaning of what was said, and if you cannot read me the riddle, I shall cut off your head.'

The minister saluted the Khalīfa and left him. First he went to his house and took a bag of gold, and secondly he went back to the fuller. To him he said, 'O my dear, Allah preserve you and your children and lengthen your life! What was the meaning of what the Khalīfa said to you and you to him!'

Answered the fuller, 'Pass on! That is nothing to you!'

Said the minister, 'My brother, my dear, if you will not tell me, the Khalīfa will cut off my head! Allah bless you, Allah preserve you! For the sake of Allah the Merciful and the Prophet, on him be peace, tell me the meaning of your conversation.'

Said the fuller, 'If for each riddle, you will give me a hundred pieces of gold, I will speak.'

The minister gave him a hundred pieces of gold.

The fuller said, 'The Khalīfa said to me, "You have twelve, do you need these three?" and his meaning was, "There are twelve months in the year, need you work during the three cold months?" and to this I replied, "For the thirty and two they are needed," and I meant my teeth. For if a poor man remains idle three months, his teeth are idle too!'

Then the minister said, 'And now the second dark saying.'

Said the fuller, 'First another hundred pieces of gold!' and the minister counted him out the hundred.

Then said the fuller, ' "The far is now near", referred to my sight, which has grown longer with age, as is usual with those getting on in life.'

Said the minister, 'And the third saying?'

Replied the fuller, 'Give me all the gold that remains in the bag and I will tell you.'

The minister handed him the bag, and the fuller said, 'The Khalīfa asked if I could pluck a goose, if he were to send me one. By the goose he meant you, and, by Allah, I have plucked you!'

And he held up the gold, and added, 'And now return to the Khalīfa!' And the minister departed, shamed.

XVIII

ANOTHER STORY OF THE KHALĪFA

ONE day the Khalīfa was walking in the streets with Abu Nowās, when he saw a man, stark naked, lying in the road asleep, and his body and limbs were painted in divers colours. The Khalīfa poked him with his foot and said, 'What is this?'

Answered the fellow, 'What business have you with me?'

Answered the Khalīfa, 'Why have you painted yourself in this manner?'

Answered the man, 'I wished to sleep. Suppose while I was asleep, one came and cut off my hand, or my leg, and took it away, how should I know them again unless they were painted?'

The Khalīfa laughed, and said, 'This poor fellow is mad!' and to him he said, 'Rise! come with me and return to my house. You can live in my kitchen and help the cook, and earn your bellyful.'

So the man was put into the Khalīfa's kitchen, and the Khalīfa ordered that he should be well fed, and that they should employ him in the kitchen on such tasks as washing plates and peeling onions.

Now one day a Sultan sent his wazīr to the Khalīfa, and when he had entered the Khalīfa's presence, the wazīr said, 'I have two riddles to propound to your Majesty from my master the Sultan. If you can explain them satisfactorily, there will be an alliance between you, and if not, there will be war.'

But the Khalīfa could not understand the riddles, and he and his wazīrs were troubled and anxious. The fool who worked in the kitchen noticed that something was amiss, and asked what was the matter.

They answered him, 'What are you, that you should understand, madman!'

The fool replied, 'I am mad, but perhaps I may be able to help them, for I see them troubled and anxious.'

And he was so insistent, that at last they went to the Khalīfa and said to him, 'The fool in the kitchen wants to speak to you, he thinks that he can help you!'

Answered the Khalīfa, 'Let him come! When there is no help in wise men, perhaps the stones will speak!'

And they brought the madman, and the strange wazīr came also, while all the court waited to see what would happen.

Now neither spoke a word, but the strange wazīr bent and traced on the ground a circle with his finger. The fool bent also, and with his finger he drew a line across the circle. Then the wazīr took from his pocket an egg and placed it in the midst of the circle. The madman put his hand into his pocket, and drew out an onion, and this he placed beside the egg.

Then the wazīr spoke and asked him to explain the meaning.

Said the fool, 'The circle that you drew was the world, and I cut it across to symbolize the two spheres. The egg with its yolk and white means the waters of the earth, and the sun which gives it life, and the onion, with its seven skins, symbolizes the seven layers of the earth.'

And the wazīr cried, 'This fool could not have known the meaning, it was Allah who spoke through him!'

And the court applauded and all saw that Allah had spoken by the mouth of the fool.

XIX

THE TRICKS OF JĀNN

MY uncle was interpreter for the police in Baghdad, and their hōsh,[1] which was 'dwelt-in' (haunted), was divided into two courts, one near the street, and the other on the river, and at night they locked the door between the two. One night, when all were asleep, my uncle was awakened by a knocking, taq-taq-taq! on the door on the river side. My uncle was a brave man, and he got up and opened the door and went into the other courtyard. He heard a wailing, a boy's voice crying *'Khatr Allah!* I am drowning! get me out! Give me your hand!' He went to the river, and there in the river he saw a boy. He stretched forth his hand to the boy, but the appearance stuck out its tongue and with a laugh it disappeared into the river.[2]

This same uncle was once in the quarter Sultān 'Ali, and came out of the *kōnak* one night at about eleven o'clock, and was returning to his house alone, when he saw a woman sitting by the roadside. She was veiled and beautifully dressed, and was weeping bitterly. How she wept, *āhu, āhu, āhu!* My uncle drew out his dagger, for before the war every one went armed, and said to her, 'My aunt, what is the matter, who has done you hurt? Why are you sitting here weeping?'

She answered nothing, but continued to weep, *ferd buka'!*

He said to himself, 'How can I leave her here alone at such an hour and weeping like this!'

At this, she suddenly lifted her veil, and put out her tongue at him, and he knew her for a jinnīya. He stuck his dagger into the ground before her, and she disappeared. But his hand remained rooted to the dagger in the ground: he could not withdraw it until there came by a man, who lifted it for him.

And my grandmother told me about a cousin who died

---

[1] See p. 29.   [2] Cf. Preface, p. xii, for the *ferij aqra'a.*

before I was in the world. Their house was in the Maidān, and that night as they were going to the vigil before Christmas, at the church they passed by the tomb of the daughter of Hasan, to which the Moslems tie rags, and at which they light candles. The boy was walking a little behind the rest, and when they came to this tomb, he saw a black dog coming from it, with two candles alight on its head. The boy began to cry, and ran after my grandmother, screaming, 'I am afraid of the dog that came out on me!'

And all through the church service that night he was trembling and crying, and from that moment he was ill, for the fright descended into his legs, and three months afterwards he died.

That tomb is 'dwelt-in' as every one knows. One evening my aunt was passing by it, and she saw a huge figure before her, like an enormously tall man. It was a *tantal*.[1] She stepped to one side: it stepped also: she could not evade it, step where she might. So she began to say 'In the name of Allah,' and to pray, and it went.

The prophets of the Moslems are often demons.[2]

[1] See Preface, p. xi.
[2] The narrator of this story was a Christian.

XX

IT WAS ENOUGH TO BEWILDER THE LION!

This story was often told to show how, during the war, a big shaikh would be imprisoned by one person in authority, and released by the next, particularly when successive waves of troops invaded his territory.

THERE was once a seller of firewood who went into a wood to get sticks to sell for a livelihood. There, whom should he see but a lion. Said he to himself, 'If this lion comes here, he will eat me, and then what would my family do with no goodman to support them!' So, taking courage, he went to the lion and said, 'What are you doing in my wood?'

The lion was so astonished at his impudence that he said, 'Your wood! Why, it is my wood, by my right as Lord of all Forests and King of Beasts.' The poor man said, 'This is my wood, where I come to pick up the firewood that I sell, and if you don't agree, we will fight the matter out.'

'Fight for it?' said the lion, more and more astonished. 'Why, what chance would you have against me?'

'True,' said the man, 'you have your claws and teeth, while I have no weapons, but, if you will allow me, I will go to my house which is not far away, and get a hatchet.'

'Ho, ho!' said the lion, 'and if I let you go, how do I know that you'll ever come back?'

Said the man, 'My name is Fās-Fūs, and the address of my house is this——' and he gave it. 'If I don't return, you can come to my house and eat me. But on the other hand, how do I know that *you* won't run away the instant my back is turned?'

The lion was overwhelmed by his impudence. 'I, King of Beasts, run away from a poor thing like you? Why, so far am I from wishing to run away, that you may tie me up, if you wish!'

Now this was exactly what the man wanted, so he tied the lion up securely and left him.

There the lion would have stayed for ever had not a mouse come by and heard him roaring.

The mouse stopped and asked him what was the matter, and the lion told him.

'That is easily put right,' said the mouse. 'I can nibble through the cords which bind you and set you free.'

'If you will,' said the lion, 'you and your family can claim the protection of the King of Beasts for evermore.'

So the mouse set to work, and nibbled at the cords until the lion was set free. It was just running off when the lion called to it.

'How shall I keep my promise if I do not know your name?'

'My name is Fsay-fís,' said the mouse, and off it went.

Said the lion, 'A Fās-fūs bound me and a Fsay-fís[1] (turkey) loosed me! There is something uncanny about this, and this wood is no place for me!' So saying, he bounded off and left the place for ever.

---

[1] Fsay-fís is the diminutive of Fās-fūs, i.e. 'Big Jack in office put me in jug, and Little Jack in office released me.'

XXI
NURSERY RHYMES
I

Khashabati nūdi nūdi
Salamīli ʿal jidūdi
Al jidūd sāfaru ʾlʾ¹ Makka
Labbasūni tōb ū kaʿkaʿ
Wal kaʿkaʿ wein adhumha?
Adhumha batn es sandūq
As Sandūq yarīd miftah
Wal miftah yarīd haddād
Wal haddād yarīd fulūs
Wal fulūs ʿand al ʿarūs
Wal ʿarūs batn al hammām
Wal hammām yarīd qandīl
Wal qandīl tāmus bil bīr
Wal bīr yarīd habl
Wal habl yarīd fattāl
Wal fattāl yarīd jāmūs
Wal jāmūs yarīd hashīsh
Wal hashīsh yarīd matar
Wal matar ʿand Allah!

An alternative version of the last eight lines:

Wal habl fōq al jebel
Wal jebel yarīd hashīsh
Wal hashīsh yarīd matar
Wal matar ʿand Allah!

My little piece of wood, nod, nod!
Salute my granddad and his dame,
To Mecca they have gone away,
And gave me dress and thread so gay,
Ball of thread where shall I keep it?
I will put it in the box
And the box will need a key,

¹ Contraction of *ila.*

And the key will need a smith,
And the locksmith wants some pay,
Who will pay it? The bride may![1]
But the bride is at the bath,
And the bath must have a light
And the candle's in the well!
And the well needs a rope,
But the rope must first be twisted,
A buffalo the twister's needing,
The buffalo needs grass for feeding,
And the grass it needs some rain,
And the rain comes from Allah.

Alternative Version

And the rope's upon the hill,
And the hill needs grass,
And the grass needs rain
And the rain comes from Allah.

II

'Andi maghzal, farreyta,
Jōwa shejer dhammeyta
Ja khāli, mā 'anteyta[2]
'Ateyt lil fahl wan nāga,
Wan nāga ma mirbūta
Illa bi qusaiyib khāli
Khāli, ya bū seyyidīya
Bahr al bahrīya
Tala 'at minha ibnaya
Al bunaya ismha 'batta'
Wa til'ab bi kureysh al hanta.
Yā rabbi! ma tasa'adha!
Sa'ad benāt al jinjil
Al jinjil bi īda risha
Itārad 'alal gadīsha,
Gadīshat 'ammi Sālim
Chetālat al awādim

---

[1] I have translated freely here to give a rhyme.
[2] *'anta*, a local form of *'ata*, to give.

Weaving grass mats, Karbala

A grass rope maker (*fattāl*), Hillah

'Andi n'aja kurdīya
Tuhlib huga wa hugīya
Ja ad dīb 'ar'arha
Wa khallat tunga majfīya!

I had a spindle, twisted it,
Beneath a tree I put it,
When uncle came, I refused it,
To the she-camel I gave it,
And the she-camel cannot be bound
But by the twisted lock of my uncle,
My uncle, wearer of the green turban![1]
From the river
Came out a little damsel
And the damsel's name was 'Duck'
And she played amidst the corn. (lit. in the belly of)
O Lord, do not help her!
Help the daughters of an anklet (i. e. those who wear
    anklets)
In the hand (of one of them?) a feather,
The feather gallops on an old mule,
The old mule of my uncle Sālim,
That old mule attacks people.
I have a Kurdish ewe
She gives me a hoqa[2] and a little hoqa of milk,
There came the wolf and barked at her,
And she left the dish upside down.

---

[1] A Seyyid, a descendant of the Prophet.   [2] hoqa = about 2 lb.

XXII

THE BITTER ORANGE

THERE was once a man and woman who had been married for some years, and Allah had given them no child. One day the woman was sitting with her friends, and she began to speak of her misfortune, saying, 'I do not know what I can do!'

One woman asked her, 'Have you taken medicine?'

She answered, 'Aye, I have drunk medicine, but it was no good.'

Another said, 'There is a way, and I will tell you what you must do. Buy a bitter orange,[1] bring it to the house, but do not let your husband see it, go into your room and eat it, and you will have a child!'

The childless woman thought that she would try this, so she went into the sūq, and bought a bitter orange, and returned to the house with it, hiding it beneath her 'aba.[1] Her husband met her and said, 'What are you carrying beneath your 'aba?'

She denied, saying, 'No, I am carrying nothing!'

Then he came to her, and took the orange from her by force.

She said, 'Do not take this orange from me, for if you do, you will become pregnant, and I shall chase you out of the house!'

He laughed and said, 'How can that be true!' and purposely he seized it and ate it before her.

After that, month by month, his belly grew bigger and bigger and the woman was ashamed and angry and would not speak to him. When the ninth month was complete, and his pains began to come upon him, she opened the door of the house, and put him outside.

He walked and walked, in the desert, and at last he sank down exhausted, and, his pains reaching their climax, he brought a daughter into the world.

As soon as he was able, he took a piece of paper, wrote

[1] See p. 1, note.

upon it all that had happened, tied it to the arm of the baby, and went away.

As for the girl-baby, Allah sent her a she-gazelle, which nourished her from her teats, and a falcon which hovered above her head and shielded her from the sun, and so she lived in the desert.

One day the Sultan's son was riding to hunt in the desert, and he saw in the distance something which glittered in the sun. He cried to his slaves, 'What is that yonder which glitters? Go and fetch it!'

They went, and on the ground they saw a little girl, sweet, sweet! as dazzling as the sun in beauty. They wrapped her up in an 'aba and brought her to the Sultan's son. The prince was delighted at her beauty and read the paper tied to her arm, and knew from it her story. He set the child before him on his mare and returned to his house, and said to his mother, 'My mother, I have brought you a lovely girl for you to bring her up like your own daughter.'

The mother brought her up, and when the girl was grown marriage-ripe, the prince took her for his wife. He loved the girl madly, and could not bear to be parted from her one moment.

Now there was a great resemblance between the foundling girl and her mother-in-law; in fact, the one was the mirror of the other, for the hair of both was golden, and their faces were so much alike that it was difficult to tell one from the other.

One day there was a war, and the prince was obliged to go and fight. He asked his mother to take care of his bride (*hallahalla bīha*) and bade them both farewell and went.

Now the mother-in-law was jealous of the girl, and began to torment her, beating her from morn to eve, and giving her no food to eat. The girl wept, but her mother-in-law said to herself, '*Māku chāra!* There is no way out of it! My son has gone to the wars—who knows if he will ever come back? Why should I keep this girl longer in the house?'

So one day, she seized her, and pushed her out into the road.

The girl roamed about in despair, not knowing what to do. In her distress, she lifted her head and said to the Lord of All things, 'My Lord! My Master, help me! Build me a house in this wilderness such as there is not in this world, and in the garden fruit-trees which shall bear fruit in winter-time as in summer-time.'

And Allah, of his mercy, built for the girl a house as she had asked, in the middle of the wilderness, and the key was beside her. She rose, and took the key, opened the gate, and went into the house. When she looked from the windows of the house, what a garden she saw—of all the gardens Allah has created this garden was the finest! Every fruit grew in it, and blossom and fruit came together, for there was no season of winter in that garden.

But in spite of this, the girl was not happy, for she loved her husband dearly, and longed for his presence. Day and night she wept for him and prayed for his return.

Now the war was over, and the Sultan's son returned from the war, and went to his house. His mother was frightened lest he should find out what she had done, so she pretended to be his wife. When he asked her, 'Where is my mother?' she answered, 'She is dead! and come to her end.'

Now the mother became pregnant from her son. She was ashamed and displeased at what had happened, but there was no way out, for she knew that if he learnt what she had done to his true bride, he would kill her. One day she went on to the roof and in the desert outside the city she saw a garden, and in it a vine in full fruit, although it was winter, and snow lay on the ground.

She came down from the roof and went to where her son was sitting, and said, 'I want some grapes, go and bring me some.'

Said he, 'It is winter, where shall I find grapes!'

Said she, 'But I have seen some in a neighbour's garden.'

Said he, 'How can that be, with snow on the ground?'

Said she, 'But there are grapes growing: I saw them with my own eyes from the roof.'

Then the Sultan's son called his slave and said, 'Diamond, go to the house of our neighbour, and say from your mistress: "O our lady, give us a bunch of grapes to satisfy our whim! (*wahima*)".'

The slave went, and knocked at the door of the girl's house, and from within the girl answered,

> 'I am Bitter Orange, daughter of a Bitter Orange.
> My mother bought me, and my father became pregnant of me.
> And the she-gazelle suckled me,
> And the falcon hovered above me.
> The Sultan's son has begotten a child on his mother,
> Does her longing remain?
> Go! I have no grapes!'

The slave returned and repeated to his master the words that he had heard. The Sultan's son began to ponder, and to understand. Then he went himself to the house, and knocked at the door, saying, 'O lady, give us a bunch of grapes to satisfy our whim!'

The girl replied in the same words, and her husband cried,

'What is this! Come down and open the door!'

The girl came down, and he saw that she was his bride. He bade her tell to him all that had happened, and she related everything.

Then he returned and sought his mother, and said to her,

'Woman, where is my mother?'

She replied, 'She is dead.'

Said he, 'Where is her tomb?'

Answered she, 'In such and such a place.'

Said he, 'Take me to it.'

The woman was confused, and wherever they went there was no tomb, and she said, 'I forgot! It is not here, it is elsewhere.'

At last he seized her and said, 'You have lied! Tell me the truth!' and she was forced to tell him all.

Then he went and brought a tin of naphtha and poured it over her and set her alight, and she was burnt up. But his own wife came back to him.

XXIII

A TALE TOLD BY A
SHAMMAR TRIBESMAN

I could not get the Shammar women to tell stories of the supernatural: they were frightened to talk about spirits, they confessed,
saying: 'If you tell stories of the Jinn in the daytime, they will
plague you by night.'

The following was told to satisfy my whim, but not willingly.

BISMILLAH![1]
There was once a man called Muhammad, and he
was riding with three companions in a ship on the
Euphrates. In the night he awoke and perceived above
him two eyes like two lanterns, like fire! Then they lifted,
and disappeared. The second and third night it was the
same, and on the fourth he sat and watched with a gun in
his hand. When the eyes descended upon him, he shot
at them, and it was a spirit in the shape of a bird, which he
killed. In time the ship arrived at the place to which it
was bound, and Muhammad descended from it and met
some sheep and with them a shepherd. The shepherd
invited him to sleep with him that night. He told him
that every night a *seʻir*[2] (ogre) with one eye came and ate
his sheep. Muhammad sat with him, and by witchcraft
he prevented the ogre from eating the sheep. The ogre
was angry and the next night he seized Muhammad and
said, 'I shall eat you!' Muhammad waited until the fire
was hot that was to roast his flesh, and then, while the
ogre was asleep, he heated a bar of iron and planted it in
his one eye, and so escaped.

One day there came to him a tribesman, and said, 'You
must marry my daughter, and live in our house. But if
she dies first and you survive her, I shall put you into the
well, and if you die first and she survives you, I shall put
her into the well.'

Muhammad said, 'Good,' and he married the girl. A

---

[1] This invocation was for keeping off evil spirits, who come if they are spoken
of.   [2] See Preface, p. xiii.

little afterwards she died, and the father put her corpse and the living body of Muhammad in the well. Beneath, in the well, he met a maiden who dwelt in the well.[1]

She said to him, 'Are you Muhammad?'

He answered, 'Aye, I am Muhammad.'

She said, 'In the night a fox will come from this hole in the side of the well, and will eat of the corpses which lie here. When he comes, seize his tail.'

It was as she had said. In the night, a fox came to eat of the dead body. Muhammad seized his tail, and the fox fled into the hole and came out the other end into the world again.

[1] The spirit of the well. See p. 11, The Story of Three Little Mice.

XXIV

SHAMMAR STORIES

I. THE SHAMMARI AND THE JINNĪYA

We had been talking of men who had disappeared with the fairies, and one of the men present in the tent said:

'AYE, one of us did enter the ground, in the cemetery belonging to Ibn Rashīd in Haïl. It was about six of the evening (i.e. midnight) and he was coming out of the house of a friend whom he had been visiting. He met an old man with immensely long beard and whiskers, who stopped him and said, "Greeting, *Marhaba*,[1] O youth, greeting, O boy, greeting, O old man!" This he said three times. The man did not understand what he meant by this speech, and was astonished. The old man then said, "Come and drink coffee with us," and he sank into the ground and the Shammari with him, and into the country of the jānn. From what he saw there he fell unconscious, and he woke in his own bed with his own people, but was ill for a long time afterwards. He said that the jānn below the ground had eyes set in their faces vertically, not like ours horizontally.'

Another man said, 'A Shammari youth, as it was told me, was going his way on a camel one day, when he met a beautiful jinnīya, alone, in the chōl. She was lovely, of great beauty. She spoke to him and said, "*Nta, min ein ent?* You, from whence are you?" He answered her, "I am a Shammari." She said, "Where are your people?" Said he, "In Najd. And you, where are your people?" Said she, "I, too, am a Shammarīya." Said he, "Why are you walking afoot?" Said she, "I was on a camel, but it broke its leg in the desert and died." Said he, "Whither are you going?" Said she, "I am going to buy some things for my people in such and such a village. Take me on your camel."

[1] A form of greeting often used between a Moslem and a person of another faith.

'The youth took her up with him on his camel, and they rode together for the rest of that day. When night came, they spent it in the desert, and she cooked him bread and they supped, and then slept on the ground, with the camel between them. In the night they were afraid of robbers, for the place was lonely, and she sank into the earth and he with her. The girl told him that she was a jinnīya, and said that she would stay with him for five years. Said she, "I shall be constantly beside you wherever you go. Should you wish to [be alone for reasons of modesty], only say 'In the name of Allah', and I will leave you! If you wish to wash yourself or change your clothes or desire privacy for other reasons, say '*Bismillah*!' and I will go."

'So it was, and when the youth wished for modesty's sake to be alone, he said, "*Bismillah*", and she left him. However, when he slept, he forgot to say "*Bismillah*", and she came to him and said, "Now you must either marry me or die, for I have been with you in bed."

'The youth said, "I am your guest! Mercy! My mother has none but me, I am the only support of the family."

'The jinnīya said, "Never, never! I have got you, I shall keep you!"

'Said he, "I accept."

'Then she married him, and kept him in a room which was always locked, so that none of the jānn her people should know that she had a human husband.

'Now her father loved her very much, and she was so beautiful that all the jānn were asking for her in marriage.

'She refused them all, and one day she said to her father, "O my father, I wish to marry one that I know."

'Her father said, "Who is he? What is his name?"

'She answered, "One that I have seen and loved."

'Said her father, "O my daughter, from which family of jānn does he come?"

'She answered, "He is no jinni, he is a son of Adam, and I have given him my protection." Then she told him about the Shammari, and her father forgave her, and went

The great tent of Shaikh ʿAjīl al Yawir. The further half is the reception tent (*mudhīf*), the nearer is the women's quarters

Shammar Tribesmen

and made the espousals, and she took the youth as her
husband openly.

'The Shammari loved her and cherished her, and after
a time she bore him a son. Ten years they lived together,
and at the end of that time she died, leaving several
children. Her father then brought him from out the
country of the jānn, expelling him from their company,
and forced him to leave his children behind him. The
Shammari returned to his people, and lived for ten years
more before he died himself.'

XXV

SHAMMAR STORIES

II. THE QARĪNA[1]

This story was told out of complaisance, because the shaikh had ordered that stories should be told. It is of the stuff that lies are made of, but is amusing as showing the rough material out of which folk-lore is made. The teller was literate, and acted as agent for the tribe in Mosul. He had accompanied the shaikh to the desert from Mosul. The tribesmen present listened open-mouthed and believed every word.

TWENTY-FIVE years I lived in Najd, and whilst there I saw and talked with a jinnīya, wallah, she put her hand on my shoulder! One night I came out of the house of Ibn Rashid in Haïl, and was returning to my own house, a distance of about fifteen minutes. I saw in the light of the full moon a girl sitting by the way. She was very beautiful, more beautiful than any daughter of woman, and wore silken garments, with bracelets, anklets, gold rings, and on her shoulders was a shaikh's white 'aba,[2] like the rays of the moon. She rose, and followed in my footsteps, and spoke to me, and said, 'Peace upon you, O Sālih!' by name, as if she had been my friend for years. I said to her, 'Of what district are you?' She replied, 'I am from the village of Nasīya, near Ibn Rashīd's property, about two hours' distance away. I am your guest.'

I answered her, '*Ahlan u sahlan*—You are welcome!' out of hospitality.[3]

We walked together, and I said to her, 'O woman, I have fear for your reputation and for mine. Walk at a distance of two minutes behind me to the house.' And she said, '*La bas!* It doesn't matter! It is night, who will see us?' and it was indeed nine and a half hours of the night. In my hand there was a sword,[4] and we walked

[1] See Preface, p. xii. [2] See p. 1.
[3] *bi dheyf*. An honourable necessity, if a stranger proclaims himself a guest.
[4] This was a protection against jinn.

shoulder to shoulder, but after a little she put her hand on my shoulder, with her arm behind my head. Her hand was as soft and light as cotton and she smelt sweet of flowers and sandalwood.

Said I to her, 'O girl, take your hand from my shoulder!' I was afraid that some one would see, for I was invited that night to an assembly of friends, and they were waiting for me in a garden, and if they had seen, they would have thought shame and ill about me.

So she took off her hand, and we walked for about two minutes thus.

Then I saw one of my friends waiting for me in the road, and I said to her, 'O woman, go behind me, for a man is waiting for me in the road, and I fear he will see you!'

She walked behind me for three minutes.

My friend came, and wished me peace, and said, 'Come, enter, all your friends are waiting for you.'

I said, 'I am going to my house, I will change my clothes first, and then come.'

My house was at a short distance from that of my friend. When I entered it, I saw that the woman was walking in my footsteps, behind me. My friend saw her and tried to seize her, but she sank into the earth, calling out, 'O Sālih! O Sālih!' My friend cried to me, 'The woman who was following you was of the jānn!'

I said to him, 'It is not true: the woman is from above the earth, no jinnīya!'

He said, 'By Allah, she was a jinnīya!'

And he brought the lantern into the shade in which she had disappeared, and moved it over the spot where she had sunk into the ground, and there, on the spot, was a piece of (gourd[1]), white, smooth and without dust. I was troubled, and felt sick and afraid because she had put her hand on my shoulder. As for my friend, who had tried to seize her, he became so ill that he nearly died.

After that, she used to come to me in the night, when

[1] I cannot read the word I took down here. It might be gourd.

I was sleeping in bed: she came to me in dreams. One night she came to me, and I rose, and went to the roof, upon which my wife and children were sleeping. The jinnīya followed me, and said, 'I want coffee and tea!' I said, '*Ana mamnūn!* I am grateful' (to do you this favour) and I went and made her tea and coffee. She drank two cups. In the end, she asked me to take her into my bed. It was five hours of the night, and my wife, hearing voices, came down from the roof where she was, and came upon us in the place of coffee. But there was only myself present, for the jinnīya disappeared.

My wife said, 'Who was with you?'

I said, 'No one was with me.'

Said she, '*Al asbāb!* But there are causes! Why are you awake and drinking coffee!'

Said I, 'I could not sleep, so I rose and made coffee.'

Said she, 'But there were noises and voices, people were here.'

Said I, 'Never! No one was with me!'

The next night she came again, and I was sleeping with my wife. The jinnīya stood by my side, and said to me, 'Your friend is ill, and it is I who caused his illness. Why did he try to seize me and touch my clothes—I—who am daughter of the shaikhs of the Jānn? I have come back to you so that you may hear that I have not cursed him without cause. Now I will tell you how to cure him. Take water, spit into it, and give your friend that water to drink, and he will be cured, and his sickness will depart from him.'

Then it was near dawn, and as soon as the light appeared the jinnīya departed. This was the second night. The third night she came to me as I was asleep, and put her arm round me as I lay in bed. I was afraid, and very afraid for my wife, who was in the room and wakened, and saw her. As soon as she saw her, the jinnīya disappeared, and my wife left her bed and came and slept beside me till morning.

My friends came in the morning, and I told them what had happened. They said to me, 'Let her become your

The coffee-maker in the guest-tent. The man standing to left is Sālih, narrator of 'The Qarina'

The women's quarters in a Shammar shaikh's tent

friend, because she will give you money and you will be a rich man.'

I answered them, 'I don't want her or her friendship because I am afraid of her.'

My maternal uncle is an 'alim, who knows how to exorcise evil spirits, so I went to him, and told him the whole story from the beginning to the end, and asked him to come to my house and read (a spell) so that she could not return to me.

He brought his books and read (spells aloud), and assembled all the sultans of the Jānn. He said,

'Fulān Fulāna (Thou So-and-so) daughter of Fulāna (So-and-so), do not come to torment Sālih, or I shall injure you sorely,' and conjured her, that she should come no more, by the power of the spirits he had raised. All this he said beneath the carpet[1] and she never returned to me from that hour.

---

[1] *Beneath the carpet.* People who speak to the *Jānn*, often lift a corner of the carpet, and put their mouths near the ground: the *Jānn* being supposed to inhabit the underworld.

XXVI
SHAMMAR STORIES

III. THE WOOD-CUTTER AND THE JINNĪYA

This story was told in good faith, and was corroborated by several of the tribesmen, whose money had been given to the man who pretended to talk with Nejma.

THERE was once a wood-cutter who lived near Damascus, and one day, when he was out cutting thorn, he met a beautiful woman who cried to him, '*Al amān, al amān!* Mercy! Save me from the wolf, and I will enrich you!' He had a gun with him, and he shot the wolf[1] who was following her. She was a jinnīya, and she was afraid the wolf would eat her, because all children of the jānn are unable to disappear into the earth if they see a wolf.

The jinnīya said to him, 'Go back to your house—do not take your thorn. My name is Nejma (Star) and each night I shall put under your pillow five golden pounds. Secondly, if any one steals your money or your clothes, I will tell you his name and where to find him. And, thirdly, I will give you a secret word, by the power of which, if you have friends who are guests in your house,

---

[1] *Wolf.* The wolf is the one animal of which the jinn are afraid, because, when he is present, they are unable to sink into the earth, and so fall a prey to his teeth and claws. A Shammarīya woman lulls her child to sleep at night with the chant,

Bismillah	In the name of Allah
Ism adh dhīb	The wolf's name
Al khotīb	The invoked one
'Ala galbak!	Upon your heart!

and thinks that thus she frightens off evil spirits. His teeth prevent coughing, and teeth and claws are worn by girls as charms, or are hung up in house or tent to keep out evil. A wolf's eye, dried and carried on the person, protects a man against surprise in sleep by an enemy or the law.

The origin of talismanic stones is thought to be this. A wolf coming one day upon a company of jinnīyāt, they were able by sorcery to escape from him by turning themselves into stones of a semi-precious description. These stones took on the magic qualities of the jinnīyāt, each having special powers, e. g. soapstone prevents heart sickness, haematite gives the wearer power, and so forth.

Of all living creatures, the wolf will be the last to die, say the Arabs, at the end of the world.

you will be able to see their loved ones however far distant they are, and tell them what they are doing, and how they are.'

The thorn-seller did not believe her, and took his thorn, and went back to Damascus, sold it as usual, and bought food for his family. When he had eaten, he slept on his bed, and in the morning, when he rose and lifted his pillow, there were five golden liras beneath it, and he knew that Nejma's words were true.

I visited this man when I went to Damascus, and paid him ten lirāt, and he talked under the carpet,[1] wiss-wiss-wiss—with Nejma, and told me that my people were with Ibn Rashīd's people, and that my father was well, and my brother a little sick but that he would be cured, and wallah, it was true.

One or two of the other tribesmen corroborated this, and said they had visited Nejma's friend in Damascus when they were there, and had paid him money for news of their respective families.

[1] See p. 111.

XXVII

HĀJIR

THERE was once a fair woman. In her prime she was fairer than the full moon and her fame was great amongst all lands. Her father married her to a rich man and in time she bore him a daughter. The name of this daughter was Hājir, and as she grew up, she became so beautiful that her mother became jealous of her.

At night, when the moon swam in the sky, the woman asked it,

> *Ya Qamr!*
> *Minu al helu?*
> *Enta, lō ani, lō Hājir Khān?*
> 'O Moon!
> Who is the fairest?
> Thou, or I, or the Lady Hājir?'

Answered the moon, as it passed like a silver ship across the roof-top,

> *Ana wein, enti wein?*
> *Hājir Khān ahlā minech wa minni!*
> 'Where am I, and where art thou?
> The Lady Hājir is fairer than thee and fairer than me!'

The woman was enraged by the moon's answer, for she wished to be lovelier than her daughter. She had an old maidservant who was devoted to her, and she called her and said to her, 'To-morrow, take Hājir Khān to the wilds, and lose her there. Return alone.'

The next day, the maidservant took Hājir away into the hills, where there were many rocks and caverns. Giving a pretext, she left the child alone in a wild place, never doubting but that Hājir would be devoured by the wolves that lived in the rocks. Then she returned alone to her mistress and told her that by now the girl must have perished.

Now when the servant had forsaken her, Hājir ran

about the rocks, and towards nightfall, seeing a large cavern, she entered it and was surprised to find that it was not like the other caverns, but was furnished with carpets, bedding, and everything necessary to a house.

'Some one must live here,' said Hājir to herself, and she hid in a corner where she would not be seen. As the sun set, there entered the cavern seven 'afarīt, who seated themselves and began to eat and drink. When they had finished, they rose up and went out. Hājir came out of her hiding-place, and when she had eaten, she began to sweep and clean the place, and finding some dirty clothes, she washed them in a stream nearby, and mended them neatly. The next morning the 'afarīt returned, and were very astonished at seeing the cavern so neat and clean. 'Who has been here? Who has done us this kindness?' they asked. In the day they slept, but towards the afternoon they went out for food, and on returning, ate as before. Said they amongst themselves, 'To-night we will leave one of our number behind in the cave, so that if any one comes, he will see him.' So when they went out, one 'afrīt stayed behind. Hājir did not come from her hiding-place until she saw that he was asleep. Then she swept and cleaned the cave, washing the dishes and setting everything in order as on the previous night. When the 'afarīt came back they asked the 'afrīt they had left behind who had done the cleaning, and he replied, 'I saw no one!' The next night another 'afrīt stayed behind, and it happened with him as it had happened with the first. So it was for seven nights, a different 'afrīt watching each night, and each night falling asleep. On the eighth night it was the turn of the first 'afrīt again, and he resolved that this time he would pretend to sleep. So after a little he feigned sleep, and when he saw Hājir he leapt up and seized her. She was afraid, but he told her that he did not wish to harm her, but to thank her. When his brothers came back, they were delighted to see Hājir, and asked her to stay with them always and be their house-mother, while, for their part, they would serve her and do everything to please her. 'We will be your brothers,' they said

to her, and Hājir agreed to their proposal. So for some
time they lived happily together.

Now when the moon was again full, Hājir's mother,
believing that her daughter was dead, went on to the roof
and asked the moon as it gazed on the house,

> *Ya Qamr!*
> *Minu al helu?*
> *Enta, lō ani, lō Hājir Khān?*

> 'O Moon!
> Who is the fairest?
> Thou, or I, or the Lady Hājir?'

Answered the moon,

> *Ana wein, enti wein?*
> *Hājir Khān ahla minech wa minni*
> *Wa'ad ha ikhwān sab'a.*

> 'Where am I, and where art thou?
> Lady Hājir is fairer than me and than thee,
> And she has brothers seven.'

When she heard the moon's reply, the mother wept
and was troubled, and she sent for the old woman, her
servant, to reproach her, saying that the girl was still
living. Said she—'I have prepared some chewing-resin.[1]
My daughter loves to eat of it, but when she eats this
resin of mine she will die, for it is poisoned. Do not return
until the girl is dead.'

The maidservant disguised herself and went to the
place where she had left the girl, and before long she
found the cavern where Hājir lived with the seven
'afarīt. When she saw Hājir there, the old woman began
to cry '*Alech zein! Alech zein!* Good resin for sale!'

Hājir came to her, and said to her, 'I want some 'alech,
give me some.'

The pretended pedlar gave her the resin, and took
payment for it, then hid herself. As soon as Hājir had put
the resin in her mouth, she fell down unconscious, as if

---

[1] Chewing gum to prevent thirst has been customary in Arab countries for
centuries; it is not an American invention.

she were dead. The old woman hastened back to her mistress and told her, 'Hājir Khān is dead. I saw her fall with my own eyes.' Then the mother rejoiced.

When the 'afarīt returned and found Hājir lying on the ground, they were much distressed. They touched her head, her hands, and her feet, and said to each other, 'Hājir is dead! We must bury her.'

Said one of them, 'Hājir is fair, let us not cover her face with dust, but wrap her in reed matting,[1] and put her on the top of the mountain.'

The rest agreed, and did as he had said, and with much sorrow they left her on the mountain.

Now, shortly after this, there passed that way the Sultan's son in the course of his hunting, and when he saw the girl's body, he was amazed at her beauty and ordered his followers that they should take her up and bear her to his city. When they reached the city, the young prince sent for a skilled physician and ordered him to examine the body. The physician did so and reported that the pulse was still beating and that, with the help of Allah, the girl could be restored. This indeed happened, and as the Sultan's son loved her like one mad, he married her and set her in a fine house.

Meantime the mother, when it was time for the full moon to appear, went to the roof and asked it the same question. Said the moon in answer:

> *Ana wein, enti wein?*
> *Hājir Khān zōjat ibn es Sultān*
> *Ahlā minech u minni!*

> 'Where am I, and where art thou?
> Lady Hājir is wife of the Sultan's son,
> And is fairer than thee and me!'

At that, the mother became ill from her spite, and died, and that was the end of her.

Now after some months Hājir Khān bore the Sultan's son a boy, and the child grew and became a fine lad. One

---

[1] In early times in 'Iraq the dead were wrapped in matting. Many of the Sumerian graves opened at Ur revealed that the bodies had been so buried.

day the boy was playing with some companions in the road at knuckle-bones[1] and during the game the princeling began to quarrel with his companions. The boys began to mock him, and sang in derision,

> *Ibn ash shaqta!*   'Son of a No-one-knows-who!
> *Ibn al laqta!*   Foundling's son!'

At that the boy ran crying to his mother, and told her of his companions' taunt. She comforted him and said, 'Next time they say that, say you to them:

> *Tug, ya cha'b, tug!*
> *Wa khālna seb'a*
> *U ūmmna bein hum neb'a.*

> "Crack, knuckle-bone, crack!
> Our uncles are seven
> And our mother bloomed amongst them." '

Now one of the 'afarīt, flying over the town, passed by the boys at their play, and hearing Hājir's son saying this, he marked his beauty and resemblance to their lost sister. He alighted, and approaching the children, said to the princeling, 'Go and fetch me water, I am thirsty!'

The boy answered, 'Come with me, I will give you to drink,' and took him to his mother's house. When they arrived, he ran to his mother, and said, 'A stranger is here asking for water: he is thirsty.' Hājir sent the child down with a cup of water, and the 'afrīt hearing her voice was now certain that it was indeed their sister. So when he had drunk the water, he drew a ring off his finger and dropped it into the cup, saying, 'Take that to your mother, boy!'

The child did as he was told, and Hājir, seeing it, recognized it as a ring belonging to the 'afrīt, and came gladly to welcome him and to tell him of all that had happened to her. The 'afrīt listened and rejoiced in her happiness, and when she had finished, said to her,

'Remember, Hājir, we are your seven brothers and ready at all times to do your bidding. If you are in sorrow,

---

[1] Knuckle-bones is a favourite game amongst the urchins of Baghdad.

we will come to you, and if your husband quarrels with you, or forsakes you, you shall return to us.'

Hājir thanked him and the 'afrīt went back to tell the good news to his six brothers, while she remained to live a long and happy life.

This is the end of the story of Hājir Khān.

> *Wa lo baitna qarīb,*
> *Kunt ajīb likum tubaq hummus wa tubaq zebib!*

'And were our house near,
I'd bring you a plate of pease and raisins!'

XXVIII

THE WOMAN OF THE WELL

IN ancient times there was an old man who was very poor, and who lived in a village at some distance from Mosul. All his life he had worked and nothing had prospered; indeed, he and his wife were often forced to beg. To add to his misery, his wife was a very Shaitan, whose tongue afflicted him from morning to night. For his misfortunes she had nothing but railing, and for his poverty she did nothing but upbraid him.

One day it happened that they had nothing in the house to eat or to sell, and as soon as the day dawned, she began to scold and abuse him.

'Here we are starving, and you look for no work! Never was a woman cursed with such a vagabond as you!'

By her stinging words she forced him to rise and go out to seek employment, and he went from one place to another, but no man would employ him, for the harvest was over and work was scant. So, not knowing where else to go, he seated himself by the roadside in heaviness of spirit, and thought how sorely his wife would use him when he came back with nothing more in his pocket than a morsel of bread which a charitable soul had given him. It was then full noon, and as he sat he watched the wheel-marks and foot-marks that flowed away over the hill like a stream, for the road led to Mosul.

'Mosul is a fair city,' said he, his thoughts following the track, 'and if Allah so willed it, it might be that wealth and fortune would await me, if my wife and I set out thither.' And then he considered, and reflecting that even with wealth his life would be a burden if she continued to plague him, he changed his thought, and said, 'Why should I not journey alone to Mosul?'

And his heart grew light, and, drawing the bread from his pocket, he rose up and set off upon the road, eating as he went. He walked until the sun was nearing the horizon, and then, seeing a well and a shady tree by the wayside, he turned aside, and after he had refreshed his thirst, he seated himself on the edge of the well to rest.

He had rested but a little while when he saw on the brow of the hill a cloud of dust. It came nearer and nearer, and then he saw that it was caused by a woman, moving swiftly, and his heart became water within him, for he knew that it was his wife who had followed him. As soon as she was within hearing, she began to scream and abuse him for deserting her, calling him a dog and the son of a dog, the child of iniquity, an eater of filth, and a doer of evil. He answered nothing, for his conscience accused him, and they sat together on the edge of the well, she reviling and he listening, until, losing patience, he struck her with his elbow and she fell into the well below.

Rising affrighted, he went again on his way, regardless of her screams, and after he had gone an hour or two his mind began to rest, and he thought that after all, what had happened was ordained, and that now, by the favour of Heaven, he was a free man. It was sunset, and he stopped to prepare himself for prayer by the wayside. But as he turned, lo, in the distance he saw a cloud of dust. It came nearer and nearer and his heart turned to water within him. But when he could perceive clearly who was approaching, he saw that it was not his wife, but a jinni, who approached him with angry looks and said, 'I am come to slay thee!'

The old man fell on his knees and said, 'What have I done to you, O Amīr of the Jinn, that you should require my life? Give me but time to say my prayers, and tell me the reason of your anger.'

'Have I not reason for anger?' said the jinni. 'For forty years I have slumbered peacefully in my well, and this day you have cast into it a woman whose tongue is a plague and her screaming like the screaming of peacocks.'

'O Amīr of the Jinn,' said the old man, 'for forty years you have had peace and quietness and for only two hours a woman's tongue. But what of my unhappy lot? For forty years I have had my woman's tongue, and but two hours have I had peace and quietness. Consider and be merciful!'

'Your lot has indeed been hard,' said the jinni, 'but what of the woman in my well?'

'O Amīr of the Jinn, leave her in the well and travel the world with me.'

The jinni was pleased with the words of the old man, and travelled with him until they got to Mosul, where they entered a khan and ordered the best that could be provided for them.

'I will pay,' said the jinni, and the next day he took a large house with many servants, male and female, where he and the old man lived together, entertaining the notables and rich people of the town and spending much money in pleasure and hospitality. But this life did not suit the jinni, who began to thirst after mischief, and after awhile he said to the old man, 'If I continue to live with you, I shall do you a harm. Better is it that we part now.'

'Alas! Without money what shall I do?' asked the old man.

'I will tell you how to win fame and fortune,' said the jinni. 'It is my fancy to enter folk and make them mad, and when I leave you, I shall enter into the daughter of the grand wazīr of Baghdad. He will reward highly the man who can cure the possessed girl, and that man will be yourself.'

'But how shall I cure her?'

'I will tell you upon one condition—that you do not again employ exorcism against me. If you do, I will enter into you and never leave you, but keep you in torment.' And with that he taught the old man the exorcism.

Thereafter he disappeared, and the old man left Mosul and travelled to Baghdad. Shortly after he had taken up his abode in the city, he heard the news that the grand wazīr's daughter was grievously ill; that a jinni had entered into her and was tormenting her with all the pains of hell. And he went to the grand wazīr's house and asked to see him, saying that he was a skilled physician with special skill in curing those possessed.

The wazīr received him with honour and asked him if indeed he could cure his daughter. The old man said, 'Sir, I can cure her, but not without reward.'

'What is your price?' asked the wazīr. 'Name it, and I will pay it though it be large.'

The old man answered, 'My price is two thousand dinars.'

When he heard the exorbitance of the sum, the wazīr was angry. 'This is indeed beyond reason,' said he. 'Are there no physicians in Baghdad beside you?' And he sent him away.

But day by day his daughter's malady increased, and all the doctors and exorcists of the town tried their skill upon her in vain. She was conducted to the shrine of Abdul Qāder al Gilāni and left there for three days and nights, she was chained to the grill at the tomb of the two Kādhims for yet another such period, the Qurān was read over her, she was anointed by magic balms and salves, and she was beaten to the point of death, but all was useless.

Then the old man went again to the wazīr and told him that he was able to cure his daughter.

'Cure her,' cried the wazīr, 'and I will pay thy price, even the two thousand dinars.'

'Sir,' said the old man, 'my price has increased. It is now the half of thy possessions.'

Then the wazīr was enraged and swore that he would not give it. He said, 'This day comes a wise man from Al Hind, and if God wills, he will cure her.'

'If God wills,' said the old man, and he went out. But the wise man from Al Hind was not able to cure the wazīr's daughter. Then the wazīr sent for the old man and said to him:

'O, old man, cure my daughter, and I will give thee half I possess.'

'Sir,' said the old man, 'my price has increased. It is now the half thy possessions and the hand of thy daughter.'

'Take what thou askest if the cure be perfect, or thou wilt leave me nothing. But if there is no cure, look to it, for I will order my servants to beat thee soundly.'

'Fear not,' said the old man, and they took him to the room where the wazīr's daughter, a very pearl of beauty, was bound down with ropes and bonds.

When he was left alone with her, he pronounced the word of power which the jinni had taught him, and with a loud scream the evil spirit departed from her. The maiden blushed at coming to herself and finding that she was alone with a man, but when she knew that he was her deliverer and promised husband, she greeted him with kindness and permitted him to loose her bonds. Then they went to her father, who was overjoyed at her recovery.

So there were marriage rejoicings for seven days and seven nights, and the old man renewed his youth in his beautiful bride, and lived happily with her for a period of three months.

At the end of that time, there came to the old man as he was sitting in the harem with his wife, a message from his father-in-law, bidding him come at once to his house. He went, and the wazīr, greeting him affectionately, said to him, 'The Commander of the Faithful has ordered me to bring thee to the palace without delay; the cause being the illness of his favourite daughter, who is possessed by a terrible jinni.'

The old man was much alarmed, for he suspected that the jinni who had taken possession of the princess was the jinni of the well. He began to excuse himself from accompanying the wazīr, but the wazīr would not hear him, and insisted that they must obey the commands of the Khalīfa. When they had arrived in the presence of the Khalīfa, the old man kissed the ground, and when he received the order to visit the princess, he said,

'O Commander of the Faithful, I am the least of thy slaves, and my knowledge of healing is insignificant. Send for thy physicians and let them heal the princess, for are they not skilled men and worthier than I!'

'The Khalīfa frowned, and said, 'What is this? and why art thou unwilling to exercise upon my daughter the skill which thou has proven upon the family of my wazīr?'

And the old man said, 'Not from unwillingness, but from incapacity, O Commander of the Faithful.'

'Thou liest!' cried the Khalīfa. 'Does not all Baghdad know thee for a skilled exorcist, for didst thou not succeed in expelling a demon from the daughter of my wazīr when all else had failed and every physician in the kingdom had tried their craft in vain? Why these evasions and excuses? Cure my daughter, or by Allah, I will hand thee over to the executioner to meet a death befitting such reluctance to serve thy sovereign.'

And he ordered his attendants to take the old man to the apartments of the princess and to strike off his head if he either attempted escape or failed in his exorcism.

As the old man was conducted through the palace towards the women's quarters, he beat his breast and wept bitterly. 'Alas, woe is me! What man can escape from his fate? It is the destiny of one to be born to sorrow and another to fortune. I have now but the choice between a miserable death and a life of torture.'

So complaining, he was led to the apartment of the princess, who lay upon her bed exhausted and like one beaten. As he gazed upon her, with the hand of the executioner on his shoulder, he thought upon the bride he had just left, and upon all the deceptions and disappointments of his life, beginning with his first marriage. And suddenly he bit on his hand, and cried, 'What an owl am I!' and hope, which a moment before had flown from him, returned to his breast.

Boldly approaching the princess, he pronounced the word of power.

In a moment the evil jinni leapt from her body, and appearing to the old man in a frightful aspect he laid hold of him crying, 'Thou old fool! what did I tell thee! Now I shall enter into thy body and torment thee until the end of thy life!'

'O Amīr of the Jinn,' answered the old man, 'one torment is not worse than the other. Enter into my miserable body—but know that my wife has escaped from the well and is even now waiting without for me.'

'What!' shrieked the jinni. 'Live beside thy wife and listen to her revilings? Never, never!' And with a loud cry he flew to the window and leapt from it into the air and was never seen or heard of in those parts afterwards.

And this is the end of the story of the Woman of the Well.

XXIX

HASAN THE THIEF

THERE was once a Sultan in this land, and in the town in which he dwelt there was a clever thief. He stole from the houses of the citizens during the night, and none knew how he entered or how he departed. Each night a fresh house was robbed, and at last the townspeople went to the Sultan and said, 'We have a complaint to make to your Majesty. There is a robber who steals from our houses by night. We know not by what door he enters, or how he leaves, but night by night it is the same, he steals first from one and then another.'

The Sultan promised that he would look to the matter, and he ordered the police to be vigilant, and set guards everywhere, but it was the same as before, and every night this thief enriched himself at the expense of the townsfolk.

One day the Sultan sat in his diwān, when a writing fell from the ceiling, on the table before him. He looked but there was none there, and on the paper was written, 'Your treasure will be stolen this night.'

The Sultan was angry and troubled. He said, 'What! I have guards and police, and have set watchmen and soldiers everywhere, and yet this insolent thief threatens to steal my treasure!' And, full of care, he rose from his writing-table, went to the women's apartment and entered his daughter's room.

She saw that he was troubled and said to him:

'*Eysh bīk, bābā?* What is the matter with you, papa?'

Said he, '*Jūzi mini, binti, jūzi!* Leave me in peace, my daughter!'

Said she, 'But tell me, bābā, what it is that troubles you!'

Answered he, 'Allah keep you, my daughter! Just now a writing fell from the ceiling before me, and on it was written that my treasure would be stolen from me to-night. I have set spies and police and soldiers and watchmen everywhere, and if my treasure is stolen it will shame

me before my people. I am the Sultan and if the thief
enters here it will blacken my face. For this reason I am
angry and troubled.'

And she said, 'O bābā, do not be anxious! Arise, eat
with me, and do not sigh, do not trouble! Allah is merciful, perhaps the thief will not be able to come and steal
your treasure!' And with her comforting words she consoled her father, and he ate supper with her, and then
went to sleep.

All the inmates of the palace went to sleep like the
Sultan, but the daughter of the Sultan went to her father's
room and took down his sword from the ceiling, where it
hung suspended, and seated herself in his treasury, beside
the treasure chest, with the sword beside her on the
ground, saying, 'I wish to see from whence the thief will
come!' She looked at the ceiling, and at the walls, and
all about her, and looked and watched, and looked and
watched. All in the house were sleeping and it was dark.
At midnight she felt the ground beneath her shake, and
she said to herself, 'Ha! the thief will come from underground!'

Then the floor opened, and a man came up through the
hole. As he reached the top she drew the sword and cut
off his head and waited for the next. There were forty
thieves, and as each man came up she cut his head off, in
silence and quietly, throwing the dead men aside. Thirty-
nine were killed in this manner, and last of all came the
chief of them, and as he climbed to the top he said to
himself:

'*La hess, la bass!* What has happened to my men?
And why have they not returned? I must go and
see!'

So he also emerged, and as she struck at him with the
sword, in her haste she only cut off the top of his scalp,
and he quickly put it back, exclaiming:

'By Allah! it is you who have killed my thirty-nine
men! Though your bones be of steel, yet I will kill you
with my own hand!'

So saying, he fled into the earth whence he had come.

The girl went and knocked at the door of her father, who started up and said, 'Who is it?'

Said she, 'I, bābā. Open the door.'

He opened the door and asked her, 'What is it, my daughter?'

And she said, 'Call the servants.'

He called, and the servants and guards and every one in the palace came running, and brought lights and arms.

She said, 'Come, see what is in the room below.'

They went to the room where the treasure was kept and there they saw thirty-nine robbers lying dead, and all exclaimed with surprise.

She told them how she had killed the thirty-nine, and how she had wounded the head of their chief, and that he had sworn by Allah that he would kill her, though her bones be of steel, and that her life was in danger.

The Sultan replied, 'How can such a man approach you! Do not think of such a thing, it is impossible that he can harm you.'

When it was day, the news went through the city that the Sultan's daughter had killed the thieves with her own hand, and all rejoiced with a great joy, saying, 'Before we were afraid to sleep, but now these bad men are dead!' Every one came into the palace to look at the corpses of the thirty-nine, and at evening they took the bodies and threw them out into the desert to be eaten of the jackals, saying, 'This night we shall sleep in peace, praise to Allah.'

Two days, three days, one month, twelve months, a year, two years, three years passed, and one day the Sultan's daughter walked upon the roof. She was very beautiful and sweet, there was none like her for beauty. She looked upon the desert, and she saw tents and soldiers, and in the midst a pavilion, and in the pavilion in a golden chair sat a Sultan with a crown on his head, and jewels about his neck, and soldiers standing about him.

She came down quickly and went to her father and asked him,

'What is this? And who is this Sultan who visits us?'

Said the Sultan: 'Which Sultan?'

Said she, 'Go to the roof and see with your own eyes.'

And he went and looked from the roof and exclaimed, '*Eya bā!* He must be an important man, this Sultan! And he has brought soldiers with him, perhaps he means war.'

He called his wazīr, and bade him come and see also, and then said, 'Go and find out who is this Sultan who comes without giving me warning, and with armed men. Is it war? Go, and find out.'

The wazīr went out of the city and came to the tents and was taken to the strange Sultan's pavilion.

He saluted him and gave him peace, and said to him, 'It is well, please God?'

And the strange Sultan answered: 'It is well,' and made him sit in his presence. And the wazīr said,

'We cannot understand why you have come to us without warning, and with this army of soldiers. We hope that you have peaceable intentions and mean no evil.'

The Sultan replied, 'Never! *Māku shey!* It is nothing! In no wise do we mean evil. I have come to ask for the daughter of your Sultan in marriage!'

And they brought coffee and sherbet and *nargīleh* (water-pipe) and the Sultan treated him with honour, and calling for a string of jewels, he gave it to the wazīr. When the visit was over, the wazīr returned, and went to his master, and said, 'This Sultan has no evil intention, and desires no quarrel with you, he has business with you, and wishes to talk with you.'

Then the Sultan said, 'Saddle my mare, I will go out and kiss his hand and greet him.'

They brought his mare, and he rode upon her outside the city, and went to the strange Sultan, and saluted him. The strange Sultan gave him peace, and made him sit beside him on his couch of gold.

Then said the Sultan, 'Why have you come? We were afraid that your intention was not peaceable when we saw the soldiers. Speak! Say what is in your mind!'

The other answered, 'No, no, no! I came because I wish to be betrothed to one of your house, and because I wished to ask you by word of mouth and face to face to give me your daughter to wife.'

The Sultan thought when he saw how rich the other appeared, 'To whom better could I give her than this one'. And he said, 'You are a Sultan, and I am a Sultan, the marriage is suitable. I will give her to you.'

Said the stranger, 'I wish for her to-morrow, for I cannot tarry here; on the fifth day of the week I must go, and I will take her with me.'

The Sultan agreed, and they brought him coffee and sherbet and treated him with all honour and respect; so he returned to his palace, and called his daughter to him, saying:

'Ha! What a thing has come to pass, my daughter! This Sultan has come to marry you. I will call the mulla, we must make immediate preparations, for he wishes you to go away with him on Thursday.'

The Sultan's daughter answered nothing, but did what her father wished. The mulla was called, the betrothal was made, and the next day the strange Sultan came to take his bride away.

He refused all that they offered him, and when they brought the escort, with gifts and horses, he declined, saying, 'I need no escort, and no gifts, I am a Sultan, I have all and need nothing: just wrap your daughter in her 'aba and give her to me, she is all that I wish.'

The Sultan was distressed, and said, '*Shlōn yasīr!* How may that be! I cannot send my only daughter away without an escort! It would be shame upon us!'

The other replied, 'I want nothing, only your daughter! I need no more.'

The Sultan said 'Never! It cannot be! *Hīch ma yasīr!* I must send an escort with my daughter.'

Then the other gave in and said, 'It matters not. Send soldiers with her, since you wish it, but make all ready, for as soon as it is midnight we shall set off.'

This. And the strange Sultan called his own soldiers, and said to them, 'When we are midway, go off, and leave me alone with the bride.'

So at midnight they set off: his soldiers before, hers behind, and in the centre rode the bridegroom on his mare with his bride on her mare, they riding and the soldiers walking. *Meshi, meshi, meshi—dī, dī, dī, dī!* they walked and they walked and they walked, and the next day, as it was agreed, his soldiers walked off and left them. Then said the Sultan to her escort, 'Come!' and they came to him. And he said, 'Turn and go back whence you came, for I do not like fuss and pomp! I wish to enter our city quietly with my bride, so return you and leave us!' And he gave them bakshīsh.

The soldiers said to him, 'We dare not go, we are afraid that the Sultan will be angry!'

But he persuaded them, and gave them money, and so they turned and went back, and so they were two, she and he, each on a mare, riding in the desert.

They went and they went: *ardh atshīlu, ardh athattu, ardh atshīlu, ardh athattu,* till *dī!* the sun set, and they came to a wood, deep and thick, and in it were jackals, and boars, and wolves, and lions, and evil spirits (*deywāt*). It was a large wood.

He said to her, 'Come, we will rest a little here, for you are weary. We will sit under the trees, and I will lay my head on your lap. When we have rested a little, we will mount again and ride on.'

She answered, 'As you will,' and they dismounted, and sat on the ground. Then he took off his turban, and reclined on the ground beside her and put his head on her knees.

Then he said, 'Put your hand on my head, and feel it.'

She stretched forth her hand, and felt his head, and then in dismay, she bit on her hand.

He said, 'You, what do you say?'

Answered she, 'There is no hair on your head,' but she had perceived the scar that was on it.

He said, 'And what then?'

Said she, 'There be many men who have no hair on their heads!'

Said he, 'Have you perceived who I am?'

Answered she, 'I have perceived.'

Said he, 'You killed thirty-nine of my men, and I am Hasan the Thief. Now I shall kill you, for you are in my two hands. Say, how shall I kill you?'

Answered she, 'I am between your two hands, and if you wish, kill me, but I ask you for one thing, I make one request, and when you have granted that, kill me.'

Said he, 'What is it?'

She replied, 'Give me a quarter of an hour alone to make my ablutions and perform my prayers so that I may not die as an unbeliever.'

He said, 'If I leave you alone, you will escape!'

Said she, 'Not so. Tie my legs with that tent-rope, and hold the other end in your hand, and you will know that I am here when you pull on the rope. And when I have washed and said my prayers, I will call you.'

Said he, 'Good!' And he took the rope which bound his tent to his mare, and undid it, and tied one end to her legs, and took the other and went a little into the forest.

As soon as he was gone, she quickly untied the rope and fastened it round a date-palm, and said,

> *Deyu yakulnī*
> *Sebʿa yakulnī*
> *Dīb yakulnī*
> *Haīyat yaʿadhnī wa amūt,*
> *Bas hūwa la yaktulnī.*

> 'An ogre may eat me
> A lion may eat me
> A wolf may eat me
> And a snake may bite me and I may die,
> But he shall not kill me.'

Then she went into the deep forest, and walked beneath and beneath the trees, till she reached a tall tree with thick foliage and branches so wide and leafy that they would have hidden ten people. She climbed it and hid herself.

Hasan the Thief waited a quarter of an hour, and he waited half an hour, then he pulled at the rope and cried, '*Yalla! ma khalasti baʿad?* Hurry up! Have you not yet done?' but there was no reply, and as it was night, he cried again, 'Have you not finished your prayers?' and pulled at the rope, and went to see why she was silent.

When he got to the place and saw no one there, he began to shout, 'Where is she, where is she?' and he found the rope tied to the palm-tree. Then he called out, 'Though your bones were of steel, I will kill you with my hands!' and he shouted and yelled, but he was afraid to enter the thick part of the wood because of the lions and evil spirits; he only searched the outskirts, and looked in the bushes. And he continued to shout with rage, saying, 'I shall kill you with my two hands!' but at last he got on his mare, and led the other, and went, *meshi, meshi, meshi*, into the desert.

From the tree she saw him depart, and when he was gone she stayed in the tree that night, and the next afternoon she came down, saying, 'Now I am rid of him,' and began to walk into the desert, not knowing whither she went, but going where Allah directed,

ardh athattu, ardh atshīlu, dī, dī, dī!

till she saw a house-of-hair[1]—and there were Arabs in that tent, an old man and an old woman. She saluted them, and they asked her what she wanted, and whence she came. She said to the old couple, 'Oh, my father and oh, my mother, let me come and live with you, and I will cook for you and look after you, just for my keep (*batni*). I will fetch your thorn and your water, and look after the sheep, and work for you and be your servant.'

The old woman replied, 'Better than that! We have no children, my old man and I are alone, you shall be our daughter, and this our tent is yours!' And they were happy and said to each other, 'She is so sweet that Allah must have sent her to us!' and they put her in a blue smock like a Bedawīya, with a coarse 'aba, and she lived with them as their daughter for three years. And she cut their thorn, and fetched their water, and milked the sheep, and made butter, and ground flour, and made bread, and worked for them.

[1] A Bedouin tent is made of hand-woven cloth made of goat's hair.

An encampment of poor Bedu

A Bedawi woman grinding corn. The mat-screen, of reeds and sheep's wool, is woven by the tribeswomen

This. Now one day the son of a Sultan who lived near that place came hunting with a single servant, and the name of the servant was Feyrūz.[1] And it was summer and hot, and the prince became thirsty, and when they saw the black tent, the prince said, 'Feyrūz, I am thirsty, go to yonder house-of-hair and ask them for water.'

Feyrūz went, and came to the tent, and asked for a little water for his master.

The girl arose, and poured him water from the skin, and when he saw her, Feyrūz marvelled and said in himself, 'I never saw such beauty before!' and his understanding flew away as he gazed at her. He went back to his master, and said, 'Oh, bey! the girl who poured me out this water is beautiful! Never have I seen such loveliness!'

When he heard these words, the prince poured the water out and took the cup himself to the tent, and said, 'Can I have a little more to drink? I am very thirsty, may I have a drink of water?'

And the girl came and answered, '*Mamnūn!* With pleasure!' and he drank and looked at her, and as he looked, his heart became dough, and he said in himself, 'Can there be anything more beautiful in the world! And this beauty is living with the 'Arab!'

And he marked that the tent was swept and carpeted and clean and well kept.

He turned and went back to his house with his slave, but he could think of nothing but the girl. 'Is there such beauty! Can such sweetness be!' and he yearned so much for her that he fell sick and took to his bed. His father sent for a physician, and one came and visited him. After he had seen him, he went to the Sultan and said, 'Your son is not ill, he is '*ashiq*, he is love-sick! Go to him, find out who is troubling his peace, and who is in his mind.'

The Sultan cried out, 'Who can it be? But I will not ask him, I will send his dāi,[2] his old nurse, before whom

---

[1] 'Turquoise'. Slaves are usually given names like Coral, Turquoise Diamond.   [2] A wet-nurse.

he will not be ashamed to speak freely, and he will perhaps tell her for whom he is yearning.'

He sent for the nurse and said to her, 'Go to-day to my son and find out what is ailing him, who has disturbed his peace of mind, and for whom he is yearning.'

So the woman went to him, and stroked his cheeks, and said, 'My darling, I am your mother, my milk is in your belly, I have been a mother to you when you were small, and I am grieved to see you thus. Tell me, what ails you?'

He replied 'I cannot tell you.'

She said, 'Tell me! For perhaps I can do you a good turn and help you.'

Then he told her, 'I was hunting, and it was hot, and I was athirst, and we went to the tents of the 'Arab there, and a girl gave me drink, and she was beautiful as the full moon! My heart became dough, and I want her for my own.'

Said the woman, 'Ey, my darling! Why did you not tell me? I will do what I can and I will speak to the Sultan. Do not sigh! Do not be troubled.'

She went her road and came to the Sultan and said, 'What shall we do? Your son is longing for a maid of the tribes, beautiful as the moon. Bring her and betroth her to him, for better that than let him die of longing.'

The Sultan replied, 'Good. Go, and take a slave with you, and betroth the girl to my son.'

The dāi returned to the boy, and said, 'What did I tell you! I have seen your father, and he has told me to go and get the girl and betroth her to you!'

How he rejoiced! How full of happiness was his heart!

The woman went with the slave into the desert, *meshi*, *meshi*, *meshi*, till they came at length to the house-of-hair, and there was the old man and his wife, who gave them peace, and called to them to enter and rest. How astonished the nurse was to see the tent so clean, so swept, so spread with mats! She entered and the slave remained without, and they brought her water, and said, 'Welcome, please to sit down and rest!' and treated her with respect and hospitality.

After greetings and inquiries after health, she said to them, 'I have a son, an only son, and he wishes to marry your daughter. I wish to take her with me, what do you say, O good old woman?'

The old woman answered, 'As my daughter wishes! If she wants to leave us she may go with you, she may do as she desires and marry your son or refuse him.'

And the old man said, 'Aye! *Keyfha!* As she wishes.'

Then the nurse turned to the girl and said, 'And what do you say, my daughter?'

The girl answered, 'First, I wish to know something. Is this young man really your son?'

The nurse answered, 'No, he is not my real son, but I suckled him when he was a babe.'

'You have come! And upon my eyes and head be it! But why did you come and not his real mother? Let his mother come, and I will answer.'

Then she gave the nurse coffee and treated her with honour and respect, and gave her peace, and the woman went her road and returned to the Sultan. She said to him, 'The girl I have seen and she is lovely, and I have never seen a tent like their tent, swept and garnished. The parents told me that all was in the hand of the girl, and when I asked her, she said, "Let his own mother come, and I will give an answer."'

The Sultan replied *'Al hākim hakīm!* The judge is wise. This can be no daughter of the 'Arab! She would not have spoken thus! Even had not my son desired her, I should have desired her for this her conduct!'

Then he went into the harem, and went to see his wife and said to her, 'Rise, take a slave with you, and go out to the desert and ask this girl who is in the house-of-hair to marry our son.'

The next day, the Sultan's wife took a slave, and went in a carriage to the house-of-hair in the desert. She descended from the carriage and entered the tent, and saw that it was swept and garnished so that any Sultan's daughter could have dwelt in it. And when she saw the girl, how sweet she was, she loved her at sight. They

made much of her, and honoured her and gave her coffee
and sherbet and cigarettes, and then she turned to the old
woman and said, 'I have come to betroth my son, my only
son, to your daughter. What do you say?'

The old woman said, 'As my daughter wishes.'

The old man said the same.

Then she turned to the girl and said, 'And what say
you, my daughter?'

The girl replied, 'You have come, and on my eyes and
head be it. I will marry your son, your only son, but
I make a condition, and if you do not carry it out, I will
stay in my place and he in his.'

Said the Sultan's wife, 'Tell me the condition. Speak!'

She said, 'I want from you a castle of crystal set in the
midst of the river, reached by a stairway that can be put
up or removed at will, and round the castle three moats
and three drawbridges, and in the outermost moat a pair
of lions that have not been fed for seven days. I will take
your son to husband on this condition, and if you cannot
fulfil it, I will stay in my place and he in his.'

This. And the Sultan's wife rose, and took her leave,
and returned with her slave to the Sultan and told him all
that she had seen and all that she had heard.

When the Sultan had listened, he exclaimed, 'Indeed
this is no daughter of the 'Arab! This is one of high
estate who has come to dwell amongst them. I will do
what she asks.'

And he rose quickly and called a builder, and told him
to build a castle in the midst of the river, as she had said,
of crystal, with a drawbridge and three moats, and hungry
lions in the third moat.

It was finished in fifteen days, and the Sultan sent and
made the betrothal, and brought the girl to the palace.
They took her to the bath and washed her and admired
her beauty, and prepared her for the reception of the
bridegroom. Then they crossed to the castle and she
entered it and sat waiting in the marriage chamber.

The story returns to Hasan the Thief. Now he was
walking that afternoon on the river-bank, and he saw the

A Shammar girl

castle, and asked of the people, 'What is that castle in the midst of the river?' They answered him, 'This, this is the castle which the Sultan's son built for his bride, and his bride is a daughter of the 'Arab,' and they told him all they knew. In his heart the thief thought, 'That is my enemy! That is she, and this night, Allah willing, I will slay her.'

It came to sunset, and the bride sat waiting in the marriage chamber. The bridegroom, for his part, went and prayed in the mosque, and afterwards came with his companions and friends to the river, and took boats and reached the castle, and there they feasted. At last he entered the bridal chamber, and found the bride sitting awaiting him. When they had greeted each other, the bride said to him, 'You are but newly risen from sickness, and are tired now, rest a little, come, lie on the bed and sleep.'

The bridegroom did as she wished, he stretched himself on the wedding-bed and went to sleep. But the girl was afraid to sleep, for she was afraid of Hasan the Thief. At one o'clock in the night, there was a noise in the roof, and she said to herself, 'He is coming by the roof!' and a little after, there was a hole in the roof, and a man appeared. Khr, khr, khr! He slid down by a rope and stood before her and said:

'How shall I kill you?'

She answered, 'You mean to kill me?'

Said he, 'With my two hands I will kill you.'

Said she, 'Why kill me here? People will hear and be alarmed. Take me into the desert and kill me there.'

Answered he, 'Yes. Walk before me.'

Said she, 'No, you walk before me and I will follow.'

So they walked together, he first and she second over the first moat, and the second moat, but when they were walking over the third moat she gave him a push with all her force and sent him over into the moat where the lions were waiting. They were ravenous, and they fell upon him and one seized one leg and the other the other and tore him in two and began to eat him up.

Then she returned to the wedding-chamber and woke the bridegroom, saying, 'Rise! We must return to your father, and tell him this story, and then I will be yours.'

And she took him to see where Hasan the Thief was being devoured, and told him that he had tried to kill her. They called to all who were in the castle, and they too beheld, and then they took a boat and went across and to the Sultan's palace. When they had entered it, they went to the Sultan's room, and knocked at the door.

He said, 'Who is it?'

The girl answered, 'I, bābā, your daughter and your son, and we wish to speak with you.'

He opened to them, and said, 'Speak!'

They entered and kissed his hands, and said, 'Come, see what lies in the moat of our castle!'

He rose and went with them, and when he saw what was in the moat he asked for explanation.

Said the girl, 'I am no daughter of the 'Arab, I am the daughter of such-and-such a Sultan, and I killed thirty-nine robbers with my own hand, and this was the fortieth.' And she told him the whole story from the first to the last. Then the Sultan answered, 'Well, I know your father, he is my great friend! Indeed I said you were no daughter of the 'Arab!'

And for seven days and seven nights they made rejoicing, and beat drums, and made feast.

> *Kunna 'adkum, wa jīna*
> *Wa lō kān beytak qarīb*
> *'Ateytak tubeg hummus wa tubeg azbīb!*

We were at their house and came back,
And if your house were near,
We would have brought you a dish of pease and
  raisins.

And the narrator added this moral exhortation:

> *'Ya hāfir al bīr! La tāhfur ghamīj* (vulg.) *bīhā*
> *Wa enta tāhfur al bīr wa enta tōqa fīha!'*

which corresponds to our proverb—'Who digs a well may fall in it himself.'

XXX

MOSES AND THE TWO MEN

THEY relate that one day of days the Prophet Moses (upon him be peace!) took into his mind to visit Allah. And on the road he chanced to meet a man who was ragged and poor. The man wished him peace, and he returned him peace, and then the man asked, 'Where dost thou journey, oh Nebi Mūsa?' The prophet replied that he was travelling to heaven to see Allah, and the poor man said: 'Thou seest my state and my poverty! I beg thee mention my name to Allah when thou reachest heaven and ask Him to take pity on my need.' Then Moses promised that he would do so. And Moses continued on his way, and after some minutes he met another man, but this man wore splendid clothing. And after this man had given him the salutation, and the prophet had returned it, he asked, 'Where goest thou, oh Nebi Mūsa?' And, as before, Moses answered that he was going up into heaven to talk with Allah. And the rich man said, 'I beg thee put a petition before Allah for me!' And Moses asked him what it was. And the rich man answered, 'I am so rich that I know not what to do with my money, and still gold pours in upon me! My petition is that Allah will lessen his gifts.' And Moses promised that he would speak of the matter to Allah. And when he reached Heaven, he fulfilled his promise and spoke of the poor man's request for more money and the rich one's request for less. Allah answered him, 'O Moses, say to them that they must be silent and again silent, *Yeskutūn yeskutūn!*'[1]

[1] This tag 'yeskutūn yeskutūn' is used proverbially to show that whatever a man does he cannot turn the tide of fortune, be it good or evil.

XXXI

AL GUMEYRA (LITTLE MOON)

A MERCHANT and his wife in a certain town once upon a time both died in one day of a mortal sickness and left behind them two children, a boy and a girl, who inherited their possessions. The name of the girl was Gumeyra, or Little Moon, and the boy, her brother, loved her very fondly for her beauty and goodness. He went to the sūq each day to buy and to sell, and the girl looked after the house. A young woman who lived near by was pleased to come in and help Gumeyra with her household tasks and to cheer her in her loneliness, and the two became great friends. One day the young woman said to Gumeyra, 'We love each other like sisters, why do you not ask your brother to marry me so that we may always be together?'

Gumeyra was delighted at the idea, and did not delay in telling her brother that it was her wish that he should marry her friend. He consented to do so; a marriage contract was made, and the wedding took place. No sooner had the bride entered the house, however, than her demeanour changed, for she became very jealous of her husband's fondness of his sister. It became difficult for Gumeyra, for her sister-in-law was always seeking quarrels with her and trying to represent to her husband that Gumeyra was her enemy.

Gumeyra became very unhappy, and when at night the moon shone into her room in a friendly way, it comforted her and she talked to it, and said:

> *Ya gumeyr yemwennes*[1] *al gharāib*
> *Bil leyl ʿandi, ou bin nahār ghā-ib!*

'O Moon that lovest far to wander
At night with me, by day thou'rt yonder.'

Her sister-in-law heard her, and said to her husband,

---

[1] *Ya muwennes*—pronounced as I have written. Lit. O Moon, O thou who amusest strangers, At night with me, by day absent.

'Gumeyra has a lover who visits her at night, and his name is Gumeyr.'[1]

The next night the brother listened, and he heard his sister speaking as his wife had said. In anger he entered, but found no one there. His sister protested her innocence, but he would not listen to her, and bricked up the window and the door, leaving only a small aperture in the ceiling through which he pushed down to her bread and water. However, the angels visited Gumeyra and gave her meat and sweetmeats, so that her beauty did not suffer by her immurement, but rather increased.

Now Gumeyra was loved by all who knew her, and when the neighbours heard of her imprisonment, they came to the brother, and begged him to release her. He had already begun to doubt his wife's tale, and when he heard praise of Gumeyra from all, he relented, took down the bricks, and set the girl free. It was now nine months after his marriage, and the young woman, his wife, was delivered of a boy; but instead of rejoicing at this event, she could think only of her hatred of Gumeyra and her anger that her husband would not listen to her when she complained to him of Gumeyra's wickedness.

One day she went out to the sūq, leaving the new-born child in the care of her sister-in-law. When she came back, both Gumeyra and the child were sleeping. The wicked wife took a knife and slew her own child, and putting the bloody knife beside her still sleeping sister-in-law, she went to summon her husband, shrieking that murder had been done, and demanding justice. He went with her to Gumeyra's room, and there was the child dead, with Gumeyra and the knife beside it. Gumeyra was aroused by the cries, and her brother, unable to doubt her guilt, sprang upon her and tore out both her eyes, then drove her out of the house with curses and blows.

Gumeyra was almost beside herself with pain and horror, and wandered far into the country outside the town, not knowing in her blindness whither she was going. At

[1] The diminutive is endearing, and Gumeyr (Little Moon) is the masculine equivalent of Gumeyra.

last she came to a big house, and when the servants of that place saw her plight, they took her in and showed her to the lady who lived there. That lady was a physician and she cured many people. When she saw Gumeyra, she pitied her, and took her into her house and performed a cure upon her, so that before long she could see as well as ever. Then the lady made her her servant, and because she was fond of Gumeyra, she told her her secrets and instructed her in the art of healing.[1]

Gumeyra abode in that place many years, helping the lady with her good work, until in time the lady died, leaving Gumeyra her house and all her possessions.

Now, for their wickedness to Gumeyra, Allah had smitten her brother with blindness and his wife with leprosy,[2] and it happened one day that a neighbour told them that there was a lady in the country near the town who had arts by which she worked the most marvellous cures upon the sick who came to her.

The husband and wife went together to the house, which was the house in which Gumeyra lived. When she saw her brother and sister-in-law, she knew them at once, and going to her brother, she used her art so well that he soon saw the light of day again and looked upon her.

Then she said to him, 'Do you know me, and do you believe that I did not kill your child?'

He answered, 'I know you, and I testify that you are innocent.'

Then she said to her sister-in-law: 'As for you, I will neither cure nor kill you: go, and trouble us no more.'

The woman fled from the place with her leprosy on her, and Gumeyra and her brother lived to old age in the house which the lady had left to her.

---

[1] I suspect that in the original story the beneficent *khatūn* was a sorceress. A sorceress is always expected to work cures, and white witches and wizards are largely employed in spells for curing various illnesses. In modern times the Baghdadi has acquired faith in the medical art: hence the substitution of the word *hakīma*. Here the lady-doctor is credited with the power of restoring sight o a person whose eyes had been torn out!

[2] Really elephantiasis, but leprosy sounds better in a tale.

XXXII

THE THREE DERVISHES
AND THE WONDERFUL LAMP

The narrator said, before we sat down to this tale: 'If you take to listening to stories in the daytime, your trousers will be stolen!'

Kān u ma kān
Wa 'ala Allah at tuklān. (3)

It may and may not have been
And God is the All-Powerful.

THERE was once a merchant who, though married for many years, had no child to his great sorrow. One day he was sitting in his shop in the sūq, when there came a darwīsh to him and said to him: 'Take this apple, peel it, cut it in half, eat half yourself, give the other half to your wife to eat, and give the peel to your mare.' The merchant did as he was bid, ate half the apple and his wife the other half, while the peel they gave to the mare. The mare and the woman both became pregnant, and in her due time the mare brought forth a foal, and the woman after nine months bore a boy, a fine child. The father was thankful to Allah for his mercy, and sent the darwīsh and his two brothers, for they were three, a present. They came to the house and cast the boy's horoscope, and foretold that one day he would find a great treasure beneath the earth.

So beautiful was the boy, and so much did his parents love him, that they did not permit him to go outside the house, he must always remain in their hōsh.[1] *Dī, dī, dī, dī!* The years went by, and the boy was fifteen years old and as beautiful as the full moon. But his father died at that time, and as there was no one left to earn money for them, the mother and son became very poor. Now the boy had for a long time yearned to go outside the hōsh. He said to his mother, 'My mother, *Aku awādim mithli?* Are there boys like me outside in the world?' And his

[1] See note, p. 1.

mother replied, 'Yes, my dear, there are boys like you outside in the world.' But when he begged her that he might go outside, she always refused. When his father died, the boy said to her, 'Now that my father is dead, will you not let me go outside? We are poor, we have scarcely enough to buy bread and meat, how shall we live if I remain here?' But the widow refused, and said, 'It was the wish of your father that you should not go from the house, and we must not disobey it.'

But one day the boy found the house-door unlocked, and he escaped outside. The first thing he did was to look carefully at the number written on the door, and at the number of the next house and the next, so that he should not lose the way, for he was an intelligent boy. He went only a little way, and there, on the ground, he saw a beshlik[1] lying. He picked it up, and bought bread, and meat, and fruit with it, and returned to his house by the way he came. When the widow saw the food, she wondered, and said, 'How did you come by this food, my son?' He answered, 'Allah gave it to us.'

Another day he did the same thing, and this time, always observing carefully which way he took, he went out again, and this time he ventured farther. A second time he found a beshlik lying on the ground, and with this, as before, he bought food. When the widow asked him whence it came, he replied that the food came from Allah. The next time he went out, he made up his mind to go to the sūq. So he walked, *meshi, meshi, meshi,* until he came to the sūq, and there he looked this way and that, admiring the fine shops and the merchants and all that he saw, while every one who saw him admired him too, for he was as handsome as the moon on the fourteenth night.

Now the eldest of the three darawīsh was sitting in a shop, and no sooner did he behold the boy than he went to him and kissed him on both cheeks, and said, 'My eye, my darling! How are you? How pleased I am to see you! How I longed to see you! You are the son of my brother, and I shall be a father to you in the place of him who has

---

[1] Five piastres.

been translated, Allah have mercy on him!' And he gave
him gold and bade him take him to his house. So the
boy brought him to his house, and ran up and told his
mother, saying, 'My father, had he a brother, oh my
mother?' And she said, 'I never heard that he had had
a brother.' He said, 'There is a man below who says he
is my father's brother, and he has given me gold.' She
said, 'Perhaps your father had a brother and I did not
know it.'

So they received the darwīsh into their house and made
him welcome, and he lived with them. He gave the boy
money to buy merchandise, and the boy started business
in a shop in the sūq, and in that shop were fine things,
silks and embroideries and rarities of all kinds. So they
had money and prospered.

One day the darwīsh said to the boy, 'Come, let us go
and hunt in the desert.' So they went, *meshi, meshi, meshi,*
far into the desert, and when they had reached a certain
spot the darwīsh said to the boy, 'Below us there is a great
treasure. When I have read my spells, the ground will
open, and you must go down into the earth. In the garden
below, you will see trees hung with crystal fruits, and
emeralds, and rubies, and cornelian, and diamonds, but
you must not pick them, for if you do, the earth will close
and you will not be able to get back.'

The boy said, 'On my head and on my eyes.'

The darwīsh said, 'You will see below an old lamp.
Put that in your pocket and bring it to me. But if you get
into trouble down there in spite of what I have told you,
rub this ring,' and he gave him a ring, which the boy
placed on his finger. Then the darwīsh lit a fire and he
read and read and read, until the earth cracked a little
and then it widened, and at last they saw steps going down
into the belly of the earth. Then the boy did as the darwīsh
bade him and walked down into the ground. When he
reached the bottom of the steps, he found himself in a
beautiful garden. Each tree was blazing with crystal, or
emeralds, or diamonds, or cornelian, just as the darwīsh
had said. The boy could not resist the sight of them, and

in spite of all that the darwīsh had said, he picked plenty of jewels, and stuffed his pockets full of them, and at last, spying the lamp, and remembering what the darwīsh had said, he pushed that behind him in his shirt under his zibūn.[1] Then it became dark, and he tried to find the opening by which he had come, but the earth had closed, and there was no way out. He searched and he searched, but there was no way of getting out.

Meantime the darwīsh waited one, two, three, four, five, six, and seven days above on the place where the boy had gone in, and when he saw that the boy did not return he was like one mad. He said to himself, 'The boy has forgotten what I told him, and has picked the fruits and has either lost or forgotten about the ring.'

And in the boy's house in Baghdad, when he did not return, they gave him up for dead. The widow said to the people, 'The darwīsh must have killed him!' And they began to wail and mourn and beat their breasts as for the dead.

Now the boy was always searching for the way out, and in climbing about on the seventh day he chanced to rub his ring on the rock. At once the earth cracked and opened, and he saw steps before him, and going up them, he came upon the light of day and the darwīsh sitting where he had left him. The darwīsh told him that he had given him up for dead. The boy told him his adventures, how that he had picked the fruit off the trees, and he emptied his pockets one by one until the jewels lay at the darwīsh's feet. Then the darwīsh said, 'But where is the lamp I bade you bring for me?' The boy thought to himself, 'If he does not value these jewels, but thinks the lamp of more worth, the lamp must be something important,' and he said, 'I forgot the lamp.'

At that the darwīsh uttered a loud cry of disappointment, and falling back, he died in his place.

So the boy went back to Baghdad, and the jewels were

[1] A gown worn over the shirt (*dishdasha*). It almost reaches the ankles, but is divided on either side for several inches to allow the wearer freedom of movement.

in his pockets and the lamp was with him as well. When he went to his house, he heard the cries of grief and the sounds of mourning, and went in and found his mother bewailing him. When she saw him she was very glad, and asked him where was the darwīsh, and he replied, 'He is dead.'

Now when the jewels were sold in his shop, the boy and his mother became very rich, and he was one of the first merchants in the town. One day, the mother saw the lamp, and saying to herself, 'That is a dirty old lamp, it must be cleaned,' she fetched a cloth and began to rub it.

When she rubbed it, suddenly there was a smoke in the room, and lo, seven *salaūn*—seven sons of the jānn—stood before her with their arms folded, so! and the chief of them said to her:

Labbeik, labbeik,	'Your will, your will!
Ana 'abid bein īdeik	I am your slave to order
Utlub ū temenna!	Ask and favour!'

But the widow was so frightened that she ran away and told her son what had happened. He went up, and took the lamp and rubbed it with the cloth, and immediately the seven sultans of the jānn stood before him, and their chief said:

> '*Labbeik, labbeik*
> *Ana 'abid bein deik*
> *Utlub ū temenna!*'

The boy was not afraid, and asked for a golden tray, and on it something of great price covered with a net embroidered with pearls. And the jinn said to him, 'Hide your eyes!' and he hid them, and when he opened them, there was the tray before him, and on it, underneath a net embroidered with pearls, were jewels that shone like the sun.

The boy called his mother, and said to her, 'Go with this tray to the palace of the Sultan, and ask to see him, and give him this tray. When he asks who sent it, say, "My son sends you this gift."'

The woman did as her son said. She went to the Sultan's house, and when she had come into the presence of the Sultan, she put the tray where his eyes would fall on it. When he saw the pearls on the cover, he asked what it was. Then the widow came forward, and said, 'My son sends you this gift, O Sultan!' The Sultan got on his two legs, and looked at the jewels and saw that they were finer than anything he had in his treasury, and was astonished at the richness of the gift. He said to his chief wazīr, 'What does this gift mean, O wazīr?'

And the minister replied, 'It must mean that the merchant's son wishes to marry your daughter.'

So the Sultan said to the widow, 'Tell your son, On my eyes and head I accept his generous gift! and that I am willing to give him my daughter.'

The widow went home, and gave her son the Sultan's message, and the young man was so happy that he spent his time in feasting and pleasure of all sorts, but he made no effort to claim his bride. *Dī, dī, dī!* A year passed, and as the Sultan's daughter was sought in marriage by a neighbouring prince, the Sultan accepted him as his son-in-law, forgetting his promise to the merchant's son.

When they told him, saying, 'There is a marriage in the Sultan's house, and to-morrow, Friday, the bride goes to the bridegroom's house,' the young man was beside himself, and reproached himself for his neglect. He rubbed the lamp and the seven jānn appeared as before, and said '*Labbeik*'.[1]

The merchant's son told them his trouble, and admitted that it was his fault, since he had omitted to claim the Sultan's promise.

The chief of the seven said, 'It does not greatly matter: you must not trouble, for the princess will be yours.'

On the Friday, the wedding being completed, the bridegroom chosen by the Sultan went at night to his bride's room, and the young couple were left to themselves. But the bridegroom no sooner looked at his beautiful bride, than he fell down—*sār khashabi*, he be-

---

[1] Repetition, omitted here.

came wood, and lay on the floor as he had fallen, all night.

When they came to ask her in the morning how the bridegroom had behaved after they had left them alone together, she replied, 'He was like a dead person.'

The second night, and the third, it was the same thing. Then the merchant's son went to the Sultan, and said, 'Why did you give your daughter to this man? Did you not promise her to me? Where is your honour?' And the Sultan bit on his finger [*the storyteller bit hers*] and said, 'I forgot! But this bridegroom is no bridegroom at all, I will send him away and she shall be yours.' So he sent for the bridegroom, and said to him, '*Ma 'andek nesīb 'andi!* Your fate is not with me!' and gave him a present and sent him away.

This for the bridegroom.

But as for the merchant's son, he married the Sultan's daughter, and the jānn of the lamp constructed him a fine house in the place of a stable that was near the Sultan's palace, so that the girl might live near her father.

And the darawīsh, as for them, they were now two, and they did not know what had become of the eldest brother. So they set out and they went from place to place, *ardh atshīlu, ardh athattu,* earth taking, earth placing, seeking their brother, and finally came to the conclusion that he had been killed by the merchant's son. So they went to Baghdad, and when they saw the fine house that had been built by the King's palace, they asked, 'Whose house is that?' And they were answered, 'That is the house of the merchant's son who married the Sultan's daughter.'

So the second darwīsh went into the sūq, and he bought a *sella* (flat basket) and many lamps, the most beautiful that could be found in all the sūq, and when he had them, he put them into the basket, and went along the streets with the basket on his head, crying, '*Khōsh lampāt! Khōsh lampāt!* Fine lamps!'

Before long he came to the house of the Sultan's daughter and the merchant's son. The bride was sitting at the window, and when she heard the darwīsh crying his lamps, she looked out, and saw them on his head, below, and sent her servants down, saying, 'Bring the father-of-lamps up, so that I may look at what he has in his basket.'

So the darwīsh came up, and put his basket on the carpet, and began to spy about him. The princess came and looked at them saying, 'That is sweet! How fine that one is! I should like that! I should like this one!' And the darwīsh said, 'Take them all, if you like them! Only give me in exchange that old lamp which is hanging up there on the wall!'

And the princess laughed, and said, 'That old lamp is very dusty and dirty, take it, father-of-lamps!'

And the darwīsh took it under his arm, and went away. Just after came in the girl's mother-in-law, the widow, and when she saw all the new lamps on the floor, she asked how they had come there, and the princess told her that the father-of-lamps had given them to her in exchange for the old lamp that hung on the wall. When she heard that, the old woman was very angry, and said, 'What have you done! That lamp was what made my son a rich man!' And the girl said, 'I did not know! How should I know?'

Now the merchant's son was fond of hunting, and every day he went out into the chōl to hunt. That day also he went hunting, and when he came back, lo! his house was no longer there, only the stable. This was because the darwīsh, when he had the lamp, went outside the city and rubbed the lamp, and when the slaves of the lamp appeared, he said to them 'Transport the house and all that is in it to my country.' And it was done.

When the Sultan saw that the house in which his daughter was had gone, he was very angry, and sent for the merchant's son, and said, 'What have you done with my daughter?' Now the young man had sought out his mother in his trouble, and she had told him that his wife had given the lamp to the darwīsh, and he understood how everything had happened. He answered the Sultan, 'The matter happened thus and thus,' and told him the story from the beginning. When he had finished his story, he said to the Sultan, 'I am going now to look for your daughter, and if I do not return before forty days, you will know that we are both dead.'

So he went out into the desert, and walked and walked until he was very tired. After he had walked some days, he came to a pool and took water in his hands to drink, and also washed his head with the water in his hands. As he did so, he chanced to rub the ring which was on his finger, and in the twinkling of an eye, there stood before him two black slaves, who said to him,

> '*Labbeik, labbeik*
> *Ana ʿabid bein īdeik*
> *Utlub ū temenna!*'

The merchant's son then suddenly remembered his ring, and cursed himself for not having remembered it until now. He said to them, 'Take me to the country of the three darawīsh, and place me on the roof of their house.'

The slaves of the ring answered him, 'We will take you, but do not ask us to do anything else, as we are afraid of the jānn of the lamp.' They said to him, 'Shut your eyes!' and he shut them, and when he opened them, the slaves of the ring had thrown him on to the roof of the second darwīsh's house, and already they were flying away, flying, flying, as quickly as an aeroplane.

Now the darwīsh was away from his house, hunting in the desert, and the Sultan's daughter was alone. The second darwīsh had told her that she must marry him, and she had said to him, 'I will marry you when the forty days of my ʿedda[1] are over. Until then, it would not be seemly for you to see my face.' And the darwīsh agreed to that.

When the merchant's son came on the roof, he went downstairs to the harem, and finding the door of his wife, he knocked. She said, 'Who is it?' He said, 'I!' and she knew his voice at once, and opened the door and embraced him. And they told to each other all that had happened. And he asked her, 'Where is the lamp?' She replied,

[1] Period of mourning.

'The darwīsh never lets it leave his person, but wears it chained to his waist, behind his body.'

Then he said to his wife, 'This evening, when the darwīsh comes back, hide me under the couch, and put a rug over it. Then when he comes to you, throw back your veil and smile upon him, and tell him that you will marry him at once, and not wait for the forty days to be over. But say to him that he must drink with you, and with your own hand give him a drink mixed with henbane.'[1]

She did as he had said, hid her husband under the couch, and when the darwīsh came to her, she uncovered her face and smiled upon him, and said, 'Welcome!' The darwīsh was pleased and delighted, and she told him that she would wait no longer for the term of her 'edda, but would marry him at once.

And she added, 'But I am accustomed to drink and make merry, so on this joyful occasion let us drink together.'

He called for wine, and, already intoxicated by her eyes, he drank. Then she put the henbane in his cup, and said to him, 'This cup you must drink from my hand!'

And he answered, 'From your hand and your beauty I will drink!' And he drank it and fell to the ground like a piece of wood. Then the merchant's son came from his hiding-place and stabbed him with his dagger, and that was finished for him.

Then they took the lamp from the body of the darwīsh, and when they had rubbed it they were transported in the moment that they shut their eyes, they and the house and all that was in it back to Baghdad.

This is what happened. And the merchant's son, when he got back, rubbed the lamp and when the seven jānn had appeared, he asked them, 'I have killed two enemies. Have I any more?' And they answered, 'Yes, there is one more, and he will seek to kill you, three days from now.'

---

[1] *Henbane (benij)* is a favourite opiate in the Middle East, and appears constantly in the *Arabian Nights*.

By this they meant the third darwīsh, youngest of the three, who, when he had sought his brother, and had not found him, had said, 'This must be the merchant's son.' So he went from place to place, *ardh atshīlu, ardh athattu, ardh atshīlu, ardh athattu,* till he came to Baghdad. And it was summer, and the merchant's son was living outside the town at Karrādah. And the darwīsh went to his house and said, 'Does the Sultan's daughter, the merchant's son's wife, go out?' And they said, 'No, she does not leave the house.' And he said, 'Does she receive visitors?' And they said, 'There is a ma-sœur,[1] one of the ma-sœurāt, who comes every Sunday to pay her visit, but, except for this woman, she receives no one.'

So the darwīsh waited until the Sunday, and then, when he saw the ma-sœur in the road, he set upon her and killed her, and then put on her corneyta[2] and dark robe. Then he went to the house, and knocked at the door, and when they called, '*Minu?*' he replied, 'I, the ma-sœur.' Now the merchant's son, being warned that the darwīsh would come on the third day, had taken down a sharp sword so sharp that it cut everything through with one blow. This sword was hung to the ceiling, but he took it down, as I have said, and hid with it behind the door.

Now the Sultan's daughter loved the ma-sœur, and she came quickly down the steps into the courtyard to welcome her, but before she could reach her, her husband leapt out from behind the door before the false ma-sœur could enter, and with one blow severed his head from his body so that it flew—flew—and rolled away into the desert.

Then the princess began to cry and said, 'Why have you killed the ma-sœur? She was my friend, and I loved her.'

He replied, 'Come and see.'

And he showed her that it was no woman, but a man

---

[1] 'ma-sœur', i.e. a nun. The Baghdadis always refer to the excellent girls' school which is kept by the French sisters (of the Order of the Presentation), in Baghdad as the 'school of the ma-sœurāt'.

[2] white coif, or *cornet*.

dressed in nun's dress. After that, he had no enemies, and all was well with him.

> *Wa lō baitkum qarīb*
> *Kunt ajīb lakum tubeg hummus wa tubeg azbīb.*

> And if your house were near
> I'd bring you a dish of pease and raisins.

or, in rhymed paraphrase:

> And if your house were only near,
> I'd bring some goodies for you, dear!

XXXIII

THE KING AND THE THREE MAIDENS,
or THE DOLL OF PATIENCE

ONE day a King was wandering in disguise about the streets of his capital, when chancing to pass beneath an open window, he heard three girls talking, and he stopped to listen. The first said,

'If I were to marry the King, I should make him a carpet so big that it would cover all his kingdom.'

The second said, 'If I were to marry the King, I would cook him a loaf so large that if all his army ate of it, there would remain some crumbs.'

The third said, 'And were I to marry the King, I would bear him two children, and on their heads silver curls and gold curls, growing side by side.'

The young man listened, and asked of some bystander who they were. The next day he sent for their father, and asked for the hand of the eldest girl in marriage. The marriage was celebrated, and as soon as he was with his bride, he asked her to weave him a carpet as large as she had promised. But she was unable to do it. To punish her for her boast, the King made her a kitchen-maid, and he sent again to the father and asked for the second daughter. When the marriage festivities were over, he ordered her to bake him a loaf as big as she had said, but she could not. So he put her in the kitchen too, and then he asked for the third daughter, and married her. For nine months they lived happily together, and then the girl bore twins, and on their heads were gold and silver curls, growing alternately all round their heads. As soon as the sisters perceived these beautiful boys, they were jealous, and told the midwife to take two puppies and put them in the bed instead of the children. When the mother asked to see her children, they said, 'They were not children, they were puppies.' And they ordered the midwife to put the two boys into a wooden chest and to cast them into the Tigris. This she did.

When the King saw the puppies and heard that his wife had brought this shame on him, he was very angry, and ordered that she should be buried up to her breast by the door of his house, and that each passer-by should throw a stone at her and spit in her face. And this was done.

There was a fisherman who lived with his wife a little way down the river, and he was the King's fisherman and took fish every day to the palace. The rest he sold in the sūq. One day, when he drew in his nets, they were very heavy, and when he saw a box in the net as he pulled it up, he was alarmed and let it fall back into the river, fearing lest a deyu should be within the box. But when he told his wife, she came with him, and bade him draw up the net again, and said to him, 'Perhaps there is treasure in the box.' They drew it up, and took the box to their hut, and when they had opened it, they saw within two boy-babes, as beautiful as angels, and on their heads curls of gold and curls of silver. The couple were delighted and, as they had no children of their own, the woman nourished them and brought them up as her own.

Now after the King had punished his third wife, he brought her two sisters out of the kitchen and lived with them, forgiving them for their boasts. One day, he bade them good-bye, and told them that he was going upon a journey across the sea, and asked them what present he should bring them when he returned. The first sister asked him to bring her a gown embroidered with pearls, and the second sister asked him to bring her a diamond necklace.

Then they said, 'Since you ask us what we should like when you come back, ask also our sister, who is half-buried beside the door.'

He replied, 'Why should I ask her? She made a fool of me, her behaviour brought shame on me.' They answered: 'Never mind, she is your wife and our sister, ask her, and hear what she wants.' So he went to his wife by the door, and asked her, 'What do you want when I come back from my journey? and she answered, 'Nothing, only that you should travel in safety and come back in happiness.' He replied, 'No, you must tell me something that you want for yourself.'

And to that she said, 'Then bring me the Doll of Patience and the Knife of Patience, which you will find in the country to which you are going. If you forget, the ship upon which you travel will not be able to move.'

The King travelled to a far country, and when he had accomplished his business there, he ordered the merchants of that place to bring him a zibūn[1] embroidered with pearls, and a diamond necklace. Then he took ship, and ordered the captain to set sail for his own country. The captain replied, 'On my head!' and he set the sails, but the ship could not move. He came to the King and said, 'The ship will not move, perhaps there is some witchcraft against which we are powerless.' Then the King remembered his third wife's words, and said, 'Wait! I have forgotten something, and before we leave I must fetch it.' He went back into the town and called the merchants, and said, 'I wish to buy the Knife of Patience, and the Doll of Patience.' But all the merchants said they had no such thing. At last there came one, and said, 'There is a man in the town who says he has the Knife of Patience and the Doll of Patience, if your Majesty goes to him, perhaps he will sell them.'

The King said, 'Take me to him.'

So they took him to the man, and the man was an old cobbler who mended old shoes, and he lived in a small, mean place. The King asked him, 'Have you the Knife of Patience, and the Doll of Patience?' And the old man answered, 'I have.' The King said, 'I wish to buy them.' And the cobbler said, 'Wherefore do you wish to buy them?' And the King told him, 'I have promised my third wife, whom I have punished for her crime against me, that I would bring them.' Then the old man said, 'I will give you what you ask for, but you must do exactly as I tell you.' And the King promised. And the old man said, 'When you give your wife the knife and the doll,

[1] See note, p. 148.

hide yourself behind the door that you may hear what
she says. You will behold this doll burst, and as soon as it
has burst, you must seize your wife's hand, or she will
kill herself.'

So the King got again upon the ship, and this time the
winds blew and the sails filled and they rushed quickly
through the waves until he reached his own country.
When he had landed, he went to his palace and gave his
two wives there what they had asked for, one the zibūn
embroidered with pearls, and the other the diamond
necklace. Then he went down to where his wife was half-
buried beside the street-door, and with his hands he gave
her the knife and the doll. He pretended to go away, but
in reality he hid himself behind the door, and looked and
listened to see what would happen.

The third wife addressed the doll, saying:

Wey, ya laʿabat es sabr,
Nti sabr wa ani sabr,
Cham dub qalbi yastabr!

'Alas, O Doll of Patience,
Thou art Patience and I am patience
How many blows my heart has suffered patiently!'

Then she began to tell the doll all that had happened,
and how her sisters had taken her children and told the
midwife to put puppies in their place, and of all her sorrows from the day of her delivery to that day. And as
the doll listened, it grew bigger, and bigger, and bigger,
till at last, with a loud crack, it burst. When the third
wife saw that, she said, 'Doll of Patience, thy heart is
broken!' and she took the Knife of Patience, and was
putting it to her heart, to pierce it through, when the King
rushed from behind the door, and seizing her hand,
prevented her from killing herself. Then he said to her,
What you have told the doll, why did you not tell it to
me?' And she replied to him, 'I was afraid that you would
harm my sisters for what they did.'

Then the King called people and bade them dig her
out of the earth, and told the servants to make her a bath

A cobbler, Baghdad

and to put new clothes upon her, and they did so. And his other two wives he put into prison. Then he called a dellāl—a crier—and bade him go through the city for seven days crying that two children with gold and silver hair must be brought to the palace.

The fisherman and his wife heard the crier, but they did nothing, for they loved the children. But on the seventh day, the fisherman's wife said to her husband, 'You are the King's fisherman, and if he hears that we are concealing the children he wants, he will be very angry, and our livelihood will be gone. Take the children to him, and we shall gain his favour, and perhaps he will give us a present.'

So the fisherman went to the King and said, 'Oh, your Majesty the King, I am your fisherman, and I bring you fish every day. One day, when I was casting my nets and drawing them in, I perceived a heavy box entangled in them, and when we drew them up, we found two children hidden in the box. We brought them up as our own, thinking no harm, but now we have heard the order.'

The King said, 'Have the children hair of gold and silver?'

And the fisherman said, 'They have.'

The King said, 'Bring them that I may see them.'

So the fisherman brought the two children, and the King was overjoyed, and sat one on one knee and one on the other. To the fisherman he said, 'You have done well, and to reward you, I will build you a house in a garden near the palace so that you may see these children when you wish.'

Then he ordered his servants to bring much firewood, and to build it up in the street over the hole where his first wife had been buried. They did so, and then he had the wicked midwife and the two sisters who had been his wives brought, and naptha was poured over them, and they were burnt alive in the big fire to punish them for their lies and wickedness. But he did not let his wife know, only telling her that he had sent them away.

As for the fisherman and his wife, they lived happily in their house and saw their foster-children every day.

XXXIV

THE MERCHANT'S DAUGHTER

THERE was once a young prince, and when his father the Sultan was lying sick at the point of death, he called his son and said to him,

'Come, my son, I have a charge to lay upon you!'

And the prince answered, 'Yes.'

And the Sultan said, 'I am leaving you all my property, all my horses and stables, and houses and gardens, and khāns and all I possess, it will all be yours. But the charge I lay upon you is this, do not drink 'araq,[1] do not gamble, and do not frequent bad company! Obey me in this, for I am going to die.'

The young man answered, 'Good, my father, I will obey you.'

Then his father died.

But he did exactly the opposite of that which his father had commanded him, and drank and gambled and frequented bad company, *dī, dī, dī!* gambling! *chalghiāt!*[2] dancing-girls and singing-boys, bad characters! *dī, dī, dī!*

And his mother said, 'Why do you act thus, my son? Why do you not heed what your father laid upon you?'

But *bōsh!* No good! he did not heed, and before long his father's money was all finished, and he began to sell the houses, the lands and the gardens, the khāns and the horses, and the money he gained from these he dissipated in evil living. *Dī!* It was all spent.

That youth was now very poor, and his mother reproached him,

'What have you done! You have squandered all!'

But it was of no use, and so poor they were that they wanted for food, they had not enough upon which to sup.

So the youth rose and said to his mother, 'My mother,

---

[1] '*Araq* is distilled either from grapes or dates: in 'Irāq usually from the latter.

[2] A musical entertainment is called a *chalghi* (Turkish). House-concerts for which a troupe of musicians are engaged for the night are a favourite form of entertainment in Baghdad, particularly with Jews and Christians.

I wish to travel. If I become a man, I will return; if not, count me as dead.'

Then he took his road, and went into the desert and walked and walked, until he came to the sea-shore, and there in the distance he saw a ship. He took his keffiyeh[1] off his head and waved it, and the ship came and took him aboard. It was loaded, but it had no crew; there was only its captain, and he was a wealthy merchant. The cargo was his and the ship was his.

The young man said to him, 'I am in need, and have travelled far, and have nothing to eat. Let me work for you for my keep, and if I do not suit you, let me depart when we get to a port. I will work and do anything you ask me to do.'

The merchant answered 'Good.'

The ship sailed off again, and the youth worked for him like a servant, baked his bread, brought him his food, and did all that he could in the ship. They came to a port, and the youth said, 'Do not trouble yourself with the unlading and charging the cargo: I can write, I will do that for you.'

The merchant was amazed at hearing the lad could write, and said to himself, 'In truth, this is a good lad, and clever and well-educated!' and he liked him still better than he had liked him at first.

True to his word, when the ship had anchored, the lad counted the bales as they went out, and paid the dues, and went to the Customs house, and did all that was necessary, while the merchant remained sitting on the ship.

Then the lad asked, 'Do you wish me to go my road, or shall I stay with you?'

The merchant answered, 'Stay with me.'

And so they went from port to port, and at last the merchant came to his own port, where he lived, and the lad did as before, and got the cargo off, and paid the dues

---

[1] Head-kerchief. In Baghdad the head-kerchief is usually of black and white, or red and white, cotton, and is kept in place by woollen or silken strands bound into a rope by threads of metal or of silk wound tightly around the strands at intervals.

and got the goods through the Customs, while the merchant remained sitting there.

And the lad said, 'Now shall I go my way?'

And the merchant replied, 'I have no son, for my own boy died, and I have only a daughter. Come to my house, and I will adopt you as my son.'

The lad answered, 'As you please,' and followed him to his house. There the merchant gave him a room, and showed him his accounts, and from that day all the merchant's business was in the lad's hand: he bought and sold, and went to the Customs, and managed all the merchant's business: as for the merchant, he sat at home, and received guests, and was at his ease, for this merchant was richer than any Sultan.

The lad remained with him one year, two years, three years, and became rich and prosperous, and everything was in his hand. At last the merchant's friends said to him, 'O Merchant effendi, everything you possess is in the hand of this lad (Melek Muhammad by name), why do you not marry him to your daughter?'

The merchant saw that the advice was good, and he rose, and called a mulla, and they made a contract, and gave him his daughter to wife. Thus all was in the hand of Melek Muhammad, and he remained with the merchant ten years. As for the girl, his wife, she was a sweet girl; she might have said to the moon, 'Be absent! I will take your place and light the world!'

Di, dī, dī! Time passed, and one day his mother came into his remembrance, and, putting his keffïyeh over his face, he began to weep. His wife came to him and asked, 'O Melek Muhammad, why do you weep, why?'

He answered, 'My mother came into my mind.'

Said she, 'Have you a mother?'

Said he, 'Yes, I have a mother.'

The girl went to her father and said, 'Melek Muhammad weeps!'

The merchant went to him and asked him what ailed him, and Melek Muhammad answered, 'I wish to see my mother: I do not know whether she is alive or dead.'

The merchant asked him, 'Whose son are you?' for until then they had not asked him.

He replied, 'I am the son of such and such a Sultan!'

The merchant was pleased to know that his son-in-law was the son of a Sultan, and said to him, 'I will give you leave to see your mother: go, visit her, and return after forty days; you must not stay longer, for all my business is in your hands, and I cannot spare you!'

He said, 'Yes,' to that, and his wife said, 'I will go with you!'

He replied, '*Adili, bedili!* You had better change your mind! you cannot come with me! for it is a long voyage. Another time when I go away you can accompany me, but this is too far.'

Said she, 'I will come with you,' and she rose, and said to her father, 'I wish to go with Melek Muhammad, and you must give me permission to go with him.'

Her father replied, 'As you wish, my daughter, if you wish to, go!'

She returned to Melek Muhammad and said, 'My father says I may, and I shall go with you!'

So they made preparations for the journey, and the merchant said to Melek Muhammad, 'Go, buy forty camels in the sūq and load them with gold and silver from the cellar.' This was done, and forty camels were loaded with treasure,

khafīf al himl, ghāli al thaman!

light in weight but precious in value!

And on them, too, he piled his baggage and his wife, and the merchant said, 'Do not delay! Come back after forty days!' and *ey!* they moved off, *meshi, meshi, meshi, ardh athattu, ardh atshīlu, ardh athattu, ardh atshīlu,* until the caravan came at last to Melek Muhammad's city.

The young man left the caravan outside the gate of the city and said to his wife that he would go to see his mother. He went, and knocked at the door.

Now his mother had dug a tomb in the cellar and she sat there every day and wept, thinking that Melek

Muhammad was dead, and thought about him beside the tomb. When she heard the knock she said, '*Minu?* Who is it?'

He answered, 'I, Melek Muhammad.'

She said, 'My son is dead this ten years!'

He said, 'I am Melek Muhammad, my mother, open the door!'

Cried she, 'That is my son's voice!' and she opened the door and encaged him in her arms, and said, 'My darling, how! where have you been? I thought you dead!' and much else.

He answered, 'I have come and brought my wife with me, for I am married.'

She called the servant and said, 'Sweep! Clean! Spread carpets! prepare for my son and his wife.'

And Melek Muhammad went, and brought his wife, and the forty camels, and they entered the courtyard, and he unloaded the camels, and when his mother saw all the treasure, she was so delighted that her reason flew from her!

Then Melek Muhammad said to his mother, 'I have only forty days here, I may not stay longer.'

But he went into the town, and all that his father had once possessed, he bought it back again, horses, stables, gardens, houses, khāns, all that he had sold, he bought back again, and his mother rejoiced and was happy.

The tale of days was counted, and at last he said to his mother, 'The forty days are over, I must return.'

Now his mother loved her daughter-in-law so well that if she needed water she went to get it for her; and had the girl wished to walk on the old woman's two eyes instead of on the ground, her mother-in-law would not have said her nay. So when the time came to depart the girl said to her husband, 'I shall not go with you, I shall remain with your mother.'

He said, 'How can that be!'

She replied, 'Excuse me! but I wish to remain here. Leave a slave with me to act as courier and bring letters from me to you and you to me, and when I wish to bring my stay to an end I will send, and you can fetch me.'

He agreed, and took farewell of her, and said to his mother, 'My mother, you look on me with one eye—look on my wife with two! take care of her well! (*tabaw'aīn illi bi 'ain wa marrati bi'ainatain*).'

She promised, and when he had gone she said to the young wife, 'I will look after you, for you have taken the place of my child. I will do everything for you, and this is your house, and your place, for I love you like my own!'

One day of days and time of times, the girl was oppressed by her restriction, and wearied, and she said, 'I wish to open a window and to gaze at the street, raise it but a little, so that I can see the people that pass to and fro.'

So the window was opened just wide enough for her to peep through and watch the people who passed by. Presently there came the qādhi, riding upon an old, lame mule, with his slave behind him. Now the qādhi was very old and misshapen, and when she saw him she laughed. When the qādhi heard the laugh, he raised his eyes and thought, 'She smiled at me! She is in love with me!' and he went to the door and knocked, and Melek Muhammad's mother came to talk with him.

He said, 'A Sultan's daughter lives here, and I want to have her as mine!'

The old woman answered, 'How, thou owl! you want a Sultan's daughter! If you want her, take her!'

He said, 'But there is a Sultan's daughter here, and she loves me, for she laughed at me from the window!'

The old woman said, 'She laughed at your crookedness and at your age!'

But the old man went home and, although he was a miser, he called wizards and witches to his house and consulted them about the girl.

His mother said to him, 'You are spending your money in vain! Why should this Sultan's daughter love you? She will never take you—you are wasting your substance.'

But he was mad from love. One day there came to him an old witch, very skilled, very clever, and he opened his state to her, and said, 'I want this Sultan's daughter and you must bring her to me.'

She replied, 'I can bring her to you to-night.'

Said he, 'Truth?'

And she answered, 'Truth.'

And he said, 'How much do you want?'

Said she, 'Five gold pounds, and this night at two o'clock, Arab time, I will bring her to you. Only leave your door open.'

He gave her the money, and she went to the sūq and bought a few sugar almonds, and tied them in a kerchief. Then she went to the Sultan's house and knocked at the door and they opened and she saluted them. Said she to the mother, 'I have come from the house of a Sultan in whose family there is a wedding,' and she gave them the comfits,[1] thus inviting them to the wedding, and saying, 'The household of the Sultan send greetings, and say there is a wedding in their house, and they invite your daughter-in-law, who is a stranger and knows not our customs here, to see how weddings are held in this country.'

The mother replied, 'As my daughter-in-law wishes! Till now she has not been outside the house, but she may please herself.'

The old woman said, 'Where is your daughter-in-law?'

The mother said, 'Upstairs,' and they called to her, 'Come down! Come!' When she had come, the old woman told her what she had told her mother-in-law. The girl said, 'As my mother-in-law pleases!'

Replied the mother, 'Please yourself! If it will amuse you, go, for you have not seen a wedding here yet.'

Asked the girl, 'Who will take me to the house?'

Replied the old woman, 'I will return at sunset and take you there, and will bring you back with my two hands.'

---

[1] *Mulabbas* (comfits) wrapped in a silk handkerchief are presented to every wedding guest at a big wedding. Unmarried girls put these sweets under their pillows to dream of their future husbands.

Said the mother, 'Go, my daughter, spend an hour or two there, see what it is like, and return.'

They then divided the comfits and agreed that when the girl had dressed and prepared herself, the old woman would return and take her to the wedding.

This. The old woman took her leave and after the sun had set, she returned. The girl had put on fine clothes, jewels, pearls, and gold ornaments, so as to be finely dressed for the wedding. She went with the old woman into the street, and they walked and they walked, for the old woman took her by circuitous routes so that time should pass.

Said the girl, 'Where is the house of the wedding?'

And the old woman replied, 'Farther yet.'

They walked, and they walked, and it became dark, and the lanterns were lit—for in those days there was no *letrīk*.

Meanwhile the old qādhi told his mother that the girl was coming, and she was very angry, and said, 'My son, you are mad! If the girl comes I will go out, I will not stay here!' So she went to her own place[1] in the house, and he remained alone in the courtyard waiting behind the door.

Presently the girl came, and the old woman said to her, 'That is the house!'

Said the girl, 'But there is no sound and all is dark!'

Answered the old woman, 'But there are three court-yards, one after the other, all in the belly of the house. The wedding is in the farthest. Here is the gate, pass in —you first and I behind.'

And she opened the door, and pulled it to when the girl had entered, and ran off.

The girl found herself face to face with the old qādhi. She bit on her hand and said, 'This is a trick!' (*Hadha nuqta 'ala rāsi!*)

The qādhi welcomed her saying, '*Marhaba! Ahlan u sahlan!* Come and sit upstairs! you are welcome, twice welcome.'

---

[1] The women's quarters.

She went, and sat upstairs on the couch, and she pondered within herself, 'What shall I do to rid myself of this accursed son of a dog?'

Said he, 'Won't you amuse yourself, and talk to me?'

Answered she, 'I am not amused thus, my uncle! Before I can talk of love I must drink, so bring every kind of drink, 'araq,[1] whisky, champagne, white wine, red wine, all you can find, and we will drink. Does this not please you?'

Answered he, 'It pleases me. All you ask you shall have, and if you ask for many kinds of drink, you shall have all kinds!'

Then he called his slave, and said, 'Come, Feyrūz![2] Bring pistachios and almonds[3] and drinks!' And he went to see after the slave.

Outside was his mother, and she said to him, 'You are a miser, and you love to hoard money, and now, see how you are scattering money, and incurring expense!'

But the old man did not listen to her but said to the slave, 'Feyrūz, go and buy all sorts of drinks in the sūq, 'araq, wines, champagne, whisky!' and he gave him five gold pounds. The slave went and returned with the drinks.

While the old man was outside, the girl pushed a head-kerchief inside her bodice. Then she called for a table and glasses, and plates for the almonds and nuts. All was brought to them, and they sat, and she poured out drinks, handing him a glass with the words, 'Drink this from my hand!' Now he had never drunk wine and knew not the taste of it, but he took the wine from her hand and drank and said, '*Hadha min 'ayūnki!* This is from your eyes!' Then they drank, but she had poured water into her glass instead of 'araq,[4] and drank, saying, 'To your eyes.' This. And he wished to talk with her and make love with her,

---

[1] See note, p. 162.

[2] Turquoise, see note, p. 135.

[3] Salted nuts are usually served at a drinking-bout. When an Oriental, untouched by Western ideas, drinks, it is usually with the intention of getting drunk.

[4] 'Araq when neat is colourless.

but she said, 'I am not yet intoxicated: the night is long, and Allah is merciful; let us drink, and when the wine has warmed us, we will amuse ourselves and make love.' And she did not let as much as his little finger touch hers. She poured him three glasses, each four fingers high, and he drank, and his head sank on his breast. Then she poured him another, saying, 'I am not yet intoxicated, drink one more!' and he took it again from her hand, and drank and fell like a log on the floor. Then she quickly took off her jewels and pearls and put them in the kerchief and put them in her pocket, and went down and looked in a room and found a razor. She returned with it and shaved his hair, his beard, and his eyebrows, then poured the wine down his open mouth and broke the bottles and glasses on his head till he was covered with blood, and said, 'Dog, son of a dog, die!' and she drubbed him severely. At dawn she opened the door softly and went out into the street, and looked this way and that, wondering which road to follow. But she remembered the way by which the witch had led her, and *dī!* came at length to the door of their own house. Her mother-in-law was waiting for her, and when she knocked, said, 'Who is it?' She answered, 'I!' and the door opened. Her mother-in-law asked, 'Did you amuse yourself at the wedding?'[1] She answered, 'Yes, I amused myself!' and went to bed, saying nothing of what had happened. Within herself she said, 'What a trick they played me!'

The next day, when she woke from sleep, her mother-in-law brought her tea, and she drank and afterwards they broke their fast. The girl reflected much, but said no word to her mother-in-law.

The story returns to the qādhi. The next morning the mother came into the courtyard and called, 'Feyrūz! where is your master? Wake him from sleep, he must go to the courts: they have come in search of him—what answer can we give them!'

Said the slave, 'I will not go, for I think he is sleeping with the woman—go you and rouse him.'

[1] Wedding festivities are carried on until the day dawns.

She went, and knocked at the door, and went in, and saw her son stretched out as if dead, his eyes covered with blood and his head all gory. The mother screamed, 'Feyrūz! come and see what has happened to my son! Ha! What did I say! No good would come of this!' and she sent for a doctor, and ordered Feyrūz, if they came from the court for her son, to say that he was in bed, sick of a fever. 'Say, "To-day the qādhi effendi will not come!"'

The doctor came, and gave him medicine, and bound up his wounds.

After three months in bed the qādhi's hair and his beard grew again, and his wounds healed, and he became well, so that he was able to get up and return to the law-courts. But he said to his mother, 'I will not rest until I have killed that girl!'

Accordingly, he called his slave, Feyrūz, and asked him if he were friendly with the slave who carried letters in the Sultan's house. He replied that he was. Then the qādhi said to him, 'When he takes a letter from his mistress to her husband, contrive that you can take out that letter from his bag and substitute one that I will give you.'

Said Feyrūz, '*'Amrkum!* As you command!'

Then the qādhi sat down and wrote a letter as if it came from the girl's mother-in-law, accusing her of bad conduct, saying that she was unfaithful to her husband, that she was wanton and entertained men in the house, and so forth. Then he sealed the letter and wrote on it 'From your mother,'[1] and gave it to Feyrūz, the slave.

Feyrūz went and sat on the road upon which he knew the messenger passed when he took letters from the girl to her husband. Presently came the fellow, who greeted him, and said, 'Ha! You, Feyrūz! why are you sitting here?'

[1] As the mother was probably illiterate, the handwriting would not be questioned. Well-bred women up to recent times were seldom literate and employed scribes or slaves to write their letters. Many women of the better classes still are illiterate: amongst the tribes it is rare for a woman to know how to read or write.

Feyrūz began to abuse his master, saying, 'What a beggar the qādhi is! what a miser! he gives me nothing to eat, he treats me badly, he is the son of a dog—I have left his service. And you, what are you doing?'

Answered the fellow, 'I am taking a letter from my mistress to Melek Muhammad.

Said Feyrūz, 'I will go with you a little way.'

Said the other, 'Good,' and they walked till they came to the post-house.

Said Feyrūz, 'Go off from the road here and ease yourself, and while you are gone, I will take care of your post-bag.'

The other left him for a moment, and while he was away, Feyrūz took out the letter and put into the bag that which his master had given him.

Then the messenger came back, and they bade each other farewell, and they parted, each going his own road.

Feyrūz returned to his master, who when he heard what had been done, cried, '*Aferim!* Bravo!' and was delighted.

As for the messenger, he went his way, and delivered the letter to his master, Melek Muhammad. When the young man took it in his hand, and saw that the letter was from his mother, he shook his head, fearing evil. Then he read it, and put it under his mattress and was very angry; however, he called the messenger, and wrote a letter to his wife as usual, as if he had heard no evil of her, and the messenger returned with it.

Now all this happened several times: each time Melek Muhammad's wife sent a letter, Feyrūz substituted one purporting to have been written by her mother-in-law.

The Sultan Melek Muhammad was beside himself with grief and wrath: his head became hot, and he said, 'What vileness has my wife brought upon me! My mother cannot have looked after her. I will kill my wife out of hand!' That night, he mounted his mare and rode fast; the mare flew, *dī-dī-dī!* until he had reached his own town. He arrived at midnight when all were sleeping, and he knocked at the door loudly.

Cried his mother, 'Who is it?'

Answered he, 'I! Open the door!'

Said she, 'That is my son's voice!' and opened the door, crying, 'What is it? Why did you not tell us you were coming! What is it, my darling, what is the matter with you?'

But he answered her not a word, and his mother, when she saw how angry he was, trembled. He was silent as a wall, and replied to her nothing, so she dared not question him more, but let him pass her and go up the stairs. Then he knocked at the door of the room where his wife was sleeping, and beat at it. She answered, 'Who is it?' He knocked again, and she opened it and cried, 'You have come! What is it? Why?' He said not a word, but attacked her with a dagger, and stabbed her.

She was unconscious (her spirit flew from her), and he took all her jewels and diamonds and ornaments, and threw them and her out into the road. It was then two o'clock of the night.

There came riding by a surgeon who was returning from attendance on a Sultan who lived in another place, and he saw a woman in the road, surrounded by jewels. He descended from his mare, and wrapped her and the jewels in his 'aba, put her on his mare, and rode with her to his house. Now this surgeon was a Jew, and clever at his craft. He called for water to be boiled, and washed her wounds, and bound them up with lint and bandages, and gave her restoratives. At last she opened her eyes, and after he had attended her for many days she recovered.

She said to him, 'See, you have cured me, and I will give you all these my jewels as payment. Now, let me go. I will make you wealthy, and God is the Bountiful!'

Answered he, 'You have been in my arms, and I want you, I love you, remain with me.'

(For, *al helu ham*[1] *balwy!* Beauty is bane!)

She gave reply, 'Never! Kill me, wound me, take all the jewels I possess, but that can never be! Loose me, and let me go!'

---

[1] Local word for 'also', 'as well.'

Said he, 'I will not loose you!' And he put her into the sirdab[1] and tied her with a rope, and beat her, and gave her nothing but bread and water. Twice a day he beat her, and gave her a bowl of water and a little barley bread, and then he locked the door and left her tied up.

All this time, he neglected the Sultan, his patron, and at last the Sultan sent, saying, 'If you do not attend me, I shall cut your head off.'

At that, he called his wife, and told her that while he was absent she was to continue to beat the girl he had shut in the cellar, and to give her bread and water. Ordering her to be obedient to this command, he left.

Now the wife did not know why her husband treated the girl thus, but obedient to his order, she took a stick, and some bread and water, and went to the cellar. When she opened the door, the girl asked her, 'What do you mean to do?'

She replied, 'I am going to beat you.'

Said the girl, 'Come! why beat me without reason?'

Said the woman, 'My husband told me to beat you.'

Said the girl, 'Did your husband not tell you why he beats me? He wished to take me and put me over your head, and I would not accept.'

Said the woman, '*Suduq?* Truth?'

Answered the girl, 'Aye.'

Then said the woman, 'I will loose you.'

And she untied the rope, and opened the door, and said, 'You are free, go!'

And the girl left the place, and walked out of the town and into the desert, walking, walking, walking, *ardh athattu, ardh atshīlu,* and walked and walked until she was weary and hungry and thirsty. At last, from afar, she saw a shepherd with a hundred head of sheep. She approached him, and when he saw her, he cried, 'From whence do you come? from the sky or the ground? What do you want?'

She answered, 'I am hungry and thirsty, give me a little to eat and drink.'

[1] See note, p. 63.

Said he, 'I want you!' for she was so lovely that all who saw her wished to have her for their own.

Answered she, 'Good, I will be yours, but first fill my stomach, for I am hungry!'

Said he, 'I am the slave of your eyes! What I have, I will give to you!'

And he gave her from his pocket some bread and dates, and poured her a little water from his water-skin.

Said she, 'Allah keep you! But I beg you, give me a little shenīna¹ and laban!²'

Answered he, 'I will go to our tent and get it, but keep your eye on the sheep.'

The tent was far, and as soon as he had gone she took the bread and cheese and dates and ran away as fast as she could, leaving the sheep to disperse in the desert. She went fast and far, and at last found a cavern in the desert, and there she remained, ate and drank, then tied up her head and slept.

As for the shepherd, when he returned with the laban, he saw that she had fled, and he set to work to collect the straying sheep.

The next day, she walked and walked until again she was faint with hunger and thirst. At last she saw a pool of water in the distance, and went to it.

Cried she, 'Praise God!' and she stopped, and washed her hands and face and drank of the water, and sat by it.

As she sat, she saw a rider approaching. This rider was the Sultan's courier with a mail-bag belonging to that Sultan.

Her heart said to her, 'I have saved myself from them all, how shall I rid myself of this one?'

He rode up, and greeted her and gazed at her; then he got down and tied his mare to a mulberry tree. In the saddle-bags were money and letters and food.

Said he to her, 'From whence did you come? from sky or earth?' for he too loved her at sight—she was so sweet.

Said she, 'I am hungry, give me, I beg you, some food.'

¹ Curdled milk and water, a favourite drink in 'Irāq.
² Curdled milk. Sweet milk is called *halīb* in 'Irāq: *laban* in Egypt.

An oasis pool, Shithātha

He replied, 'On my eyes!' and took down his saddle-bags from the mare, and took out chicken, and eggs, and bread; then he spread his head-kerchief on the ground, and set the food on it. Then they sat down and ate together, and the more he looked at her, the more he loved her.

Said he, 'I want you!'

She turned pale, and thought what was best to do. Then said she,

'Good. As you will. But first, you must wash and I will wash, and we will both say our prayer. After that, I will be yours.'

He agreed, and took off his clothes and entered the pool, and she, pretending to amuse herself, took his clothes and said, 'Come! I will put on your clothes and be a man!' He laughed and said, 'Put them on!' Said she, 'And now I will put on the bags and mount your mare and be like a postman!' Said he, 'As you like!'

She put on his clothes, and then she mounted his mare, and away she flew.

Cried he, 'For the sake of Allah! stop! I will not harm you; return, or the Sultan will take off my head!'

Said she, 'Never!' and off she went, and the courier remained naked and bereft in the middle of the desert.

Dī, dī, dī! she and the mare flew together, until she reached a town. When she had entered it, she addressed a passer-by and asked him, 'Where shall I alight? I am a stranger.'

He answered her, 'In such and such a khān.' She went to the khān, and engaged accommodation, and tied her mare and entered her room, and opened the saddle-bags. In one bag she found money and letters, and with the money she bought food in the sūq, and ate. When she listened to the people in the sūq, she learnt that the Sultan of that country was dead, and that they were going to make another Sultan in his place. They told her, thinking that she was a man, 'After seven days, we are all going out into the desert, and they will loose a bird bearing in his beak the Sultan's robe. Upon whose head the bird lets the robe fall, he will be Sultan.'

Said she, 'I will go with the people into the desert and watch to see who is made Sultan.'

And after several days she went with the crowd outside the city, where a great press of people were gathered together, wālis, qādhis, muftis, ministers, all waiting there for the bird of fate.

Then they loosed the bird, and it flew high and higher, and very high, like an aeroplane, and all waited and gazed and waited and gazed. Then it descended and flew around and above the crowd, and at last it dropped the Sultan's robe on the head of the girl—who was dressed in the courier's clothes.

All cried, 'Who is that youth? from whence does he come?'

They answered, 'He is a stranger and has only been in the town seven days.'

Then they seized the bird, and gave him the robe again, and for a second time they loosed him and he flew up. And this time also he let fall the robe on the head of the girl, and a third time.

Then all the people clapped their hands, and they played music, and put a crown on her head, and said, 'Allah has sent you to be our Sultan.'

And the girl became Sultan over that city and acted with justice and ruled with wisdom, so that all the people praised her, saying, 'What a good Sultan Allah has given us!' All loved her.

One day she rose, and caused an artist to come and take her likeness. Said she, 'I wish you to take my picture in women's clothes. Make four photographs of me, all alike, and then break the plate.'

He answered, 'Aye.'

She retired, and put on her women's clothes, and the jewels that her husband had given her, which she had kept all this while in her pocket, and he took her picture —four copies, and no more, and these four she put up on the four gates of the city, so that all who passed in and out would see them. By each picture she placed two policemen. To these she said, 'If you hear any one addressing this likeness, seize them and bring them to me.'

It was done, and after some days there came to that city the qādhi who had played her the sorry trick. When he saw the picture he was amazed, and stopped before it, and addressed it, saying,

'Where are you? Are you alive or dead? I would that I knew!' and the two police seized him and brought him before the Sultan.

He began to excuse himself, saying, 'I did no harm, I was looking and thought the picture pretty, and talked to it. I beg you, let me go!'

Answered she, '*Kheyr!* No! Take him and imprison him in a cage.'

The next day her husband came to that place, for he heard the truth from his mother, and was repenting his deed, and was looking for his wife. He saw the picture, and stayed before it, and wept and said, 'What did I do! Pardon! I did not know what I was about! Your image is always before me!'

They seized him like the first and brought him to the Sultan. She knew him at once, and told them to put him into a room in the serāi. Said she, 'This one has a request to make, and I will consider it presently.' The next to come and speak to the picture was the courier whose mare she had taken, and after him the shepherd, and these two she placed in prison, but when the Jewish surgeon came, him she placed in a cage, like the qādhi.

She then appointed a day, and said, 'On that day I will hear the cases of these prisoners, and will judge them.' And at three o'clock of that day, there was a sitting in her diwān, and many people came to listen to the trial of the prisoners.

First of all, they called the qādhi, but her husband she caused to be present so that he could hear all that took place.

When the qādhi had come, she said to him, 'Tell us the truth, why did you talk with that picture? You must tell the whole story from the beginning to the end, or I shall cut off your head.'

The qādhi rose, and he told all, from the beginning to the end; how he had procured the girl through the witch, how she had treated him, and how he had revenged himself by changing the letters.

And while Melek Muhammad heard, he marvelled, and said, 'Surely this is my story!'

When the qādhi had finished, the Sultan turned to the assembly and said, 'What does this fellow deserve?'

Answered they, 'He deserves to have his head taken off!'

She summoned the executioner, and he struck with his sword: the qādhi's head flew off, and he died.

Whom did she call next? The surgeon!

To him she said what she had said to the qādhi, 'Speak the truth, or lose your head.'

The surgeon spoke and told her all, how he had found a girl lying in the road, and cured her of her wounds, and afterwards asked her favours, and the whole story from the beginning to the end, saying, 'Since I left her in my house I have not seen her.'

The Sultan turned and asked the people, 'What does this fellow deserve?'

They answered, 'He deserves to have his head cut off.'

And his head flew off like the qādhi's.

Next they called the shepherd, and he told his story, saying, 'A girl came, and I loved her, and gave her to eat, and wished to make her mine, and she asked for curds, and I went to get them and told her to mind the sheep, and when I returned she had fled.' And as he told his tale he trembled, for he saw that those before him had suffered death.

But to him the Sultan said, 'You can go free!' and she told them to give him a qirsh[1] and let him depart.

Next was the turn of the courier, and he too told the truth.

When he had finished, the Sultan said to those about her.

'Go, fetch the mare from the stable, and the saddle-bags.'

---

[1] Halfpenny.

They brought the mare and the saddle-bags, and she showed them to the courier, and said, 'Are these yours?'

Said he, 'Aye.'

Said she, 'Count the money and letters, is all there?'

Said he, 'All is there.'

Then she said, 'Loose him too.' And they let him depart with his mare and the bags.

Who remained? The girl's own husband.

But she did nothing then, she said, 'Take him back to his room, and I will hear his petition later.'

Melek Muhammad began to fear, thinking within himself, 'All these stories I heard at the trial concern my wife! What will happen to me when I relate my tale?'

That night, when it was midnight and all the world slept, the girl rose, put on her man's clothes, and her crown, and went to the room where her husband was and knocked at the door.

Said he, 'Who is it?'

She answered, 'I, the Sultan. I have come to visit you.'

He opened, and she entered and sat on the bed, and said, 'Come, sit by me!'

He did not dare, for he was afraid.

But she said, 'Sit!' and he sat.

Said she, 'Did you understand the stories told at the assembly to-day?'

Answered he, 'Yes.'

Said she, 'And what do you say?'

Said he, 'I have committed a great crime.'

Said she, 'How is that, tell me.'

He answered, 'My head was hot! and I am the son of a Sultan and my name is Melek Muhammad,' and he told her the story of himself and his wife, and how he had tried to kill her.

Said the Sultan, 'I know your wife, and that she still loves none but her husband. Heard you not the tales of those men?'

He said, 'Aye, I heard.'

Said she, 'Do you know me?'

He replied, 'No, your Highness!'

Then she stood up, and threw off her Sultan's robes, and put the crown on the table.

Then he knew her, and fell before her with his head on her two feet and cried, 'I did thus to you, do not the same to me!'

Said she, '*Kheyr!* Nay!' And she put the Sultan's robe upon him and the crown on his head, and said, 'Now we will bring your mother and my father here, and we will live in this country always, and you shall be Sultan in my place.'

> *Kunna ʿadkum wa jīna*
> *Wad daff umgargʿa wal arūs hazīna*
> *Wa lo beytna qarīb*
> *Kunt ajīblak tubaq hammas wa tubaq zebīb!*

> We came to you and went away,
> The tambourine makes music gay,
> The bride sits weeping all the day;
> And if our house were only near,
> Sweet dishes I would bring you, dear!

XXXV

WUDAYYA (LITTLE WHITE SHELL)

THERE lived in Baghdad a man called Hamad, and his wife, and they had an only child, a girl-baby, whom they named Wudayya or Little White Shell. The summer after the birth of their child, the woman sickened with a mortal sickness, and on her death-bed she called to her husband, bade him make her clothes and her wedding 'aba together into a bundle, and suspend the bundle by a rope from the ceiling so that it hung about the height of a tall man from the ground. He did as she asked. Then she said to her husband, 'O, my husband, vow me a vow.' He answered weeping, 'All that you ask I will vow to you, my beloved.' She said, 'Vow to me that you will not take another wife until our daughter has grown so high that she can touch the bundle that you have hung from the ceiling.' Hamad vowed to his wife as she requested; then the woman died and wailing was heard in the house. Wudayya was now motherless, but her father saw to it that she was tended, and as for himself, he grieved so bitterly for his dead wife that he had no wish to take another woman. When Wudayya was seven years old, he apprenticed her to a woman who taught sewing (*ista al khayyāta*), and this woman, who was a deep schemer, showed herself so kind to the child that Wudayya began to love her. Like all the neighbours, the sewing-mistress knew of the widower's vow, and one day she called Wudayya, and standing her upon a chair, said to her: 'Oh, my darling, touch the bundle that hangs from the ceiling!'

When she was stood upon the chair the child was just high enough to touch the bundle with her fingers. Then the sewing-mistress said to her, 'You are motherless, my daughter, and your father lacks a wife. When he comes back to-night, say to him, "My father, I lack a mother, and you a wife. Marry the sewing-mistress, whom I already love as a mother."'

When her father returned, the child did as she had been bidden, and repeated the words that the sewing-mistress had taught her. When she spoke thus, her father sighed and said, 'The time is not yet, my daughter. I vowed a vow to your mother that I would not marry for a second time until you had touched the bundle that hangs from the ceiling.' The child answered, 'To-day I touched it, oh my father.'

The next day the widower sent his mother to the house of the sewing-mistress to make negotiations for the marriage, for he thought it was the will of God that he should remarry. In due time, the sewing-mistress was brought as a bride to the house and herself took the wedding 'aba threaded with silver[1] that was in the bundle with the rest of the dead wife's possessions.

Wudayya much resembled her mother in beauty and grace, and the sewing-woman, now that she was installed as lady of the house, began to be jealous of her step-daughter. Day by day the beauty of the child increased, and day by day the hatred of the step-mother towards her grew and was bitter. She could not endure the tinkle of the bell-adorned anklets which the child wore when Wudayya ran about the house.

There came a day when the man must take a journey, and the heart of the step-mother was light, for she thought that now she would have opportunity to rid herself of Wudayya. So, some days after his departure, she said to the girl, 'Put on your 'aba, we will take an arabāna and drive into the desert to meet your father.' The girl gladly went with her step-mother and they set forth into the desert and drove for many miles. Then the woman said, 'Wait here while I go to see if I can espy your father.' The girl sat down as she was bidden, while the woman went away in the arabāna. But instead of returning, she drove back to Baghdad, and left the girl alone in the desert, thinking that she would surely perish there. On her arrival in Baghdad, she killed a sheep and wrapped it

---

[1] A wedding 'aba is usually of a deep puce colour, and is heavily interthreaded with silver.

in a shroud and buried its body and was glad to think that she had got rid of Wudayya.

Meanwhile Wudayya, when she perceived that she had been abandoned, wandered about in the desert, hungry and thirsty. But God the Merciful ordered that she should find a stream at which to quench her thirst, and floating in the stream she found a loaf. So she ate and drank and was refreshed, and slept that night by the stream. In the morning she awoke, and lo, near her, coming to drink, was a wolf. Wudayya was very frightened, and seeing a tree close by she climbed into it, and called aloud for her father in these words:

¹Udʿayya ib janājilha²
U jāha ad dīb yakulha!
Sōda bi wijhak
Hamad, ya abūya!

'Wudayya with her anklets (is here)
And the wolf has come to her and will eat her,
Thy face is black (with shame),
Hamad! oh my father!'

Now it happened that her father returned earlier than they had thought, and the place to which the child had wandered was on the road he was travelling, and he heard her voice from afar. Hastening to her, he rescued her, and when he had embraced her, she told her story. When he heard it he was amazed and angry, and said to her, 'I have here a chest in which are some rich stuffs that I was bringing to my wife as a present. Get into the chest and hide beneath the silks, and take this needle. When she who betrayed you opens the box, prick her with the needle on her hand.'

So the girl got into the chest, and it was strapped to the mule again, and they came to Baghdad. When Hamad arrived at his house, his wife met him with a sober face and told him that Wudayya was dead.

---

¹ The reversal of syllables used vulgarly in Baghdad is seen in Wudayya's verse. *Bi* becomes *ib*, Wudayya—udʿayya, and so forth.

² *Janājil* are anklets of silver with little bells attached. They are often worn by children, so that their mothers know by the tinkling where they have strayed.

The man feigned great grief, and then said, 'Didst call in our friends for the mourning?' The woman answered, 'No. I told no one. The girl died in the night and I was afraid, so I buried her. I will show you the tomb.' And she took him to where she had buried the sheep and pretended to shed tears of sorrow. Her husband said, 'This will be shame upon us! Inform our friends and call them to the house that we may make 'azza[1] for my daughter.'

So she sent to all their friends, and in the meantime he told his wife that he had brought her a chest filled with enbroideries and silks. All eager to see them, she had the chest brought up, and opened it in the presence of her husband, thrusting in her hands to pull out the stuff. When she did so, Wudayya, who was within, pricked her finger, and when the woman shrieked, her husband bade her see what was in the chest. When she looked, lo! Wudayya was inside.

The step-mother was astounded and frightened, and then her husband took her to the cemetery and forced her to open the grave. When it was open, and the shroud undone, within it was revealed the dead body of a sheep.

When the mulla arrived to read prayers for the dead, and their neighbours were assembled for the mourning, the man told all the company of the evil behaviour of the woman, and all agreed that she had deserved death. However, he contented himself with pronouncing the threefold divorce, and the woman departed with shame from the house and never returned.

(At the end of this story, the relator pronounced the moral, 'This story is a proof of the trickery of women!')

[1] An *'azza* is the general gathering of friends to bewail the deceased.

XXXVI

THE POOR GIRL AND HER COW

THERE was once a couple who had an only child, a
daughter, of whom they were very fond. In time the
mother died, leaving her cow to her daughter, and the
father married again, his second wife bringing him another
daughter. The two girls grew up together, but the step-
mother did not love the first wife's child and made her
life very difficult.

Now the orphaned girl discovered that the cow which
her mother had left her had a wonderful gift. If she gave
it cotton to eat, it returned it all spun. This she took to
the Sūq al Ghazl, the Market of the Spinners, and sold it.
Each day the girl took the cow into the desert, and there
the cow spun her cotton.

The step-mother was angered with the girl for her
absences, and said to her husband, 'That girl takes her
cow every day and goes off into the desert. You must kill
the cow!'

Answered the father, '*Khatiya!* That would be a sin!
The girl has done nothing evil, and the cow was left to
her by her mother. What good would it do if I were to
kill it?' And he refused.

One day, when the girl was in the desert, two pieces
of the cotton which the cow was spinning for her flew
away on the wind, and the girl ran after them till they
reached a cave, before which there ran a water-channel,
and in this cave was a s'ilūwa[1] milling flour between two
stones, her teats thrown backwards over her shoulder, after
the fashion of the s'ilūwat.

The girl picked up some of the flour which had fallen
out, and sucked some of the s'ilūwa's milk.

The s'ilūwa turned round and said:

'Had I seen you before you had drunk of my milk and
eaten of my flour, I should have made one mouthful of
you, but as it is, you are my daughter. Now, I wish to

[1] See Preface, p. xi.

sleep at the mouth of the cave. I will put my head on your lap, and you can take the lice from my head, and all that you catch, bite them up!'

The girl looked this way and that, and she spied some loose grains of corn lying about, and she picked up a handful of them.

Then the s'ilūwa reclined, and put her head on the girl's lap, and said,

'If the water runs white, rouse me,
If it runs yellow, rouse me,
But if it runs black, do not rouse me.'

Answered the girl, 'As you order, my mother, sleep!'

And the s'ilūwa slept, and the girl began to pluck the lice out of her head, and what a lot of horrid creatures they were! Black, white, large, small! From time to time the girl put the wheat into her mouth and said, 'How sweet your lice are, my mother! I am enjoying them.'

Presently, she saw that the water in the channel ran white, and she roused the s'ilūwa, saying, 'The water is white!' Said the s'ilūwa, 'Rise, go and wash in the water.'

The girl did as the s'ilūwa told her, and when she came out of the water, *subhān Allah!* she was as fair as the morning! The girl returned, and the s'ilūwa slept again with her head on her lap, while the girl picked the lice from her head. Presently the channel ran yellow, and she roused the s'ilūwa and told her, 'The water runs yellow!'

The s'ilūwa said, 'Rise, go and dip your head in it.'

The girl dipped her head in the water, as she was bid, and when she lifted her head and shook the water from it, her hair was yellow as kalabdūn,[1] glittering like gold, and so long that it reached her knees.

But when the girl saw it, she was afraid, and said to the s'ilūwa, 'Alas, why have you done this to me? When she sees me, my step-mother will ask me what I have been doing and will perhaps be angry with me.'

---

[1] The gold wire used in embroidering 'abas, especially round the neck, and at the edges.

Said the s'ilūwa, 'Tie up your head in a rag and go back. Do not fear! Your step-mother will kill your cow.'

When she heard that, the girl began to cry.

And the s'ilūwa said, 'Do not eat of its flesh, but put the bones and skin and all that remains of the cow into a bag, and go to the place where she spins cloth from the cotton, and bury the bag there and leave it there for forty days. At the end of that time, take it out, and whatever you find in the bag is yours.'

So the girl left the cave and returned to her cow and drove it back to her father's house. When she saw her, the step-mother began to abuse her and revile her, saying, 'Where have you been? Why have you dallied so long? You bring shame on us. I shall tell your father, and ask him to kill your cow.'

The girl began to weep, but the step-mother went to the father and said, 'Your daughter is always gadding and gives the excuse of her cow. So now you must slaughter it.'

The father said, '*Khatiya!* That would be a sin! My daughter loves her cow, and it was the gift of her mother who is dead.'

Said the step-mother, 'Either you kill it, or I leave the house.'

So the father rose, and went to the cow and slaughtered it, and skinned it, and cleaned it, and threw the head and skin and hoofs and entrails away. Then the step-mother cooked the meat, but the girl refused to eat of it.

They said to her, 'Eat, eat! The flesh is good.'

She said, 'Never! I will not eat of the cow!'

And she went secretly, and put the skin and bones and head and tail and feet and entrails into a bag, and took it out into the desert, and buried it in the place where her cow used to graze and spin her cotton. Then she returned to the house, and every day she wept about the cow.

One day she wished to comb her hair, so she went on the roof, and took off the rag about her head and combed it.

The step-mother came out to see what she was doing

on the roof, and the girl's hair was streaming out like the rays of the sun, and shining like gold.

Said the step-mother, 'How did you get your hair like that?'

[1]Answered the girl, 'It was the s'ilūwa,' and she told her how she had followed the two pieces of cotton to the s'ilūwa's cave, and all that had happened to her there.

The step-mother said, 'Go, return to the cave, and take my daughter with you to the s'ilūwa, and ask her to make my girl's hair like yours.'

So the girl went with her step-sister, and on the road she told her all that had happened, so that the girl might know what to do.

The other girl was stupid, and she said, 'I cannot remember all this!'

When they came to the cave, the second girl did as her sister had told her, and ate of the flour on the ground, and sucked the s'ilūwa's milk from the dugs that hung over her shoulder.

Then the s'ilūwa turned and said to her, 'Child of Adam, if you had not drunk of my milk and eaten of my flour, and become my daughter, I should have made one mouthful of you.'

Then she said as she had said to the first girl, 'Sit by the mouth of the cave, and I will put my head in your lap so that you may pick out the lice while I am asleep.'

The girl sat down, and the s'ilūwa put her head in her lap, and the girl began to pick out the lice. But when she saw what was in the s'ilūwa's hair, she began to scream, and said, 'What creatures! I am afraid.'

Then the s'ilūwa said,

'If the channel runs black do not rouse me,
If the channel runs yellow, rouse me,
If the channel runs white, rouse me.'

Then she went to sleep. Presently, the girl, who had not listened well to what she said, roused her, saying, 'The channel has run black.'

---

[1] Repetition of story here.

The s'ilūwa answered, 'Rise, go and wash your head in it.'

The girl rose, and went and plunged her head into the water. And when she withdrew it, there were two black horns on her head!

The s'ilūwa said, 'Did I not tell you "do not rouse me if the water is black".'

And she sent the girl away, and the two sisters returned weeping, and the younger uglier than before.

When the step-mother saw her daughter, she was very angry and asked what had happened. Said the first girl, 'It was not my fault, I told her what to do.'

Said the second, 'She told me, but I forgot.'

The step-mother was angrier than ever, and said to her own daughter, 'You owl! Why did you not listen!'

Now the elder girl was counting the days, and *dī, dī, dī!* they passed, until it was the fortieth. Then she went into the desert and dug in the place where she had buried the bag.

When she had uncovered it and opened it, what did she see! The skin had become an 'aba all embroidered with gold, the tail had become a dress of silk, and the bones and the rest were changed into jewellery, each bone a piece; chains of pearls, bracelets, and precious stones, and amongst the rest were a pair of clogs set with diamonds and emeralds. Never was there such an outfit in all the world!

The girl was so delighted that she put on her finery and admired herself in the brook, and when she had pleasured herself enough, she took them off, and put them in the bag, and buried them again. Then she returned to her house in her old clothes.

Every day she returned to the place, and put on her finery and looked at herself in the brook, and then took it off and returned home.

One day when she was so arrayed and adorned, there came by the son of the Sultan, whose house was near that place, and he watched her. When she had finished adorning herself, she changed her clothes, and folded up her 'aba and jewellery, and hid them in the sack and buried them. But as she was hiding them she saw that some one was looking, and in her haste she forgot one clog, which slipped into the brook.

When she had gone, the Sultan's son called a servant, and said, 'In the brook there is a clog, go into the water and get it.'

The servant went into the brook and searched for it, and found it. He wrapped it up and brought it to the Sultan's son.

When the Sultan's son saw it, he exclaimed, 'What a clog! Such a fine one I have never seen.' Then he went to his mother and said to her, 'My mother, I wish to marry the owner of this clog.'

His mother answered, 'Good, my son.'

She took a slave, and she went into the town, and she tried at one house after another, but the clog fitted no girl: for one it was too long, for another too short, for another too broad, and for another too narrow. At last she came to the house where the two sisters lived; it was the last house.

When she knew that the Sultan's wife had come to find a bride for her son, the step-mother took her step-daughter, and put her in the oven,[1] and shut the cover down on her; but her own daughter she adorned, and dressed in fine clothes.

When the Sultan's wife saw her, she said, 'Is this your only daughter?'

The woman answered, 'Aye, I have no other, this is the only girl.'

And the girl in the oven cried out, 'Oh, oh, oh, Fatma Khān! My feet stick out of the hole.'

The step-mother cried angrily, 'Hush! Hush!'

---

[1] One type of 'Iraqi oven resembles a large clay amphora without handles, and is heated by wood burnt inside it. When it is hot, the flat rounds of bread are plastered to the sides. Sometimes a square oven is built, with a hole beneath it, and the jar-like oven above the hole, so that it can be heated from below. The oven of the story must have been this kind. Beduins make a large hole with smoothened sides in the ground, and use this as their oven. In each case the bread is slapped flat and round and then plastered to the hot sides of the oven.

The Sultan's wife said, 'Who is that? Let her speak.'

The girl cried out again, 'Oh, oh, oh! Fatma Khān, my feet are sticking out.'

Said the Sultan's wife, 'I think there is a girl in the oven.'

Said the step-mother, 'No—that is a cat.'

Said the Sultan's wife, 'No, but I hear her,' and she went to the oven, and there were the girl's feet sticking out. So she opened the oven and bade her come out.

Said the Sultan's wife, 'Put the clog on the foot of this one.'

And the girl put the clog on her foot, and it fitted perfectly, as a ring fits on a finger.

Then the Sultan's wife said, 'I will take this one for my son.'

And they called the mulla and made the betrothal and there was a marriage for seven days and for seven nights.

XXXVII

THE PRINCE AND THE DAUGHTER
OF THE THORN-SELLER

THERE was once a Sultan who died leaving an only son, aged about fifteen. The youth's mother came to him, and said to him, 'Take a wife, so that I may rejoice in you!' but he would not accept.

One day the young man went out to hunt, accompanied by his slave, and they came to a brook. The prince stooped to drink, and as he did so, his eye fell on a piece of paper lying beside the brook. He lifted it, and gazed at it, and straightway his spirit left him for a time, and he was unconscious. Said the slave to his master, when he had returned to himself, 'O my master, what is it? What ails you?'

Answered the youth, 'Take me back to the palace, for I shall not hunt to-day.'

They returned, and the prince's mother cried to him when she saw him, 'How now! How quickly you have returned from your hunting!'

The prince said to her, 'My mother, do you wish me to marry?'

She answered, 'Aye.'

He said, 'Then I will marry the original of this picture,' and he showed her the paper, for it was a picture that he had found lying on the ground.

Said the mother, 'Oh, my son, your paternal uncle has seven daughters, will you not espouse one of them?'

Answered the youth, 'My cousins are all ugly: and unless I can marry the original of this portrait, I will marry no one.'

The mother was distracted, but she answered, 'Good!' and the next day she went out with a slave, and inquired from door to door if the original of the portrait lived there, but found her not.

Everywhere she looked and inquired, but she met no one who had seen the original of the picture.

Said the mother, 'In the town there is no girl to compare with the beauty of this portrait: I will go out into the chōl.'

So she fared forth into the desert, and in time she met a maiden who saluted her and asked her, 'O bībī, why have you come out into the desert, why have you travelled so far from the town?'

Answered the mother, 'I have come to search for the original of this portrait, for my son is sick of longing for her, and will marry none other.'

Said the girl, 'O bībī, you have reached your goal! In yonder house lives a thorn-seller, with three daughters. The eldest is the original of the portrait, the middle sister is even sweeter than she, and as for the third, when you see her, your understanding will fly from you and you will lose all knowledge of your surroundings.'

Said the queen, 'Truth?'

Answered the maiden, 'Yes, bībī, there is the door, go, and you will find her whom you seek.'

The mother went to the door and knocked and the thorn-seller's wife opened, and bade her welcome, 'Deign to enter!' and gave her a mattress to sit on. Then the woman called her eldest daughter, saying, 'Our guest is tired, bring her water.'

The girl came with water, and the dame looked at her and then at the picture, and lo! it was the two halves of a bean!

Then the woman called to her second daughter, and bade her bring sherbet, and when the dame saw the second girl she perceived that she was even lovelier than the first. Then the woman called her youngest daughter, and told her to bring the coffee, and when the dame perceived this third daughter, she was rapt out of herself, and exclaimed, 'Can such beauty exist in this world!' and she could not endure to look at the girl, being abashed in the presence of such loveliness, for the girl might have said to the moon, 'Absent yourself, and I will shine in your place.'

Then the dame opened her mind to the thorn-seller's wife, and said, 'I have an only son, and I have come to betroth your daughter to him.'

Replied the thorn-seller's wife, 'I and my daughters are before you! Take which of us you wish!'

Said the dame, 'I will take the youngest! Do not give her gear or presents, for I will give her all that she needs, and she shall be adorned with pearls and diamonds and gold. After fifteen days, when I have arranged the house, and prepared a wedding feast, and bought her clothes, and invited the guests, I will send for the girl.'

Said the thorn-seller's wife, 'As you command!'

And the dame returned to the palace, where her son was awaiting her.

Said he, 'Ha, did you find the owner of this picture?'

Answered his mother, 'I have found her! I went into the desert, and to the house of a thorn-seller, and this picture is of his eldest daughter. The second is even lovelier than she, and as for the third, the youngest daughter, she is so exquisite that when I saw her my senses left me and I swooned away.'

Said the prince, '*Suduq?* Truth?'

Answered she, 'Aye! And I shall call the mulla and betroth you to the youngest of the three.'

The next day the mother began her preparations: she called a painter and told him to paint the house, and a carpenter, and told him to make furniture, and a flocker and told him to flock a mattress, and the servants she told to clean the house and spread carpets and prepare for a feast. From the jeweller she ordered jewels, and from the robe-makers dresses, and from the 'aba-makers, 'abas. The wedding-chamber was complete by the end of the fortnight, and guests were invited for the coming of the bride. How pleased she was that her son was to marry!

The day came when the bride was to arrive, and when she came to the house, all the guests were astonished at the beauty of the girl, one gazing after the other, and crying, 'Was there ever such a lovely creature!'

The prince went to the hammām with his slave, and as he was returning, he had to pass beneath the windows[1] of

---

[1] *shenāshīl*—windows jutting out over the street, and protected by

his uncle's daughters. They saw him, and began to talk as if they knew not that he could hear them.

Said the eldest, 'Did you see our cousin's bride?'

Said the second, 'Yes, and never did I behold such ugliness!'

Said the third, 'She is crooked!'

Said the fourth, 'She is blind!'

Said the fifth, 'She is black!'

Said the sixth, 'Her nose is awry (*kachma*).'

Said the seventh, 'She has no teeth.'

The young man stopped and heard what they were saying, and he said within himself, 'My cousins seem to have had a glimpse of the bride as she passed by, and I fear that my mother has deceived me. My bride is not the beauty that she led me to expect, but as ugly as they have said!'

And he was very angry, and sent his slave to the palace with this message to his mother:

'You have brought a bride hither, marry her to whom you will, I will have none of her!' and he went to his country house[1] without the town and came not to the palace where the wedding guests were assembled and the bride waiting.

The slave went to the palace, and going to the prince's mother, he said to her, 'My master says, "You have brought a bride to the house, marry her to whom you wish, for I will have none of her!" and he has gone to his country house in anger.'

The prince's mother was greatly troubled, and asked the slave,

'With whom did he speak? Whom has he seen?'

The slave replied, 'He has spoken with none.'

She did not know what she should do, for the guests were there, and the music was playing, and a feast being prepared, and the bride ready in her chamber. She knew

---

lattices. This type of window is common in Baghdad, and is especially for the use of women, who can see without being seen.

[1] *qasr* is the term used for a large house: it does not mean castle, as it is sometimes translated.

her son's nature, and that when he was angry he was so obstinate that nothing would change his mind, so she said nothing, but returned to the guests and told them, 'My son will come afterwards,' and did not let them know that which had passed. When all had gone, she went to the bride and said, 'My daughter, my son is angry with me, and perhaps he will not come to you to-night! To-morrow, if God wills! And you, go, take off your clothes, and go to bed.'

The girl did as she had said: she took off her clothes, and folded them, and that night she slept alone.

The next day it was the same, the prince remained in his house, and the bride and her mother-in-law in the palace, and so it was the second day, the third day, the first week, the first month, one year, three years! And all the while his mother knew nothing of what had angered him.

Now one day the son of a neighbouring Sultan was to be married, and his mother and relatives sent to the palace to invite the ladies to be present. According to the custom of that country, a guest to a wedding must spend seven days with the hosts, and the prince's mother wished to go to the marriage. But her daughter-in-law could not go, for a bride may not visit a bride: it is shame.[1]

So the woman said to her daughter-in-law, 'My daughter, I am invited to a wedding, and am obliged to leave you here alone. I shall pray to Allah that my son may be appeased and reconciled to us! And as for you, stay here: here are the keys of the house, open whatever you like, and amuse yourself as best you can, and after seven days I shall return. Perhaps my visit may bring us better fortune.'

Answered the bride, 'Go, my mother, go! Do not trouble about me!'

So the mother-in-law took her road, and the bride was alone in the house.

---

[1] It brings ill fortune to both, and magic must be employed to undo the evil. I shall give the details of the charm in a future book, as they are too lengthy for a foot-note.

A street in Baghdad
with jutting windows (*shenāshīl*)

Spinning cotton. The clay ovens are being dried in the
sun before being baked

The next day the girl called her groom, and said to him, 'Can you keep a secret?'

Answered the groom, 'Yes, lady, whatever you wish!'

Said she, 'I will enrich you, and Allah is the Bountiful! What I ask is this, go and get me a handsome mare, the finest mare that you can find.'

Said he, 'On my eyes and head!' and departed and brought the mare.

Then she opened a chest, and took out a rich zibūn,[1] an 'aba, an embroidered belt, and a handsome fīna,[2] and a purse of gold, and she put on these male clothes, and put the purse in her bosom. When she was ready,

> *Subhān Allah ar rabb, al khāliq*
> *Wal khāliq ahsan!*

> Praise to God, the Lord, the Creator,
> He who creates is better than his creation!

she was a youth so exquisite, that as she rode the mare through the streets, the passers-by gazed bemused and could not take their eyes from her. Said one to the other, 'What sweetness! What beauty!'

So she came to the house of the prince, and knocked at the garden gate. Cried the gardener, 'Who is it?'

Answered the girl,

> *Ana khashab al azhar*
> *Kul men yashūfni yiskar*
> *Shedda warid asfar*
> *U bi ghāzi[3] dhahab āhmar*

> 'A spray of blossom is this elf (*lit.* am I),
> Who sees me straight forgets himself (*lit.* becomes intoxicated),
> (O you who in this garden delve,)
> For yellow flowers, here 's golden pelf.'

The gardener opened the gate, and when he saw the beautiful youth, he was as if intoxicated, and he gathered the bunch of yellow flowers which the youth asked of him.

---

[1] See note, p. 148. [2] Skull-cap, of red felt.
[3] Ghāzi is a small gold coin.

Whilst he was so employed, the youth rode his mare backwards and forwards amongst the flowers, slashing at them with his stick, and treading them underfoot. Then he came back to the gardener, took the bouquet, threw him a handful of gold, and left.

The Sultan's son looked out of the window of the harem and saw that there was havoc in the garden. Roses lay here, and lilies there. He called the gardener and said to him,

'Gardener! What is this? Who has done this to the garden? And where were you?'

Answered the gardener, 'Oh, Sultan! My son was sick, and I went to him. He died and I had to bury him, and when I got back the garden was as you see!'

The young man said, 'Put the garden straight,' and the gardener worked and swept the paths, and put the flower-beds in order, and watered it, and did all he could to repair the damage.

The next day the girl called to the groom, 'Go, bring the mare as before,' and when he had brought it, she dressed herself in man's clothes and rode through the town until she came to her husband's house. There she knocked at the garden gate, and the gardener cried, 'Who is it, who?'

She answered,

'A spray of blossom is this elf,
Who sees me straight forgets himself,
Oh, you who in this garden delve,
For yellow flowers, here's golden pelf.'

The gardener opened the door, and he went to pick her the flowers she asked, while she, as before, rode hither and thither over the flowers, striking them down with her stick and trampling them under her mare's feet. Then she went to the gardener, took the flowers, threw him a handful of gold, and went.

Then the Sultan's son looked out of the window, and saw the garden in worse case than ever, such havoc had been wrought, and he was furious and sent for the gardener.

Said he, 'Dog! Son of a dog! Come here, you accursed one! Who is dead to-day? Is it your mother?'

Answered the gardener,

'Sultan! Give me your judgement and mercy!'

He said, 'Speak!'

Spoke the gardener, 'For the past two days, there comes to this garden a youth, such a youth! Sweet, sweet, sweet! From the day I was born never have I clapped eyes on such beauty! He comes and knocks at the door and says,

"*Ana khashab al azhar
Kul men yashūfni yiskar
Shedda warid asfar
U bi ghāzi dhahab āhmar!*"

and when I open to him, and pluck him flowers, he rides his mare over the garden and makes havoc as you have seen.'

Asked the prince, 'Why did you not tell me this yesterday?'

Answered the gardener, 'O Sultan, I was afraid, and I thought he might not come another day!'

Said the prince, 'If he comes to-morrow, tell him, "His highness wants you," and if you do not bring him before me, you shall lose a hand!'

Answered the gardener, 'Good.'

The third day the girl called the groom as before, and bade him bring the mare, and when he had brought it, she donned man's clothes and rode through the streets to her husband's home. There she knocked at the door, and when the gardener asked, 'Who is it?' she answered with the same verse.

He opened to her, then he ran and told his master, 'The boy has come!'

The prince followed him, and when he saw the lad, astonishment overcame him, and he cried:

'Does this world possess such loveliness?' and he embraced him, and said, 'You are my guest, welcome!' and was undone and amazed by the boy's beauty, and led him to his diwān.

There he plied him with sweets, and jam, and sherbet, and coffee, fondling him and endearing him, and saying to him,

'Come every day, we will amuse ourselves together!'

Answered the lad, 'Good, gladly will I come! But I ask your pardon for that I did to your garden!'

Said the prince, 'I and my garden and the gardener are at your feet, do with us as you will. Only come here every day and amuse yourself with us.'

The boy asked after a little, 'Do you know how to play chess?'

Replied the prince, 'Yes, I know.'

Said the lad, 'We will play, you and I, but on a condition.'

Said the prince, 'Your pleasure! What is it?'

Said he, 'If I win, make a feast for me in your palace!'

Answered the prince, 'I do not go more to the palace, for I have quarrelled with my mother, but for your sake I will do what you ask!'

They played chess, *dī, dī, dī!* and at last the lad won, but in moving a piece, he managed to scratch his finger. So enamoured was the prince of his guest that he took off the costly embroidered shawl which was round his waist, and tore off a piece to bind the finger, and wrapped it round tenderly. Great was his love for him!

At last the lad said, 'My people will wonder where I am tarrying, I must return.'

Said the prince, 'It is early, and I cannot endure to part with you!'

Answered the boy, 'I have been long away, and must return.'

Said the prince, 'This night you are invited to my palace, will you come?'

Replied the lad, 'I will come, why should I not come? Gladly! This night I will come to you!'

And the prince walked with him to the door of the garden, entreating him, and watched him till he was out of sight, for indeed he was like a madman for love of the

boy[1] and could think of nothing else. As for the lad, the
bride in disguise, when she returned, she took her man's
clothes off, and gave a handful of gold to the groom.

This. And as for the mother-in-law, who was at the
wedding, she had told the women there of her trouble,
and they had comforted her, saying, 'Allah is the Opener!
He is the Merciful! Perhaps our wedding will bring you
good fortune.'

And the mother sighed and said, 'My son is obstinate,
but, *min sā'a ila sā'a farj!* (78) But hourly God works
deliverance!'

As for her son, he called his slave, and said 'Feyrūz!
Go to my palace, and tell my mother that there will be
a feast at the palace to-night. They must prepare the
dishes and make all ready!'

When he heard that, the slave was delighted, and rejoiced, and ran until he reached the door of the palace.
There he knocked and cried, 'My lady, my lady! My
master has sent me to say that there will be a party to-
night in this house.'

They answered him, 'Our mistress is away at a
wedding!' and they told him where to find her, saying,
'Go, tell her!'

The slave went to the other Sultan's house and knocked
at the door, and when he saw his lady, he cried, 'My lady,
my lady, my master wishes to make a party to-night in
the house, and wishes you to see that everything is
ready!'

How the mother rejoiced! Her joy was immense! and
the ladies her friends said, 'Did we not tell you our
wedding would bring you luck!'

She went quickly to the house, and sent for the cook,
and told the servants to kill and prepare a lamb, and geese,
and ducks, and chickens, and turkeys, and to make pilaus,[2]

---

[1] Said the narrator, parenthetically, in explanation,

'Allah yahibb al helu!
God loves the beautiful!'

[2] A dish of meat or chicken cooked in melted butter with rice, almonds, and
sultana raisins.

and 'bitter-sweet',[1] and every dish and sweetmeat necessary for a feast.

Then she said to the bride, 'Go to the bath, and put on your wedding dress, for your husband is coming.'

And they set tables, and decorated the rooms.

When all was ready, the bride sat in the marriage chamber adorned with jewels and diamonds—she and the letrïk shone together in the room!

Dï! At two hours after sunset the Sultan's son came from his house, and walked up and down on the upper terrace[2] waiting impatiently for the boy. In his walking he passed by the bridal chamber, but thought not of his bride.

Presently as he passed he heard a sound of moaning, and at last he cried, 'Is there pain? Does your heart pain you?'

Answered the bride from within, 'There is pain. And he tore his shawl and bound my finger!'

He understood her words, and opened the door, crying, 'Allah, was it she?'

And when he beheld her, his understanding fled from him, and he fell at her feet, crying, 'Was it you?'

She answered him, 'My husband, why have you kept me imprisoned and alone these three years?'

Then there were wedding festivities for seven days and seven nights, and guests were entertained, and the drums beat, and the music played.

And the bridegroom cried, 'O all you who love me and wish my presence, bring straw and bitumen and oil, and put them in the stable cistern!'

They brought them, and then he caused his cousins to be fetched thither, and put them into the cistern with the bitumen and oil, and burnt them all alive.

---

[1] A Turkish dish, a meat stew with sweet dried fruit, cooked together.

[2] The *tarma* is the gallery which runs round the upper story above the courtyard.

XXXVIII

UHDEYDĀN, UCHʿEYBĀN, AND UNKHEYLĀN

Kān u mā kān
ʿAla Allah at Tuklān.

THERE were once three brothers, called Uhdeydān, Uchʿeybān, and Unkheylān (Little Iron, Little Knucklebone, and Little Bran). One day they said to each other, 'Come, let us build ourselves houses.' Said Little Iron, 'I will build my house of iron, and the door of iron.' Said Little Knucklebone, 'I will build my house of knucklebones, and the door of knucklebones.' Said Little Bran, 'I will build my house of bran, and the door of bran.' And each brother built himself a house and lived in it.

Now a sʿilūwa[1] lived near them, and one day, feeling hungry, she came to eat them up. First she went to the house of Little Bran, and cried outside his door.

'Little Bran, Little Bran, open your door, I have come to give you a treat!'

But Little Bran knew her voice, and he called out:

> 'Fūti! adurrati, u dam adurrati
> Inshaqqi wa atkhaīyati!
>
> (Untranslatable abuse)
> Go away! . . . Tear yourself
> And sew yourself up again!'

The sʿilūwa said 'Oh! You talk like that, do you!' and she blew at the door. The bran flew in all directions, and she went in, ate him up, and went away.

The next day she felt hungry again, and so she went to Little Knucklebone's house, and knocked at his door, crying,

'Little Knucklebone, Little Knucklebone, open your door so that I may come in and give you a treat!'

---

[1] See Preface, p. xi.

Little Knucklebone answered,

'Go away. . . . Tear yourself and sew yourself up again! Why should I open the door for you to come in and eat me up?'

Said the sʿilūwa, 'Truth?' and she butted with her head at the door. It fell down, and she entered, ate him all up, and returned to her home.

The third day she went to Little Iron's[1] house, and she said, 'Little Iron, Little Iron, I am invited to the Sultan's house! Come with me: there is a wedding there, and there will be a feast, with lots of good things!'

Little Iron replied, like his brothers, 'Go away. . . . Tear yourself and sew yourself up again! You want to eat me! Go you to the Sultan's palace, but I won't come with you!'

The sʿilūwa left his house, and went to the Sultan's palace. She seated herself near the door, and began to eat the bones and dirt that they threw out into the road. Little Iron had followed her, and hid close by. When she was not looking, he took up a big bone that had been thrown out on to the road, and hurled it at the sʿilūwa's head. The blood ran down her face, and she licked it with her tongue and said, 'How good this blood tastes! Ah! Little Iron's blood will taste like this!'

Little Iron burst out laughing, and ran back to his house and locked the door securely.

After a little she returned to Little Iron's house and began to wail outside the door, 'Little Iron, Little Iron! I've been to the Sultan's house, to the wedding feast, and I've eaten kubbeh,[2] and lamb and turkey and pilau,[3] kebāb and many other good things and succulent dishes. Come! There is still some for you!'

He replied, 'Off with you! Off with you! You have been eating refuse outside the Sultan's palace, and I threw a bone at you which made your forehead bleed, and you said, as you licked your own blood, "How good Little Iron's blood will taste!"'

---

[1] *Iron*, and even the utterance of the word iron (*hadīd*) is supposed to rob the *jinni* world of their power. See notes on 'The Crystal Ship', pp. 293–4.

[2] See note 2, p. 3.   [3] See p. 203.

The sᶜilūwa cried '*Eya bā!* It was you who threw it? It was you?'

Little Iron said, 'Aye, it was I? so off with you!'

She went, but the next day she returned and knocked at his door, and said, 'Little Iron, Little Iron! I am invited to the Sultan's garden to eat fruit. There are mulberries there, quinces, apples, grapes—every fruit that can be found in the world is in his garden. Come with me, and we will eat our fill!'

Little Iron said, 'Go away, eat your fruit, I am not going with you.'

So she took her way, and fetched her daughter, (for she had a daughter), and went to the Sultan's orchard.

Little Iron disguised himself, and went quickly to the orchard after them. It was as the sᶜilūwa had said, there was fruit of every kind in the orchard, melons and watermelons and the rest, but the gardeners would not allow the sᶜilūwa to eat of the fruit on the trees. So she and her daughter crept about eating the rotten fruit and the peel which had been thrown away.

Little Iron watched her from a distance. Then he took a very large water-melon, cut it in half, scooped out the fruit, got inside it, and put the other half on top of him, so that it looked like whole fruit. When the sᶜilūwa espied this big melon lying beneath the trees, she cried to her daughter to come and carry it home.

The sᶜilūwa's daughter came, and tied the big melon up in her ᶜaba, and put it on her head. Then she and her mother set out for their house. On the road, Little Iron wished to make water, and he did so. The sᶜilūwa's daughter cried, 'O my mother, O my mother, Little Iron has made water on me!'

But the sᶜilūwa answered, 'Pass on, pass on! Little Iron is in his house, how could he make water upon you? If Allah pleases, one day we shall eat him.'

They went on, the sᶜilūwa's daughter grumbled to her mother, 'How heavy this melon is!'

When they reached their house, the sᶜilūwa said to her

daughter, 'Go and wash that water-melon, for we shall eat it for supper.'

The girl opened her 'aba, and took out the melon, and as she was about to cut it, out sprang Little Iron!

The sʻilūwa's daughter cried to her mother, 'There! Didn't I tell you that Little Iron had made water upon me?'

How glad they were that they had got Little Iron at last! They seized him and held him and the sʻilūwa said, 'Now we will eat you up! My daughter will have one half of you, and I the other half!'

Little Iron said, 'You would be foolish to eat me now! See how thin I am—there is hardly any flesh on my bones. Keep me for a week, and fatten me up, then I shall be worth eating!'

The sʻilūwa said, 'Aye! Truth! We'll leave him a little.'

Her daughter said, 'Don't leave him, you had better kill him now.'

But the sʻilūwa wished to fatten him, so she kept him tied up. At the end of three days, she said, 'I am going to the garden of the Sultan to get a few vegetables to eat with Little Iron when we stew him. Make ready a pot of water, and let it boil, and when it is boiling, throw Little Iron into the pot and let him cook. Then you and I will eat him.'

The daughter answered her, 'Aye.'

When the sʻilūwa had gone, her daughter went and brought the big pot, and lit a fire, and set the pot over it. After a while the water began to boil, and she went to Little Iron and brought him to it.

Little Iron said, 'Before you put me in the pot, let me put on your clothes, and you mine! I want to see if I am like you in your clothes, though you are a handsome girl.'

She agreed, and they changed clothes. He said to her, 'Now I am really a little like you, handsome as you are!' Then he said to her, 'Now throw me in the pot, but first see that the water boils, for I want to die quickly.'

She said, 'Aye!' and went to look in the pot. As she

did so he seized her from behind, and threw her into the pot. Then he sat down and waited for the sʿilūwa. Presently she came to the door, and cried, 'My darling! My dear!'

Little Iron answered, 'Yes, mother.'

Said the sʿilūwa, 'Have you boiled Little Iron?'

Said he, 'Aye, mother, I have boiled him.'

Said the sʿilūwa, 'Then bring bread, so that we can put the meat upon it and eat, for I am very hungry.'

She sat down, and he went to the pot, and put on the bread a slice of the head, with the ear attached, and set it in front of her, and then he went off and hid on the roof.

The sʿilūwa had only taken a mouthful or two before she bit on something hard, and she spat it on to her hand, and saw the ear-ring of her daughter.

She cried, 'What is this! This is my daughter! Woe, woe! I have eaten some of my daughter's head!' She began to mourn and mourn and rushed on to the roof to make hōsa,[1] and acquaint the world with her grief.

But when she reached the roof, she burst—Boom! with her grief, and that was the end of her.

As for Little Iron, he went and took his way to his own little iron house.

---

[1] An outcry. The word is also used in a joyful sense, as when tribesmen come to the shrines on pilgrimage, and dance and chant in the streets.

XXXIX

MELEK MUHAMMAD AND THE OGRE[1]

THERE was once a ruler who had two wives. The one bore him thirty-nine children, but the other only one, and all the forty were sons. The thirty-nine were not clever, and not very amiable, but the fortieth and youngest, whose name was Melek Muhammad, was unusually intelligent and quick, and the ruler loved him more than all his brothers. Time was, and these forty children grew up and became marriageable, but their father, who had grown very old, made no arrangement to marry them. So one day the elder brothers said to Melek Muhammad, 'Go you, as our father loves you so much, and say to him, "My brothers wish to get married. Give each his portion, so that he may take a wife."'

Melek Muhammad did as they asked, and said, 'Bābā, my brothers wish to get married, but they have no portion wherefrom to endow the bride.'

The King said, 'Truth. I will divide my kingdom and give to each his inheritance now, so that he can marry.'

So he divided his property, and gave each brother his portion, saying, 'Go and get married.' To Melek Muhammad he gave nothing, because he had asked nothing.

Then the brothers made up their minds to go out into the world, and Melek Muhammad, too, thought that he would travel. So each set out into the chōl, the brothers together, and Melek Muhammad by himself. Melek Muhammad walked and walked, *meshi, meshi, meshi*, until he came to a country ruled by a Sultan. Melek Muhammad went to the Sultan, and said to him, 'I am a stranger and I wish to earn my bread here. Can I become your servant, and work for you?' The Sultan accepted him into his household, and soon became very fond of him, for he was such an intelligent, capable boy. Before long, the Sultan was always calling for him, and would have none to serve him but Melek Muhammad, for none was

[1] *Deyu.* See Preface, p. xiii.

so clever and willing as he. Now Melek's brothers had also come to that country, and one day he went to see them, and salute them and ask them how they did.

The brothers answered him, 'We have done nothing since we got here, we have been amusing ourselves, and we have spent all our money—not a para remains. Help us to live, for we have nothing left.'

Melek Muhammad promised to do what he could for them, and he went to the Sultan and said to him, 'There are thirty-nine young men come here, they are very poor and have no money left. I beg you let them come to our house and work for you and become your servants.'

The Sultan said, 'Melek Muhammad, as you wish! whatever you wish!' So Melek Muhammad went and fetched his brothers, and they worked with him in the Sultan's house. After they had been there for two days, they became jealous of Melek Muhammad, and went secretly to the Sultan and said, 'You prize Melek Muhammad for his understanding and cleverness. Well, now, if he is so clever and devoted, why does he not get the ogre's tray for you?'

The Sultan said, 'What tray?'

They said, 'There is an ogre who lives in the desert not far away, and he has a tray which, if it be struck, will produce enough food for thousands.'

Said the King, 'But of what use would such a tray be to me?'

Said they, 'Your Majesty, it would feed all your army.'

Said he, 'Aye, truth, that would be very useful to me.'

Then the Sultan called Melek Muhammad and said to him, 'Melek Muhammad!'

He answered, 'Yes!'

Said the Sultan, 'I want you to bring me the ogre's tray.'

Melek Muhammad knew that the Sultan's order must have proceeded from his brothers, but he replied, 'Yes, your majesty, I will go and get it! But I have a request to make of you before I leave.'

The Sultan said, 'Speak!'

Melek Muhammad said, 'While I am gone, I ask your Majesty to shut up those thirty-nine youths that I brought in to work for you. Put them in the sirdab[1] and give them only one loaf of barley bread and a little water apiece for three days. If at the end of the three days I have not returned, kill them all!'

For in his heart, Melek Muhammad thought that he would surely be killed by the ogre, and he wished to be revenged on his brothers.

The Sultan did as he wished, and imprisoned the thirty-nine young men, being ignorant that they were Melek Muhammad's brothers.

The first day passed, and they were given nothing but barley bread and water. And that day Melek Muhammad went, *ardh athattu ardh atshīlu*, until he reached the ogre's cave. Before the cave ran a deep water-channel, and the ogre was inside, sleeping near the tray, which was leaning against the wall of the cave. Melek Muhammad crossed the water, and crept into the cave, then he seized the tray, which began to sing out, 'Tangq! Tangq! Tangq!' Melek Muhammad fled, and jumped across the water,[2] just as the ogre woke and asked, 'What is this? Who is trying to steal you that you are crying out like this?'

The ogre looked, and saw no one, for Melek Muhammad had hidden himself. Then he went to sleep again, and Melek Muhammad came a second time and seized the tray. It cried out as before, and the ogre woke, but Melek Muhammad was so quick that he had leapt the stream and was hidden. Said the ogre, 'Why do you wake me like this? One would imagine that Melek Muhammad had come to steal you! And there is no one here!'

A third time Melek Muhammad came, seized the tray, and it cried out. Again he fled and hid, and this time the ogre, seeing no one, was very angry and said to the tray, 'Why will you not let me sleep?' and he seized the tray

---

[1] See note 1, p. 63.

[2] A *deyu* does not like to (or cannot) cross running water.

and beat it soundly, while Melek Muhammad peeped from his hiding-place. Then the ogre covered his head and slept again, and when Melek Muhammad crossed the bank and seized the tray for the fourth time, it was so indignant that it made no sound. He crossed the stream (sāqia)[1] with it and went back across the desert, to the city of the Sultan. As soon as he had received it, the Sultan was delighted, and clapped him on the shoulder saying, '*Al 'āfiya*, my son! Well done!' and he went to his dīwān with it, and set it on the floor, and struck it. As soon as he had done so, a black slave stepped from the tray and said,

> '*Labbeik, labbeik*
> *Utlub ū temenna!*'

The Sultan said, 'Be filled!' and immediately on the tray there appeared mounds of rice and lambs roasted whole, kubbeh,[2] chickens, creams, sweets, bread, and every kind of food. When they took this away, more appeared, and, just as they had said, the Sultan was able to feed his whole army.

Meanwhile Melek Muhammad freed his brothers from the sirdab, but although he gave them no further punishment for their treachery, they hated him more than before. They went to the Sultan in a few days' time, and said to him, 'O Sultan, Melek Muhammad brought you the ogre's tray without difficulty, why did he not bring the ogre's mare as well?'

Said the Sultan, 'What should I need with a mare? I have mares of the best blood in my stables.'

Said they, 'This is a sea-mare,[3] and it flies through the air like a bird—wherever its rider wishes to go, it flies there!'

Then the Sultan called Melek Muhammad, and he answered 'Yes!'

Said the Sultan, 'Melek Muhammad, I want you to bring me the ogre's mare also.'

---

[1] A *sāqia* or vulg. *sājia* is a small irrigation-channel. A large one carrying pumped water is called a *mahmūl*. A *jedwal* is a wide water-channel or canal. A *qanāt* is a channel flowing underground.

[2] See note 2, p. 3.   [3] See notes, pp. 302 and 303 on story XLVII.

He replied, 'I will go,' but he knew in his heart that his brothers had told the Sultan about the mare. So he said to the Sultan, 'Put those thirty-nine youths in the sirdab and give them nothing but barley bread and water for three days. If at the end of that time I have not returned, kill them.'

The Sultan said, 'As you wish,' and he shut up the nine and thirty in the sirdab. Then Melek Muhammad wished him peace, and set off over the desert to the ogre's cave. When he got there, the ogre was sleeping, and the mare beside him. Melek Muhammad leapt the stream, and placed his hand on the mare's neck, and she whinnied. Melek Muhammad leapt back and hid himself, and the ogre woke and said, 'Has Melek Muhammad come that you are whinnying thus?' Then he went to sleep again. This happened a second and a third time, and the fourth time the ogre, seeing no one, was angry, and cried '*Eysh bīki?* What 's the matter with you?' and beat the mare with his stick. He beat the mare, beat it, *beat* it! Then he went to sleep again (and the sleep of a deyu is very heavy). Melek Muhammad came again and took the mare, and because she was angry with her master, she made no sound. As soon as they had crossed the water, he told her to fly to the Sultan's palace, and she flew in the air until she reached the palace and came down in the courtyard.

The Sultan was delighted, and kissed Melek Muhammad, and cried, 'What a beautiful mare! So handsome and full of race! *'Āl!*'[1] And he put it in his stable.

When he had released his brothers from the sirdab, one said to the other, 'How did he escape from the ogre this time?' Another said, 'There is still a box belonging to the ogre, he will surely not let that be stolen! We will tell the Sultan about the box!'

So they went to the Sultan, and said, 'O Sultan, Melek Muhammad does not serve you well, or he would have brought you the ogre's box.'

Said the Sultan, 'But what should I want with a box?'

[1] A common exclamation indicating 'height of perfection!'.

Said they, 'Ah, this box is the best of all the ogre's treasures! In it is a vast army and wealth therewith to pay them their wages. It would be very useful to you and your Government.'

The Sultan sent for Melek Muhammad, and said to him, 'Melek Muhammad, there is still a box which you have not brought me. Go and bring me the ogre's box.'

Melek Muhammad pondered for a while, and then he answered the Sultan, 'Yes, I will go and fetch the box, but I ask for forty days to perform this task. Imprison the nine-and-thirty for this period, and when it has expired, if I do not return, cut off their heads.'

The Sultan said, '*Zein!* Good!' and imprisoned the brothers as before.

As for Melek Muhammad, he took his way and travelled to the ogre's cave. As before the ogre was sleeping, with his wife beside him, and Melek Muhammad saw that the box was between them, and fastened to the ogre's leg by a chain.

Melek Muhammad crossed the brook, and pondered, 'How shall I take it? How?' He seized the chain, but the box began to cry so shrilly that the ogre rose and asked, 'What is it?'

The box said, 'Melek Muhammad is taking me!'

Said the ogre, '*Shlōn?* How? There is no one here!'

He went to sleep again after a while, and Melek Muhammad came again and touched the chain, and the box cried out, 'He is taking me, he is taking me!'

The ogre said, 'There is no one here!'

Said the box, 'You are not quick enough, he was here and has gone away again! Next time, I shall not cry out, but I will prick you in the leg so that you will wake!'

When he saw the ogre asleep again, Melek Muhammad crossed the stream once more, and took the chain, and the box pricked the leg of the ogre, but kept silence.

The ogre rose, and seized Melek Muhammad before he could escape. He was very angry and roared out, 'How shall I eat you? I have eaten thousands like you!

You stole my tray and my mare, and now you are stealing my box! How shall I eat you?'

Now the sons of Adam are cleverer than demons, and Melek Muhammad answered him, 'No! Don't eat me now! I am thin and ill-nourished! Keep me and fatten me, then I shall be a good meal for you. I am here, if you tie me I cannot get away.'

The ogre replied, 'True!'

So he and his wife brought him game and food of all sorts, and he ate them and grew fat. The ogre said to his wife, 'At last Melek Muhammad is fat, so I will summon my friends to a feast, and we will eat him to-day. We will boil him and feast all our friends and relations!'

His wife said, '*Zein!*' (Good.)

The ogre went and set out to invite his friends and relations, and said to them, 'Come! We are going to eat Melek Muhammad!'

The ogre's wife was left to prepare the feast. She set a large copper pot (siferīya) on the fire, and put fire beneath it and kindled it. Then she brought Melek Muhammad, and said, 'Now I shall put you in the pot.'

Said he, 'First loose me, for I must say my prayers.'

She loosed him, and he said, 'Now see that the water really boils, for if I must die, I wish to die quickly!'

She turned to look at the pot, and he came behind her, and pushed her into the boiling water so that she died. Then he took some of her clothes, and put them on.

The ogre returned, and asked his wife, 'Have you done as I ordered, for our friends are coming?'

Melek Muhammad answered, 'Aye, husband.'

The ogre dipped his hand in to see how the meat was cooking. He drew out a piece of flesh, and in it was an ear-ring! When he saw that, he understood that it was his wife who was cooking there, and in his grief and anger he tried to spring after Melek Muhammad, who had quickly leapt the stream with the box under his arm. The ogre fell into the stream, and was drowned, and that was the end of him.

Melek Muhammad went his way with the box, and as he walked the jinnīya of the box spoke to him and said, 'Are you mad (possessed), or are you simply foolish?'

Said Melek Muhammad, '*Shlōn?* How that?'

Said the jinnīya of the box, 'You owl, why do you give me to the Sultan? Why should you take all this trouble for him, when you could keep me and the treasure that I hold?'

Melek Muhammad began to reflect and said, 'Truth! Why should I?'

Said the jinnīya of the box, 'Why do you not use the army which I contain to master the kingdom? If you are the victor, all the people of the country will come to kiss your hand, and the Sultan will follow their example. You will be a king of kings!'

Melek Muhammad began to think to himself, 'Yes, indeed, I should not have performed these tasks but for the enmity of my brothers! Why should I not profit by it?'

He set the box on the earth and struck it, and out came seven Sultans. Each cried to him:

> '*Labbeik, labbeik*
> *Ana ʿabid bein īdeik!*'

He said to them, 'I have decided to make war with the Sultan, my master, and I need an army so big that it will cover the desert.'

In an instant the army was there. Melek Muhammad rode at its head and came to the wall of the Sultan's city and said that he must speak with the Sultan.

All took him for a strange Sultan, and all were greatly afraid when they saw the huge army that was with him.

When the Sultan had come, Melek Muhammad said to him, 'Resign your kingdom to me, and you shall live in peace all the days of your life: refuse, and you shall die.'

The Sultan did not know him, and he answered, trembling,

'I resign, and thank you for sparing my life.'

Melek Muhammad went to the palace, and took

possession of it, and the tray, and the mare, and took the Government into his hands. He treated the Sultan with such kindness that the Sultan kissed his hands and said, 'My people and I are grateful to you!'

As for Melek Muhammad, he ruled long and well and he made his thirty-nine brothers ministers beneath him.[1]

[1] And so acted piously. One of the clogs on the wheels of progress to-day in 'Iraq is that a man is considered a member of his family rather than an individual. If he takes office, he is expected to do all he can for members of his family, and if he lets family interests influence his judgements or appointments, he is merely fulfilling a natural and pious instinct.

XL

ER RŪM

THERE was once a King and he had a tailor who was very clever at making clothes. Hearing that the tailor had been boasting of his skill, the King sent for him, and when he hastened into the royal presence, the King told him that he must accompany him on a walk without the city. Much flattered, the tailor bowed to the ground, and walked beside his royal master until they were outside the city walls. While they were walking in the desert, the King said to the tailor, 'Pick me up that stone!' and the tailor, wondering, picked up a stone that lay by the wayside.

'Take the stone home with you,' said the King, 'and show your skill by making me a stone coat.'

The tailor was frightened, and protested that no man could make a coat of stone, but at his first word the King feigned great anger and cried, 'If you do not make me a stone coat in three days, I shall hand you over to the executioner.'

In great alarm, and convinced that the King had but invented an excuse to kill him, the tailor returned to his home, and told his family that he was certainly doomed to die as there was no hope that he could contrive a coat out of a piece of rock.

His wife and his three daughters listened, and all but the youngest wept with him as he bewailed his fate. But the youngest daughter sat thinking, and after a little she said to her father,

'Do not weep, my father, I have a plan by which you can escape the anger of the King.' And she instructed her father in what he should do.

The next morning the tailor demanded audience of the King, and when he was admitted bowed low before his Majesty, placing a bag on the ground before him.

'What is this?' asked the King.

Said the tailor, 'Your Majesty, I have completed the

cutting out of the stone coat, and it promises to be a handsome affair. But your Majesty has not furnished me with suitable thread. So I have brought some sand in this bag. If your Majesty will kindly have it manufactured into thread, I will start on the completion of the coat.'

The King burst into laughter, and commended the tailor for his ruse. 'You have saved your head,' said he. 'But you are a fool and cannot have thought out this jest by yourself. Confess who helped your wits.'

'Your Majesty is too astute,' said the tailor. 'In truth, it was not my own thought, but that of my youngest daughter.'

'What is her age?' asked the King.

'Her age is fourteen.'

'Then I will marry this maiden for her wit and she shall live in a handsome house near my own.'

The tailor went home and informed his family of the honour which the King was doing them, and in due time the marriage contract was completed and the bride taken to her new house with much rejoicing and many presents from the bridegroom. But when the moment came for the bridegroom to present himself, he did not come, and the bride waited in loneliness day after day. The King had not seen her, and thought little more about the affair, except that when he went to hunt, he tapped at his bride's window and said, 'O tailor's daughter, how do you do?' And to that she replied that she did very well.

The tailor was grieved for the slight put on his daughter, but for the whims of princes there is no accounting, and the maiden was well provided with gear and money, so that it was not a bad business.

The day came when the King decided to take a voyage to the country of Rūm; and travelling by land and sea he came at last to a fair valley in the pleasant land of Rūm, and there set up his tents.

As soon as she heard that her lord was voyaging, the tailor's daughter disguised herself, and following him, she came to the same place, and set up for herself a magnificent tent. In the evening she walked abroad unveiled, and reached the place where the King had pitched his camp. The King's coffee-maker was sitting by the fire when she passed by, and he was making coffee for the King. When he saw the beauty of the tailor's daughter, his under-standing flew, and without knowing what he did, he put salt instead of sugar into the coffee. When the King tasted the coffee he was angry and sent for the fellow. The coffee-maker confessed his fault, but excused his distrac-tion, by saying that a damsel fairer than the moon had passed as he was making coffee and had cast her glance at the tents. The King was curious when he heard this, and instructed his servants to find out where the beautiful girl lived. They reported to him that she lived in a fine tent in the same valley, and the King at once made haste to visit her. He was hospitably received, and was so charmingly entertained that he could not leave that night, but stayed with his sweet hostess three days and three nights. The third night they played chess, but the King was so deeply enamoured that he thought of his opponent more than of the game, and the lady won. As a prize for her victory, he drew from his finger a costly ring and placed it on hers. At the third dawn, when he still lay sleeping in her tent, the tailor's daughter packed up and set out on the journey home. The King could find no more pleasure in his journey after the disappearance of the beautiful lady, and he too went back to his own country. But he paid no more attention than before to his young bride, unless it were to ask her how she did from below her window when he rode a-hunting.

A year later he sought to allay the restlessness of his heart by another voyage. This time he visited the land of Armenia, and stayed in the town of Erzerūm. Again his forsaken wife followed him, and sending him a mes-senger, she invited him to visit her. Overjoyed at finding the lady he so much loved, the King repaired to her house, and they spent three nights in endearments and merry-making. On the third night, as before she challenged him to a game of chess, and again the King lost. This time he paid for his defeat by giving her the jewelled dagger from his belt, and as on the first occasion, she fled at dawn, leaving the King asleep. Again the disconsolate King returned to his own country and sought to distract his sorrow, but in vain, and a third time he set off for a far country. Once more his neglected wife followed him in disguise, and again he was transported with joy when he rediscovered her. Three days and nights were spent in delight and joy, and the third evening as before she challenged her husband to chess and won the game. As prize he gave her the gold-broidered kerchief from off his royal head, and strove that night not to sleep so that she might not elude him. But she had put henbane in his drink and when he was in a deep sleep, she left him, and returned to her own country, and he, too, angry and disappointed, travelled back to his own land.

For seven long years the young King mourned the fickle lady and then, resolving that he would think no more about her, he resolved to marry a new wife who should bear him children and cause him to forget his heart-sickness. A suitable lady, the daughter of a neighbouring prince, was selected, marriage contracts drawn up, and on the appointed day, the people lined the streets to see the bride and her cavalcade ride in to the city.

Now each year, after her meeting with the King, the tailor's daughter had borne him a child. The eldest was a boy, and she named him Rūm, after the country where she had known her husband. The second, too, was a boy, and him she called Erzerūm. To the third, a girl, she gave the name of Shelhām.

On the day of the King's marriage, she told her children to stand on the steps of the palace, one above the other, near the place where the King was to wait to receive his bride, and she instructed them carefully what to say. Besides this, she placed the ring she had won on the finger of Rūm, the dagger she thrust into Erzerūm's belt, and the kerchief she placed upon Shelhām's head. The three children obeyed their mother's orders, and as soon as the King had arrived, and the cavalcade of the bride was approaching, Rūm cried to his brother, 'Oh, Erzerūm, take care of my sister Shelhām, lest the she-mule step on her!'

Hearing the child's cry, and wondering at what he said, the King called the three to him, and asked them their names. At the same time he saw and recognized his three gifts, and commanded the children that they should tell him how they came into their possession.

The boy Rūm answered boldly, and told him that his mother had bidden him speak as he had spoken, and had girt them with the ring, the dagger, and the kerchief.

'Where is your mother?' asked the King, and he was taken by the three children to the place where their mother sat veiled. The King soon understood that she was in truth the lady to whom he had given his heart in the land of Rūm, and he gave orders forthwith that the bride who had arrived for him was to be sent back to her father's house.

So the tailor's daughter was made happy, and she and her three children were the joy of the King's heart.

XLI

THE COTTON-CARDER
AND KASILŪN (LAZY-BONES)

THERE was once an industrious woman who earned a
living for herself and her family by carding cotton.
Her husband earned nothing, for he was a lazy lout who
did nothing but sleep in the courtyard of the house, and
never went without. All that he did was to clamour for
food, and if his wife did not bring it to him, he would beat
her with his thick stick, which he kept greased with fat
stolen from her kitchen. This stick he called *Al Madhūna*,
'the Greased One', and if she dared to reproach him for
his laziness, he would reply 'Bring me the Greased One',
and as he was powerful and strong she quickly stopped
her scolding and ran off lest she should be beaten.

One day when she was in the sūq, she told a friend of
her troubles, and complained that her husband had become an intolerable burden.

The friend was a wise woman, and said to her, 'Endure
his laziness no longer! When he has left the house, lock
the door and refuse to let him enter until he comes with
money in his hand!'

The cotton-carder[1] said, 'How shall that be, seeing that
he never leaves the house. He never leaves our courtyard,
wallah, the whole day he sleeps!'

Said the old woman, 'Has he a favourite dish, my
sister?'

Said the cotton-carder, 'He is very fond of pācha.'[2]

Said the old woman, 'He is a dog, the son of a dog, and
like the dogs must be led by the nose. Cook some pācha
and throw it outside the door and entice him into the
street, and then close the door upon him.'

The cotton-carder followed the advice of her wise friend
and bought some pācha, which she cooked very suc-
culently. When it was ready, she scattered a little in the

---

[1] *naddāfa*.   [2] See note, p. 28.

courtyard near the corner where her husband slept, and the rest outside the door of their house.

Then she shook him, and while he was yawning and still half asleep, she cried, '*Ya* Kasilūn! See! In the night it has rained pācha!'

He rubbed his eyes and took up the pācha and began to eat.

'Leave this here,' cried his wife, 'Go outside, there is abundance there, and if we don't get it, the neighbours will eat it!'

So he ran to the door, and while the stupid fellow was still gathering up the pācha and cramming it into his mouth, his wife closed the door upon him and bolted it.

'Hey wife,' cried Kasilūn, 'I have picked up pācha enough—come you and get the rest. Open the door, I want to go to sleep again.'

'No, not I!' replied the cotton-carder from within the door. 'I will not open to you until you return, as a man should, with money in your pocket!'

'Bring me the Greased One!' shouted Kasilūn in a great rage, and when she threw him the stick from a window, he rattled at the door and made such a noise that the neighbours gathered to laugh at him. At last, mad with anger, he set off, all bareheaded as he was, and walked far into the desert.

At nightfall, when he was far from Baghdad, he saw a fire, and as he was cold and hungry, he went towards it. Round the fire were sitting seven 'afarīt, and upon the fire a pot was boiling. Now 'afarīt are addicted to human flesh, and when they saw Kasilūn approaching, they said, 'Here is good fortune! This man will make us a meal to-morrow!'

As for Kasilūn, when he saw the pot and smelt the hot meat, he was very pleased, for he had eaten nothing since the pācha that morning; so, approaching them, he wished them peace. They gave him the salutation, and invited him to join them.

Said he, 'I will eat with pleasure, for since it rained pācha this morning, I have not eaten a crumb!' and so saying, he dipped his frozen fingers in the pot and drawing out the lamb that was seething therein, he tore it in half, and devoured it.

After he had eaten he fell asleep, and the 'afarīt, seeing how fat and big he was, decided to kill him the next day so that they would have fresh meat to last them for some time.

The next morning they roused him and said, 'We are going to kill meat soon; go, take this water-skin and fill it with water and return to us so that we can fill the pot ready for the broiling.'

'This will never do,' thought Kasilūn when he saw the big skin that they gave him to fill. 'They will make a water-carrier of me!' So when he had reached the river, he bent as if he were filling it, but in reality he put his lips to it and blew until it was swollen with air and appeared full to the brim. Then, tying it, he began to return with the skin on his shoulders. The 'afarīt expected to see him bowed under the weight of the water, but lo! he walked as if the skin were but a feather. When he was near their tents, however, he sat down, and putting his mouth to the skin, he made as though he were emptying it, and did so until the skin was deflated.

'What sort of a man is this?' said the 'afarīt. 'He drinks more at a draught than an ordinary man in a week!'

They went up to him, and when he saw them, he said that he had drunk the water and was still thirsty, and would go down and refill the skin.

'We will send one of our number,' said the 'afarīt. 'But as you are a strong fellow, we will send you to get the wood to make fire for the pot.'

'Where shall I find the wood?' asked Kasilūn.

'There is a coppice of trees[1] at a little distance from here. One of us will show you where it is.'

'This is very bad,' thought Kasilūn, 'they are making a beast of burden of me!' and he asked for a very long

---

[1] *zōr.* As is explained on p. 38, the term is often applied to a thicket of bushes. I have translated it here 'coppice of trees' because the intention was to illustrate the strength of Kasilūn.

rope. When they had reached the coppice, he said to the 'afrīt who had accompanied him, 'Take this end of the rope and walk round the coppice and come back with it here.'

'Why must I do that?' asked the 'afrīt, but Kasilūn insisted, and as the 'afrīt was afraid of the strength of a man who could drink a water-skin at a draught, he did what was required of him. Then Kasilūn tied the two ends of the rope and bent his back.

'Now we have the wood tied together,' said he, 'hoist it on my back!'

'How can I hoist living trees!' cried the 'afrīt.

'That is nothing,' said Kasilūn. 'I shall do the real work when I carry it back! Hoist the wood on my back and be quick about it!'

'But,' said the 'afrīt, 'we only want a few faggots!'

Then Kasilūn pretended to be very angry. 'What is this?' he said. 'You refuse to hoist a few light trees on to my back? Am I to do all the work? Then I refuse to carry them at all!'

He went back to the camp and told his story as if he were in the utmost indignation.

The 'afarīt became more than ever afraid of him when they heard he had wanted to carry the coppice on his back, and made up their minds to kill him in the night when he was asleep, lest he should prove too much for them.

So that night they took him to their house, and pretending to welcome him, they put him into the best room.

'There is something in this,' thought Kasilūn, who had become suspicious of their intentions, and, when night came, instead of sleeping beneath the fur mantle which they gave him to cast over himself, he went and hid in the tannūr, or oven,[1] from which hiding-place he contrived to overhear his hosts discussing their plot of killing him.

As soon as he understood plainly their intention, he went back to the room, arranged the fur mantle over some

---

[1] See note, p. 192.

carpets so that it had the appearance of a sleeping man, and hid himself in another part of the house. At midnight, the ʿafarīt came with daggers and sticks and attacked the heap all at once, and went out making sure that their guest was dead.

In the morning, Kasīlun greeted them as if nothing had happened, and told them that he had been a little disturbed by mosquito-bites during the night, but that towards morning he had slept peacefully.

The ʿafarīt then resolved on a fresh attempt to kill him. They had in their house a cupboard lined with scimitars, which closed upon the victim when a button was touched without. But Kasīlun overheard their plan from his hiding-place in the oven, and made up his mind that they should die in their own trap. The next day they led him to the door of the cupboard and told him that if he went in, he would find gold and treasure, which would be his from henceforth.

'I am a big man,' said Kasīlun, 'and I could not get into the cupboard.'

The ʿafarīt assured him that he could. 'Why,' said they, 'it would hold six of us!'

'I will believe that when I see it,' said Kasīlun.

So in they went, and when they were safely inside, he pressed the button and the knives closed together and killed them.

There was only one ʿafrīt left, and Kasīlun began to think that as he had disposed of the others so easily, he need not fear him. Indeed the case was entirely otherwise, as the ʿafrīt came to him and implored him to save his life, saying that if he did so he would show him where his brothers had kept their treasure, for it had been their practice to rob caravans in the desert and take possession of the goods of their victims after they had killed and eaten them.

Kasīlun filled a large sack with the stolen gold, and told the ʿafrīt to carry it, for he was going back to his home. Thus they set off together; Kasīlun clad in the rich robes which he had found amongst the stolen goods, and the 'afrīt walking behind like his servant with the sack of gold on his shoulders.

'Life in the desert does not suit me,' said Kasilūn to the 'afrīt. 'There is too much hard work there! One is better off in a town.'

At nightfall he came to his house in the city, knocked at the door, and bade his wife open, telling her that he had returned bringing her some money.

Though she could scarcely believe him, the cotton-carder opened the door.

'Here is a guest, wife,' said Kasilūn; 'and here is a sack of gold. Make us a good meal, for I have hardly had a bite since I went away.'

The cotton-carder prepared a sumptuous meal and they spent three days in feasting and music.

At the end of the three days the 'afrīt said to Kasilūn, 'I want to have a furwa (a skin cloak or coat with hair inside) made, for it is cold.'

Said Kasilūn, 'Go to Hasan the tailor, he will make you a furwa.'

The 'afrīt went and gave the order to the tailor, but each time the 'afrīt went to see if the furwa was ready, the tailor answered '*Bācher!* To-morrow!' At last the 'afrīt went to Kasilūn and said, 'The tailor will not make the furwa that I need for my journey.'

Kasilūn said to the 'afrīt, 'Tell him you are the guest of Kasilūn, and that he must hurry with the work.'

The 'afrīt went to the tailor and said, 'I am the guest of Kasilūn, and you must hurry to finish the furwa!'

The tailor knew Kasilūn as a good-for-nothing and lazy man, and when the 'afrīt said this, he began to laugh in the 'afrīt's face, saying, 'I am not afraid of Kasilūn! He is always asleep! Come, we will go together, and will talk to him in his own house!'

So the tailor and the 'afrīt went together to Kasilūn's house, and the tailor knocked at the door and calling to Kasilūn bade him open the door as he was not afraid of him. When Kasilūn heard, he roared out to his wife, 'Wife, bring me the Greased One!' And the tailor had his hand on the door to open it, the 'afrīt being beside him. When the 'afrīt heard Kasilūn call for his stick, however, he pulled the tailor back in fear, and Kasilūn coming out and seizing the tailor by the other hand, the tailor was torn in two pieces, and the 'afrīt took one half and ran away in mortal fear and never came back!

XLII

BUNAYYA

THERE was once a shaikh, a wealthy man, head of a tribe connected with the Shammar. He had several wives, but none of them had a son which survived, although seven daughters lived out of the children which they bore him. But when the shaikh was getting on in years, one of his wives became pregnant, and bore a son, to whom they gave the name Bunayya, which means Little Girl, so that the 'Breath'[1] should not blight him. He was strong and grew big, and the shaikh, who prized him above all that he had, sent him while still young to Constantinople, so that he should learn to read and write and become acquainted with the ways of the world. Every month he dictated him a letter by the hand of his mulla (for he himself could not read or write), and sent him money, and the boy remained in Stambūl. There he learned to live like the Franks, and to wear Frankish clothes, and to read many books. He was intelligent and loved his studies, and when he had reached the age of eighteen, and his father wrote to him to come back to his people, he wept and wrote that he would rather remain where he was. But his father was troubled, for he knew that his son must become shaikh in his stead when he was dead, and he did not wish him to forget his people: moreover, his heart yearned for the boy. So he sent him a letter urging him to come back, and promising him that if he returned to the tribe he might go again from time to time to Stambūl. Bunayya was forced to fall in with his father's wishes, and, as his father had said that he might bring some friends

[1] Bunayya (or Ibnayya) is commonly used in 'Iraq for a girl-child. 'The Breath' is like 'the Eye' (or evil eye), it is ill-luck brought by envy, whether innocent or malignant. To give a boy (in public) a girl's name, or to dress him like a girl in order to avert ill-fortune is a common practice in 'Iraq. The tribes (especially Marsh Arabs) are fond of giving their children extraordinary names indicating worthlessness or uselessness with this purpose, e.g. 'No-Good', 'Whooping-Cough', 'Dog', 'Jackal', 'Fox', 'Not-Wanted', and 'Flea'. The car having now become a commonplace, 'Buncture' has recently become popular, both as a term of reproach and as a nickname.

with him, he brought four or five boys of his own age, with servants to look after them, a cook to give them the food to which they were accustomed, camp-beds, meat and fruit in tins, Frankish bedding, chairs, and other things from Stambūl. They travelled, and when the father knew by his agent in the nearest town that they had arrived, and would travel out to the tribe the next day, he and his horsemen rode to meet them. When they saw them, they galloped backwards and forwards on their mares, and fired their guns into the air, and made a fantasīa.[1] So they rode together back to the place where the tribe had their houses of hair. That night they made a big feast in the guest tent for them; sheep were killed and roasted whole, and dishes of rice and kishk[2] and kirsha[3] were served, with plenty of laban[4] and shenīna.

The shaikh ate with his son and his guests, and for Bunayya and the strangers they set spoons and forks, since they were not accustomed to eat with their hands in the manner of the Bedu. Bunayya's friends were very pleased with their entertainment: it was the first time they had ever known life in the desert; and they went riding, and took hawk and salūgis and chased bustard and gazelle, and in the evening they played the 'ūd,[5] or listened to the Arabs playing the rebāba[6] and singing, and amused themselves and laughed and sang. They praised the life of the chōl, and then, after about ten days, they went away, and said farewell to Bunayya and his father.

Bunayya enjoyed himself very much while his friends were there, but when they were gone, what could he do? He read in his books a little, but he wearied of riding and hunting, and there was no cinema or coffee-house, no friends to whom he could talk. He found the men ignorant, for they knew nothing of the books from which he had been taught. He thought them animals: wild and

[1] Display of horsemanship.   [2] A kind of porridge-cake.
[3] Haggis. Rice is put into the haggis, but, of course, no spirit.
[4] See notes, p. 176.
[5] Lute. This is an instrument shaped like a mandoline, and often very elaborately embellished.
[6] A kind of fiddle, held like a 'cello, except that the player sits on the ground.

boorish. His mother and the women he found worse still: they were yet more ignorant than the men, and they were dirty and foolish in his eyes. He grew tired and wearied, and wished for Stambūl.

His father saw it, and was sad. He pondered as to what he should do to keep his son with him. And one day he called Bunayya and said, 'Bunayya, I am old, and I want to see your son. I want you to marry.'

Bunayya replied, 'I am young: I do not wish to marry.'

Said the shaikh, 'But I am afraid that I shall die, and I wish you to beget me a grandson. Marry and rejoice my heart.'

Said Bunayya, 'Whom should I marry here? Let me return to Stambūl, and I will marry a girl there.'

The shaikh replied, 'That cannot be, until you have a son of our own blood. First marry a cousin, so that she may bring you a son, and afterwards you can take a Turk or a Frank or whomsoever you desire.'

They talked, and the boy was angry, but in the end he had to accept what his father said, and agreed that he would marry, if the next year he might return to Stambūl on a visit.

The shaikh, his father, began to make inquiries everywhere among their kin for a bride for him. He wished to find a girl who was more than usually beautiful and intelligent, so that his son might love her, and wish to stay for her sake. He asked, and they told him, 'Your cousin, Ibrahīm of the Beni——, has one daughter among seven sons. He loves her very much, and she has been brought up like the light of his eyes. He loves her more than the breath in his body. The girl is beautiful, and for intelligence there is not her equal. She knows how to write, her father's mulla has taught her all that he knows, she can read the Qur'ān, and she can strike the lute.'

Bunayya's father was pleased with what they told him, and he sent to his cousin her father and asked him to give her, and her father consented.

On the day appointed they brought the bride, and a great company of her kinsfolk and servants rode with her,

and she arrived, seated within her canopy[1] on a camel.
They took her with cries of joy to the bridal tent, which,
as custom orders, is apart from the rest. They washed
her, and they washed her hair and greased it with butter
boiled and strained, and rubbed into it rashūsh.[2] They
put henna on her hands and feet, they placed on her head
the watīa, the gold head-dress, they threaded gold ornaments and beads into her plaits, they adorned her with
ornaments and pearls, they placed a necklace round her
neck and chains of wrought gold to fall on her bosom.
On her toes were fatkhāt[3] (toe-rings) and they perfumed
her clothes with oil of roses and oil of jasmine. Her 'aba
was embroidered with needlework, her hāshimi[4] was of
woven silk, her dishdasha[5] was of fine linen. Such is the
way we dress brides in our tribe! She was sweet, sweet,
sweet! and her age was twelve years.

But the boy, Bunayya, was sad and angry. He said,
'These Bedu women are animals! they are dirty: they have
lice, they put their hands in the rice and it remains sticking
in their rings!'

Only because his father had insisted, had he agreed
to the marriage. When they brought him to the bride,
he did not even look at her. They said to each other, 'He
is shy before us!' and they went and left them alone, for
he told them to go.

The bride sat on her mattress and he sat on another and
smoked a cigarette and said no word to her. He was
dressed in Frankish clothes. He wore a fez on his head,
a coat and trousers, and collar and tie; but they had made
him carry a fine dagger[6] with a handle studded with

---

[1] The canopy is formed of wooden hoops covered with woven cloth or wool.

[2] Pink roses dried and powdered between two milling stones and then mixed
with saffron or musk.

[3] The word *fatkha* is more usually applied to a certain kind of ring worn on
the forefinger. The ordinary word for toe-ring is *'athra*. It is usually worn on
the great toe and attached to the khilkhal or anklet by a thin silver chain. This
was in great vogue amongst nomadic and semi-domesticated Arab women some
twenty years ago, but is now démodé.

[4] Outer robe; with the tribes, hand-embroidered.   [5] Chemise.

[6] A metal instrument keeps away evil spirits (see note on 'The Crystal Ship',
pp. 293, 294), and the blue of the turquoise averts the evil eye. In Baghdad it is

turquoises to keep off the jānn. There they sat, the one with the other, and neither said a word. Presently he put out the lantern and slept on the mattress upon which he had been sitting. The bride, whose name was Māi, saw him and she loved him. She waited until she was sure that he was asleep, and then she called to an old woman of her family who was waiting outside the tent, and she spoke with her, and persuaded her to put pigeon's blood on the mendīl.[1] She told the woman that it was better so, lest there should be talk, and she knew that she would be secret.

In the morning, the boy Bunayya rose early and went out, and presently they came to her and said, '*Tawennestum?* Had you pleasure together?' and she answered, 'We had pleasure.' To them she pretended to be happy, but her heart was anxious, and she said to herself, 'Perhaps to-night.'

But when the night came, it was the same. He came, and smoked, and read his book a little, then he went to sleep, and to Māi, the unfortunate! he did not raise his eyes. She said to herself, 'If my father and brothers were to know that he slights me, they would be very angry, and they would insist on a divorce. Better that I say nothing: perhaps in time he will love me.'

The sisters of Bunayya made much of Māi and she behaved as if she were happy lest they should suspect the real state of things. She laughed and answered them gaily when they asked her, 'How is he? Do you love him?' No one knew how it was between them. When they perceived that he never approached her before them, and never looked at her, they thought, 'In Stambūl it is perhaps shame for a bridegroom to look at the bride or talk to her before the people.'

So it was for three months: then the boy said to his father, 'My father, I wish to go to Stambūl, and after a little I will come back again.'

customary to place a knife between the upper and lower mattress of the bridal bed on the day of the bride's arrival at her husband's house, or beneath her pillow.

[1] The proof of virginity produced the next morning and shown to the bridegroom's family. The *mendīl* (kerchief) is often placed by the bridal bed in a silken cover.

His father said, 'And Māi?'

Said Bunayya, 'Let her return to her people for a little.'

His father was sad, and reasoned with him, 'Your wife is not yet pregnant, will you go away now?'

He replied, 'She is yet young, and I will come back.'

He went, and travelled to Stambūl, and there he stayed for two years. His father sent him money every month, and wrote him letters by the mulla asking that he should come back, but Bunayya did not wish to leave Stambūl. At the end of two years, at the beginning of the spring, he yielded to his father, and set off on the journey to his home, and he brought ten friends with him. As before, they brought with them their own tents, and carpets, and camp-bedsteads, and food in tins, and a cook and servants. Bunayya's father was rich, and he did not stint him in money.

As on the first occasion, the tribesmen came to meet them, and they made fantasīa, riding their horses and firing their guns into the air. It was the spring, and the flowers of the desert were in bloom and the 'ushub[1] was high and the air was fresh and sweet. His friends said to Bunayya, 'How lovely the desert is! how fine is the life of the Bedu! how pure is the air!' The shaikh made them a great feast and treated them with all welcome and hospitality, and day after day passed in hunting and riding.

Now the story returns to Māi. She, the unfortunate one, when she returned to her people, who met her with great joy and fired their guns for her, made a good face, and answered their questions 'I am happy! My husband is kind to me. I love him.' They said to her, 'Are you yet pregnant?' She replied, 'I have not yet become pregnant.'

Now Māi's eldest brother, 'Aun, when Māi was only a little child, had married a girl called Latīfa. This Latīfa had loved Māi like her little sister, and Māi had always been constantly with her in 'Aun's tent. The night after Māi's arrival to her people, Latīfa came after the others had gone to sleep to talk with Māi, and said to her, 'Truly, oh Māi, are you happy with Bunayya?'

[1] Spring herbage.

Shammar tribesmen eating

A shaikh's wife and her servants. She is the central standing figure

Then Māi's eyes fell, and she began to weep, and she wept bitterly.

And Latīfa said, 'Do you love him, oh Māi?'

Māi replied, 'I love him, but he does not love me, and he has never taken me.' Then she told Latīfa the whole story from the night of her wedding till her return. Latīfa said, 'You must tell your father this. Who is Bunayya, that he should put this blackness upon you, the daughter of your father? We are no common tribe: the blood of the Prophet is in your father's veins!'

Māi answered her, 'For the sake of Allah, say nothing! If my father knows it, he will be very angry and will make me divorce Bunayya, and I love him! Even for me to look at him is something, though he will never look at me. My father and brothers must not know, or they will want to kill Bunayya. Tell no one!'

So Latīfa told no one, not even 'Aun her husband, though her heart was hot for Māi's unhappiness. When her family saw Māi sometimes sad, they said, 'The poor one! she loves her husband, and he is forced to leave her!'

So the two years of Bunayya's absence passed.

When Bunayya returned, his father said to him, 'Will you go and fetch Māi from her people?'

Bunayya answered, 'I cannot fetch her now that my friends are here.'

His father was silent, not wishing to cross him so soon after his arrival. The days went on, and it was the middle of April, when the 'ushub was highest, and the flowers most plentiful. The young men agreed that they should make a journey of a day or two to a place named Tās where there was plenty of game, so that they could get better sport than where they were camped. So they took tents, military tents for themselves and houses-of-hair for the servants, and tribesmen who went with them, and horses, and salūgis,[1] and all that was necessary, and they set off, the young men and their following, but the shaikh did not go with them.

Now Tās, the place to which they went, was not far

---

[1] Persian greyhounds.

from the tents of Māi's people. Māi heard of their
coming, and that Bunayya had gone there hunting with
his foreign friends, and her father heard of it also, and
said to her, 'Your husband is perhaps coming for you,'
and she replied, 'He is with his friends; he will not come
for me now.'

To Latīfa she said, 'He is so near! I must see him!
Let us put on men's dress and pass by their camp!'

Latīfa would not agree: but it was spring, and in the
end she agreed that they would go for a few days if they
took servants and some of the other girls in the camp with
them, for sometimes the daughters of a shaikh will make
expeditions of this kind in the spring when the year is at
its best.

So the next day Māi and 'Aun's wife dressed as young
men and went off riding upon horses, accompanied by
some of the girls of the tribe, and a few servants to look
after them. They went, and when they were approaching
the place in which Bunayya and his friends were camping,
some of Bunayya's people saw them, and fearing a raid,
urged him to send some one to see who the 'Arab were.
So one of the servants galloped out to them, and met them
and asked them, 'Who are you? From whence coming,
whither going? Have you come in enmity or in peace?'

They answered, 'We are of the Beni—— and we are out
hunting. Our shaikh is called Ahmad.'

The Beni—— are a large tribe like the Aneyza, and
Māi was of this tribe,[1] but Bunayya did not ask more, for
most of the 'Arab of that part of the desert are of the
Beni—— and their sub-tribes.

Latīfa and Māi spread their tents not very far from
those of Bunayya, and they sent some one to ask Bunayya
and his friends to eat with them that evening. So about
sunset, Bunayya and his companions came over to the
tents of the 'Arab, and Māi was sitting, dressed like a
young shaikh. She rose and greeted them, 'Be welcome!'
and all sat in the guest-tent. Presently they brought food
—a lamb and rice in a large dish, and all sat round and

---

[1] A discrepancy. She was Bunayya's cousin, and he was of the Shammar.

ate. Bunayya thought 'Ahmad' a handsome lad, and he and his friends made merry and laughed and talked with Ahmad till it was late. At the end of the evening Ahmad asked Bunayya to come again and eat with them the next evening, and they replied that they would.

Now the friends of Bunayya had talked much about the beauty of the Bedawīya girls that they had seen since their arrival in the desert, and when Bunayya told them that the women of the Beni——— are renowned for their good looks, they looked about them on leaving, to try to see the women that Ahmad had brought with him. Ahmad had told them that he was not married, but that he had a sister with him, and they hoped to see the sister, thinking that if she resembled the young shaikh she must be beautiful. But they saw no one, but one or two of the girls who had accompanied Māi, and they returned to their tents. But when Bunayya had gone into his tent, he thought of Ahmad's sister and the moon was full, and he felt compelled to wander out into the desert. He went out, and the air was sweet, and the moon was high. He went towards the black tents of the young shaikh Ahmad, and all was silent there. Then he saw that some one came out of Ahmad's tent, and walked as women walk. He went quickly, and he saw Māi, who had felt restless and ill at ease and had put on her woman's gown and come forth. So they two met, and the moment Bunayya looked on her face, he loved her. It was two years since he had seen her and she had grown tall and when they were married he had scarcely glanced at her. He said to her, 'Who are you?' She answered, 'I am the sister of Ahmad, and my name is Hayya.'

He replied, 'I am Bunayya, and this night I supped with your brother.'

They talked, each not daring to gaze much in the other's eyes, for they were shamed with their love.

She said, 'I must return, or there will be evil spoken.'

He said, 'Come to my tent. I will wait all the night for you.'

Replied she, 'Not to-night, it is shame upon me.'

He said, 'You will come to-morrow night. I will change the place of my tent, and set it apart a little, so that you will know it, and will not be seen.'

So they parted. The next morning, Māi told Latīfa of what had happened, and Latīfa was angry, and said,

'You cannot go to him, for that would be shame upon you! We will strike our camp to-morrow and return to your father.'

Said Māi, 'Where is the shame? He is my husband, why should I not go to him?'

Said Latīfa, 'He slighted you, and you will go to him now?'

Answered Māi, 'I love him, and I will go.'

In the end she persuaded Latīfa, who consented to remain.

The next night Bunayya came with his friends and supped again in the black tents. But he was not so happy as the former evening, for he was thinking of the young Hayya, and wondering if she would come to him. They stayed awhile, and then they returned, and Bunayya went to his tent. He waited there and looked into the desert. Presently she came to him, and he received her like one mad with love. Before dawn she returned to her own place, taking with her his ring, and she found that Latīfa was waiting for her, displeased and angry.

Said Latīfa, 'We shall strike our tents at dawn and return, for this has been shame upon you.'

Answered Māi, 'Bunayya is my husband, why should I not love him?'

But the next morning, they struck their tents early, and went away. When Bunayya rose, they told him that the 'Arab who had camped by them were gone. He was angry, and cursed himself, for he knew nothing of the girl more than her name, Hayya (Modesty), and the name of her brother Ahmad, and he could not find out whither they had gone, nor more of them. He was constantly thinking of Hayya, but he said nothing to his friends or his father. After a while his friends departed, but some of them said that they had enjoyed their visit so much that they would return the following spring. Bunayya's father said, '*Mamnūn!* And you are welcome!' but Bunayya remained that year with his tribe.

Now shortly after her visit to Tās, Māi perceived that she was pregnant, and she told Latīfa. By this time Māi's father was angry with Bunayya because he had not come to fetch his wife, and she dared not speak of him. When the time came that Māi could not hide her condition, Latīfa said to the shaikh, 'O our father, Māi is ailing, I will go with her to our kinsfolk that she may spend the heat of the summer with them,' for Latīfa was of another tribe. The shaikh said, 'Go with her.'

So Latīfa rode with Māi and brought her to the tents of her people, and left her with a woman there to look after her. In time, Māi brought forth a son, and him she named Tās. They sent word secretly to Latīfa, and Latīfa came, and fetched Māi back to her people. So it was until the next spring, when Bunayya's friends came on another visit according to what they had said.

Again they went out to hunt. First they went to Tās, but there were no 'Arab there, and Bunayya, hearing that there were Beni—— farther north, moved his tents nearer to Māi's tribe at a place named Tāūs. Māi came and pleaded with Latīfa to do as they had done on the former spring, and seeing her weep, and plead, Latīfa was unable·to withstand her, and they went as before.

What joy there was when Bunayya saw their tents, and knew when he asked of them that the shaikh Ahmad was there! He visited them at once, and ate with Ahmad that night, he and his companions. When they had gone, Māi put on her woman's dress, and looking, she saw that Bunayya's tent was apart from the rest. So she went to him, and he received her with mad love, for he had longed for her all that year.

He reproached her for having left so quickly the former year, and she made excuses and said the shaikh her brother had willed it so. They talked and had joy of each other all the night, and when dawn was approaching, she took his dagger[1]

---

[1] See note 6, p. 234.

from him, and said, 'To ward off the jānn (from our love)!' and they parted.

The next morning, Latīfa struck the tents early, fearing for Māi's good name, and they returned. This time, too, Māi had a child in her womb, and Latīfa did as before; she persuaded the shaikh to send Māi with her to her own tribe. There Māi brought forth a second boy, whom she named Tāūs,[1] and leaving it with the first in the tent of the woman who had given her shelter, she returned to her people.

The third year came, and the spring, and again some of Bunayya's friends returned to the desert to hunt with him. This year they went to a place called Rumeyla, a short distance from the part of the desert in which the Beni—— pasture their herds and flocks, and there they put their tents. Māi heard of their coming, for her father was angry that Bunayya made no effort to come and fetch her, and would have sent to attack them, if she had not dissuaded him. Once again, she persuaded Latīfa to go out with her into the desert at a spot near Rumeyla. It was the same as before, and Māi, as the Shaikh Aḥmad, received Bunayya with friendliness, and entertained him and his friends. That night she again spent with her husband, who reproached her bitterly for deserting him the former year. But she said nothing, knowing that she must go the next morning, and remembering that he had never come for her as his wife. She would tell him nothing more of herself, but her name, Hayya, and before she left, she took his scarf, and put it amongst her clothes.

A third time she became pregnant, and Latīfa, helping her as before, she went to the same woman of Latīfa's tribe, and bore a daughter in her tent. The daughter she called 'Rumeyla' (sandy dune).

When she returned, she said to Latīfa, 'It is finished, I shall not seek for Bunayya more. I have three children by him, and that is all that I ask. From now I shall live at peace.'

So it was, and though Bunayya tried to find out who was

[1] Here meaning verdant country.

the Shaikh Ahmad, and where he lived, he discovered nothing, nor did he see him the next spring, or the next, or the next.

Five years passed, and each year Māi went to see her children. The boy Tās was now eight years old, his brother Tāūs seven, and the girl Rumeyla six.

Bunayya's father was now very old, and he said to Bunayya, 'You deserted Māi, and her people are angry. You must take another bride of our blood, and have a child by her, for I will soon die, and you have no son.'

Bunayya agreed, and it was settled that he should marry a girl from a family to whom they were related. The marriage was fixed, and the news of it came to Māi and her people. Māi went to Latīfa and said, 'Bunayya's children shall go to their father's wedding.'

Said Latīfa, 'How! Are you mad? You will send your children to the marriage of that man who has treated you so ill?'

She answered, 'Aye, I shall send them.'

She was not to be dissuaded, and Latīfa journeyed with her to the woman with whom she had left her children. There her children greeted her, 'Oh our Mother!' and embraced her, and she them. Said she to the children, 'Your father is to be married, and I shall send you to the wedding.' So she prepared them good clothes and travelled with them until she came to a wādi[1] near to Bunayya's people. Then she sent them with a servant, and ordered that they should be taken into the madhīf[2] during the wedding festivities. But first she spoke with the children, and told them how they must behave. On Tās's finger she put the ring which his father had given her, in Tāūs's belt she placed Bunayya's dagger with the turquoise-studded hilt, and round Rumeyla's head she twisted the scarf. She told them that when they saw their father Bunayya, they were to sit where he could see them.

---

[1] A slight, or deep depression, or the bed of a stream, when dried.

[2] *madhīf*, the large reception tent. This is often enormous, and several hundreds of guests can be accommodated in the tent of an important tribal shaikh. In the marsh-district the *madhīf* is usually a large house of reeds.

Tās was to display his ring, and Tāūs his dagger, while Rumeyla was to finger her scarf. She said to them, 'If he notices you and speaks to you, call him 'Bābā' and kiss his hand.'

The children were clever and understood what they were to do, and the servant took them and rode with them until they reached the camp of Bunayya's tribe. When people came and asked whose were the pretty children, the servant answered, 'They are the children of a shaikh, and their mother has sent them to see the wedding.'[1]

The children were taken into the guest-tent, and sat down, all three together. Every one noticed them, and asked whose children they were, for they were lovely to look on. To all questions the servant replied, 'They are the children of a shaikh,' but gave no name. Presently Bunayya entered the tent, and the servant, when he knew that it was Bunayya, told them, 'That is the bridegroom!'

Bunayya came and seated himself, and seeing the children, he at once noticed their good looks. He asked who they were, and receiving the same answer as the others, he called Tās, 'Come, come!' The boy rose, and came and sat beside him, and following came his little brother and the sister. Bunayya took the boy's hand, and said to him, 'What is your name, my son?' The child answered, 'My name is Tās, *ya Bābā!*' Bunayya looked at him, and the boy showed his ring. Then Bunayya began to wonder and to be moved in himself, for a father when he meets his son, feels something within him stir, he knows not why. Then he turned, and saw the second boy, whose hand was on the dagger. Bunayya saw the dagger, and he knew it for his.

He asked the second boy, 'What is your name?'

The boy answered, 'My name is Tāūs, *ya Bābā.*'

The little girl said, 'My name is Rumeyla.'

Bunayya saw the scarf round her head, and he knew it for his. His understanding flew from him, as he thought of the meaning of the coming of these children.

[1] Any person may come to a wedding-feast, invited or uninvited.

He asked them, 'Your mother, where is she?'

Said Tās, 'She is in the wādi not far away.'

Bunayya arose, and said to the servant who was with the children, 'Come, show me where these children live.'

The servant went with him and the children to the wādi where Māi was awaiting them. Bunayya came to her tent, and she stood there to meet him.

He said, 'You are Hayya.'

She answered, 'I am Māi, your wife, and these are your children and mine.'

Then he entered, and bowed his head before her and said, 'Pardon, pardon!'

Then they sat together, and he wept and asked her forgiveness, and she told him all that had happened to her, and how she had come to him in the guise of Ahmad, and as Hayya.

Then Bunayya returned with her and his children to his father, and said to him, 'My father, these are your grandchildren, and this is Māi!'

The old man rejoiced exceedingly, and embraced the children and blessed them.

Then, as Bunayya had no need of a second bride, they sent the new bride back to her people, and Māi lived with her husband, nor did he ever take another.

XLIII

THE CAT

THERE was once a girl whose parents were dead, and she had nothing in the world but her cat. This cat was called 'Aisha, and it was very clever, for it brought her food and drink and everything that she needed. One day the cat went and brought her back a golden comb.

The girl took it and went to the hammām. She took off her clothes, but she had no soap, nor towel, nor loofah, nor friction glove, nor bath wrap—nothing but her comb, which she put in her hair and sat there naked. A merchant's wife saw her sitting there with the fine comb in her hair, and noticed that she did not soap or wash herself. She came to her and said, 'O my daughter, whose daughter are you?' She answered, 'I am the wife of Mahmud,' naming a merchant of the place. Said the merchant's wife, 'Why do you not wash yourself?' Answered the girl, 'My maid who brought me here went from here and took my clothes, and soap, and all that is necessary for the bath, leaving me nothing but this comb.'

Said the merchant's wife and her family, 'You are the wife of Mahmūd the Merchant—we cannot see you in such difficulty. Come, sit by us, and we will lend you loofah and soap.'

She came and sat by them, and they helped her bathe herself and wash her hair. When that was over, she had no towel to dry herself, and they lent her towels and bath wrap, and all that was necessary.

Now she had thrown her dirty old smock in a corner, and pretended that her maid had taken her clothes also, so they said to her, 'We can provide you with clothes!' and they gave her shoes and stockings, clothes, and an 'aba to place over all. Then they said, 'Now we will take you to your house, where is it?'

She dared not tell them where her real house was for it was nothing but a little mud hut, and she had said that she was the wife of Mahmūd the Merchant. So she was obliged to go with them to Mahmūd's house.

When they arrived there, they heard the sound of wailing[1] (*chaīna*), and when they entered and asked the servants what was the matter, they answered, 'Oh woe, woe, our mistress, wife of Mahmūd, is dead!'

The women who had brought the girl replied, 'How can that be? Mahmūd's wife is here, we brought her with us—she was at the bath with us!'

So they went up with the girl to the room where the bereaved merchant sat mourning. They said to him, 'Mahmūd, is this your wife?' and uncovered her face.

The merchant saw that she was beautiful, and loving her at sight, and wishing to protect her, he replied, 'Aye, this is my wife!' and he went out and said to the neighbours who had gathered together to weep, 'Do not stay! My wife has returned.'

So she remained with him, and he sent for the mulla and made a marriage contract with her so that she really became his wife, and the merchant was so devoted to her that he could not bear to be parted from her a single instant of the day or night. He allowed her to do no menial task, and treated her with the utmost kindness.

Soon after her marriage she became pregnant. The cat heard of her mistress's marriage, and went to live with her. When the girl saw her cat again, she was overjoyed, and said,

'O cat, I am pregnant, and have a longing to make myself some dough-cake. Go, and bring me some dough.'

The cat answered, 'O daughter of the poor, you have everything here in your house, flour, leaven, and all that is necessary! Make your dough-cake here and eat it, why should I bring you dough from outside?'

Said the girl, 'My darling cat, bring it to me! for the sake of Allah, bring me some dough!'

So the cat went off to a baker's and managed to steal some dough for her mistress, and brought it in her paws

---

[1] See note 2, p. 44.

and said, 'There is your dough, rejoice! I have brought it for you.'

That day when the merchant had gone to the sūq, the girl made a pretext to get the maids out of the way, so as to go secretly to the kitchen and bake her dough. Just as she was about to bake it, the merchant knocked at the door of the courtyard and opened the door and coming in, found his wife in the kitchen.

When he saw her there, he cried, 'Why are you here in the smoke and the grease? What are you doing in the kitchen?'

In her confusion, she hid the dough in her lap, and said, 'Go up, go up, I will follow in a moment!'

He replied, 'No! You must not stay here in the grease and smoke!' and he drew her to her feet, and the cake on her lap fell to the ground and was broken.

When he gazed to see what had fallen, he saw pieces of gold jewellery ornamented with pearls lying on the ground, and he cried, 'From whence have you these?'

She answered, 'From my father's house.'

Said he, 'You—have you a father?'

Said she, 'Aye, in Damascus: he is a merchant.'

They went upstairs, and all was happiness between them.

But the cat said to her, 'Do not tell such lies!'

Shortly after this she said to the cat, 'My cat! Bring me a haggis (*kirsha*)!'

Answered the cat, 'How shall I bring you a haggis? All these people here, they will see me!'

But she insisted, and in the end the cat went, and stole for her a haggis. When the merchant had gone to the sūq, she told the maids, 'I have some work to do in the kitchen,' and sent them out. Then she washed the haggis and prepared it nicely, and was just going to put it in to cook, when her husband came to the door, for he had returned.

Said he, 'Why have you come down into the dirt and smoke?'

Answered she, 'I came to see what the maids were doing!' and she hid the haggis in her lap.

He pulled her up by the hand, and the haggis fell, and it became a solid lump of gold all studded with jewels.

Said he, 'From whence have you this?'

She answered, 'This is from my father!'

Said he, 'How rich he must be to send you presents like this so often!'

Said she, 'Aye, he is richer than you are!'

So all was well, and they went to eat together.

The cat said to her, however, 'I am tired, because of you! I have worked all my life for you, and so hard that I am worn out, and shall most likely die. Now when I am dead, in return for my faithful service, you must wrap me in your husband's coat and bury me.'

The girl promised, and the cat lay down, and feigned to die.

When she saw that, the girl said to her servant, 'Come, throw the cat on the rubbish-heap, for she is dead.'

The servant took the cat by her tail, and threw her on the rubbish-heap. The cat stayed there for a little, and then rose and entered the house again and said to her mistress, 'O daughter of the poor, do you treat me thus? I have always worked well for you, and this is the way you reward me—you take me and throw me on the rubbish-heap!'

The girl said, 'Pardon! I was thoughtless!'

Replied the cat, 'Let it be this time, but you must not do it again.'

A little while after this the girl was annoyed with her husband about something, and she called out in her rage, 'Your beard is no better than the broom in my father's house!'

The merchant was angry, and said, 'Why do you say that my beard is no better than the broom in your father's house,' and he quarrelled with her and would not speak to her.

The girl went to her cat and said, 'My husband is very angry with me, and I am afraid he will divorce me. Do me a favour, for the sake of Allah!'

And she told the cat what she had said in her anger. The cat said, 'This time I will help you, but you must not use such language to your husband in future.'

The cat went to Damascus and heard there that a wealthy merchant was dying. She entered the merchant's house, and contrived to slip into his room. Just as she did so the merchant died. She slipped beneath the coverlet of the bed, and when his eldest son came near the bed to see how his father was, she spoke from beneath the coverlet and said, 'O my son! I have a daughter who is married and lives in Baghdad. Her husband is chief of the merchants there and he lives in such-and-such a street. I lay upon your obedience that you send her eight camel-loads of money, and five brooms with handles of gold and hairs of pearl: and you must give her a fifth of my lands as well.'

Said his son, 'O my father, till now, you have never told us that we had a sister.'

Answered the cat from the dead merchant's bed,

'I was once in Baghdad, and I married a woman there, and then divorced her. This girl is that woman's daughter. I lay upon you as my dying wish that you should not forget what I have told you. Send her the money and the brooms, and say, 'Thy father is dead!' As long as you live, you must look after your sister, and it will be better if you live with her in Baghdad.'

Said the son, 'How many years have passed and you never spoke to me about this sister in Baghdad!'

Said the cat, 'I was afraid to tell you, but I have always sent her money and presents.'

Then the cat was silent, and the merchant's son, approaching the bed, perceived that his father was dead. They washed the merchant, and mourned him, and put him in the tomb, while the cat returned to her mistress and said, 'I have done what you asked.'

Soon after a telegram came from Damascus, addressed to the girl, which said, 'Our father is dead (we hope that) you are well.'

When the merchant her husband opened this telegram,

he began to repent having quarrelled with so wealthy a
wife as his must now be, and made up his mind to be
reconciled to her. So he went to her and said,

'*Abūch māt, nti tayyiba!* Your father is dead, may you
be in health!'

She answered him, '*Nta tayyib!* [1] May you be in health!'
and began to throw up her arms and wail. While the
seven days' mourning was in progress the eight camels
and their drivers arrived, and they were laden with money
and the five brooms on the top of all. Upon each of the
brooms the name of the girl was written. When her
husband beheld them, he was overjoyed, and taking one
of the brooms in his hand, he said, 'When you compared
my beard to the broom in your father's house, I confess
I was angry, and thought it an insult, now I know, my
dearest wife, that you paid me a compliment!'

A short time after this the poor cat fell sick (Allah have
mercy on you!)[2] and after a few days it died. The girl,
thinking it might be shamming death, was afraid to throw
it on the rubbish-heap, so she took her husband's coat,
wrapped the cat in it, and laid it in a box. After a few
days she said to herself, 'I must see if the cat is well or
if it is really dead!' So she opened the box, unwrapped
the cat and saw to her surprise that the cat was changed
into a cat of solid gold, and that a sweet odour emanated
from it. She lifted it out, and set it on the table of her
reception room, and was delighted to have such a handsome ornament. Her husband entered the room, and
asked her, 'From whence have you this fine model of a
cat?' She replied, 'It has been sent me from my father's
house.' The merchant said, 'What beautiful things they
have in your father's house!'

Said she, 'I beg your permission to go to visit my
brothers there!'

Said he, 'You may go, and I will accompany you.'

---

[1] *Nta tayyib!* You are in health!' is a way of announcing death to a relative
of the deceased.

[2] The mention of misfortune should be accompanied by a pious phrase. See
p. 274.

They sent a telegram to her brothers, 'We are leaving Baghdad and coming to pay you a visit.'

When the brothers received this news they were delighted and said, 'We are delighted that our sister is coming, for we want to see what kind of a woman she is!'[1]

In due time the girl and her husband arrived in Damascus. The eldest brother came to meet her: he was a very wealthy man like his father, and he was rejoiced to see her and welcome her. They held seven days' mourning for the death of their father, and at the end of that time she said to her husband, 'My brothers would like us to remain here with them always.'

Answered he, '*Shlōn!* Am I to leave all my property in Baghdad? That cannot be! I must return to my own country.'

Then she said to her brothers, '*Mā yukhālif!* It matters not! We must go back to our own country.'

They replied, 'Oh sister, go with your husband! But we love you so well that we shall sell our possessions here and come with you.'

So they all travelled to Baghdad, and that was the end of them!

Kunna ʿadkum wa jīna!

---

[1] Literally, Shlōnha, what colour she is.

XLIV

THE FISH THAT LAUGHED

THERE was a Sultan, and, as it had been foretold to him that a daughter would bring shame upon him, each time that his wife bore him a girl baby, he slaughtered it. Now he had a wazīr, and one day this wazīr was riding his mare, when they passed five or six boys playing knucklebones by the roadside. The boys made a noise, and the mare shied, and the wazīr clapped his legs against her sides.

Cried one of the boys who were playing, 'Shame! Why do you so? Unbeliever! why mistreat your mare!'

Said the wazīr, 'What business is it of yours?'

Answered the boy, 'The mare will bring forth a foal, which would be worth a treasure had you not rendered it blind of one eye by that blow you have given her.'

The wazīr thought within himself, 'How is it that a boy so young knows that my mare is with foal!' and he went his way.

A little afterwards the mare had a foal, a beautiful creature, but its right eye was blind. The wazīr said to his wife, 'What a clever boy that was! Yesterday, as I was passing him, I struck the mare with my foot, and he cried to me that the foal which the mare would bring forth would be blind in one eye! What an intelligent boy!'

Answered his wife, 'There be many sharp boys in the world!'

Said the wazīr, 'But how did he know that the foal would be blind. His words came true—what a clever boy!'

Now the Sultan's wife was pregnant, and she was afraid that the child she would bring into the world would again be a daughter, and that the Sultan would kill it, and she resolved to go to the Sultan and beg him to spare the child if this time it should be a girl. So she went into the presence of the Sultan, and seized his two hands.

He said, 'Sit!' and she sat.

Said he, 'What do you want?'

Answered she, 'I beg you, in the name of Allah, that if this time I should bring a girl into the world that you will not kill her,' and she pleaded so long that he said at last,

'Go, and I promise that if this time your baby is a girl, I will not kill her.'

In due time the woman was delivered of a daughter, and after the babe was three days old, the mother brought her to the Sultan and said, 'I have a daughter. I beg you, keep your word, and do not kill her!'

Answered he, 'Good, I will not kill her!' But he took her from the mother, and placed her with a wet-nurse in a castle which he built beside his own. No man was allowed to enter the castle, and the child was not allowed outside it. But in order that he might send messages and food and all that was required into the castle, he sent for a blacksmith, and ordered him to make a man of iron (*ādmi yashtaghal bil yāi*, a man working by springs), which was wound like a clock, and passed from the dīwān of his castle into the dīwān of the castle of his daughter.

The child grew and grew, *dī, dī, dī!* and reached the age of twelve, thirteen, and fourteen. The wet-nurse left her, and she learnt from female professors reading and writing, but never left the interior of the castle. To amuse herself, she wrote a chronicle of all that happened in her father's castle and of the news which was brought to her of the world, but she did not go out.

And thus she reached the age of twenty.

Now the Sultan had a fisherman, whose duty it was to catch fish for his table, for the Sultan ate much fish and preferred it to meat or fowl. For supplying the fish the fisherman was given a wage, and what fish he caught over and above the Sultan's needs, he was permitted to sell in the sūq. One day of days the fisherman took his net, and threw it, and when he drew it up there was no fish in it, not one. He furled his net, and threw it again, and again there were no fish in it. This happened many times, and the fisherman became very troubled, saying, 'If I bring the Sultan no fish, he will be angry and I may lose my head!' *Dī, dī, dī!* he threw and he threw till at last when he drew in his net he saw in it two fishes, a pair, about the length of half your arm. He was very glad, and said, '*Yā ruhān!*[1] Allah has saved me from the Sultan! and I will take him these!' As he was examining them, and noticing how curiously decorated the scales of the fish were, the fish laughed.

Said he, 'These are indeed astonishing fish! Truly, I will lay them before the Sultan.'

He went, and entered the Sultan's presence, and said, 'All the night I threw my net and caught no fish, but at last I caught this pair, and never before in my life have I seen such fish! for they laugh. Let your Majesty gaze upon them, for I have brought them for you to see.'

The Sultan said, 'What a strange thing!' and calling a servant, he told him to fill a basin with water, and to bring it to him. It was done, and the fish were thrown into the bowl. The fish began to swim about and to laugh.

Cried the Sultan, 'This is indeed a marvel! I will send them to my daughter to see.' So he called for the iron man, and wound him up and put the fish in his arms, and wrote upon a piece of paper, 'I send you these for your amusement. Never have I seen such marvellous fish!' Then he touched the spring, and fr-r-r-r! the iron man went into the daughter's castle, into the presence of the young princess. When she had read the note, the girl called a servant and bade her bring a bowl of water. No sooner were they in the water than the fish began to laugh. The girl pondered, and then she wrote to her father,

'Oh, papa, I was very amused by the fish, but I want to know why they laugh?'

Then she wound the man up and sent him back.

The Sultan took the note, and read it, and then called his wazīr, and said to him, 'Oh, wazīr, tell me, why do these fish laugh.'

The wazīr was unable to reply. Then the Sultan said,

---

[1] A pious exclamation of relief.

'I will give you three days to find out why the fish laugh. If you do not find out in that time, I will take your head off.'

The wazīr was very downcast when he heard these words, and he returned to his house, without appetite or spirit. His wife asked him what was the matter, and when he told her, she consoled him, saying, 'Do not be troubled, my husband; Allah is merciful, perhaps, by inquiring here and there you will find some one who will be able to explain the meaning of this miracle.'

The wazīr went to all the learned men, and the old men, and he asked in the mosques, in the baths, in the shops; of the wizards and the doctors, and the barbers, but all replied to him, 'There is no meaning in it that we know.'

The evening of the first day, and the evening of the second day, came, the wazīr said to his wife, 'There has been none to explain the miracle, oh woman! not one!' They could neither eat or sleep. The evening of the third day came, and the wazīr sat weeping, 'O woman, I have found no answer!'

His wife pondered, and at last she exclaimed, 'O my husband, I have a word for you! You have asked all the wise men in the city, and they have been able to tell you nothing. But you have not remembered that boy who told you not to beat the mare: perhaps he will know, for he was an intelligent boy.'

Said the wazīr, 'Aye, woman, true! I have not asked him.'

Said she, 'Go and find him.'

Answered the wazīr, 'I do not know his name, nor where he lives, but I know one of the boys who was playing knucklebones with him, and he may know where to find him.' And he rose and said, 'Go, fetch my clothes, I will go to that boy.'

He put on his clothes and went to the house of the boy whom he knew, and said to him, 'My dear, one day I was riding past on my mare and I saw you playing knuckle-bones with some other boys, and one of them called to me not to beat my mare. Do you know his house, and can you guide me to it.'

Answered the boy, 'Yes, I know his house and will guide you to it.'

And he came with the wazīr and showed him the house, and knocked at the door.

The boy's mother called out, 'Who is it?'

The wazīr answered, 'I! Open the door. Is your son here?'

The mother called, 'Come down, my son, a man wants you at the door!'

The boy came, and when he saw the wazīr, he knew him.

Said the wazīr, 'My darling, my son, I have a word to speak with you!'

Answered the boy, 'Speak! what do you want?'

And the wazīr told him of the fish that the fisherman had brought to the Sultan, and that the Sultan had demanded that he should tell him why they laughed, so that he might tell his daughter. Said the wazīr, 'If you can tell me the reason, so that I may save my head, I will enrich you (and Allah is the Enricher).'

Said the boy, 'When you came and called me, I was afraid. But your business is a simple matter—it is nothing!'

Said the wazīr, 'Then tell me.'

Answered the boy, 'No, that I will not! But if you will take me to the Sultan, and say to him, "I cannot tell why the fish laughed, but this boy knows, and will tell you," all will be well.'

The wazīr said, 'Good.'

Said the boy, 'To-morrow early I will come to your house and fetch you and we will go together to the palace.'

So it was, and the boy came to the wazīr's house and they went together to the Sultan's palace.

When they arrived, they went in and the wazīr took the boy, who was about twelve years old, into the Sultan's presence, and he said to the Sultan,

'O your Majesty, I was not able to discover why the fish laughed, but I have found this boy, and he knows.'

The Sultan lifted his head and looked at the boy and said, 'You know why the fish laughed?'

Answered the boy, 'Yes, I know.'

Said the Sultan, 'Tell me, oh my son! What is the meaning of it?'

Answered the boy, 'Nay, I will not tell you.'

Said the Sultan, 'Why will you not tell me?'

Said the boy, 'I will tell your daughter, and none other!'

The Sultan looked at the boy, and said to himself, 'This boy is as yet a child, he is no grown man, I will let him go to my daughter!'

So he called for the iron man, and told the boy to get upon him, then he wound the iron man up, and the iron man passed with the boy from the Sultan's palace to hers, from his dīwān to hers, and with him a word to tell who the boy was.

The princess read her father's letter and looked at the boy.

Said the boy, 'What does your highness want of me?'

Said the princess, 'I wish to know why the fish laughed.'

Answered the boy, 'If I tell you, you will regret it.'

Said she, 'Nay, I shall not regret it!'

He repeated, 'You will not repent it?'

'No, I shall not repent it!'

Said the boy, 'To-day I will tell you a short story, and then, if you wish, to-morrow I will tell you the meaning of the fish which laughed.'

Said she, 'Tell me.'

Said the boy, 'There was once a man who had a falcon, and went hawking with it. A falconer he was, and his life was bound up in that bird. Day and night he held the falcon on his wrist, and he lived by what it caught for him. One summer's day he went hawking. It was very hot, and after a while he became thirsty. He walked and he walked, with the falcon on his hand, but water there was none to be found. Presently he came to a high rock, and as he watched, a drop of clear water fell from the top of the rock. He watched, and after some time, there fell another drop. So he drew a cup from his pocket, and set it where the drops would fall into it. The cup was filling, when the bird flapped its wings and upset it. Now the man was half

A hawker, Najaf

A fisherman on the Tigris, throwing his net

dead from thirst, and his tongue was dry, so he set the cup again to catch the drops. When it was nearly full and he was about to drink it, the bird again flapped its wings and the cup overturned. A third time he set the cup, and waited, and a third time the falcon overset the cup. Then he was very angry: he seized the bird by its neck and hurled it to the ground, and it died.

'Then the falconer began to think, "Why did the bird upset the water? From whence does it come? I will ascend the rock and see."

'When he got to the top of the rock he saw a serpent panting with open mouth upon the top of the rock, and the venom from its mouth ran and fell down from the rock. And he repented his act—and if I tell you why the fish laughed, you too will repent, like the man.'

She replied, 'Nay, I shall not repent.'

Then the boy said, 'For to-day I shall wish you peace, and to-morrow I will return and tell you why the fish laughed.'

Then the boy went away, and the girl sent word to her father that the boy had left her.

Asked the Sultan, 'Did he tell you why the fish laughed?'

She replied, 'No, but to-morrow he will tell me.'

The second day came, and the boy went to the Sultan's palace, and mounted the iron man, and went to the princess. When he saw her he asked her, 'What do you want from me?'

She replied, 'I want you to tell me why the fish laughed.'

Said he, 'O my sister, if I tell you, you will regret it!'

Said she, 'Nay, but I shall not repent it.'

Said he, 'Let me but tell you a small story, and to-morrow I will tell you why the fish laughed.'

Answered she, 'Tell it, my brother.'

Said the boy, 'There was once a man and wife, who, though they were married for twenty years, had no child. At last, Allah gave them a son, and he was their joy and blessing. Now this pair also had a dog named Jāk, and this dog loved the baby, and slept beneath its cradle, and rocked it to sleep. The child was always with the dog, and played with it, and the man and his wife were fond of the dog as they were fond of the child. One day the woman said to her husband, "My head is dirty, I want to go to the bath: keep your eye on the boy!" and she went out, leaving her husband in the house, and the dog beneath the cradle rocking the baby. Said the man to himself, "I will sit by the house-door and watch for my wife, and the dog Jāk will guard the boy and rock his cradle." So he went and sat at the house-door. There came a serpent, and coiled itself around the cradle and the baby, and tried to bite the child. Jāk, when he saw it, was very angry, and fought with the serpent and killed it. He stretched it out dead by the cradle, and then returned to its rocking. Came the woman from the bath, and when he heard her voice, Jāk, his face all covered with blood, ran to meet her, very pleased because he had killed the serpent.

'The woman called the man, and cried, "See the blood on the dog's face! O father of my son, he has killed our boy!"

'The man drew out his hanger and killed the dog. Then they went upstairs, and there was the serpent stretched out by the cradle dead, and the cradle was still rocking as the dog had left it.

'In that hour, did the man and his wife repent over Jāk, or did they not?'

Answered she, 'They repented, bitterly they repented!'

Said he, 'My dear, if I tell you why the fish laughed, you too will repent bitterly.'

Answered she, 'Nay! I shall not repent! Never!'

Said the boy, 'Not to-day, but to-morrow, I will tell you. But in your dīwān there must be assembled your father, and his ministers, and all his court. Then I will tell you why the fish laughed.'

With that he mounted the man of iron and returned to the Sultan's palace.

The Sultan said, 'Did you tell my daughter why the fish laughed?'

The boy replied, 'No, I shall tell her to-morrow, but

you must be present, and your wazīrs, and your officials, and your qādhis: to your daughter alone I shall not say it.'

Said the Sultan, 'Good.'

And on the next day, the Sultan, and his advisers and his court and the qādhis, assembled in the dīwān of the princess, and the princess sat on a couch in the midst.

Then came the boy, and the Sultan said, 'Speak, my son, for all are here.'

Answered the boy, 'For two days I have spoken to your daughter in parables, telling her that she will repent if I tell her why the fish laughed, and she has answered me each time, "Nay, I will not repent." And now I will tell you all in two words, and see how you will regret it!'

They all answered, 'Nay, we shall not regret it!'

He asked the princess for the last time, 'And you, will you not regret it?'

She answered, 'No.'

Then said he to the princess, 'Rise, quickly! Stand up!'

The princess said, 'I have repented!' and remained sitting.

The boy said, 'Nay! Rise!' and she rose.

Next he said, 'Lift the couch!' and they lifted it, and at his bidding they removed the carpet and the matting. Then he told them to lift the marble slab beneath, and they lifted it, and below it there were steps leading into the cellar.

They went down the steps, and behold, in the cellar they found forty men, the lovers of the princess.

Then said the boy, 'That fish laughed at the intelligence of your father, who thought to keep you from evil by shutting you up and letting none but a man of iron go in to you: the while you received nightly these forty men, who came in from the desert by an underground passage and made love to you, and you amused yourself with them!'

The Sultan lowered his head for shame, and called his executioner, and said to him, 'Take off my daughter's head, I do not want her any more as daughter of mine!'

And it was done as he had said.

Then he called the boy and said, 'Children I have none now, and because you are so clever, I will make you my son, and you shall inherit all that I have.'

And he took off his crown and put it upon the boy's head.

Kunna ʿadkum wa jīna
Wad daff umgargʿa wal arūs hazīna!

XLV

THE HONEST MAN

THERE was once an honest man, upon whom Fortune never smiled. His wife deceived him, his sons robbed him, and when his beard was white he found himself without either money or honour.

He complained of his ill fortune one day in the sūq to a friend, who counselled him to make a pilgrimage to the tomb of a holy man, as this had been known to bring children to the childless, wealth to the penniless, and success to the unfortunate. The old man decided that he would go, and taking his staff and a little bread, he set out the next day. He had not gone very far on the road before he came to a rocky place, and there was a lion, his head between his paws, roaring as if with pain.

The honest man was merciful, and cared not to see beasts suffer, so he stopped and asked the lion, 'Why are you roaring, O Abu Khumeyis?'[1]

'Wallah!' said the lion, 'I roar because my head pains me. For the past sixty days I can neither eat nor sleep for pain. And you, where are you going?'

Said the man, 'I am going on a pilgrimage in the hope of mending my fortunes.'

Said the lion, 'And which shrine do you visit?'

Said the man, 'The shrine of the two Kādhims.'

Said the lion, 'I beg you, if while you are there, you can learn how I may best cure my pain, you will tell me on your return!'

'Mamnūn! Thankfully!' answered the honest man, and he went on his way.

Presently he came to a lake. In the lake were many fishes, and they were all at play, diving and swimming, save one large fish, which floated on the water like a ship.

'Peace on you!' said the man. 'Why, oh fish, do you not dive and swim like your fellows?'

Said the fish, 'Alas, I cannot! Some sickness has taken

---

[1] See note 2, p. 81.

me, and I cannot swim below in the cool water, but must float above in the sun. And you, where are you going?'

Said the man, 'I am going to visit the shrine of the two Kādhims, so that they may reveal to me a way of mending my fortune.'

Said the fish, 'Friend, mention my trouble also, I beg you.'

And the honest man promised not to forget it.

He went farther along the road for a day or two and he came to a field, and in it he saw three men, digging hard so that the sweat ran down their faces.

'Peace be upon you!' cried the honest man, and they answered him, 'And on you the peace!'

'The sun is hot,' said the old man, 'why do you labour so hard?'

'Our father left us this piece of land which he said would bring us great riches, and though we toil, as you see, with spade and plough as he bade, the land is salty and yields nothing. And you, where are you going?'

'I go to Kādhimain to pray at the tomb of the Imams who will, God willing, reveal to me the way to fortune.'

Said the brothers, 'And Allah with you! Remember us also in thy prayers, uncle, so that our toil may be rewarded.'

And the honest man promised to pray for them.

After some days of travel, he reached the city of Kādhimain,[1] and paid his visit to the holy tombs, and made his prayer there. And the third day he fell asleep by the tomb of the holy Mūsa al Kādhim, and it seemed to him that he saw standing before him a reverend man, who wore a green turban, and had an aspect of authority. And he knew him for the Imām. And the Imām said to him, 'Peace, my son! What can I do for thee, to put thee in the way of happiness in this world and in the next?'

And the honest man said, 'Peace and prayer upon thee! Before I tell thee my troubles, holy one, permit me to relate the trouble of three men whom I passed upon the road.' And he recounted what the three brothers had told him of their father's inheritance.

[1] Near Baghdad.

'That is easy,' said the Imām. 'They must dig very deep in the centre of the field and there they will discover a chest of marble containing a treasure. Thus will their father's words be fulfilled. And now, my son, tell me thine own trouble.'

'I thank thee,' said the honest man, 'but I have yet another promise to redeem. Farther back, I saw a fish, which suffered the greatest misery because it could not dive beneath the surface, but must swim like a ship in the heat of the sun. I vowed that I would ask thee concerning the matter.'

'Know,' said the saint, 'that thou must call her to the bank and smite her on the head with my staff. She will then recover. And now, what is it that thou desirest for thyself?'

'Wait a little,' said the honest man, 'there is yet another matter that I promised to lay before thee. This concerns Abu Khumeyis, the lion, who has suffered from a headache these sixty days and can neither eat nor sleep.'

'His case is also easy,' answered the Imām. 'All that he has to do is to eat the head of a fool, and he will instantly be cured.'

'And now,' said the man, 'I beg thee for myself, for lo! I prosper in nothing!'

'Go in peace,' said the saint. 'I have already told thee that which is necessary to end thy troubles.'

With that, the vision disappeared, and the old man prepared for his homeward journey, his mind at rest about the future because of the Imām's kind words.

He soon reached the field in which the three brothers were at their fruitless labours. He hailed them, and told them what the saint had said concerning their heritage. As soon as they heard his words, they took their spades and dug into the centre of the plot, and behold! there was the marble chest, even as the Imām had said, and when they opened it, they saw that it was full of gold and jewels.

In the heat of their gratitude they said to the old man,

'You are the cause of our happiness, and therefore it is but just that you should be the partaker of our gain. Take half this treasure for yourself, old man!'

'But the honest man replied, '*Lā! ma yasīr!* No, that cannot be! Far be it from me, my sons, to take that which your father intended to leave you! Enjoy the good fortune which Heaven has sent you, and I will go on my way!'

So he parted from them and walked on and on until he came to the lake. There was the fish, swimming disconsolately on the surface as before. Calling her to the side of the pond, he told her of the saint's message, and she begged him to use his staff, and placed her head upon the bank that he might smite it.

Thereupon, he hit a shrewd blow, with the result that a blister in the fish's head broke, and a large diamond fell out on the bank. The fish swam off, and with the utmost joy began to dive and plunge with her fellows.

'Stop, stop, my sister!' cried the old man. 'You have left a costly diamond here on the bank where robbers can seize it!'

The fish put her head out of the water to say, 'What is that to me? I have no use for diamonds!' And she plunged below again.

'Yet it were a pity to have it stolen!' said the old man, and he cast it after her into the middle of the pond.

Then he went on his way, and at last he came to the rocks where the lion lay roaring in his pain.

The honest man approached the lion, and said, 'Oh Abu Khumeyis, I saw the Imām and fulfilled my promise.'

'Tell me all,' said the lion.

And the honest man told him all his adventures, from the beginning to the end.

'What said the Imām concerning me?' asked the lion, with attention.

'He said, my brother, that thou hadst to eat the head of a fool, and thy troubles would cease.'

'And with them, thine, *inshallah*!'[1] roared the lion, and he sprang upon the honest man, bit his head off, and devoured it.

[1] Please God.

XLVI

THE GENEROUS MAN AND THE NIGGARDLY MAN

THERE were once two brothers, and the one was generous and the other niggardly. Both were poor, and had so little in their pockets that they made up their minds to go out into the world to improve their fortunes. Said the generous brother, 'Come! we will go out into the chōl and see what we can find. Before we go let us bake bread, so that we may have something to eat on the road. If my food is finished first you can give me some of yours, and if yours is finished, I will give you some of mine. Perhaps Allah will provide for us if we go elsewhere, for here times are bad, and we cannot earn our living.'

Said the other, 'As you will, my brother.'

Each brother went to his mother[1] and asked her to bake some bread, saying, 'We are going away to look for work.'

The mothers rose, made dough, baked bread and gave to them, and each man put his loaf in his bag, and then they set off together into the chōl.

They walked and they walked, and when they were hungry they ate. After a while the generous one said to his brother, 'My brother, I have finished my bread, give me a little morsel of yours as we agreed before we left home.'

The other replied, 'Oh, that agreement is far away! I shall not give you any of my bread.'

Said the generous one, 'What is this! I am your brother, and I am hungry, and you promised that we should share our provisions. I only ask a morsel!'

Said the greedy one, 'Never! I can't spare you even a crumb!'

The generous one replied, 'If you refuse even a crumb, our roads part here! I will go one way and you the other, and I will know you no more!'

---

[1] They were brothers by different wives.

So they parted—one went in one direction and the other in the other. The generous one walked and walked, *ardh athattu ardh atshīlu, ardh athattu, ardh atshīlu,* until it was evening. He looked about for a place where he might shelter that night, and saw a cave. Said he to himself, 'I will spend the night here. Should a lion, or jackal, or deyu attack me, God is my protection!' And he entered the cave, and wrapped up his head and slept there.

When night fell, a pair of lions entered the cave.

Said one to the other, 'There is a smell of man (*beni Adam*) here, my brother!'

Replied the other, '*Fūt!* how can *beni Adam* be here? No man would come hither! Perhaps we smell ourselves, for we have eaten man.'

When he heard the lions, the man awoke, and began to tremble with fright.

The lions lay down, and presently one lion said to the other,

'I have something to tell you.'

Said the other lion, 'Tell me!'

Said the first, 'There is a rat in this cave, and in his hole there is a heap of gold. He has a gold tray in his hole also, and every morning, at dawn of day, he takes the treasure out of the hole so that the rays of the sun may fall on the gold, and he plays on it, and presently takes it back to his hole. If we kill the rat we can take the gold, and I will tell you what we can do with it. In the town which lies a league off there is a Sultan whose daughter is afflicted by a jinni. Her father is seeking for one to come and cure her. Now there are some 'Arab camped not far away, and one of them has a black dog. We will take the gold, buy the dog, kill it, and put its blood in a jar. If the princess be bathed in the blood of this black dog, she will be cured—and this is the only cure for her malady.'

The man listened to what they were saying, and understood it.

Replied the second lion, 'That is not lion's work, it is work for a son of Adam!'

The first lion repeated, 'I tell you this: the Sultan's daughter can only be cured by the blood of this black dog.'

They conversed a little more, and then went out. The man waited till it was dawn and the rays of the morning sun struck the entrance to the cave, and then he took a big stone and laid it ready to hand beside him. Presently, from a hole in the rock a rat came out, dragging in its teeth a tray. He placed it at the mouth of the cave, and then fetched out some pieces of gold which he placed in the tray. Then he began to play amongst the gold pieces, scattering them, and heaping them, and enjoying himself amongst the yellow gold. He played and played, and tiring after a while, he stopped and rested. The man then took the stone, aimed at the rat, and threw it as hard as he was able. Dum—m—m! It hit the rat and it died. How delighted the man was! He took off his cheffīyah and tied up the gold in it and set off walking. He asked each man that he met, where the 'Arab were camping, and they guided him, saying, 'There are 'Arab in such and such a place.'

He followed their directions and presently he came upon the houses of hair. He went to one of them, and entered it and sat, saying, 'Peace upon you!' They answered him, 'Upon you peace.' Presently he took out a piece of gold[1] from his pocket and said, 'I am hungry: give me some laban[2] and bread and shenīna.[2]

They brought him food and drink and said, 'We are 'Arab, we do not want your money! Be pleased to eat!' He ate, and they brought him a pipe and he smoked, then he lay down to sleep.

When he rose the next morning, he went and walked about the place, and he saw a big black dog, as large as a ram, tied to one of the tents by a chain.

He asked, 'Who is the master of this *bait*?' and a man answered him, 'I.' He said, 'Will you sell this dog?'

The man answered, 'No—why should we sell him? He

---

[1] He was a townsman and was not familiar with the usage of the desert.

[2] See notes 1 and 2, p. 176.

is a faithful dog and a strong dog, and we do not wish to part with him.'

Said the generous man, 'But I want your dog, and I will pay a good price for him.'

The Bedawi replied, 'Never! I will not part with him.'

Said the other, 'Name your price! Even if it is high, I will pay it.'

'I will not sell him!'

'I will give you ten gold pieces!'

'*Ma yasīr!* It cannot be!'

'Fifteen!'

'It cannot be!'

'Twenty!'

'It cannot be!'

and so it went on until he said, 'Fifty!'

Then the Badawi could not resist the offer, and said, 'Take the dog!'

He gave him the gold, and took the dog on a chain, and a jar, and he went into the chōl, walking, walking, walking, until he came to a hole. He put the dog into the hole, killed him there, and let his blood fall into the jar (*tunga*). Then he rose and walked until he came to the town where the Sultan lived. He entered it, and began to cry, 'A doctor! a healer!' through the streets. They heard him in the palace, and went to the Sultan and said to him, 'A new physician has come to the town, he is crying, "A doctor, a healer!" through the streets. Shall we fetch him in?'

The Sultan replied, 'What is the use! I have employed fifty physicians and wise men in the effort to cure my daughter, and not one of them has succeeded. Why should this one be more useful than the others?'

The Prime Minister said, 'You have employed fifty, let this one be the fifty-first. Is there not a saying,

Hajarat elleti ma yirdha lik bīha, tifchakh![1]

Let us call him, and we will see.'

The Sultan said, 'Call him.'

[1] The stone which you thought useless will strike. *Tifchakh* should be *tiffakh*.

Some of his people went, and brought the man into the presence of the Sultan, and the Sultan said to him,

'I have a daughter who is possessed of a jinni. She is chained below in the cellar. If you can cure her, say.'

Replied the man, 'With the permission of Allah, I will cure her.'

Said the Sultan, 'If you do not cure her, I will take off your head!'

Replied the man, 'You have laid down a condition for me. I will lay down one for you!'

Said the Sultan, 'Speak!'

Answered the man, 'If I cure your daughter, I will take her to wife. If I do not, you may take my head off!'

Pens and paper were brought, and the agreement was written down and the Sultan and the healer set their seals to it.

Then the healer said, 'Let the bath be heated to fever heat.'

They heated the bath, and he said,

'Where is the Sultan's daughter?'

They answered, 'She is chained in the sirdab,'[1] and took him down to the cellar, and unlocked the door. Within the princess lay naked, and cried out upon him.

Said the healer, 'Rise, at once!'

She rose to her feet, shrieking with fright, and they seized her and bore her by force to the bath. Then he bade them leave him there alone with her, and they went and left him alone with the girl. He took the jar and poured the dog's blood on her head, and rubbed it over her skin, until her body was completely imbrued with the blood.[2] She sat there dumb for an hour, and then she lifted her head and cried out, 'What is this strange man doing

---

[1] See note 1, p. 63.

[2] This must be a *fedu* or 'ransom' ceremony. A black animal, or bird, often appears in Semitic magical ceremonies as the 'ransom' whose sacrifice averts misfortune.

Comp. the 'purification by blood' which appears so often in the Bible, e.g. Hebrews x. 22.

A favourite charm in Baghdad is a shell which has been dipped in the blood of seven slaughtered sheep at 'Id al Dhāhia. It is pierced and worn as an amulet against sickness of various kinds.

here?' and began to call for her maids in a tone of alarm, 'Jaffarāna! Khazarāna! Come! I am here alone with a man!' The slaves heard her calling in her natural voice, and came running and rejoicing and crying, 'Our bībī is cured! Our bībī is cured!' They entered making joy-cries, and washed her and clothed her and combed her, and took her up to her apartments. She was as sane as she had been before, and the madness had left her.

As soon as the wazīr knew it, he went into the Sultan's presence and said, 'Deign to come and see your daughter and how she is!'

The Sultan entered his daughter's dīwān, and she rose, and took his hand and kissed it. Her father was overjoyed. He sat down and began to converse with her, and then the healer entered his presence, and said,

'Your Majesty, what was our agreement?'

The Sultan replied, 'Aye, true! O wazīr, call the mulla, and draw up the marriage contract!' So the wedding was celebrated with great rejoicing, and when it was over, the Sultan took off his crown and put it on his son-in-law's head, and said, 'You are my son, and you shall reign in my stead.'

See how Allah prospered this generous man!

The new Sultan reigned well and wisely, and a day came, and a day went (*jā yōm, rāh yōm, jā yōm, rāh yōm*), until a long time had passed. One morning the Sultan looked out and he saw passing below the window of the palace a darwīsh, begging for food from the passers-by. When he gazed at the man, he saw that it was his brother —the greedy one. The Sultan called a servant and said, 'Go, fetch me that darwīsh, I wish him brought into my presence.' The servant went out and called, 'Bābā darwīsh, bābā darwīsh, come! Our Sultan wants to speak to you!'

Answered the darwīsh, 'Why does he want me?'

The servant answered, 'Come, come!' and took him and brought him into the palace. There they set food before him and sherbet and coffee, while the Sultan looked on.

The darwīsh did not recognize his brother in the Sultan,

and feared that it was intended to play a trick upon him. When he had eaten and drunk, the Sultan called him, and said, 'Do you know me?'

The darwīsh replied, '*Showkatli*—your Majesty—how should I know you? I am a poor darwīsh, but just arrived from the desert, how should I know you?'

Said the Sultan, 'Do you not know me at all?' (*Hīch ma taʻrifnī?*)

'I do not know you at all!'

Said the Sultan, 'I am your brother—to whom you refused a morsel of bread. See what Allah has done for me, and how he has treated you!'

The darwīsh fell upon his knees and besought the Sultan, 'Do not use me with hardness, as I used you!'

The Sultan replied, 'Never!' and raised him, and treated him as a guest.

Said the darwīsh, 'How did you become rich like this? Tell me, so that I can enrich myself also.'

The Sultan said, 'No, that may not be.'

But the darwīsh pressed him, saying, 'Only tell me for the story's sake.'

At last the Sultan told him how it had happened, and the darwīsh exclaimed, 'I will go also to the lions' cave and perhaps I too shall get rich!'

The Sultan replied, 'No! You are my brother and I forbid you to go, for if you do, evil will befall you and the lions will eat you. Now that we have found each other again, stay with me here. Do not think of undertaking to go to that place. Take my advice, for I am your brother and wish you well.'

But the darwīsh would not listen to him, and one day, taking some food and money with him, he set off and journeyed until he came to the lions' cave.

Now when the first brother had slain the rat and departed with the gold, the lions returned and found the dead rat lying by the mouth of the cave with a stone beside it, and one lion said to the other, 'Did I not tell you that a son of Adam was in the cave? He must have overheard us, and killed the rat!'

When the lions entered the cave the night after the darwīsh had hidden himself in it, one stood still and swung his tail so that it knocked dum! dum! dum! on his belly. Said he, 'I smell Man!'

The other said, 'How should a man be here?'

Answered the first, 'You said that last time, but a man was here and took the treasure!'

So they hunted and smelt about, and found the darwīsh where he lay hidden. Cried they, 'How shall we eat you? It was you who killed the rat and took the treasure!'

Said the darwīsh, 'No, no, it was my brother!'

Said they, 'How shall we eat you?'

Then the darwīsh saw that there was no hope, and he said, 'I deserve to die for being such a fool and not accepting my brother's advice!'

Then the lions sprang on him, and one seized one shoulder and the other the other shoulder, and they tore him into two halves and ate him all up.

Kunna ʿadkum wa jīna!

XLVII

THE BOY AND THE DEYUS

A̱KU māku ferd sultān! There was, was not, once a
Sultan who had three sons and three daughters. One
day he fell grievously sick (the name of Allah upon you!)[1]
and was near his death. He said to his sons, 'My sons,
I fear that I am dying, come and listen to my dying
wishes and will!'

His sons came to the bedside, and when they had
assembled there, the Sultan spoke to his eldest son and
said, 'My son, when I am dead you will be Sultan in my
place.'

He answered, 'O bābā, do not speak thus: I do not
want to be king, we wish you to remain with us always.'

Said the Sultan, 'That I cannot do. Now I lay upon
you my dying wish. You have three sisters. Shortly after
my death three darawīsh will come. They will not ask for
money or food. To the first give your eldest sister as a
bride, to the second your middle sister, and to the third
your youngest sister. As for me, when I am dead you
must watch my tomb for three nights after the seven days'
mourning, as I have enemies who, though they may not
injure me while I am living, may seek to do so when I am
dead. I fear that they will steal my body and throw it
outside.'

The sons promised to do what their father commanded,
and soon after the Sultan died and was buried. All the
sons wept for their father, but the youngest more bitterly
than his brothers, for he had loved his father more than
they all. When the funeral guests had departed and the
seven days mourning was over, the youngest prince said
to his elder brothers,

'Oh my brothers, what did our father command us to
do? We must spend these next three nights in vigil at
his tomb.'

---

[1] The name of Allah should be invoked when mentioning death. People say
'*Ba'id 'anak insh'allah*' ('Far from you, please God!'). See note, p. 251.

Said the eldest brother, '*Wallah*, he is dead: what is the use of spending the night by his tomb?' and when the youngest brother persisted that they must do so, he became angry, and said, 'We will not go!'

The youngest prince was very troubled, *khatya!* poor boy, and without any more speech with his elder brothers, he took his sword and his dagger, and went as soon as night had fallen to the tomb. He scraped a little hole in the ground beside the tomb, and covered it with thorn so that no one would see him, and there he hid. In the middle of the night the moonlit sky was darkened. He looked and saw a black cloud, descending. It came nearer, and he saw that it was a black deyu[1] seated on a coal-black mare. The deyu alighted, and roaring, 'While you were alive I had no power over you, but now that you are laid low, I will grind you to powder!' he dismounted from the mare and approached the tomb.

The boy was afraid, for he was alone, poor boy!

The deyu opened the tomb, and while he was bending to lift the dead body from its resting-place, the boy took courage, came out of his hiding-place, and struck with his sword at the deyu's neck. So hard did he strike that the deyu's head fell from his body at a single stroke. Then the lad took his sword, and cut out the lips, the eyes and the nose,[2] put them in his head-kerchief and tied them up. After that, as soon as he had taken up his father's body and replaced it decently in the tomb, he approached the black mare, seized her by the bridle, and placing into the saddle-bag the deyu's weapons, his black garments, and the kerchief containing the nose and mouth, he mounted her and rode her to his old nurse's house, throwing the kerchief as he passed into the river. He woke her, and confided the deyu's arms and mare into her keeping, saying, 'My mother, keep these for me in trust, and say no word of them to any one.'

Then he returned to his house and slept. The next morning a darwīsh came to the house. The elder brothers

---

[1] See Preface, p. xiii.
[2] Disfigurement of the dead has its magical significance.

wished to send him away, but the youngest said, 'Have you forgotten, my brothers? This has happened as our father said it would, and we must give this darwīsh our eldest sister.' So they gave the eldest sister to the darwīsh, and he went away with her, no one knew whither.

That night, the youngest prince said to his brothers, 'Will you not watch with me to-night?' but said nothing of his fight with the deyu. They refused, and saying to himself, 'Even though I should be killed, I must keep the vigil by the tomb,' he went at nightfall and hid as before in the hole by the tomb. At midnight the brother of the first deyu appeared in the sky like a red cloud. He descended, riding upon a red mare, and going to the tomb like the first, he began to drag the body from the grave. The prince said to himself, 'How can I let my father's body be taken out of the tomb!' and conquering his fear, he came behind the deyu and smote his head from his body. He did with him as he had done with the first, throwing his nose and lips into the river, and took his red clothes, arms and mare to his old nurse, binding her to silence. The next day came the second darwīsh and he took away the second princess. At sunset the young prince said to his brothers, 'Will you not watch to-night by our father's tomb?' and they answered him, 'We will not go; as for you, do as you please!' And he went again and hid in the hole. At midnight he saw a white cloud in the sky, and when it came nearer he saw that it was the third brother of the deyus, and he was white and rode a white mare. Him he slew just as he had slain the other two, and put his arms and the white mare with the others in the safe keeping of his old nurse. The next day came the third darwīsh, and took away with him the youngest princess. So were all the dead Sultan's wishes fulfilled, and the eldest brother ruled in his father's place. Some little while after that a crier came to the Sultan's capital, and proclaimed in the streets that his master, a neighbouring Sultan, had three beautiful daughters. He proposed to marry the eldest daughter, but to test the skill of the suitors, he had dug a hole in the ground, forty cubits deep and forty cubits wide, in which he would place her, and the man who could discover a means of getting her out should marry her. The princes heard the offer, and the two eldest said at once that they would ride off to try their luck. The youngest prince said to his brothers, 'Give me a mare too, I want to come with you.'

The other two laughed, and the eldest said, 'Who are you, to get the girl out of the pit?'

All the young men of the country set off with the princes to go to try to win the princesses, each boasting, 'I will win her!' and at last the elder brother, seeing that the youngest was bent on coming, said to him, 'There is an old dirty jade left in the stable, take her and ride with us if you will.'

The lad set off with the rest of the company, but when he had got half way to their destination, he turned and rode back to his nurse. There he put on the black clothes and arms of the first deyu, and mounting the black mare he touched her, and she rose, flying like a bird in the air, until they reached the country of the three princesses. There was a great concourse of people gathered together about the pit in which the first princess was immured, and when they saw the black horse and rider in the clouds, they cried to each other, aghast, '*Wallah!* A deyu has come to take the maiden!'

The youth rode the mare low over the hole, seized her hand, lifted her into the saddle and flew up again, while the assembled suitors gazed and wondered. Some of them fired guns at him, but it was useless, he disappeared, and the people were troubled.

The prince rode with the girl until he reached his old nurse's house. There he guided the black mare to the ground, and dismounting, he gave the girl into the safe-keeping of his old nurse, saying, 'Keep her as the apple of your eye, and keep silence!' She replied, 'I will keep her as the apple of my eye, and wherefore should I not keep silence?'

He returned to the house, and there at sunset his brothers returned, weeping and downcast.

He asked them what was the matter, and they replied, 'We went and we saw the princess, who was as pretty as a rose, but before we had a chance to try to get her from the pit, a deyu came from the sky, and flew down and seized her.'

Said the youngest, 'Come and eat your supper!'

They answered, 'We cannot eat, we are too sad.'

The youngest reproached them, 'When our father died you did not weep as you are weeping now!'

They replied, 'This maiden is worth more to us than our father or our grandfather!'

So the youngest son ate and slept.

The next day the crier returned to the town and announced that his master would now place his second daughter in the pit, and that she should belong to the suitor who could get her out. The two elder brothers at once decided to go and try if they could win her. The youngest said, 'Why do you not give me a good horse? Perhaps I might be able to win her.'

They answered, 'You would not have a chance. See what happened yesterday!'

The lad answered nothing, but when they had all been gone some time, he went to his old nurse's house, and put on the red deyu's clothes and arms. Then he mounted the red mare, and she flew, flew until they reached the place where the pit was with the maiden within it and the suitors about it. It happened as it had happened the day before: he seized the maiden as he flew down over the pit, and bore her through the air to his old nurse, bidding her keep the girl, and to hold her peace.

She replied, 'Good, my dear, I will keep her as the apple of my eye.'

He returned at sunset to his own house, and he found his brothers sitting in the dīwān and weeping. He asked them why they wept, and they replied that the second maiden, who was even fairer than the first, had been carried off by a red deyu.

Said the youngest, 'Do not trouble, perhaps one of you will obtain the third maiden, for they will put her into the pit to-morrow.'

The next morning the elder princes rose early, put on their finest clothes, rode their fine mares, and set off to try to win the third princess. As for the youngest, he went to his old nurse, and put on the white deyu's clothes and arms, and mounted the white mare. Again, as before, he flew through the air, and swooped into the pit and took out the third princess, who was more beautiful than the full moon. He took her to his old nurse, and bade her look after her well and put her with her sisters.

At sunset he returned to his own house, and he found his elder brothers downcast and weeping. Said they, 'It was as before, we had not even an opportunity to try to take the princess out of the pit. There came a white deyu from the sky on a white mare, and he seized the girl and went off.'

Said the youngest, 'Come, do not weep, rise and eat supper with me: for I have that which will rejoice you!'

They replied, 'We have no heart to eat to-night.'

But the youngest said to them, 'Come and eat, and I will find brides for you both!'

They came and ate with him, and after their supper, the youngest prince went to his nurse's house, and set the three maidens on the backs of the three mares, and led them to the palace. He called his brothers, who were astounded to see the three princesses, and he said to the eldest, 'Take you the eldest princess!' and to his other brother, 'Take you the middle princess!' and as for himself, he took the hand of the youngest princess, who was the loveliest of them all, and said, 'This one shall be my bride.'

The two elder princes thanked their brother and kissed him saying, 'You are a lion of strength and a serpent for cunning! You have always been better than we are—did you not go to keep vigil by our father's tomb and we refused to accompany you!' And the eldest said to him, 'You are better than I, you shall rule in my father's place and not I.'

Then they brought musicians and made a feast, and the eldest prince married the eldest princess. When the seven days' festivities were over, the middle prince married the middle princess, and the rejoicings lasted for another seven days. Then it was the turn of the youngest to marry the youngest princess. They called the mulla and the contract was made, and then the women took the bride to the bath so that she should be ready to receive the bridegroom. Carpets were spread over the whole length of the road between the door of the Sultan's palace and the entrance to the hammām. They washed the bride and put henna on her hands and feet, and braided her hair, and then they set off to return to the palace. But while they were on the road, the sky was suddenly darkened, and a deyu appeared, who, seizing the bride, threw her upon his shoulder and flew away with her into the air. Instead of returning with rejoicing to the bridegroom, the women now returned with lamentation, and told the tale of her disappearance.

The youngest prince was overcome with grief, but he immediately exclaimed, 'I will go to look for her, though it were in the utmost ends of the earth.'

He set out to look for his lost bride, and he walked and walked and walked for leagues and leagues, until, unknown to himself, he came to the place where his eldest sister lived with the first darwīsh, who was a powerful magician. The prince was worn out with fatigue and sorrow, and seeing a spring with trees growing by the brink, he wrapped up his head, lay down, and slept by the cool water.

Now his sister who lived in the castle close by needed some water, and she said to a servant, 'Go and fetch water from the spring.' The servant went, and when he reached the spring, he saw a young man sleeping by the well, whose likeness to his lady was so clear that he was astonished. He sat down and gazed at him, and at last his mistress, tired of waiting for him to return, said to another servant, 'Go and see what has happened to the first, he has been an hour gone and has not returned from the spring.'

The second servant went and found the first, and reproached him for his dilatoriness. They both returned together, and the lady sent for the first servant, and asked him why he had tarried.

He replied, 'O lady, I saw a lad sleeping by the well who was as like you as your mirror.'

She exclaimed, '*Hāi shlōn!* Can it be that my brother is here?' She put on her 'aba and went out to see for herself who the stranger was. As soon as she set eyes on him, she knew him for her youngest brother, and waked him, saying, 'My brother, what has brought you here?'

He replied, 'O my sister, *jūzi minnī*, leave me in peace! I will tell you of the trouble that has brought me here.'

Said she, 'What is it?'

He replied, 'I took a bride, and as they were bringing her to me from the hammām a deyu came and carried her off. Now I have gone to seek her, for no matter where she may be, I must get her back!'

She cried, 'O my brother, if you are going into the deyus' country harm may befall you!'

Said he, 'I will not be turned from my purpose until I have my bride.'

She took him back with her to her castle, and at sunset her husband the darwīsh came back, and when he entered her dīwān, she saw that his face was gloomy.

She said to him, 'O darwīsh, I fear that you are displeased because my brother has come?'

He answered, 'No, by Allah, I am not distressed at seeing your brother here. He shall be the apple of my eye! The cause of my sadness is that to-day I saw a fair maiden, sweet as a flower, being borne away by a deyu on his shoulder.'

The prince said, 'The maiden that you saw must have been my wife, for whom I am seeking until I find her.'

Said the darwīsh, 'Your way to get her back will be long and difficult!'

The prince replied, 'I will bring my wife back, or I will leave my head behind!'

His sister began to persuade him against his journey, saying, 'What is this woman! There are other brides in the world! I fear you will be killed on the road!'

Then the darwīsh said, 'If you are resolved upon this journey, I will give you seven pairs of shoes made of iron. They will lead you to the place where your bride is, and all seven pairs will be worn out before you find her!'

The prince thanked him, and put on one pair of iron shoes, and the others he put in his bag for the future. He wandered and wandered till the first pair were worn out, and when the seventh pair was all but worn through he came to a strange country, and entered the town in which the Sultan of the place lived. He asked the name of the country and they told him, 'This is the country of Ibn Qāra al Farn.'

The lad looked at his shoes, and thought, 'Perhaps I am at the end of my journey!'

He passed along the road, and saw an old woman with a kindly face sitting by the door. She was very old, but he stopped to speak with her and wish her peace, and asked her, 'Do you wish for a guest?'

The old woman answered, 'If you will excuse the poverty of my house, I will keep you like the apple of my eye.'

The lad took a handful of gold liras from his pocket and gave them to the old woman saying, 'This is for my keep.'

They sat down to eat, and as they ate he heard the noise of a chalgheh,[1] musical instruments, and merry-making.

He asked what it was, and the old woman told him that the Sultan's palace was close by, and that the sounds he heard were those of a wedding. Said she, 'The Sultan is served by a deyu whose devotee he is, and this deyu brought him a beautiful girl as a bride seven months ago. She refused to marry him, but now he will wait no longer for her consent, but is taking her by force.'

The prince exclaimed, 'That is my wife!' and he told the old woman his story from the beginning to the end, saying, 'What I tell you, tell no one!'

Said the old woman, 'No, my son!'

---

[1] See note 2, p. 162.

Said the prince, '*Wallah*, my mother, this girl brought by the deyu must be my wife, on whose account I have travelled hither.'

The old woman answered, 'Trouble not, I can bring you to her, and if she is your wife, I will help you.'

Asked the prince, 'And how will you take me to her, my mother?'

She replied, 'I was wet-nurse to the royal family and I can go into the harem when I please. Wait for three days, and I will take you with me.'

Said he, 'How can that be, and I a man?'

But the old woman went and brought a barber, and shaved off the lad's whiskers and beard. Then she brought women's clothes, and dressed him in them, putting women's shoes on his feet, and an 'aba about him. Then she went to the palace of the Sultan Ibn Qāra al Farn, and going to the women's quarters, she said to the Sultan's mother, 'I have a daughter who married and left me years ago to live in another country. Now she has returned, and I should like to bring her to see the bride.'

The lady replied, 'Let her come, as she is your daughter.'

The old woman went home, and presently she returned with her supposed daughter.

Said they, 'She will not see the bride, for she has locked herself in her room, and will see no one.'

However, they were taken to the room, and the old woman knocked at the door and said, 'Open the door!'

The princess within replied, 'I will open the door to no one, for I wish no one to see my face!'

Then the old woman said to the young man, 'Speak with her in the tongue of her country.'

No sooner did the princess hear her own tongue, than she opened the door quickly and let him in, and said, not knowing him,

'What brought you here?'

He replied, 'I am your husband, and I swore an oath that I would bring you back or leave my head behind me!'

Said she, 'O my husband, in two nights' time the Sultan's son comes to take me by force!'

Said he, 'How shall we escape?'

She replied, 'There is a way. Go to the sea-shore this night, and you will see a sea-mare [1] come out of the sea to eat the spring grass. Seize her and halter her, and bring her to the palace below my window. I will break the window and we will both fly away on her back.'

The prince returned to the old woman and they went out.

That night he went down to the sea-shore, and out of the sea there came a mare, with wings on her back. He seized her and bridled her and returned with her to the palace where he waited below the princess's window. She was waiting for him, and broke the window and sprang down to him on its back. Then the mare rose into the air, and so they flew and they flew until they reached their own country.

Meanwhile the Sultan went to visit his bride, and when he came and found the window open and his bride vanished, sent for the old woman, and said to her, 'How is this! My bride and your daughter have gone!'

The old woman was cunning and to avert his anger she cried out, 'Aye! true! How many years I had been longing to see my daughter, and this year she came, but I had no sooner seen her than your bride took her away! I want my daughter! I want my daughter!' and she lamented, so that they should not suspect her.

Then the Sultan went to the deyu and said, 'My bride has disappeared, where is she?'

Said the deyu, 'I will discover her and bring her back.'

Meanwhile, when the prince and his bride arrived in their country they found his brothers in black clothes, for they had begun to mourn him as dead. When the princes saw them, they were overjoyed, and threw away their mourning, crying, 'Praise God, you and your wife are back in safety! Now we will finish the wedding!' And they made a great feast, and made merry.

[1] See notes on this tale.

The deyu in his search flew straight to the place where he had found the bride, and when he came there, he heard sounds of a wedding. He entered the house, and there sat the bridegroom with his bride. Now the bridegroom had put on the clothes of the white deyu, and when the wicked deyu entered, he drew the white deyu's sword and smiting the enemy on his shoulder, he killed him at a stroke! So he was freed from the deyus, and lived with his bride all the years of his life.

XLVIII

THE SHEPHERD AND HIS BROTHER

Āku māku ferd walad ethnein!

ONCE on a time there were, were not, two poor lads who were brothers. One herded cattle, and each day he gave a loaf of bread to the poor for Satan's sake. One day Satan said, 'This lad gives a loaf of bread every day to the poor for my sake, I must do him some good turn in return.' So Satan gave him a reed pipe (*matbij*).[1] As soon as the shepherd began to play it his sheep began to dance, and all the animals within hearing danced too. Now there was an old woman who possessed one cow, and she got her living by selling its milk and the butter she made of it. When her cow heard the pipe it began to dance with the others, and it danced so hard that it broke a leg, *khatīya*! At sunset, when all the cattle were driven back, the old woman came for her cow, and she saw that its leg was broken. The old woman went to the herdsboy and said to him, 'Why have you broken my cow's leg?' The herdsboy answered, 'I did not break it, *wallah*, she broke it herself, dancing!'

The old woman said, 'How can that be! Cows don't dance!' and she was angry and said, 'I shall take you to the court of justice!'

The lad replied, 'O my mother, accuse me if you please, but I didn't break your cow's leg!'

He was soon summoned before the judge. The judge said to the lad, 'My son, why did you break the leg of the old woman's cow? It was a sin, for her sole means of livelihood is her cow.'

The herdsboy replied, 'My lord, I did not break the cow's leg: she broke it herself, dancing.'

The qādhi said, 'How now! Cattle don't dance!'

Said the herdsboy, 'If you will let me bring some sheep to the court, I will prove to you that they do!'

The qādhi said, 'Good—go and bring them.'

---

[1] Two reeds bound together by string and pitch.

The boy went and returned with some sheep, while the qādhi and the court waited. The herdsboy drew the matbij from his pocket and began to play. At the first notes the sheep began to caper and dance, and not only the sheep, but the qādhi rose from his bench, and the clerks from their seats, and the old woman, and the people who were in the court. The Sultan who was passing heard the sounds and he came in and began to dance, and the ministers who were sitting in conclave near by danced, and the people passing in the street and the horses in the arabānas—all capered and danced, and leapt and turned.

Cried the qādhi, 'Stop, my son, stop! We are tired!' and the lad stopped playing. Then the qādhi said to the old woman, 'The boy spoke truly, oh old woman! Your cow broke her leg by dancing.'

Then the qādhi said to the boy, 'You have won your case, but you must give me the matbij!' The boy gave him the matbij and the qādhi broke it into pieces, saying, 'It shall do no more harm.'

Then the shepherd boy took his sheep, and drove them through the town and into the chōl. At noon when he was resting on the ground, he began to scrape the earth with his hand, in idleness. He found something hard, and when he looked to see what it was, it was a glazed *bastūga* jar. He took it out of the earth, and behold! it was full of gold pieces. The boy had never seen gold money before, and he said, 'What fine red stuff this is!'

He took it back to his hut at night and showed it to his brother, who was as simple as he, and said to him, 'My brother, look! see what I found in the ground! What can this pretty red stuff be?'

Said his brother, '*Wallah*, I know not! Let us divide it between us, half to me and half to thee!'

Said the shepherd, 'How shall we divide it evenly?' for he knew not how to count.

Said the brother, 'I will go and borrow some scales from the Sultan's kitchen.'

He went to the Sultan's kitchen, and said to the people there, 'Lend me your scales: we found some pretty red

A Bedawi shepherd, Northern 'Iraq

things in the ground and want to weigh them so as to make a fair division!'

The Sultan's people were curious to know what the brothers had found, and so they melted a little bitumen, and daubed a little on the scales. The brothers weighed out the gold in the scales and divided it equally, then they returned the scales to the Sultan's house. A gold lira had stuck to the bottom of the scales, but they did not notice it. The Sultan's wife took the scales to the Sultan, and said, 'These shepherds have found a treasure! they borrowed our scales to weigh it out!' Then the Sultan told the police, and they came to the shepherds' hut and confiscated all the gold, and carried it to the Sultan.

The shepherd said to his brother, 'The Sultan's wife has taken what we found! we will not stay longer in this country, but will go to another place.' So they rose up and set out. They had not gone far before the shepherd's brother said, 'If we leave the door of the house unprotected, the Sultan will enter it!'

The other said, 'Aye! We must not leave the door unguarded! Go, fetch it and we will have it under our eye.'

So the shepherd's brother went back, took the door off its hinges[1] and returned with it on his head. They walked and walked all that day and when night fell they were in the chōl, and no shelter near but a big mulberry tree.

Said the shepherd to his brother, 'Oh my brother, the sun has set, and I am afraid a wolf will come and eat us if we lie to sleep on the ground. Let us climb into the tree and spend the night there.'

They climbed into the tree, and the shepherd's brother had the door bound to his shoulder. The two sat in the tree.

In the night some 'Arab arrived, people of the houses of hair. They put up their tent beneath the tree, and sat in it, and knew not that there were two men in the tree above them.

Presently the shepherd's brother said, 'Oh, my brother, I must make water.'

Said the shepherd, 'Shlōn! How now! if you do that

[1] See note, p. 5.

upon these people, they will draw their weapons and let off a gun at us!'

But the other could not contain himself.

Said the Bedouin one to the other, 'How strange! from whence does this rain come?'

Then the shepherd's brother said, 'Oh, my brother, my shoulder is aching! I must get rid of this door!'

Answered the shepherd, 'If you let the door drop, it will fall upon the folk beneath us and kill them!'

But the shepherd's brother let the door fall, and it crashed upon the tent.

The 'Arab below were frightened, and cried, 'The sky is falling upon us!' and leaving their tent and their donkey and all that they possessed behind them, they fled quickly out into the desert and ran away.

The next morning the brothers descended from the tree, took all the gear that the 'Arab had left behind them, put it on the back of their donkey, and set off again on their journey. Towards nightfall they reached a village, and finding a ruined house there, they took refuge in it, and there they lived for some time.

One day the shepherd said to his brother, 'I do not like sitting in a house, I want to return to my trade of shepherd.'

Said his brother, 'As you will.'

The shepherd went to the house of a farmer, and said to him 'Do you want a shepherd?'

The farmer said, 'Aye, we want a shepherd, but I shall make a condition of service if you work for me.'

Said the other, 'What is that?'

Replied the farmer, 'If you ever lose your temper, you must permit me to cut a piece of skin from your throat. If I lose mine, you can do the same to me.'

Said the shepherd, 'Good.'

He returned to his brother and said, 'I have become shepherd to the people of that house.'

The other said, 'Good, my brother.'

The next morning the shepherd rose early and took the farmer's sheep into the chōl. The farmer gave him nothing to eat, and sent him nothing to eat, and when the shepherd returned back at night, he was very hungry.

Said he to the farmer, 'You left me hungry all day!'

Said the farmer's wife, 'Are you angry about it?'

He answered, '*Wallah!*'[1]

Then the farmer said, 'You have lost your temper, so I must cut a piece of skin from your throat.'

So they brought a knife and cut skin from his throat, and the shepherd died, *khaṭīya!*

When his brother learnt what had happened he was very angry, and said, 'These people have killed my brother. I will become their shepherd and will play them a trick they will not forget!'

So he went to the house of the farmer and said, 'Do you want a shepherd?'

The man said, 'Yes. But there is a condition of service: and that is, if you lose your temper you must suffer me to cut a piece of skin from your throat. If I lose mine, you may do the same to me.'

Said the other, 'Good.'

The next morning when he went to take the sheep, they gave him no food, and they sent him no food. The shepherd said, 'Why should I remain hungry with meat about me?' He took a sheep, and slaughtered it, and made a roast and ate.

When he returned he said to the farmer and his wife, 'You gave me no food, so I killed a sheep and ate it. Are you angry?'

The farmer answered, 'No, my son, we are not angry! May it give you health!' (*Bil 'āfiya.*)

But when they were alone the farmer said to his wife, 'Give him a loaf to-morrow, or he will eat a sheep every day!'

The next day they gave him some bread when he took the sheep, and he brought them all home safe at sunset. He slept with the farmer and his family, and in the night one of the children woke and cried and said, 'I want to go into the yard.'[2]

---

[1] A way of saying 'Indeed, it is so.'

[2] In Arab houses the privy is either in the yard or upon the roof.

The other children woke up, and the master of the house said to the shepherd, 'Now take them all into the yard so that they will be quiet till morning.'

So the shepherd rose and took all the four children into the yard, and there he killed them in revenge for his brother's death.

When he returned to the house, the master of the house said, 'Where are the children?'

Said the shepherd, 'I killed them all, to keep them quiet. Are you angry?'

The farmer was afraid, and said, 'No, why should I be angry?'

The next morning it was snowing and hailing, and it was impossible to take the sheep into the chōl.

The farmer said, 'A pity! The sheep cannot go out to-day. Take them and give them chopped straw, and let them get their heads well into the trough.'

The shepherd said, 'Good!'

He took the sheep, and cut off their heads, and put the heads into the straw and said, 'Eat your fill!'

Then he returned and said to the farmer, 'They are eating well!'

The farmer went presently to see, and he found all the sheep slaughtered. He said to the shepherd, 'Why have you done this, my son?'

Answered the shepherd, 'Are not their heads well in the trough? Are you angry?'

The farmer could not hold himself and said, '*Wallah*, I am angry. You killed my sons and now you have killed my sheep: of course I am angry!'

Cried the shepherd, 'Now I want the flesh of your throat!' and he took his knife and cut the throat of the farmer so that he died.

His wife came running and said, 'Why have you done this to my husband and children?'

He replied, 'You killed my brother, and I have taken my revenge. Do you need me more as your shepherd?'

She answered, 'I do not want you—go away! I have no sheep now!'

NOTES

The following works are referred to in the notes by abbreviated titles:

Persian Tales, translated by D. L. R. and E. O. Lorimer. London, 1919. *Türkische Märchen*, translated by Fr. Giese. 1925. *Türkische Volksmärchen aus Stambul*, translated by Dr. Ignaz Kunoz. *L'Orient inédit*, by Minas Tchéraz. Paris, 1912. *Contes Arméniens*, translated by Frédéric Macler. Paris, 1905.

I. *The Crazy Woman.* This tale was told me by the Baghdad Christian whom I have mentioned in the Preface. Some incidents in this tale recall 'The Story of the Shawl-Weaver' in *Persian Tales*.

II. *The Goat and the Old Woman.* A children's tale related by the same woman. Its resemblance to the English 'The Old Woman whose Pig wouldn't jump over the Stile' needs no comment.

III. *Three Little Mice.* Another children's tale. It was related by a Moslem lady of a well-known family in Mosul.

IV. *The Sparrow and His Wife.* The same lady told this charming little tale.

V. *Dungara Khsheybān.* This story was told by a Mosul girl, a Moslem and literate. She was unaccustomed to story-telling and the tale is evidently imperfect. The ingredients are well worn. The fairy godmothers with their gifts recall 'Sleeping Beauty'. The same theme occurs in a Turkish folk-tale 'Die Geschichte von der Dilber, die nicht erreichte was sie wollte', in *Türkische Märchen*, and in another, 'Die Rosenschönen' in *Türkische Volksmärchen aus Stambul*. In this Turkish version three dervishes come from the wall. The supplanted bride is also a well-worn theme, e.g. 'The Goose-Girl' in Grimm's *Household Tales*. In the Turkish tales above mentioned, the bride is supplanted by a servant and the stories are more or less parallel until the point where the eyes are restored, when they part company again. The wooden dress seems to indicate some Dryad legend.

VI. *The Crystal Ship.* A young Moslem girl in Mosul told this tale. A similar folk-story is told in Armenia. The ship that will not move out of port until a promise made by a passenger has been redeemed occurs in other stories, e.g., 'The Doll of Patience' in this volume. Sisters' jealousy of the *jinni's* bride is another common theme. The journey to the country of the *jānn* in iron shoes and with an iron staff in hand occurs in many stories, e.g. 'Enfant-Serpent, Enfant Soleil' in a collection translated by

F. Macler (*Contes Arméniens*), iron being a protection against harm from *jānn*. E. S. Hartland says in *The Science of Fairy-Tales*, pp. 306–7:

'The retention of stone instruments in religious worship was doubtless due to the intense conservatism of religious feeling. The gods, having been served with stone for so long, would be conceived of as naturally objecting to change; and the implements whose use had continued through so many revolutions in ordinary human utensils, would thereby have acquired a divine character. Now the traditional preference on the part of supernatural beings for stone instruments is only one side of the thought which would, as its reverse side, show a distinct abhorrence by the same mythical personages for metals, and chiefly (since we have long passed out of the bronze age) for iron.'

The doves talking in the tree, and thus sealing their own doom, is also a familiar incident. It occurs in an Armenian tale, 'Théodore le Danseur' in *L'Orient inédit*.

The dove is called a *cucūkhti*. The reference is to a well-known children's rhyme in 'Iraq:

Cucūkhti	Coo-oo my sister,
Wein ūkhti?	Where is my sister?
Bil Hillah.	In Hillah.
Eysh takul?	What eats she?
Bajilla.	Beans.
Eysh tishrab?	What drinks she?
Māi Allah.	God's waters.
Wein tanām?	Where sleeps she?
Bāb Allah.	At the Gate of God.

The cries of birds and beasts are often thought to convey a warning, or are translated into human speech by tradition. The swallow is supposed to chatter the Surat al Qāf. The owl cries '*Ya ghāfilīn! idhkaru Allah!*' 'Oh, heedless ones, remember God!' The bulbul murmurs, '*Jīb, baba, jīb! shedda warid, warid! Jīb warid, abu al warid!*' 'Bring, daddy, bring a bunch of roses! Bring roses, father-of-roses!' (i. e. rose-seller). The hen pigeon cries '*Ya karīm*', 'O Merciful One'; the cock pigeon replies '*Ya Allah!*' The sand-grouse proclaims its presence, '*Guta, guta, guta*'. The crow cries "*Aqa, 'aqa!*' 'I fall, I fall!' Stories of understanding the talk of beasts are common. Children are told that the beasts hold an auction sale of the house. The cow moos, '*Abi'a ad dār, dār, dār!*' 'I sell the house!'. The cat bids, '*Khams mīa—au, khams mīa—au!*', 'Five hundred!' The dog outbids her, '*B'alf B'alf!*'

'A thousand!' The cock says '*Ma abi'a ū-ū*', 'I won't sell it!', but the sheep bleats, '*Mb'a-'a-'a, mb'a-'a-'a*', 'Sold!'.

VII. *The Old Couple and Their Goat.* This children's story was told me by a Christian woman in Baghdad. A well-known European fairy story about a wolf is recalled.

VIII. *Shamshūm al Jabbār.* This interesting piece of folk-lore was told me by the same woman, who was illiterate. The story is of course that of Samson and is a sun-myth. Shamshūm is the sun, and his hair represents the rays of the sun which are cut short by winter. During that time he is weak and partially buried, but as his rays grow longer, his strength is regained, he seizes his sharp sword and lays low his enemies. The serpent devouring the eaglets and attacked by the sun-god is a myth which appears in many forms, perhaps the latest being an incident in *Alice in Wonderland.* The story of the Eagle and the Serpent on two fragmentary tablets from the Royal Library at Nineveh, now in the British Museum, should be compared. In the Assyrian account the Serpent destroys the Eagle's brood and later vanquishes the Eagle with the help of the Sun-God. For the journey to the island which 'is beyond seven seas' compare Tablets No. 13–17 from the Royal Library of Ashurbanipal (British Museum); for the description of Etana's journey to Heaven clinging to the eagle's neck (heaven also being of seven regions). Compare also an incident in a Bakhtiari tale, 'The Merchant of Isfahān', in *Persian Tales.* I heard this story later from a young Moslem girl, in a form similar to the version given by the Christian.

IX. *Husain an Nim-Nim.* This story is very well known to Moslems (though not to Christians) in Baghdad and Mosul. The union of human men and women with river demons is to this day credited as possible, and the existence of the *s'ilūwa* is not questioned by people of the ignorant classes. Even amongst those who are semi-educated there are many who believe in her existence. I have described her fully in the Preface. The theme of the human midwife summoned to the birth of the water-spirit's child is a common one in folk-stories (see Chap. III of the *Science of Fairy-Tales* by E. S. Hartland), and an identical incident is quoted by J. T. Brent in *The Cyclades, or Life among the Insular Greeks* (p. 46), the mother in this case being a Nereid. (In view of the theory that gipsies have been largely instrumental in disseminating folk-lore it is interesting to note that in folk-stories of fairy births the human midwife is often paid by the gift of a piece of coal, the coal being transformed later into money, and that the English gipsy word for both coal and money is the same—*wongar* or *vongar*.) The payment of the midwife by onion-skin and garlic (by a *peri*) occurs in an Armenian story in *L'Orient Inédit*, entitled 'L'Accouchée et le Nouveau-Né'. Like Ūmm Bāji, the woman threw the gifts away in disdain, but found later that pieces that had remained unnoticed had changed into gold and silver. Tchéraz comments that onion and garlic are the *peris'* gold and silver. The story of Husain an Nim-Nim is so universally known, that in Baghdad, to call a man a 'Husain an Nim-Nim' is equivalent to saying that he is puny, for Husain is supposed to have issued very thin and weak from the embraces of the *s'ilūwa*. Supposed descendants of Husain an Nim-Nim are fairly plentiful, and I have come into contact with several people who have had in their houses persons claiming the gift of curing sore eyes by spitting into them; the magical power being theirs by virtue of their descent from Husain an Nim-Nim. The magic property of spittle is an ancient Semitic belief. (See Doughty, *Arabia Deserta*, vol. i, p. 527, and Mark viii. 23.)

X. *The Blackbeetle who wished to get Married.* This little fable is perhaps the most generally told of all children's tales in 'Iraq. It was related to me first by the same narrator as that of the two previous stories, but I have heard it since from several other persons. There is resemblance here and there to a Kermāni fable in *Persian Tales*, but the Baghdad story is complete in itself, and much more charming.

XI. *The Thorn-seller* or *Shawwāk*. For discussion of the bird-man see Preface, p. x. The silence which must be observed by the bird-prince's wife occurs in a whole group of fairy-tales (see *The Science of Fairy-Tales* by E. S. Hartland, p. 312, on similar taboos, and *The Golden Bough*, by Sir J. G. Frazer). In a Turkish folk-tale 'Die Geschichte vom schönen Halwaverkaufer' in *Türkische Märchen* there is a story of a dove-lover who visits a princess, and similar incidents occur in Armenian and Persian folk-tales. The present version was given me by the woman who related the three preceding tales. A woman-slave in Sayyid Abdallah al Gilāni's house in Baghdad told me the same story, but with the variations that it was the pots and pans in the kitchen that wept and laughed with the *jinni* prince, who appeared in the guise, not of a bird, but of a white snake. The jealous sisters threw his snake-skin into the fire while he was with his bride. A Moslem girl in Mosul told me another, and shorter, version in which a bird flew down, seized the comb of the Sultan's daughter, and flew away. The story is the same from the point where the old beggar-woman is washing her clothes on the river bank, except that it was a stallion which filled the water-skins. Part of the story is worth quoting:

'The old woman crept under the couch and went to sleep. She was awakened by the rustling of wings, and saw that a bird had descended by the pool of water. It took off its feather dress and stepped out of it a youth, so beautiful that there was not his like in the mortal world (Subhān Allah!). This youth sat on the couch and drew from his pocket a comb and said to it:

Yā min mishthā ʿandī	"Oh thou whose comb I have,
Wa ʿainī mā tarā hā	Upon whom my eyes may not rest,
Yā ashjār, yā anhār	Weep, oh trees, of rivers,
Ubchu ʿala nahwat al buchā	For I am near tears!"

'This he repeated three times and then he and the trees began to weep, the drops falling from their leaves and from his eyes.' The story is very widely spread.

XII. *The Blind Sultan.* (The same narrator.) The opening will recall 'Androcles and the Lion' which is possibly a tale of Buddhistic origin. Some of the incidents of this story may be discovered in 'The Story of the Colt Qeytas' (*Persian Tales*). Compare also 'The Water of Life' (Grimm's *Household Tales*). The old man spinning day and night occurs in a Turkish folk-tale translated by Dr. Ignaz Kunoz: 'Der Windteufel' and the three roads are a common feature in Oriental tales.

XIII. *Jarāda.* This is a story well known, not only in 'Iraq but in neighbouring countries: compare 'The Story of the Fortune-Teller' (*Persian Tales*), and 'Der Obersterndeuter' (*Türkische Märchen*). In Grimm's *Household Tales* the story appears as 'Doctor Know-All'. I heard it from a Moslem schoolmaster, who had it from his mother.

XIV. *The Stork and the Jackal.* This was told me by ʿAbd al ʿAzīz Beg Mudhaffar. The fable is spread over the East, and appears in Aesop. Its Baghdad version is worth repeating.

XV, XVI. *'It is not the Lion's Fur Coat.'* This story and the next were told me by a Moslem clerk in Baghdad.

XVII. *A Story of the Khalīfa Hārūn ar Rashīd.* The narrator was a Christian woman in Baghdad.

XVIII. *Another Story of the Khalīfa.* (The same.) The story is widespread: compare 'Le Tisserand Intelligent' in *Contes Arméniens*, etc.

XIX. *The Tricks of Jānn.* These anedcotes were related by an illiterate Christian woman in Baghdad. She told the stories as personal experiences of her family.

XX. *It was Enough to Bewilder the Lion.* This story was told me by Mr. J. F. Levack, who had it from a Moslem in Baghdad.

XXI. *Two Nursery Rhymes.* The first recalls 'The House that Jack Built'.

XXII. *The Bitter Orange.* A Moslem lady told this in Mosul.

XXIII. *Tale told by a Shammar Tribesman.* He was illiterate and his tale is fragmentary. The first part recalls the Cyclops, and the story of the one-eyed giant whose eye is put out with a living brand occurs in the folk-lore of many countries: compare 'Les Cyclopes', *L'Orient Inédit.* As for the incident of the living husband interred with the dead wife, see the Fourth Journey of Es Sindibad the Sailor in the *Arabian Nights* for a similar incident, and in Lane's translation his note on the same. It is mentioned as a tribal custom in a Turkish folk-tale ('Der Vielgeprüfte Prinz': *Türkische Märchen*), and occurs in the German story of 'The Three Snake Leaves' (Grimm's *Household Tales*).

XXIV. *Shammar Stories.* These anecdotes hardly need comment. I heard them when staying in a Shammar camp.

XXV. *The Qarīna.* This story was related one evening as I sat in Shaikh 'Ajīl al Yawir's guest-tent. For details of the Qarīna see the Preface.

XXVII. *Hājir.* Told by a Moslem schoolmaster who had it from his mother (in Baghdad). This story is also widely spread. In Europe it appears as 'Snow-white and the Seven Dwarfs'. Compare Dr. Ignaz Kunoz's story 'Die Zaubernadel'.

XXVIII. *The Woman of the Well.* This story was related by an ex-Cabinet Minister in Baghdad to explain a remark made by him about a member of the Chamber of Deputies, of whom my friend said that he scolded like 'the Umm al Bīr'. The story, or one resembling it, was translated by Dr. Ignaz Kunoz under the title of 'Das Brunnen Gespenst'.

XXIX. *Hasan the Thief.* This was told me in Baghdad by an illiterate woman. The trick employed by the prince in tying the *deyu's* rope to a tree instead of to her ankle occurs in other folk-tales, e.g. 'Die Geschichte vom schönen Halwaverkaufer' (*Türkische Märchen*): the incident of cutting off the heads of the robbers as they appear (from the ground or over a wall) is a common one in Oriental tales.

XXX. *Moses and the Two Men*. This tale was told by a Moslem clerk in Baghdad to explain the common phrase *'yeskutūn yeskutūn'*.

XXXI. *Al Gumeyra*. This was told me by a schoolmaster in Baghdad, who had it from his mother.

XXXII. *The Three Dervishes and the Wonderful Lamp*. This is exactly as related to me by an illiterate woman in Baghdad, and is interesting as showing the form which the well-known Arab story of 'Ala ad Dīn and the Lamp takes when related in the family circle, and the manner in which modern details become absorbed into the ancient tale.

XXXIII. *The King's Son and the Three Maidens, or the Doll of Patience*. The version I have given here was told in English by an Armenian lady in Baghdad, but I heard another version of the same story in Arabic (with the title of 'The Khalīfa and the Three Maidens') from a Moslem schoolmaster, who had it from his mother. The principal differences were that, instead of being buried in the ground, the wronged mother of the miraculous children was killed, while the third sister (who escaped the vengeance of the Khalīfa for having said, 'Should the Khalīfa ask me as his bride, I should not accept him unless he were to bring me my garments with his own hands and put my slippers ready for me to wear') was the eventual accepted consort, through a series of events which led to the Khalīfa fulfilling her conditions. The children with hair of gold and silver in this version were really drowned by the third and wicked sister.

The story is widely spread, particularly the two incidents of the substitution of puppies for the queen's twin children. Compare 'The Story of the Two Jealous Sisters' (*Persian Tales*); 'The Three little Birds' in Grimm's *Household Tales*, and a similar story which occurs in the *Arabian Nights*. Also 'Cheveux d'Argent et Boucles d'Or' in *Contes Arméniens*, 'Théodore le Danseur' in *L'Orient Inédit*, 'Die Goldhaarigen Kinder' (Dr. Ignaz Kunoz), and 'The Golden-haired Twins' in Mme Mijatovich's *Serbian Fairy Tales*.

The incident of the Doll of Patience and Knife of Patience is also found in other folk-tales, e.g. 'The Story of the Marten Stone' (*Persian Tales*) and in 'Die Geschichte von der Schönen, die das erreichte, was sie wollte' (*Türkische Märchen*). In this tale the true bride and false bride ask for presents, the latter asking for the Patience-Stone. The prince goes on his voyage, but cannot leave the port because he has forgotten the request of the true bride (who has become the false bride's slave). He then procures the stone, and on his return watches out of curiosity to see what the girl will

do with the stone. She relates her story to the stone and it swells
and bursts, as in the version given here. Compare also Dr. Ignaz
Kunoz, 'Geduldstein, Geduldmesser'.

XXXIV. *The Merchant's Daughter.* This was told me by an
illiterate woman (a Christian) in Baghdad. Several well-worn folk-
themes occur in this tale, such as the recognition of a portrait as
a means of identifying a stranger and the choice of a king or leader
from auspices. Choice of a king by means of a bird which alights
on the head of a candidate for the throne is an incident which is
found in several Persian folk-stories and Armenian stories; see
Persian Tales and a tale which appears as 'L'Oiseau' in *L'Orient
Inédit*.

XXXV. *Wudayya.* The relator of this tale was a Moslem
schoolmaster, who had it from his mother.

XXXVI. *The Poor Girl and Her Cow.* This story, which was
related to me by an illiterate Christian woman in Baghdad, is
among the most-told folk-tales of the Middle and Near East.
Incidents which appear in the present version will be found in
Persian dress in 'The Story of Little Fatima' and 'How Fatima
killed her Mother' in *Persian Tales*. The cow, the visit of
the two sisters to the water-spirit's cave, the different action of
each when the water ran black and white, and the incident of the
clog or shoe are found in an Armenian tale 'Cendrillon' (*L'Orient
Inédit*). In another Armenian tale (*Contes Arméniens*) a boy is
befriended by a female demon, who would otherwise have eaten
him, because he had sucked her teats. The well-known 'Cinderella'
of European folk-lore is a version of this tale. The incidents of the
girl and her wonderful cow occur in Grimm's *Household Tales*
('Mother Holle'), while in his notes to that story Grimm mentions
a tale from Hesse in which a water-nixie has her hair combed by
a girl whom she would have kept as a slave had not the girl eaten
some crumbs of her food. A Thuringian story quoted by W.
Reynitzsch in 'Über Truhten und Truhtensteine' has similar incidents. Grimm mentions that Mademoiselle Villeneuve, in a
volume translated in 1765 into German, has a story of a water-
nixie and two girls. The treasure found where the remains of the
cow were buried is another common theme. Grimm mentions
several of them in his notes to 'One Eye, Two Eyes, and Three
Eyes' in which tale a gold tree springs from the entrails of the
slaughtered animal. For a Serbian version, cow, water-spirit,
slippers and all, see *Serbian Fairy Tales*, 'Papalluga: or the Golden
Slipper'.

XXXVII. *The Prince and the Daughter of the Thorn-seller.* This was related by the same narrator as the above.

XXXVIII. *Uhdeydān, Uchʿeybān, and Unkheylān.* (The same narrator as the above two tales.) Another widely-spread folk-tale. In European versions the *sʿilūwa* appears as a wolf.

XXXIX. *Melek Muhammad and the Ogre.* Here we have the 'Iraqi version of what is in European fairy-tales 'Jack and the Bean-stalk'. The narrator was the same as that of the three preceding stories. Compare also some incidents in 'Der Lachende und der weinende Apfel' in *Türkische Volksmärchen aus Stambul.*

XL. *Er Rūm.* The narrator was a Moslem schoolmaster in Baghdad, who had it from his mother. The opening incident of the stone garment occurs in other tales. R. Campbell Thompson, in his *Semitic Magic,* quotes from Waldenspurger who, writing in 1893 (Palestine Exploration Fund), quotes the following story:

'Iblīs once sent his son to an assembly of honourable people with a flint stone, and told him to have the flint stone woven. He came in and said, "My father sends his peace and wishes to have this flint woven." A man with a goat-beard said, "Tell your father to have it spun, and then we will weave it." The son went back and the Devil was very angry, and told his son never to put forth any suggestion when a goat-bearded man was present, "for he is more devilish than we".'

The latter part of the story much resembles the story of Bunayya which appears in the present volume.

XLI. *The Cotton-Carder and Kasilūn (Lazybones).* (The same narrator as preceding tale.) The theme is an old one in folk-lore and many stories related to this tale can be discovered, e.g. in Grimm's *Household Tales* we have 'The Valiant Little Tailor', 'The Giant and the Tailor', and 'Jack the Giant-Killer'. Dr. Kunoz in his *Türkische Volksmärchen aus Stambul* has 'Kara Mustafa, der Held', a Turkish tale akin to these.

XLII. *Bunayya.* I got this charmingly-told story from a Moslem lady of tribal origin, who had it from her wet-nurse when she was a child. The narrator was not literate to a high degree, for with praiseworthy enterprise she taught herself to read and write late in life. The likeness to story XL will be apparent.

XLIII. *The Cat.* A Kurdish girl told me this story in Arabic.

XLIV. *The Fish that Laughed.* This story was told me by a Baghdad Christian woman (illiterate). The fables told by the boy to the princess are of ancient derivation. The story of the faithful dog which protects the baby from a wild beast or reptile and is slain by its father is familiar to most children as the story of 'Gelert the Faithful Hound'. In the *Pancha-Tantra Fables* it appears as 'The Brahmin and his Mongoose'. In *The Fables of Bidpai* both fables appear, as they do in the Persian version of the fables 'Anwār as Sohaili'. The Arab version of the fables, 'Kalīla wa Dimna' (Ibn Al Muqaffa''s translation of these Indian animal stories), is familiar to every Arab schoolboy. The stories have passed into Armenian and Turkish folk-stories; compare 'Der König und seine Falke' in *Türkische Märchen*.

XLV. *The Honest Man.* Mr. Levack told me this story. He had it from a Baghdadi. It appears in slightly different form in two Persian folk-tales, 'The Brother whose Luck was Asleep', and 'The Man who went to visit his Luck' (*Persian Tales*).

XLVI. *The Generous Man and the Niggardly Man.* The narrator was a Baghdad woman, a Christian and illiterate. The tale has points of resemblance with an Armenian tale in *Contes Arméniens* entitled 'Dieu donne à celui qui donne', but the 'Iraqi story is richer in detail. Similar incidents also appear in 'The Story of Roads and Short-Cuts' (*Persian Tales*).

XLVII. *The Boy and the Deyus.* A Kurdish girl narrated this tale (in Arabic). The watch by the tomb is interesting. The removal of a corpse from its tomb amongst most races of the human family, but especially amongst Semitic races, is considered a disaster, since the spirit which once tenanted the desecrated body has henceforth no rest. See Jeremiah viii. In the *Epic of Gilgamish* (translation from the tablets in the British Museum) Eabani says:

'The man whose corpse lieth in the wilderness,
Thou and I have often seen such a one,
His spirit resteth not in the earth.
The man whose spirit hath none to care for it. . . .
The dregs of the vessel, the leavings of the feast
And that which is cast out into the street are his food.'

The watch three nights by the tomb or dead body of the deceased occurs in European folk-tales, e.g. 'The Grave Mound' (Grimm's *Household Tales*). In the latter story it is the devil who attempts to carry away the dead man. The sequence of colour of the *deyus* is also significant, and recalls the coloured stages of the Sumerian ziggurat. Here the colours possibly symbolize the evil spirits of the underworld, earth and air.

With regard to the sea-mare upon which the prince eloped with his bride, Lane, in his note to the 'First Voyage of Es-Sindibad of the Sea', quotes Al-Kazwīni:

'The water-horse is like the land-horse, save that he is longer in the mane and tail, and more handsome in colour; and his hoof is cloven like the hoof of the wild ox . . . and his size is smaller than that of the land-horse, but larger than that of the ass, by a little.'

Sindibad (First Voyage) describes how at the time of the herbage the sea-horses come out of the sea, at which period King Mihraj sent his grooms with swift mares which they tied on the shore so that they might attract the sea-stallions. Compare also *Türkische Volksmärchen aus Stambul*, pp. 137 and 270.

XLVIII. *The Shepherd and His Brother*. This was related by the same Kurdish girl as the preceding story. The magic pipes, which make all living creatures dance to their music, are too well-known a folk-theme to need comment: compare 'The Jew Among the Thorns' in Grimm's *Household Tales*, the nursery rhyme 'Over the Hills and Far away', &c. The gold which sticks to the measure which has been daubed with pitch is another incident which occurs in many other tales, e.g. 'Ali Baba and the Forty Thieves', 'Simeli Mountains' in Grimm's *Household Tales*, &c. The inhuman demand of the farmer recalls Shylock. The shepherd-brother's revenge through pretended misunderstanding of his master's orders is found in other folk-stories, but it would be difficult to match the superb bathos of the last sentence. Compare also 'Mehmed, der Kahlköpfiger' in *Türkische Volksmärchen aus Stambul*.

A CATALOG OF SELECTED DOVER
BOOKS IN ALL FIELDS OF INTEREST

CONCERNING THE SPIRITUAL IN ART, Wassily Kandinsky. Pioneering work by father of abstract art. Thoughts on color theory, nature of art. Analysis of earlier masters. 12 illustrations. 80pp. of text. 5⅜ x 8½. 0-486-23411-8

CELTIC ART: The Methods of Construction, George Bain. Simple geometric techniques for making Celtic interlacements, spirals, Kells-type initials, animals, humans, etc. Over 500 illustrations. 160pp. 9 x 12. (Available in U.S. only.) 0-486-22923-8

AN ATLAS OF ANATOMY FOR ARTISTS, Fritz Schider. Most thorough reference work on art anatomy in the world. Hundreds of illustrations, including selections from works by Vesalius, Leonardo, Goya, Ingres, Michelangelo, others. 593 illustrations. 192pp. 7⅛ x 10¼. 0-486-20241-0

CELTIC HAND STROKE-BY-STROKE (Irish Half-Uncial from "The Book of Kells"): An Arthur Baker Calligraphy Manual, Arthur Baker. Complete guide to creating each letter of the alphabet in distinctive Celtic manner. Covers hand position, strokes, pens, inks, paper, more. Illustrated. 48pp. 8¼ x 11. 0-486-24336-2

EASY ORIGAMI, John Montroll. Charming collection of 32 projects (hat, cup, pelican, piano, swan, many more) specially designed for the novice origami hobbyist. Clearly illustrated easy-to-follow instructions insure that even beginning papercrafters will achieve successful results. 48pp. 8¼ x 11. 0-486-27298-2

BLOOMINGDALE'S ILLUSTRATED 1886 CATALOG: Fashions, Dry Goods and Housewares, Bloomingdale Brothers. Famed merchants' extremely rare catalog depicting about 1,700 products: clothing, housewares, firearms, dry goods, jewelry, more. Invaluable for dating, identifying vintage items. Also, copyright-free graphics for artists, designers. Co-published with Henry Ford Museum & Greenfield Village. 160pp. 8¼ x 11. 0-486-25780-0

THE ART OF WORLDLY WISDOM, Baltasar Gracian. "Think with the few and speak with the many," "Friends are a second existence," and "Be able to forget" are among this 1637 volume's 300 pithy maxims. A perfect source of mental and spiritual refreshment, it can be opened at random and appreciated either in brief or at length. 128pp. 5⅜ x 8½. 0-486-44034-6

JOHNSON'S DICTIONARY: A Modern Selection, Samuel Johnson (E. L. McAdam and George Milne, eds.). This modern version reduces the original 1755 edition's 2,300 pages of definitions and literary examples to a more manageable length, retaining the verbal pleasure and historical curiosity of the original. 480pp. 5⅚₆ x 8¼. 0-486-44089-3

ADVENTURES OF HUCKLEBERRY FINN, Mark Twain, Illustrated by E. W. Kemble. A work of eternal richness and complexity, a source of ongoing critical debate, and a literary landmark, Twain's 1885 masterpiece about a barefoot boy's journey of self-discovery has enthralled readers around the world. This handsome clothbound reproduction of the first edition features all 174 of the original black-and-white illustrations. 368pp. 5⅜ x 8½. 0-486-44322-1

STICKLEY CRAFTSMAN FURNITURE CATALOGS, Gustav Stickley and L. &
J. G. Stickley. Beautiful, functional furniture in two authentic catalogs from 1910. 594
illustrations, including 277 photos, show settles, rockers, armchairs, reclining chairs,
bookcases, desks, tables. 183pp. 6½ x 9¼.   0-486-23838-5

AMERICAN LOCOMOTIVES IN HISTORIC PHOTOGRAPHS: 1858 to 1949,
Ron Ziel (ed.). A rare collection of 126 meticulously detailed official photographs,
called "builder portraits," of American locomotives that majestically chronicle the
rise of steam locomotive power in America. Introduction. Detailed captions. xi+
129pp. 9 x 12.   0-486-27393-8

AMERICA'S LIGHTHOUSES: An Illustrated History, Francis Ross Holland, Jr.
Delightfully written, profusely illustrated fact-filled survey of over 200 American lighthouses since 1716. History, anecdotes, technological advances, more. 240pp. 8 x 10¾.
                                                                            0-486-25576-X

TOWARDS A NEW ARCHITECTURE, Le Corbusier. Pioneering manifesto by
founder of "International School." Technical and aesthetic theories, views of industry, eco-
nomics, relation of form to function, "mass-production split" and much more. Profusely
illustrated. 320pp. 6⅛ x 9¼. (Available in U.S. only.)   0-486-25023-7

HOW THE OTHER HALF LIVES, Jacob Riis. Famous journalistic record, expos-
ing poverty and degradation of New York slums around 1900, by major social
reformer. 100 striking and influential photographs. 233pp. 10 x 7⅞.   0-486-22012-5

FRUIT KEY AND TWIG KEY TO TREES AND SHRUBS, William M. Harlow.
One of the handiest and most widely used identification aids. Fruit key covers 120
deciduous and evergreen species; twig key 160 deciduous species. Easily used. Over
300 photographs. 126pp. 5⅜ x 8½.   0-486-20511-8

COMMON BIRD SONGS, Dr. Donald J. Borror. Songs of 60 most common U.S.
birds: robins, sparrows, cardinals, bluejays, finches, more–arranged in order of
increasing complexity. Up to 9 variations of songs of each species.
                                               Cassette and manual 0-486-99911-4

ORCHIDS AS HOUSE PLANTS, Rebecca Tyson Northen. Grow cattleyas and
many other kinds of orchids–in a window, in a case, or under artificial light. 63 illustrations. 148pp. 5⅜ x 8½.   0-486-23261-1

MONSTER MAZES, Dave Phillips. Masterful mazes at four levels of difficulty.
Avoid deadly perils and evil creatures to find magical treasures. Solutions for all 32
exciting illustrated puzzles. 48pp. 8¼ x 11.   0-486-26005-4

MOZART'S DON GIOVANNI (DOVER OPERA LIBRETTO SERIES),
Wolfgang Amadeus Mozart. Introduced and translated by Ellen H. Bleiler. Standard
Italian libretto, with complete English translation. Convenient and thoroughly
portable–an ideal companion for reading along with a recording or the performance
itself. Introduction. List of characters. Plot summary. 121pp. 5¼ x 8½. 0-486-24944-1

FRANK LLOYD WRIGHT'S DANA HOUSE, Donald Hoffmann. Pictorial essay
of residential masterpiece with over 160 interior and exterior photos, plans, eleva-
tions, sketches and studies. 128pp. 9¹/₄ x 10¾.   0-486-29120-0

THE CLARINET AND CLARINET PLAYING, David Pino. Lively, comprehensive work features suggestions about technique, musicianship, and musical interpretation, as well as guidelines for teaching, making your own reeds, and preparing for public performance. Includes an intriguing look at clarinet history. "A godsend," *The Clarinet,* Journal of the International Clarinet Society. Appendixes. 7 illus. 320pp. 5⅜ x 8½. 0-486-40270-3

HOLLYWOOD GLAMOR PORTRAITS, John Kobal (ed.). 145 photos from 1926-49. Harlow, Gable, Bogart, Bacall; 94 stars in all. Full background on photographers, technical aspects. 160pp. 8⅜ x 11¼. 0-486-23352-9

THE RAVEN AND OTHER FAVORITE POEMS, Edgar Allan Poe. Over 40 of the author's most memorable poems: "The Bells," "Ulalume," "Israfel," "To Helen," "The Conqueror Worm," "Eldorado," "Annabel Lee," many more. Alphabetic lists of titles and first lines. 64pp. 5³⁄₁₆ x 8¼. 0-486-26685-0

PERSONAL MEMOIRS OF U. S. GRANT, Ulysses Simpson Grant. Intelligent, deeply moving firsthand account of Civil War campaigns, considered by many the finest military memoirs ever written. Includes letters, historic photographs, maps and more. 528pp. 6⅛ x 9¼. 0-486-28587-1

ANCIENT EGYPTIAN MATERIALS AND INDUSTRIES, A. Lucas and J. Harris. Fascinating, comprehensive, thoroughly documented text describes this ancient civilization's vast resources and the processes that incorporated them in daily life, including the use of animal products, building materials, cosmetics, perfumes and incense, fibers, glazed ware, glass and its manufacture, materials used in the mummification process, and much more. 544pp. 6⅛ x 9¼. (Available in U.S. only.) 0-486-40446-3

RUSSIAN STORIES/RUSSKIE RASSKAZY: A Dual-Language Book, edited by Gleb Struve. Twelve tales by such masters as Chekhov, Tolstoy, Dostoevsky, Pushkin, others. Excellent word-for-word English translations on facing pages, plus teaching and study aids, Russian/English vocabulary, biographical/critical introductions, more. 416pp. 5⅜ x 8½. 0-486-26244-8

PHILADELPHIA THEN AND NOW: 60 Sites Photographed in the Past and Present, Kenneth Finkel and Susan Oyama. Rare photographs of City Hall, Logan Square, Independence Hall, Betsy Ross House, other landmarks juxtaposed with contemporary views. Captures changing face of historic city. Introduction. Captions. 128pp. 8¼ x 11. 0-486-25790-8

NORTH AMERICAN INDIAN LIFE: Customs and Traditions of 23 Tribes, Elsie Clews Parsons (ed.). 27 fictionalized essays by noted anthropologists examine religion, customs, government, additional facets of life among the Winnebago, Crow, Zuni, Eskimo, other tribes. 480pp. 6⅛ x 9¼. 0-486-27377-6

TECHNICAL MANUAL AND DICTIONARY OF CLASSICAL BALLET, Gail Grant. Defines, explains, comments on steps, movements, poses and concepts. 15-page pictorial section. Basic book for student, viewer. 127pp. 5⅜ x 8½. 0-486-21843-0

THE MALE AND FEMALE FIGURE IN MOTION: 60 Classic Photographic Sequences, Eadweard Muybridge. 60 true-action photographs of men and women walking, running, climbing, bending, turning, etc., reproduced from rare 19th-century masterpiece. vi + 121pp. 9 x 12. 0-486-24745-7

ANIMALS: 1,419 Copyright-Free Illustrations of Mammals, Birds, Fish, Insects, etc., Jim Harter (ed.). Clear wood engravings present, in extremely lifelike poses, over 1,000 species of animals. One of the most extensive pictorial sourcebooks of its kind. Captions. Index. 284pp. 9 x 12.   0-486-23766-4

1001 QUESTIONS ANSWERED ABOUT THE SEASHORE, N. J. Berrill and Jacquelyn Berrill. Queries answered about dolphins, sea snails, sponges, starfish, fishes, shore birds, many others. Covers appearance, breeding, growth, feeding, much more. 305pp. 5¼ x 8¼.   0-486-23366-9

ATTRACTING BIRDS TO YOUR YARD, William J. Weber. Easy-to-follow guide offers advice on how to attract the greatest diversity of birds: birdhouses, feeders, water and waterers, much more. 96pp. 5³⁄₁₆ x 8¼.   0-486-28927-3

MEDICINAL AND OTHER USES OF NORTH AMERICAN PLANTS: A Historical Survey with Special Reference to the Eastern Indian Tribes, Charlotte Erichsen-Brown. Chronological historical citations document 500 years of usage of plants, trees, shrubs native to eastern Canada, northeastern U.S. Also complete identifying information. 343 illustrations. 544pp. 6½ x 9¼.   0-486-25951-X

STORYBOOK MAZES, Dave Phillips. 23 stories and mazes on two-page spreads: Wizard of Oz, Treasure Island, Robin Hood, etc. Solutions. 64pp. 8¼ x 11.
0-486-23628-5

AMERICAN NEGRO SONGS: 230 Folk Songs and Spirituals, Religious and Secular, John W. Work. This authoritative study traces the African influences of songs sung and played by black Americans at work, in church, and as entertainment. The author discusses the lyric significance of such songs as "Swing Low, Sweet Chariot," "John Henry," and others and offers the words and music for 230 songs. Bibliography. Index of Song Titles. 272pp. 6½ x 9¼.   0-486-40271-1

MOVIE-STAR PORTRAITS OF THE FORTIES, John Kobal (ed.). 163 glamor, studio photos of 106 stars of the 1940s: Rita Hayworth, Ava Gardner, Marlon Brando, Clark Gable, many more. 176pp. 8⅜ x 11¼.   0-486-23546-7

YEKL and THE IMPORTED BRIDEGROOM AND OTHER STORIES OF YIDDISH NEW YORK, Abraham Cahan. Film Hester Street based on *Yekl* (1896). Novel, other stories among first about Jewish immigrants on N.Y.'s East Side. 240pp. 5⅜ x 8½.   0-486-22427-9

SELECTED POEMS, Walt Whitman. Generous sampling from *Leaves of Grass*. Twenty-four poems include "I Hear America Singing," "Song of the Open Road," "I Sing the Body Electric," "When Lilacs Last in the Dooryard Bloom'd," "O Captain! My Captain!"–all reprinted from an authoritative edition. Lists of titles and first lines. 128pp. 5³⁄₁₆ x 8¼.   0-486-26878-0

SONGS OF EXPERIENCE: Facsimile Reproduction with 26 Plates in Full Color, William Blake. 26 full-color plates from a rare 1826 edition. Includes "The Tyger," "London," "Holy Thursday," and other poems. Printed text of poems. 48pp. 5¼ x 7.
0-486-24636-1

THE BEST TALES OF HOFFMANN, E. T. A. Hoffmann. 10 of Hoffmann's most important stories: "Nutcracker and the King of Mice," "The Golden Flowerpot," etc. 458pp. 5⅜ x 8½.   0-486-21793-0

THE BOOK OF TEA, Kakuzo Okakura. Minor classic of the Orient: entertaining, charming explanation, interpretation of traditional Japanese culture in terms of tea ceremony. 94pp. 5⅜ x 8½.   0-486-20070-1

FRENCH STORIES/CONTES FRANÇAIS: A Dual-Language Book, Wallace Fowlie. Ten stories by French masters, Voltaire to Camus: "Micromegas" by Voltaire; "The Atheist's Mass" by Balzac; "Minuet" by de Maupassant; "The Guest" by Camus, six more. Excellent English translations on facing pages. Also French-English vocabulary list, exercises, more. 352pp. 5⅜ x 8½. 0-486-26443-2

CHICAGO AT THE TURN OF THE CENTURY IN PHOTOGRAPHS: 122 Historic Views from the Collections of the Chicago Historical Society, Larry A. Viskochil. Rare large-format prints offer detailed views of City Hall, State Street, the Loop, Hull House, Union Station, many other landmarks, circa 1904-1913. Introduction. Captions. Maps. 144pp. 9⅜ x 12¼. 0-486-24656-6

OLD BROOKLYN IN EARLY PHOTOGRAPHS, 1865-1929, William Lee Younger. Luna Park, Gravesend race track, construction of Grand Army Plaza, moving of Hotel Brighton, etc. 157 previously unpublished photographs. 165pp. 8⅞ x 11¾. 0-486-23587-4

THE MYTHS OF THE NORTH AMERICAN INDIANS, Lewis Spence. Rich anthology of the myths and legends of the Algonquins, Iroquois, Pawnees and Sioux, prefaced by an extensive historical and ethnological commentary. 36 illustrations. 480pp. 5⅜ x 8½. 0-486-25967-6

AN ENCYCLOPEDIA OF BATTLES: Accounts of Over 1,560 Battles from 1479 B.C. to the Present, David Eggenberger. Essential details of every major battle in recorded history from the first battle of Megiddo in 1479 B.C. to Grenada in 1984. List of Battle Maps. New Appendix covering the years 1967-1984. Index. 99 illustrations. 544pp. 6½ x 9¼. 0-486-24913-1

SAILING ALONE AROUND THE WORLD, Captain Joshua Slocum. First man to sail around the world, alone, in small boat. One of great feats of seamanship told in delightful manner. 67 illustrations. 294pp. 5⅜ x 8½. 0-486-20326-3

ANARCHISM AND OTHER ESSAYS, Emma Goldman. Powerful, penetrating, prophetic essays on direct action, role of minorities, prison reform, puritan hypocrisy, violence, etc. 271pp. 5⅜ x 8½. 0-486-22484-8

MYTHS OF THE HINDUS AND BUDDHISTS, Ananda K. Coomaraswamy and Sister Nivedita. Great stories of the epics; deeds of Krishna, Shiva, taken from puranas, Vedas, folk tales; etc. 32 illustrations. 400pp. 5⅜ x 8½. 0-486-21759-0

MY BONDAGE AND MY FREEDOM, Frederick Douglass. Born a slave, Douglass became outspoken force in antislavery movement. The best of Douglass' autobiographies. Graphic description of slave life. 464pp. 5⅜ x 8½. 0-486-22457-0

FOLLOWING THE EQUATOR: A Journey Around the World, Mark Twain. Fascinating humorous account of 1897 voyage to Hawaii, Australia, India, New Zealand, etc. Ironic, bemused reports on peoples, customs, climate, flora and fauna, politics, much more. 197 illustrations. 720pp. 5⅜ x 8½. 0-486-26113-1

THE PEOPLE CALLED SHAKERS, Edward D. Andrews. Definitive study of Shakers: origins, beliefs, practices, dances, social organization, furniture and crafts, etc. 33 illustrations. 351pp. 5⅜ x 8½. 0-486-21081-2

THE MYTHS OF GREECE AND ROME, H. A. Guerber. A classic of mythology, generously illustrated, long prized for its simple, graphic, accurate retelling of the principal myths of Greece and Rome, and for its commentary on their origins and significance. With 64 illustrations by Michelangelo, Raphael, Titian, Rubens, Canova, Bernini and others. 480pp. 5⅜ x 8½. 0-486-27584-1

CATALOG OF DOVER BOOKS

LIGHT AND SHADE: A Classic Approach to Three-Dimensional Drawing, Mrs. Mary P. Merrifield. Handy reference clearly demonstrates principles of light and shade by revealing effects of common daylight, sunshine, and candle or artificial light on geometrical solids. 13 plates. 64pp. 5⅜ x 8½.   0-486-44143-1

ASTROLOGY AND ASTRONOMY: A Pictorial Archive of Signs and Symbols, Ernst and Johanna Lehner. Treasure trove of stories, lore, and myth, accompanied by more than 300 rare illustrations of planets, the Milky Way, signs of the zodiac, comets, meteors, and other astronomical phenomena. 192pp. 8⅜ x 11.

0-486-43981-X

JEWELRY MAKING: Techniques for Metal, Tim McCreight. Easy-to-follow instructions and carefully executed illustrations describe tools and techniques, use of gems and enamels, wire inlay, casting, and other topics. 72 line illustrations and diagrams. 176pp. 8¼ x 10⅞.   0-486-44043-5

MAKING BIRDHOUSES: Easy and Advanced Projects, Gladstone Califf. Easy-to-follow instructions include diagrams for everything from a one-room house for bluebirds to a forty-two-room structure for purple martins. 56 plates; 4 figures. 80pp. 8¾ x 6⅜.   0-486-44183-0

LITTLE BOOK OF LOG CABINS: How to Build and Furnish Them, William S. Wicks. Handy how-to manual, with instructions and illustrations for building cabins in the Adirondack style, fireplaces, stairways, furniture, beamed ceilings, and more. 102 line drawings. 96pp. 8¾ x 6⅜.   0-486-44259-4

THE SEASONS OF AMERICA PAST, Eric Sloane. From "sugaring time" and strawberry picking to Indian summer and fall harvest, a whole year's activities described in charming prose and enhanced with 79 of the author's own illustrations. 160pp. 8¼ x 11.   0-486-44220-9

THE METROPOLIS OF TOMORROW, Hugh Ferriss. Generous, prophetic vision of the metropolis of the future, as perceived in 1929. Powerful illustrations of towering structures, wide avenues, and rooftop parks—all features in many of today's modern cities. 59 illustrations. 144pp. 8¼ x 11.   0-486-43727-2

THE PATH TO ROME, Hilaire Belloc. This 1902 memoir abounds in lively vignettes from a vanished time, recounting a pilgrimage on foot across the Alps and Apennines in order to "see all Europe which the Christian Faith has saved." 77 of the author's original line drawings complement his sparkling prose. 272pp. 5⅜ x 8½.

0-486-44001-X

THE HISTORY OF RASSELAS: Prince of Abissinia, Samuel Johnson. Distinguished English writer attacks eighteenth-century optimism and man's unrealistic estimates of what life has to offer. 112pp. 5⅜ x 8½.   0-486-44094-X

A VOYAGE TO ARCTURUS, David Lindsay. A brilliant flight of pure fancy, where wild creatures crowd the fantastic landscape and demented torturers dominate victims with their bizarre mental powers. 272pp. 5⅜ x 8½.   0-486-44198-9

All books complete and unabridged. All 5³⁄₁₆" x 8¼", paperbound. Available at your book dealer, online at **www.doverpublications.com**, or by writing to Dept. GI, Dover Publications, Inc., 31 East 2nd Street, Mineola, NY 11501. For current price information or for free catalogs (please indicate field of interest), write to Dover Publications or log on to **www.doverpublications.com** and see every Dover book in print. Dover publishes more than 500 books each year on science, elementary and advanced mathematics, biology, music, art, literary history, social sciences, and other areas.